ROBERT SILVERBERG's many novels include *The Alien Years*; the most recent volume in the Majipoor Cycle, *The King of Dreams*; the bestselling Lord Valentine trilogy; and the classics *Dying Inside* and *A Time of Changes. Sailing to Byzantium,* a collection of some of his award-winning novellas, was published by ibooks in 2000; *Science Fiction 101—Robert Silverberg's Worlds of Wonder,* an examination of the novellas that inspired him as a young writer, was published in March 2001. He has been nominated for the Nebula and Hugo awards more times than any other writer; he is a five-time winner of the Nebula and a four-time winner of the Hugo.

AVAILABLE NOW

THE ALFRED BESTER COLLECTION
The Deceivers • The Computer Connection
re: demolished

THE ARTHUR C. CLARKE COLLECTION
The Sentinel • Tales from Planet Earth

THE HARRY HARRISON COLLECTION
Bill, the Galactic Hero
THE EDEN TRILOGY
West of Eden • Winter in Eden • Return to Eden

THE ROBERT SILVERBERG COLLECTION
Sailing to Byzantium
Science Fiction 101: Robert Silverberg's Worlds of Wonder

THE ROGER ZELAZNY COLLECTION
The Dream Master • Damnation Alley
The Doors of His Face, The Lamps of His Mouth

ISAAC ASIMOV'S ROBOT CITY
Volume 1 by Michael P. Kube-McDowell and Mike McQuay
Volume 2 by William F. Wu and Arthur Byron Cover
Volume 3 by Rob Chilson and William F. Wu

ISAAC ASIMOV'S ROBOTS AND ALIENS
Volume 1 by Stephen Leigh and Cordell Scotten

ISAAC ASIMOV'S ROBOT MYSTERIES
by Mark W. Tiedemann
Mirage • Chimera

WILD CARDS
Edited by George R.R. Martin
Wild Cards
Wild Cards II: Aces High

Arthur C. Clarke's Venus Prime: Volumes 1, 2, 3, and 4
by Paul Preuss

Battlestar Galactica: Resurrection
by Richard Hatch and Stan Timmons

CRONOS

ROBERT SILVERBERG

ibooks
new york
www.ibooksinc.com

DISTRIBUTED BY SIMON & SCHUSTER, INC

An Original Publication of ibooks, inc.

An ibooks, inc. Book

Distributed by Simon & Schuster, Inc.
1230 Avenue of the Americas, New York, NY 10020

ibooks, inc.
24 West 25th Street
New York, NY 10010

The ibooks World Wide Web Site Address is:
http://www.ibooksinc.com

ISBN 0-7434-2390-9
First ibooks, inc. printing August 2001
10 9 8 7 6 5 4 3 2 1

Cover design by J. Vita
Cover art by Gustav Klimt; copyright © 2001
Interior design by Westchester Book Composition

Printed in the U.S.A.

CRONOS: AN INTRODUCTION

by Robert Silverberg

The theme of travel in time has been central to me, both as reader and writer, throughout my lifelong involvement with science fiction. I first encountered it in H.G. Wells' *The Time Machine* when I was ten or eleven years old, more than half a century ago, and came away stunned by Wells' visions of future eras, which culminates in this unforgettable depiction of the very end of time:

"The darkness grew apace; a cold wind began to blow in freshening gusts from the east, and the showering white flakes in the air increased in number. From the edge of the sea came a ripple and whisper. Beyond these lifeless sounds the world was silent. Silent? It would be hard to convey the stillness of it. All the sounds of man, the bleating of sheep, the cries of birds, the hum of insects, the stir that makes the background of our lives—all that was over. As the darkness thickened, the eddying flakes grew more abundant, dancing before my eyes; and the cold of the air more intense. At last, one by one, swiftly, one after another, the white peaks of the distant hills vanished into blackness. The breeze rose to a moaning wind. I saw the black central shadow of the eclipse sweeping toward me. In another moment the pale stars alone were visible. All else was rayless obscurity. The sky was absolutely black. . . .

"Then like a red-hot bow in the sky appeared the edge of the sun. I got off the machine to recover myself. I felt giddy and incapable of facing the return journey. As I stood stick and confused I saw again the moving thing upon the shoal—there was no mistake now that it was a moving thing—against the red water of the sea. It was a round thing, the size of a football perhaps, or, it may be, bigger, and tentacles railed down from it; it seemed black against the weltering blood-red water, and it was hopping fitfully about. . . ."

Soon after, I encountered John Taine's *Before the Dawn,* which provided a glimpse of that long-lost age when dinosaurs walked the earth, and H.P. Lovecraft's *The Shadow Out of Time,* which told me of the grotesque intelligences that would inhabit the world millions of years hence. And then I found Robert A. Heinlein's dazzling story "By His Bootstraps," which introduced me to the perplexing paradoxes that time travel engenders.

I was hooked—forever, as it turned out. I knew that my own time on earth was finite; but here was a kind of fiction that pierced the veil of the future. Out of an aching curiosity to know what lies ahead, not merely seven months or eleven years or even two centuries ahead, but millennia, thousands upon thousands of millennia, I searched out all the science fiction I could find, looking in particular for tales of time voyages, wanting desperately to believe, at least for the nonce, in Wells' argument that "A civilized man . . . can go up against gravitation in a balloon, and why should he not hope that ultimately he may be able to stop or accelerate his drift along the Time-Dimension, or even turn about and travel the other way?"

INTRODUCTION

It was inevitable that when I began writing science fiction myself, just a few years later, I would turn my developing skills to time-travel stories almost from the first. The earliest I can recall was a piece called "Vanguard of Tomorrow," pretty much a straight imitation of "By His Bootstraps," which I wrote when I was fourteen, and which, I am relieved to say, never has seen publication. A rather more skillful job was "Hopper," which I wrote when I was nineteen, and then the time-paradox story "Absolutely Inflexible," a few months afterward. I sold both of these to magazines and they were published in 1956, "Hopper" appearing in the appropriately named *Infinity* and "Absolutely Inflexible" in *Fantastic Universe.*

Over the years I have returned again and again to the theme, eventually producing not simply imitations of classics by my betters, but original contributions to the literature of my own. Among these I would class "Hawksbill Station" of 1967 and the novel *Up the Line* of 1969, *Son of Man* of 1971, "When We Went to See the End of the World" of 1972, and "Many Mansions" of 1973; and I have continued writing time-travel stories ever since, with the most successful of them, perhaps, being "Needle in a Timestack" (1983), "Sailing to Byzantium" (1985) and "Enter a Soldier. Later: Enter Another" (1989).

The volume you now hold provides three examples of my fascination—obsession, if you want to call it that—with time travel. *The Time Hoppers,* which I wrote in the spring of 1966, just as I was beginning to find my mature voice as a writer, was an expansion of my 1954 short story "Hopper" to book length—a story that reflects the use of time travel not so much as a means of exploring other eras as of escaping from one's own. *Project Pendulum,* from 1986, was one more attempt at wrestling with the time-paradox concept, a book that involved me, somewhat to my own dismay, in a structure that could have easily been employed in a novel ten times the length of the one I actually wrote. It was a struggle to hold it to the dimensions I had intended, but I think that doing so increased the dizzying effect of the story. And *Letters from Atlantis,* which I wrote in 1988, is not only a time-travel story but also plays with another idea I have been poking at, on and off, for many years, my not very seriously proposed speculation that the legend of Atlantis is derived from memories of a lofty technology-based civilization that existed on earth in Neolithic or even Paleolithic times. I'm pleased to have the opportunity to restore these three books to print in this new edition.

Robert Silverberg

LETTERS FROM ATLANTIS

. . . it waits for that serene moment when the brain is just in the apt condition, and ready to *switch on the other memory,* as one switches on the electric light with a turn of the switch. . . .

—Kenneth Grahame

. . . now in the island of Atlantis there was a great and wonderful empire, which had rule over the whole island and several others, as well as over part of the continent; and besides these, they subjected the parts of Libya within the Columns of Heracles as far as Egypt, and of Europe as far as Tyrrhenia. . . . But there occurred violent earthquakes and floods, and in a single day and night of rain the island of Atlantis disappeared, and was sunk beneath the sea.

—Plato: *Timaeus*

1.

The prince is sleeping now. Dreaming, no doubt, of the green and golden island of Athilan, its marble palaces, its shining temples. All unknown to him, I have borrowed his body—his good strong right arm—to write this letter for me.

So:

From somewhere in what I think is Brittany or Normandy, on what I think and assume is Christmas Eve in the year 18,862 B.C., greetings and merry Christmas, Lora!

(Will this ever reach you, out there in the frosty eastern land that will someday be Poland or Russia? Less than a fifty-fifty chance, I suppose, even though you're right here in the same prehistoric year I am. But a whole continent separates us. With transportation what it is here, it's almost like being in different worlds.

I'll cause the Prince to slip it into the regular diplomatic pouch that leaves next week, and the royal Athilantan courier will take it with him when he sets out across the tundra to the trading post where you're supposed to be stationed. With any luck you'll actually be there, and whoever you're riding in will be someone who routinely has access to the royal documents that the courier brings. Considering that I'm writing this in English, he won't have the remotest notion of what it's all about. But you will, looking at it through his eyes. And maybe you'll even be able to write back to me. My God, that would be wonderful, getting a letter from you! We've only been apart a little while and already it seems like forever.)

I suspect that the chances of my actually working out any sort of regular communication with you back here—or any communication at all, really—are very very slim. But I can try, anyway. And at the very least, setting down these accounts of what I've been experiencing here ought to provide me with a good way of bringing it all into clearer focus. Which should help me make better sense and order out of it when I'm home again in our own era and undergoing debriefing.

This is the seventh day of the mission. So far everything's moving along pretty well.

First there was the time-hop trauma to deal with, of course. That was a stunner, though actually not as bad as I was expecting; but naturally I was expecting the worst. This is such a big jump we've made—the biggest jump either of us has ever done, by far. During the training period the most I ever did was something like ninety years. This is a jump of one hundred eighty centuries. So I figured I'd come slamming into the Prince's mind behind a head of steam strong enough to knock me cold for a week. And in fact it was pretty rough, let me tell you.

The tuning was perfect. Of course the purpose of all the preliminary time-search scouting work was to locate a member of the royal family for me to use as my host. And they managed to land me right in the mind of nobody less than the heir to the throne himself!

I won't ever forget the moment of landing, which felt to me the way I'd expect to feel when hitting the water after a very clumsy dive made from a very high diving board. There was pain, real pain, a lot of it. It would have knocked the breath out of me if there had been any breath in me in the first place.

Then came the total strangeness of that wild moment when the minds are fusing, which you know all too well yourself–that time when you can't really tell whether you're you any more or somebody else–and then I blanked out.

So did the Prince, evidently.

We were unconscious for perhaps a day and a half, possibly a little more. That's why I'm not sure whether this is really Christmas Eve. Once I came to, and had made enough linguistic connections to be able to understand what I was hearing, I tried to figure out how long the Prince and I had been under, going by some of the things that the courtiers were saying to him:

"We rejoice, Highness, that the darkness has ended for you."

"Two days and a night did we pray, Highness! Two days and a night you were gone from us!"

But it hadn't been quite as long as that. As you've probably discovered yourself by now, their system of days and weeks isn't much like the one we use, what with a "day" being considered just the time between dawn and sunset, and the dark hours being called a "night," and the next biggest unit being a group of ten "days" and "nights" together, which works out to a five-day week on our scale, unless I still have it wrong. And two Athilantan days and a night would be a day and a half. But I do think this really is

Christmas Eve, counting from the day we set out from Home Year and figuring up the total time that I believe has elapsed since then.

(A question, Lora: Is it really proper to regard this day as Christmas Eve, considering that we're currently living at a time thousands of years before Christ's birth? I suppose it is. We did set out from an A.D. Home Year, after all. But still the idea strikes me as a little peculiar. Then again, everything about this venture seems a little peculiar, starting with the fact that you and I have been converted into nothing more than nets of electrical energy and have been hurled thousands of years into the past, leaving our bodies behind in deepsleep. But telling myself that this is Christmas Eve makes it feel just a little homier for me here. God knows I need to have things feel a little homier right now. So do you, I imagine, out there in the frozen wastelands of the mammoth-hunter people.)

I have a very good link with the Prince's mind. I can read his every thought, I can understand the things he says and the things that are said to him, I can monitor his heartbeat and his respiratory rate and the hormonal output of his glandular system. I am able to anticipate the movements of his body even before he consciously knows he's going to make those movements. I pick up impulses traveling from his brain to his muscles, and I feel the muscles getting ready to react. I could, whenever I choose, override his own conscious commands and get his body to do whatever I felt like having it do. Not that I'd do any such thing—not while he's awake and aware. I don't want him to start thinking that he's been possessed by a demon, even though that's essentially what has happened to him.

How does it feel, Lora, thinking of yourself as a demon? Not so good, eh? But that's what we really are. That's the truth, isn't it?

The Prince doesn't have the slightest suspicion, I'm sure, that he's been invaded this way, that an intruder from the distant future is inside him, wrapped around his entire nervous system like a blanket of undetectable mist.

I know that he felt me arriving. It wouldn't have been possible for him not to feel the impact of that. But he had no clear notion of what was actually happening.

"The fingertip of a god has touched my soul," he told his companions. "For a time I was thrown into darkness. The gods chose to touch me, and who can say why?"

Some kind of stroke, in other words. And then a day and a night and a day of unconsciousness.

Well, the gods work in mysterious ways. So far as anyone knows, the Prince has made a complete recovery from whatever it was that smote him. I remain hidden, crouching invisible within his mind, a mysterious web of electrical impulses safe from any Athilantan means of detection.

And now he sleeps. I can't read his dreams, of course—that layer of his mind is much too deep to reach—but his body is at peace, very relaxed. That's why I think he's dreaming of his homeland, the warm sweet isle of Athilan. Most likely he thinks he's lying in his own soft bed.

But he isn't.

A little while ago I picked him up and sleepwalked him over to his fine shining desk, made of rare and strange timber from the southern lands—something black that may be ebony inlaid with strips of several bright golden woods—and right now he's sitting upright, hard at work writing this letter for me. Taking dictation, so to speak. A royal prince, taking dictation. But how could he ever know that?

The only clue he could possibly have is the stiffness that's building up in his right arm and hand. The shape of the letters we use is very different from the Athilantan curlicues and spirals he's accustomed to, and his muscles are straining and cramping as he writes. When he wakes up, though, he'll never be able to guess why his arm is a little sore.

We're near the seacoast, getting ready to break camp and take ship for Athilan itself. The Athilantans have a fairly big outpost here, perhaps three or four hundred people. The name of the place seems to be Thibarak. There are little primitive mainlander encampments scattered widely through the countryside all around. The mainlanders, who come to Thibarak to trade with the Athilantans, regard the powerful island people virtually as gods. I imagine that's true all over Europe, for as far as the Athilantan empire reaches.

The landscape here is pretty grim and forbidding, though I suppose nothing like the way it is where you are in Naz Glesim. No glaciers here, no ice-fields—the ice has all retreated to the north and east by now—but the ground has a raw, scraped look to it, bare and damp, rough and rocky. The weather is very, very cold. I doubt that it's been above freezing at all since I've been here, though the days are bright and sunny. Still, it's evidently a lot warmer than it was a few hundred years ago, or than it is right now out where you are, which must be still pretty much in the grip of the ice. We have some birch and willow trees here, and a few pines. I've seen occasional mammoths and bison, but not many: the big Ice Age animals don't like these new forests, and have wandered away to colder country where the grazing is better.

The Prince's name is Ramifon Sigiliterimor Septagimot Stolifax Blayl, which means, approximately, Beloved of the Gods and Light of the Universe. But nobody calls him that, because it would be sacrilegious. I learned it by rummaging around in the basement of his memory. His parents call him Ram, which is short for all the rest. His brothers and sisters call him Premianor Tisilan, which means First of the Family.

Everybody else calls him Stoy Thilayl, which means Your Highness.

He is eighteen years old, dark-haired and olive-skinned, and very strong, with enormous shoulders and forearms. He's shorter than he'd like to be, though–in fact, not very tall at all, even by Athilantan standards–and he's not too happy about that, though he knows it can't be helped. Generally he seems good-natured and very capable. Some day, if all goes well for him, he'll become Grand Darionis of the Island of Athilan. Or, in other words, King of Atlantis.

I wonder what he'd think if he knew that his magnificent island of Athilan, which has built such a glorious empire and rules the entire Ice Age world, is doomed to be destroyed in another few hundred years. So thoroughly destroyed, indeed, that the people of future ages will come to think of its very existence as nothing more than a pretty myth.

For that matter, I wonder how he'd react if he were to learn that the people of future ages are sending observers back across a gulf of nearly twenty-one thousand years to find out something about this Athilantan Empire, and that one of them is currently sitting right inside his own mind.

Well, I'm not likely to discover what he would make of that. The last thing I'm going to do is tap the Prince on the shoulder and say, "Hi, Prince, guess who's here!"

I hope that everything is fine for you out in the frozen hinterlands. I think of you all the time and miss you more than is really good for me. Write to me, if you can. Tell me everything that's happening to you. Everything!

More later.

Much love–

–Roy

2.

Four days have gone by since my last.

I mean four of our 24-hour days, not the half-day "days" that the Athilantans use. We're still here on this barren, frosty coast. The Athilantan ships are waiting in Thibarak harbor to take us to the island, but there are all sorts of rites and rituals that have to be performed first. Mainlander people in startling numbers–there must be thousands of them–have turned up to bid farewell to the Prince as he makes ready to set out for home. I suppose it isn't a common thing to have a prince of the royal blood visiting here. And so every day we have bonfires blazing, bulls being sacrificed, chanting going on and on. Prince Ram presides over it with terrific aplomb. It's plain that he's been raised from childhood to rule the empire, and he knows exactly what needs to be done.

But though I haven't been able to budge yet from my starting point, this place, provincial as it is, has plenty of fascination of its own. Maybe it isn't glittering wonderful

Atlantis, but it's the past, Lora, the remote and weird prehistoric past!

It's astonishing just being here. Every minute brings something new. I want to turn to you and say, "Look at that, Lora! Isn't that incredible?" But of course you aren't here. You're way over there in eastern Europe. If only we could have made this trip together! (I know, I know, we are together, sort of. But I'm here and you're there, instead of our both being in the same place. And don't bother telling me that it would be unnecessary duplication of resources to send two observers to the same place as well as the same time. I know all that. I still wish you were here, close enough for me to talk to every day.)

But since you aren't, I'll tell you what I'm learning. And one of these days maybe I'll be lucky enough to hear what you've been up to, too.

The difference between the Athilantans and the mainlanders is enormous. I don't just mean the cultural difference, which is even wider than the gap, say, between the Romans of Caesar's day and the savages who lived in the forests of Germany and France. That was Iron Age versus Bronze Age; this is Iron Age versus Stone Age. But I mean the physical difference. You must be seeing it, too. They're two different types of people altogether.

Correct me if I'm wrong, but my impression is that the mainlanders here at Thibarak are the people that archaeologists call the Solutreans, who lived in this part of Europe a couple of thousand years after Cro-Magnon times. These Solutreans are tall, slender, fair-haired people with a sort of Viking look about them. They wear leather clothes very finely stitched together, and they use stone tools that look pretty elegant to me, long and thin and tapering, with a lot of fine little chip-strokes around the edges. Mostly they make their homes in shallow caves or beneath shelters of overhanging rock, though I see from Prince Ram's mind that in the warmer seasons they also build little flimsy wickerwork huts for themselves.

The Athilantans are nothing remotely like them in any way.

The island folk tend to be much shorter and stockier than the mainlanders, with dark hair and somewhat swarthy skins. Their eyes are brown or black, never blue. It's basically a Mediterranean look, Greek or Spanish, and yet there's something not quite convincingly Greek or Spanish about them that I can't put my finger on. Their cheekbones have an oddly slanted look, their mouths are a little too wide, the shape of their heads is a little strange. Maybe you've noticed it too, even though there are only five or six Athilantans out there in Naz Glesim, and I have hundreds to observe here.

My theory, for what it's worth, is that the Athilantans actually are the ancestors of the Mediterranean folk of our Home Era, but modern Mediterranean people look a little different from Athilantans because of the changes that have taken place during all the thousands of years of evolution and interbreeding since the destruction of Athilan. I realize, though, that that's only a guess and may be very wide of the mark.

What amazes me most is how advanced the Athilantans are, technologically speaking, over the mainlanders. Atlantis really was a magical kingdom! It's almost unbelievable, when you stop to think about it—a wealthy and far-flung maritime empire that understands the use of iron and bronze, a civilization at least as advanced as those of Greece and Rome, way back here in the Upper Paleolithic Era!

How strange that archaeologists have never found any of their artifacts. No bronze swords or daggers mixed in with Cro-Magnon stone tools, none of their sculpture, no fragments of the buildings they erected on the mainland of Europe at outposts such as the ones you and I are currently at. Part of the answer, I guess, is that even though modern-world archaeologists have been digging up ancient ruins in a serious way for the past few hundred years they've still only scratched the surface of the buried remains of the ancient cultures and simply haven't had the good luck to come across any Athilantan artifacts so far. And maybe bronze daggers will rust beyond discovery in twenty thousand years, whereas stone tools last forever. But that can't be the whole explanation.

Well, I have a theory about that, too, Lora.

What if—after the fall of Athilan—the oppressed people of mainland Europe arose and systematically rounded up every last trace of their Athilantan masters, every weapon and tool and bit of sculpture they could find, and carried the whole business out to sea and dumped it all? Every scrap. Out of some tremendous vindictive urge they blotted the Athilantans from the face of the Earth. And twenty thousand years of ocean silt did the rest.

What do you think?

Sooner or later, time research will give us the answer. We can be pretty certain of that. We'll pinpoint the exact date of the destruction of Athilan and send observers into Europe to see what happened after that. But for the moment, I think my idea's as good as anything that's been suggested.

I have a lot of time to sit here thinking up these theories, right now. And I have to confess, despite what I said a little earlier, that I really am getting tired of this place. I want to get moving. I want to see Atlantis.

How tremendously frustrating it is to know that the royal ships are waiting in the harbor, ready to carry us off to that warm and beautiful and fabulous land out in the ocean, and instead I'm stuck in this chilly miserable place somewhere on the coast of France while the endless rituals and sacrifices are performed and rivers of bulls' blood run along the rocky ground. Prince Ram stands on top of a wickerwork tower, smiling and waving and scattering handfuls of grain to the groveling mainlanders. Imagine it, grain, in Paleolithic Europe, where farming isn't supposed to have been invented for another ten or fifteen thousand years! As the prince tosses the grain, long lines of the local folks keep coming on and on to snatch it up, more people than I ever would have guessed there were in the whole world at this time.

I really don't want to be here in this two-bit provincial trading post any longer. Yes, it's fascinating in its way, I suppose. But it's also cold and raw and primitive, and it isn't Atlantis. I want to see Atlantis. Lord, do I want to see Atlantis! It'll be just my luck if the whole place sinks into the sea before I get there. We aren't sure, after all, precisely when the final cataclysm is due to happen. It could even be next week, though I like to think there's more time than that. Nevertheless here I sit. Here I wait.

Miss you so very much.

Until next time–

–Roy

3.

Written at sea. I'm embarrassed to report that I've already lost count of the days, but I'm sure that we are just past the turning of the year—going by the Home Era calendar, that is. By the Athilantan calendar too, for that matter, because I've learned that the Athilantans begin their year on the day of the winter solstice, our December 21. That makes sense: the day the sun begins its return, the day when the days begin to grow longer.

(If you've done a better job of keeping track of time than I have, Lora, can you help me out? When and if you answer this, give me a clue, in terms of the phases of the moon or something, to the exact date in Home Era time. Not knowing the exact calendar time right now doesn't matter all that much, but I can see that it could cause big problems for me as the time draws near to return to our own time. I shouldn't have messed up like this. Dumb of me, dumb, dumb, dumb!)

Anyway, I'll assume that by our own calendar today is January 3, 18, 861 B.C. I can't be more than a day or two off.

So: Happy New Year, Lora! (Give or take a day or two. . . .) Happy New Year! But it's really difficult to keep converting Athilantan days into our days, and really dumb to use a calendar that has no relevance whatever back here. I suspect that you're using the Athilantan calendar now, although you've most likely been keeping track of the Home Era time as well. Since I can't really be sure of the right Home Era date any more, I might as well switch over to the local system. And–well–by Athilantan reckoning, I see by Prince Ram's mind, this is Day 13 of the Month of New Light in the year of the Great River. So be it.

Starting over, then–

Day 13, New Light, Great River. Aboard the imperial Athilantan vessel Lord of Day, bound from Brittany toward the isle of Athilan!

You ought to see these ships, Lora! You wouldn't believe them for a moment.

What I expected, considering the general cultural level of these Athilantans as I've come to know it in the short while I've been here, was something along the lines of the Greek or Roman galley, with two or three banks of oars and maybe a sail. Or, maybe, a vessel more like a merchantman–you know, a pure sailing ship, square-rigged or possibly with a lateen sail.

Lora, this is some kind of steamship. I'm not kidding. A steamship. In the Paleolithic!

Unbelievable. Incomprehensible.

I said last time that the Athilantans were an Iron Age people living in Stone Age times. That was an understatement, by plenty. I hadn't had a chance yet to study my surroundings carefully enough. These people aren't simply on a cultural par with the Greeks or the Romans, as I used to think–no, they've got at least a nineteenth-century technology, and maybe something even more advanced than that. I wasn't able to see that on the mainland, and you probably can't see it out where you are. But this ship is an eye-opener.

I'm not sure that there are actual steam engines down below. For all I really know, the engine room is staffed by a team of sorcerers who keep giant turbines going round and round by uttering spells. Truth is, I don't know what's down there, and neither does Prince Ram. Princes don't need to bother with such technological details, apparently. I'd like to sleepwalk him down belowdecks so that I could have a look around, but I don't dare. Not until I'm completely sure that my control over his mind is good enough to keep him asleep as long as I want. I don't want him suddenly waking up and finding himself down in the engine room, where somebody of his high rank ordinarily has no reason to go. And then starting to wonder if there's something funny going on inside his brain.

This much I can tell you, though. The ship is big, as large as a good-sized yacht, long and tapering, with a flat stern and a very high keel. The hull is of metal: iron, probably, but for all I know these people may be capable of fabricating steel. You may balk at that idea, but just keep on reading.

There's a mast, a big one, but no sign of any rigging or lines. Either the mast has some sacred purpose or it's some kind of antenna, but it isn't used to support sails. There are also two funnels, or smokestacks. I never see any smoke coming out of them. I can feel a very light but steady vibration, as though engines of some sort are at work. That's all I know.

Oh, one other thing. These people use electricity.

I know, I know, I know. It sounds nutty. The first time I saw the lights coming on, I thought the Prince was hallucinating. Or else that I must be misreading the data, coming up with false sensory equivalents for what was passing through his mind. Or maybe I was the one who was hallucinating. I tell you, Lora, it hit me like an earthquake. I was rocked by it. Flustered, bewildered, disoriented. For a moment I wondered whether I could believe anything that I was perceiving. Maybe it was all equally cockeyed. Paleolithic electricity?

But I checked and doublechecked, and the signal was coming through clear and true from him to me. What I was perceiving was what Prince Ram was seeing, to the last decimal place. So it wasn't any fever dream. It was electric lighting, Lora. However incredible that sounds.

Where I was on the mainland, everything was lit by properly prehistoric-looking oil lamps, smelly and smoky, and no doubt it's the same out your way. But every corridor of this ship that I've seen so far, and every stateroom too, I suspect, has electric lights. I suppose they simply haven't bothered to set up generators in the mainland outposts, or maybe there's no ready supply of fuel for them there. But they must have some kind of generator aboard ship, cranking out the kilowatts just like at home.

The light-globes are big and awkward, and the light they give is harsh and glaring, but there's no question that it's electrical. I've seen Prince Ram turn the light in his cabin on and off by touching a plate in the wall.

With no effort whatsoever I could make myself believe that I'm aboard a twentieth-century vessel—a peculiar one, true, designed by someone from an obscure country who has invented the whole concept of the oceangoing ship from scratch without ever having seen one from Europe or the United States, but corresponding to them in all the important details. And yet I know that I'm back here at the tail end of the Ice Age, with woolly mammoths and shaggy rhinoceroses still wandering around where Paris and London will someday be.

Who are these Athilantans, anyway? How could they possibly have achieved all this, tens of thousands of years out of the normal human sequence of cultural evolution? It doesn't make any sense. Suddenly, in the midst of a world that still uses flint axes and choppers, for a society to spring up that has mastered metals, engineering, architecture, even electricity–it's crazy, Lora. I don't get it. The old myths said that the Atlanteans were a great people, but not that they were miracle-workers.

Well, let that be for now. I have plenty of other things to tell you.

I'm pretty sure now that the place we set out from was the coast of Brittany. We all knew in advance back at Home Era, when we began focusing on members of the ruling caste as my target, that important members of the royal family made regular inspection tours of the coastal provinces and that if they aimed me at the mind of one of the high princes I was just likely to come down in ancient France as in Athilan itself.

Certainly the stone tools that the mainlanders were using were the sort of things used in France at this time. And the harbor was a good one. Whether Thibarak was Cherbourg or Le Havre, I can't say; but unless I have my geography all cockeyed we have just sailed out through the English Channel–on the clear days it seemed to me I could see the English shore to the north–and now we are running far into the Atlantic, curving down past Portugal toward the mouth of the Mediterranean. Which is just where our archaeologists had decided was the most likely place for Atlantis to have been, of course–somewhere between the Canary Islands and the Azores.

The weather gets milder and warmer every day. Birds, soft breezes (even in the middle of an Ice Age winter!), drifting masses of seaweed. There is a lot of rain, virtually daily, but it's a gentle kind of rain and when the sun comes out afterward the rainbows are heartbreaking. Especially when I stop to think that Atlantis lies at the end of them.

Life aboard ship is–

Uh-oh–trouble–

Six or seven hours later, same day.

A narrow escape. I was using the Prince to write this letter, and I almost got caught.

Ram was in his stateroom, sitting in one of the hammocklike things that they use on this ship. I had him under trance, and I was telling you all about the weather at sea when suddenly his personal steward came in. To tidy up the room, I suppose.

It isn't the custom among the Athilantans to knock on doors. They make a kind of high whistling noise when they want to enter a room. I was so preoccupied with dictating my letter that I didn't even notice. So in walks the steward, and he sees the heir to the imperial throne sitting bolt upright in his hammock with a weird trance look on his face.

"Your Highness!" he says. And then, in real terror, "Your Highness?!?"

He rushes over, seizes the Prince, shakes him hard. Well, you can bet I broke contact with the Prince's mind right away. He snapped out of it and looked around in confusion and got angry with the steward for bothering him while he was trying to take a nap. That part went all right.

But I couldn't put the Prince back into trance until the steward had left the cabin. And the steward took just long enough to get out of there so that the Prince had time to look down at the sheet of vellum he was holding, and stare at the nonsensical marks scribbled all over it.

So when the steward finally was gone, there was Prince Ram sitting there, wide awake, holding a sheet of vellum in one hand and an ink-stylus in the other, and the vellum was covered with strange marks. Marks that were, in fact, a script that nobody on Earth is going to be able to understand for another good many thousands of years.

He was absolutely mystified. He held it up close to his eyes, turned it upside down, shook his head in bewilderment. And I heard his thought loud and clear:

—What in the name of all the gods is THIS?

Well, I put him back to sleep and tried to get down into his mind and eradicate all memory of what he had just seen. As you know, that isn't the easiest thing in the world to do. You poke around in your carrier's short-term memory, trying to blot out a particular incident, and if you're not really careful, you can blot out half a day of other stuff, or a whole week, or even start ripping up the basic memory framework before you realize what you're doing. I didn't want to leave him feeling like an amnesia victim. So I tiptoed around in his memory bank, slicing here and there, doing my best. I think I did the job as nicely as anybody could have; but when I was done, I wasn't entirely confident that I had completely cleaned things up.

I hid the letter. And then I hid myself, getting down into stasis and just sitting quietly in a subconscious corner of the Prince's brain all afternoon. I didn't try to make contact with his cerebral levels in any way whatever.

(That's the hardest thing of all to do, I think—when you have to lay low, sitting tight, doing nothing. After all, we aren't capable of going to sleep. And disembodied entities like us can't just head out for a long walk to kill the time. So there we sit, unable even to twitch. Like prisoners in a cage no bigger than a human brain, absolutely immobilized, counting off seconds and minutes for lack of anything else to do. It's maddening, isn't it? It's almost unbearable.)

I guess I could have used the time to prowl through the

Prince's basic memory storage to pick up a little useful data about the Athilantan civilization, but I didn't dare. He might just be able to detect me poking around—a curious itchy feeling in his mind, let's say. I didn't want to arouse any more suspicions than I already had. And it seemed to me right then that there already was an odd new edge to the Prince's mind, a kind of prickly wariness.

I've seen that happen before. But on other occasions, when my carrier has been allowed to get an inkling of the real situation, it has passed in a few hours. Sure enough, that's what happened this time. Ram began to relax, the edge on his mind went away, he went about his princely duties as though nothing had occurred. And ten minutes ago he returned to his cabin to relax. I put him under trance and got this unfinished letter out of its hiding place.

What a strange business this is, hitchhiking through the past inside someone else's mind! I've done it a dozen different times now, and I'm still not fully used to the idea. I'm not sure I really like it very much—treating another human being as a mere vehicle, moving him this way and that for your own convenience, going through his most intimate thoughts and memories as though he were nothing more than software available for scanning. Sometimes it seems a little ugly. Like being a spy, in a way. What it amounts to is that nobody who ever lived has any secrets from us time-traveling, twenty-first century nosybodies.

On the other hand, since it's physically impossible for us to travel through time except as intangible electrical impulses, this is how we have to do it. And it does allow us to recapture all kinds of astounding knowledge that otherwise would have been lost forever in the bottomless sea of the past.

Anyway—picking up where I left off so many hours ago—

We are obviously moving into subtropical seas. Even in the Ice Age, it seems, the midsection of the world had pretty decent weather, much rainier than it is in Home Era but not particularly cold. There's a springtime tenderness in the air that everyone aboard ship is responding to. The Prince and his whole retinue have been on the chilly mainland more than a year, and they're as eager to get back to Athilan as I am to see it for the first time.

This afternoon the Prince was working on a report to his royal father about the current status of Athilantan trading posts on the mainland—evidently the thing that he was sent to Europe to investigate. There was a map open on his desk as he worked, and I was able to see the whole layout of the empire.

Incredible!

They've got outposts strung all along the southern half of Stone Age Europe as far east as Russia, and down into North Africa and the Middle East. Most of the trade is done by sea, but a network of roads links everything together inland. It's awesome how they have it all connected, couriers going back and forth over an elaborate network of highways. (No, I don't think they use automobiles—all I saw while I was in Brittany were chariots, some drawn by small, sturdy, fierce-looking horses, and some by what looked like enormous reindeer.)

And all this will be lost. All this will be totally forgotten, as though it had never been. The memory of it will survive only as fable and myth, which no one will really take seriously until the coming of the age of time exploration. It's heartbreaking to think about it.

The Athilantan highway system runs up as far as what I think is the middle of Germany, then zigs and zags through Central Europe, avoiding the most heavily glaciated areas. One of the roads goes straight to Naz Glesim, where you are, the easternmost outpost of the empire. It gave me a funny feeling to see that name on the map and know that you're there at this very moment.

Thibarak, the coastal trading post where I was, in Brittany, is a sort of headquarters for the imperial mainland operations—at least the Western European branch. Couriers go back and forth between Thibarak and Naz Glesim all the time, bearing directives from the home government and reports from the provincial governor. The trip takes a couple of months each way. I should be able to slip these letters into the diplomatic pouch, and if you really did make it into the mind of Provincial Governor Sippurilayl as they planned it when they did the preliminary time-search, you'll eventually get to read them. Or not, as the case may be. Try to arrange it so that Governor Sippurilayl sends letters back to Prince Ramifon Sigiliterimor. That way I'll see them sooner or later. Then, of course, we both will have to wipe out of our carriers' minds all memory of the strange messages in unknown gibberish that they keep getting from each other. But with practice that won't be too hard.

I think we'll reach Atlantis in another four days or so. At sundown the Prince was standing on the deck wearing only a light tunic and mantle, and soft warm breezes were blowing out of the south.

Poor Lora! You must be freezing your butt off out there on the barren Russian steppes while I sit here telling you about the sweet springlike weather we're enjoying. Well, I don't mean to rub it in, you know. It was just the luck of the toss that sent me to Atlantis and you to Naz Glesim, and I'm well aware that a mere matter of heads instead of tails and I'd be the one stuck in the back woods right now. And next trip it may be the other way around for us.

(A pity that they won't ever send us to the same locale when we make these jumps. I know, I know, they want to spread us out over the maximum territory. The best we can hope for is to go to the same era but in different geographical regions. Which I guess is better than nothing. As they told us when we volunteered for this, time travel works best when two people who have a strong emotional connection are sent out as a team. And they're right. Simply knowing that you're here–thousands of miles away, sure, but in the same era–gives me a warm, comfortable feeling. And that helps immensely in fending off the terrible isolation that would otherwise come with knowing that I'm so distant in time from everything and everyone that I care for. All the same, I'd like to be able to see you once in a while. I'd like to be able to touch you. I'd like to be able to–oh, well, never mind. At least I can write to you. And maybe one of these days the courier will get back from the eastern part of the empire and there'll be a letter from you to me.)

Meanwhile Atlantis gets closer every second.

Until then–give my regards to all my good friends in Naz Glesim, if there happen to be any, which I doubt.

Miss you miss you miss you miss you.

–Roy

4.

Day 27, Month of New Light, Year of the Great River—Atlantis, Lora! I'm in Atlantis!

The island of Athilan, I should say. It came into view in the middle of the night, while Prince Ram slept. There came a whistling at the door and they woke him up, because he had to perform the Ritual of Homecoming. We went out on deck. And then at last I saw it, gleaming in the moonlight right in front of us.

It's a lofty island, rising high out of the Western Atlantic. The great mountain in the middle, which is called Mount Balamoris, is as I think you know the volcano that sooner or later is going to blow this whole place to oblivion. Later rather than sooner, I profoundly hope. But obviously Mount Balamoris has been inactive for hundreds or even thousands of years, and a fantastic city has been built on its vast slopes and down along the broad plain that runs to the sea.

What was on my mind as we made our final approach to Atlantis was the description of it that Plato gave in his dialog *Kritias*, which you and I studied while we were in training. That Atlantis was a "continent," rich and beautiful, with an abundance of trees and shrubs, flowers and fruits, animals both wild and tame, and precious minerals. And that the capital city, on the southern coast, was a huge metropolis, fifteen miles around, having the form of two circular strips of land divided by three wide canals, with great walls of stone, bridges, towers, and palaces. At the center of the city was a holy quarter within an enclosure of gold, where the temples were covered with gold and silver and their roofs were made of ivory.

I can hear you reminding me that nobody in modern times takes Plato's account seriously as history. Well, yes, I know that. I haven't forgotten that he wrote it around 355 B.C. and even he says that Atlantis had been destroyed 9,000 years earlier. Which means he can't possibly have any hard data about it, because 9,000 years before Plato's time Greece was deep in prehistoric darkness. I'm aware that it's been the general scholarly belief for a long time that Plato probably made the whole story up himself—that all it is is a fantasy, just a pleasant work of fiction.

But is it? I wonder. Now that I've had a look at Atlantis with my own eyes, I'm not so sure that Plato was simply making it all up from scratch.

One thing we know, thanks to time exploration, is that Atlantis actually existed. As recently as the twentieth century it was thought to be purely mythical. But no: we have proof now that a spectacularly great island-city really did exist in the middle of the Atlantic Ocean thousands of years before Plato's time, and that it really was destroyed by a gigantic cataclysm. So it certainly isn't beyond belief that memories of the place and its horrendous destruction might have passed into legend, or that tales of fabulous Atlantis could have been told and retold for generation after generation, across time immemorial. And some confused bits and scraps of those ancient legends might still have been circulating in the Mediterranean region at the time when Plato lived.

The strange thing is how much the real Atlantis, the place that I'm staring at even as I write this, actually does resemble the one that Plato described.

It isn't a continent, of course. It's a just a very large island, maybe the size of Borneo or Madagascar. But how can you tell, when you see some enormous landmass in front of you that stretches a vast distance out of sight in both directions, whether you're looking at a continental shore or simply a big island? Plato wasn't that far off the mark. Certainly Atlantis was much bigger than Great Britain or Cuba or Iceland.

He was wrong about other details. For example, the capitals's not on the southern shore. It's on the western one. But the city does have a circular layout, with huge walls made up of giant stone blocks laid one atop another. The masonry work was done with fantastic precision, too. It's absolutely perfect. There are waterways and bridges inside the walls, and splendid boulevards that no city on Earth could have equalled until modern times. Perhaps no city of modern Earth does.

And I tell you, Lora, this waterfront district right here is amazing. If you could only see it! There's a tremendous semicircular harbor with a massive quay of black granite faced with pink marble, and stone piers jutting far out into the water. All around me are Athilantan ships that have come in from all over the world, and right at this minute I'm watching them unloading what must be absolutely fabulous cargoes. Officials are checking everything out on shore, boxes and boxes full of precious metals and jewels, spices, furs, strange animals, rare woods.

Then, over to one side of the harbor, there's the Fountain of the Spheres, which shoots an enormous jet of water into the sky every quarter-hour. On the other side is the Temple of the Dolphins, a white marble structure that has the most incredibly pure, balanced design. Believe me, it makes the Parthenon itself look a little shoddy.

A broad street, the Street of Starwatchers, runs just back of the waterfront. At the head of the Street of Starwatchers there's an imposing domed tower, the Imperial Observatory, and just behind it begins a tremendous avenue, the Concourse of the Sky, which cuts through the city for miles, leading to—yes, a central zone of sacred buildings, just like Plato said, set on a sloping hill. The walls of the temples are covered with white marble, not Plato's silver and gold, but when the afternoon sun strikes them the entire city blazes with reflected light.

The city continues on the far side of the sacred zone, sprawling right up into the foothills of Mount Balamoris. Beyond are parks, farms, the mines where copper and iron and gold are found, and a huge forest preserve full of all manner of wild beasts, including a herd of elephants. I don't mean the woolly mammoths that are roaming around in Ice Age Europe out where you are, but plain old ordinary elephants, very much like the ones we can see in the zoo, except I think these are even bigger. They've got ears the size of tents.

The climate here is extremely gentle. Judging by the fact that night and day are just about equal in length even in midwinter, I'd say that Atlantis is located smack on the Tropic of Cancer, or else not very far north of it. There's a little rain just about every day, but it clears off fast and in a little while the sun is out again and everything's nice and warm. The air is mild and beautifully transparent, the sky is a delicate blue, and wherever you look you see flowers in bloom. It's hard to believe that at this very moment most of Europe and North America is buried under ice. Or that enormous shaggy shambling mammoths and rhinos are grazing in the places where our great cities are going to be built some time in the far future. Or that little bands of men clad in furs are out there trying to hunt them with crude weapons made out of stone.

No wonder shimmering memories of this place continued to glow in the minds of people like Plato thousands of years later. In every human tribe the wise old storytellers must have passed vivid legends of it down and down and down through the eons, across all those thousands of years of darkness that followed the time of destruction. That great lost city, that barely remembered paradise, that vanished realm of miracles and wonders—what tales they must have told of it! And went on telling, year after year, century after century, while the ice slowly retreated, and mankind rediscovered the skills of farming, and learned to build towns and villages, and eventually, in Sumer and Egypt and China, began once more to approach the level of accomplishment that we call "civilization."

The astounding thing, the utterly unbelievable thing, is this: that the old legends didn't even begin to tell the full story of how miraculous Atlantis really was. The actual Atlantis of the year 18,862 B.C., with its steamships and its electricity and its astonishing architectural and engineering marvels, is tremendously more fantastic than any of the Greek or Roman talespinners ever imagined.

I mean it. So far as technology goes, it's right up there with today's New York or Paris or London in many ways, only much more beautiful than any of them. And it existed all the way back here in Stone Age times, when no one else in the rest of the world had managed to get very far beyond living in caves and fashioning knives and axes out of pieces of flint.

Right now I have no explanation of how this could have been possible. None whatever.

Prince Ramifon Sigiliterimor's return to the isle of Atlantis involved him in so much ritual and formality that I began to think I was never going to get to see the city at all. We remained cooped up on the ship for an incredible length of time. It was almost as crazy-making as those days of waiting around at Thibarak harbor for the end of the departure rituals so that the royal fleet could finally set out.

First came the Ritual of Homecoming. In this one the Prince gave thanks for his safe voyage home with a lot of praying and burning of incense and the sacrifice of a bull. The Prince performed the sacrifice with his own hands. I hated having to watch at such close range, but I didn't have any choice. At least he killed the animal fast. He's evidently had a lot of practice. He used a jewel-hilted blade made of what almost certainly was steel. I find that fascinating in a creepy sort of way, don't you? That they'd use high-technology stuff like a steel weapon to perform a barbaric rite like animal sacrifice, I mean. A weird mix. The bull was actually an aurochs, that extinct ancestor of modern cattle, an enormous beast with terrifying black-tipped curving horns at least a yard long.

I thought we'd be going ashore then, but no, after a lot of chanting and parading around, and a feast of charred, half-raw aurochs meat that made me glad the Prince was putting it in his digestive tract and not in mine—though it's sometimes hard to tell the difference when you're a time-trip passenger, you know—the Prince went belowdecks and busied himself in front of a little shrine in the captain's cabin, invoking this god and that, for hours. A team of priests came on board and took part in this; but when they left, Prince Ram remained on the ship.

Night fell. Crowds stood along the quay, singing and hailing the Prince. He waved back at them from the deck of his flagship. There was a fireworks display such as I've never seen in my life.

In the morning, the Prince's younger brother and sister came to give him the official family welcome. Princess Rayna is about fifteen, I'd say, and Prince Caiminor maybe thirteen. They look very much like Prince Ram, stocky and short, olive-hued skin, dark eyebrows.

Their reunion with their brother was all very formal, with touching of fingertips taking the place of kissing. The Ritual of Greeting lasted right on into mid-afternoon. Then at last they escorted him from the ship, and—by courtesy of my carrier, Prince Ramifon Sigiliterimor Septagimot Stolifax Blayl, Premianor Tisilan of Athilan, I got a chance finally to set foot on the shore of lost Atlantis.

But I didn't get very far. Off we went to the nearby Temple of the Dolphins, where a kind of tent had been set up for the Prince just inside the outermost row of perfect marble columns. Here he had to be purified, purged of any taint that he might have picked up while dwelling among the grubby uncivilized people of the mainland.

This Rite of Purification took another day and a night. They bathed him in milk and covered him with the petals of red and yellow flowers and chanted again and again, "May you be free of all uncleanness. May you be free of all uncleanness." On and on and on. "May the dirt of the mainland no longer cling to your skin," they chanted. "May you be free of all uncleanness." Over and over, until I thought I'd lose my mind.

But it taught me something important about this place.

There's real four-star racism here. That's what the Rite of Purification is all about. The Athilantans have deep contempt for the mainlanders. They are the dirt of the mainland from which the rite is supposed to cleanse the Prince.

The Athilantan name for the mainlanders is "the dirt people."

My command of Athilantan grammar isn't yet as strong as I'd like it to be, so I'm not sure whether they mean that the mainlanders live in dirt (that is, their scruffy caves and lean-tos) or that they actually are dirt. But I think it's the latter.

So these noble, splendid, magnificently civilized Athilantans regard the people of Stone Age Europe as not much more than animals. Have you noticed that, too, out in Naz Glesim? Maybe it's different there, where just a handful of Athilantans live in the midst of hundreds of mainlanders. They'd have to be more careful there. But here, where there isn't a mainland face to be seen, the Athilantans don't even try to hide their scorn for them.

"We thank you, O Gods, for the return of our beloved Prince to the human realm from the land of the dirt people."

Get that little distinction, Lora. The Prince has returned to the human realm.

I suppose we can't really blame the Athilantans for feeling superior, considering that they live in amazing marble palaces with electric lighting and indoor plumbing while the rest of the world lives in crude Stone Age ways. Still, it's going too far, I think, to insist that the Stone Age people on the mainland aren't even human. Backward, yes, by Athilantan standards. But to say that they aren't human? That's sheer arrogance.

When you take into account how deeply the Athilantans seem to despise the mainlanders, my earlier notion about why there haven't been any Athilantan artifacts found in any of the Paleolithic sites our archaeologists have excavated makes even more sense. If you've been ruled for thousands of years by a superior race that regards you as dirt, and suddenly the homeland of that superior race gets blown to kingdom come by a volcano, that gives you a good opportunity to rise up and kill all the surviving overlords. And then you might just want to take every last scrap of material belonging to your former masters that reminds you of your subjugation—every jar and dish and sculpture and even their tools, useful though they might be—and dump it all in the ocean while you're at it. Makes sense to me.

We need to check it out via time-search. Once we've begun our studies of the actual destruction epoch of Athilantan history, we ought to try to find out what happened afterward on the mainland, whether there really was the kind of purge of the hated masters that I'm suggesting. I think it stands to reason that there was, considering the ugly racist attitudes I've started to uncover in the Athilantan culture.

Anyway: I ought to go on with my story. I'm here to observe, not to judge.

The Ritual of Purification came to a glorious finale, with Prince Ram clambering into an alabaster tub filled with wine and honey and coming forth dripping wet while choirs of priests and priestesses sang hosannas. Servants robed him in a kind of toga of fine-spun white cotton trimmed with blue, which is what everyone wears here. (The white-and-blue color scheme, like the marble buildings with the fine stone columns, helps to reinforce the general Greek atmosphere of Athilan. As does the sunny springlike climate.) And off he went, with me watching goggle-eyed from my vantage point within his mind, down the whole tremendous length of the Concourse of the Sky on foot to pay his formal respects to his mighty father, Harinamur, Grand Darionis of Athilan.

The procession took all day. The Concourse of the Sky is lined on both sides by splendid majestic buildings of classical design—it's as grand a street as the Champs Elysees, or Fifth Avenue, or Piccadilly—and people looked down from every window as the Prince went by. He was bareheaded and wore nothing but that toga and sandals. The sun was very strong as he set out, but by midday the sky darkened and the usual daily rain came, a terrific downpour. He didn't seem even to notice. I don't know how long a walk it was—miles—but he never gave a hint that he might be getting tired.

And eventually he reached the imperial palace, a splendid many-columned marble building that sits high up on a huge stone platform overlooking a great plaza, at the far end of the Concourse of the Stars.

He paused there, at the foot of a flight of what must have been at least a hundred immense marble steps, and looked up and up and up. At the top of this colossal stone staircase was a broad porch. His father the King was waiting there for him. And Prince Ram, who had just walked something like ten or eleven hours through the streets of the city to reach this place without resting even for a moment, unhesitatingly began to climb those hundred gigantic steps.

"Hail, O One King," the Prince cried. "Harinamur, Grand Darionis! And then—in a softer voice: "Father."

"Ram," the king said. And they embraced.

It was incredibly touching. Mighty father, invincible son: so happy to see each other again, so intensely happy. I was always fairly close with my own father, you know. But I never felt, with him, anything remotely like the powerful force of love that was passing between these two as they hugged, in full view of the Athilantan multitudes, on that gleaming marble porch atop those hundred giant stairs.

It was a little embarrassing, too, eavesdropping on Prince Ram's feelings in this moment of reunion. But you have to force yourself not to think about things like that. As I've said before, and hardly need to point out to you, being a time-traveler involves being a sneak and a snooper and an eavesdropper on somebody else's most private moments, and there's simply no way around it. Since we can't go to the past ourselves, we have to invade the minds of its inhabitants without their knowing it, and you can't pretend that there's anything very nice about that. But it's necessary. That's the only justification there is. If we're going to salvage anything out of the vanished past, we have to do it this way, because this is the only way there is.

The King is the most awesome human being I have ever seen. In grandeur and presence and authority he is like a combination of Moses, Abraham Lincoln, and the Emperor Augustus. He's very tall, particularly for an Athilantan, with long white hair and a thick, full, white beard. He has a look of such nobility and wisdom that you want to drop down before him and kiss his sandals. This day he was dressed in purple robes woven through with thread of gold and silver, and he wore a crown made of laurel leaves set on golden spikes.

With immense solemnity he took Prince Ram in his arms and held him close, and then he stepped back so that they could look in each other's eyes; and in the King's dark shining eyes I saw such warmth, such depths of love, that I actually felt sad and envious, thinking that no one else on Earth could ever have been loved by his father the way this prince was.

"We have missed you every day of your absence, and every hour of every day," the King said. "We have asked the gods daily to preserve you and bring you safely back to us. And now our prayers have been answered."

"Father. Grand Darionis. One King. My thoughts have ever been upon you while I traveled abroad."

They touched fingertips, very quickly and delicately, in the formal Athilantan manner.

Then six priests appeared, leading out another aurochs, and father and son slaughtered the poor beast right then and there, each of them wielding one of those jewel-hilted swords. A fire was lit; the meat was cooked; the priests hacked chunks off the carcass and brought them to the King and the Prince, who fed each other with their own hands.

It was, I know, meant as a ceremony of renewed love. But to me it also seemed a bloody, barbaric business, and I was glad when it ended and the Prince and his father went side by side into the royal palace.

You would not easily believe the splendor of the place. The lavish draperies, the carvings in ivory and jade, the many-colored stone pillars and filigreed window openings—it's your basic Arabian Nights palace made real. You look at it and your heart aches, because you can't help telling yourself that all of it is doomed to wind up at the bottom of the Atlantic Ocean, buried under thousands of years of muck and silt. You stand amid all this fantastic dreamlike loveliness and you know that its days are numbered, that it's not going to last beyond next month, or next year, or maybe next century at best, and it hurts to think about it. (The ruins of the palace must still be down there on the ocean floor somewhere! But could we ever find them? And would any shred of their beauty still remain?)

Each member of the royal family has a private suite of rooms within the palace. Prince Ram's suite is in back, on the second floor, looking out over a courtyard and garden.

It's grand enough to make any king happy. I wonder what the King's own rooms are like, if this is what a prince gets.

By this time Ram was so groggy with fatigue that I was having trouble making sense of his thoughts. Everything that was passing through his mind was reaching me in blurred and woolly form. He tried to pretend that he was fine, and for a time he and the King sat together in one of Ram's rooms, discussing some important governmental matters that I couldn't follow at all.

But it was obvious to the King that Ram wasn't able to keep his eyes open, and after a little while he bade his son goodnight and left. The Prince ran through the usual set of end-of-day prayers in one almighty hurry and dropped down on his bed like a dead man.

I let him rest for half the night. But there was too much that I wanted to tell you. So I took control of him and we went looking for writing materials, and found them, and for the last two hours I've had him setting all this down on long strips of vellum. His mind is still asleep, so he's getting the rest he needs. But he's going to have an awfully sore hand tomorrow from this much scribbling. I think I'd better stop now, though. It's close to dawn. Out where you are, thousands of miles to the east, the sun is already up. I hope you're okay. And that you get a chance to see this fantastic place for yourself some day.

Signing off–

–Roy

5.

Day 36, New Light, Great River.

One more letter, sent off into the unknown. Will it reach you? Will you ever write back to me? Who knows?

I might as well admit it: I haven't really been doing too well lately. Now and then I get spells when I begin to feel lost and gloomy here, cut off, out of contact with anything real. All too aware that what I am is a floating ghost implanted in another man's body while my own lies sleeping in a laboratory at the other end of time.

And then I remind myself of what a privilege it is to be here—to have been allowed to conduct part of this amazing exploration of times lost and, so we all once believed, forever irrecoverable. To be experiencing the sights and sounds and wonders of this incredible era, an era of whose very existence we once had only the most pathetic distorted notions. How remarkable that is—how much I am to be envied—!

I suppose I don't really need to be saying things like this to you. You're in the same boat I am. Forgive me for being dull or obvious. These matters weigh on my mind.

Sometimes I wish we'd never volunteered for any of this, Lora, that we were back in our own real time right this minute, you and I walking hand in hand in the park, or running along the beach, or just sitting quietly together having a pizza. Ordinary trivial things that everybody takes for granted. Home Era is starting to seem unreal to me. I have to stop and remind myself what an ice cream sundae tastes like, or what kind of sound a guitar makes, or even—God help me—what color your eyes are. And then everything starts to cut pretty close.

Well, the moods come and go. They can't be helped.

But I know we'll get home eventually, if everything goes right. There'll be plenty of time for pizza and ice cream then, and all the rest. Meanwhile the basic thing to remember is that we're in the middle of the most fantastic adventure anybody could imagine. There you are in Stone Age Europe with mammoths walking around on the tundra—and here I am waking up every morning to the golden sunlight of fabulous Atlantis—

How could anybody dare to feel gloomy even for a moment, doing what we're doing? The idea's practically obscene.

Busy days here. Lots of new information.

This is what I've learned about the Athilantan system of government in the past few days:

The King is an absolute monarch, and I mean absolute. Whatever he says, goes. There's no council of nobles, no senate, nothing that remotely challenges the King's authority. He's got courtiers and bureaucrats, sure, but the whole empire is essentially his own private property, to rule as he pleases.

It sounds like a recipe for disaster. Certainly such an arrangement always has been, in historical times. No empire can hope to have an unbroken string of capable rulers. This king or that one might be all right, and maybe as much as a century can go along without any troublemakers reaching the throne. But sooner or later some madman is bound to come along, a Nero or a Caligula or a Hitler, somebody who won't be able to handle absolute power, who runs amok and causes terrible chaos.

Why hasn't it happened here? How has the Athilantan empire managed to survive for so many hundreds of years without producing a power-crazed tyrant who brings everything crashing down?

The clue, it seems, is in the title that they give the King. Grand Darionis literally means The One King, and by that they mean that he is the only king that Athilan has ever had. The present ruler is considered to be the reincarnation of everyone who has ever held the throne, all the way back to the time of the first Harinamur who founded the kingdom back in legendary times. When each king dies, all his memories pass into the soul of his successor, so that he embodies the accumulated wisdom of the entire dynasty. Or so they say. I don't yet know if that's literally true, or just a picturesque way of asserting the strength of tradition here. I can tell you that the look in King Harinamur's eyes is not a look I have ever seen in anyone else's. He seems almost superhuman.

I think this One King business is at least in part responsible for the unusual degree of closeness that exists between the King and Prince Ram.

After all, Ram is the heir to the throne. If I understand

these things correctly, when it is his time to become Grand Darionis he will in effect become identical with his father. The King may already regard Ram as nothing more than a literal continuation of his own identity. And Ram may already have come to see himself as the actual reincarnation of the King, the older man in a new body.

I don't really know how this works, yet. Do they have a way of transplanting the entire memory files of the King into his son? (Or daughter. As in England, the throne usually goes to the oldest child, male or female.) If so, it has to be done while the King is still alive, right? Unless they do it in the moment of death.

Or possibly, there's no literal transfer of memory at all, and the whole concept is just a kind of convention, a political fiction, like calling the Emperor of China the "Son of Heaven." If that's so, all the kings may have the same name, and they may be very closely imprinted with the beliefs and values of their predecessors, but they can't actually be regarded as identical to all the kings who have gone before them.

So far, I've probed Ram very cautiously about this whole matter. It may be a really sensitive area for him, in which case he might become aware of me as I go poking around in his mind. That's the last thing I need.

What I've learned, though, seems to indicate that they really do have some way of merging minds, personalities, stored memories, and such. And it's done in stages, each one marked with a big ceremony.

First comes the Rite of Designation, in which the young child is named as heir apparent. This is done at the age of ten.

Then there's the Rite of Joining, at thirteen. I don't quite understand what this is, but it involves creating some kind of deep bond between the ruler and his heir. My guess is that it's the opening of a sort of mental conduit through which psychic impulses flow from the older one to the younger—the beginning of the transfer.

The third step is the Rite of Anointing. That happens when the heir apparent is eighteen, which means the Anointing of Ram ought to be due to take place very soon now. In this, the Prince enters full adulthood and heavy responsibility. He receives certain mystic powers, which are so secret that not even Ram himself seems to know what they are yet. He gets to live in a palace of his own. And he becomes a kind of viceroy of the realm, a junior king, with areas of authority and obligation far beyond anything he's had to undertake before. Once this rite is performed, he is permitted to marry. Is expected to marry, as a matter of fact.

(As far as I can tell, Prince Ram, with the Rite of Anointing just around the corner, has no particular woman in mind to become his Princess. Perhaps she'll be chosen for him by his father and her identity won't be made known to him until the official moment. Brrr!)

The fourth and final rite is the Rite of Union. This, I assume, is the ultimate transfer of identity from king to prince, as the time gets close for the handing over of the throne to the chosen heir. When this takes place, or how, I don't know. All details concerning this rite are buried so deeply in Prince Ram's consciousness that I'd need to do major excavation to get to them. Obviously it's something he doesn't want to think about, or isn't allowed to.

What will it be like for me, I wonder, when Prince Ram experiences the Rite of Union? What will it feel like when all those additional mental impulses come flooding into his mind? Pretty chaotic, I imagine. I suspect it'll be something like sitting up in the top of a tall tree while a hurricane is going on all around you.

But of course I might not even be here by the time he

does the Rite of Union. We've only got a six-month assignment here, after all. As I say, I have no way of telling how soon Ram is due for the fourth rite, but my guess is that it's going to be more than six months down the line.

Some real mixed feelings here. On the other hand I'm uneasy about the impact of the Rite of Union on me if I'm still inside Ram's mind when it happens. On the other hand I suddenly realize that I'm hoping Home Era will let me stick around long enough to observe it, regardless of the dangers. The rite would probably give me answers to a lot of the questions I'm starting to ask myself about Athilan. I don't want to be yanked back to our own time until I'm good and ready to go. Until I've soaked up everything I can possibly learn about this place.

But of course I've got no control over that. When the time's up, back to Home Era I go, whether or not I want to. I return to "reality." I return to you. But I give up Atlantis. Don't misunderstand me, Lora. I'd give anything to be with you again after this separation. And yet, and yet—to be here for the Rite of Union—to have a ringside seat when all the accumulated memories of all the kings of Athilan go pouring into Prince Ram's mind—

Well, we'll see. It's entirely out of my hands. I don't care for that very much. There are times when I feel like a puppet on a string. Which I know is a dumb attitude. It was understood from the start that we were here only for a specific length of time and then we'd be brought back to Home Era. That was the deal, and no use complaining about it now. All the same, I have a funny feeling that I'm going to resent it when they yank me back, because it's going to come just as something tremendously important is about to happen.

Why am I worrying so much? All this fidgeting and dithering about things?

Just lonely, I guess. Thinking of you. Missing you.

Maybe sending "emotionally connected pairs" on these trips into the past isn't such a great idea after all.

The Prince is an active and vigorous young man, and his days are full ones.

He's up at dawn. Prayers, first. (These Athilantans are very devout. They seem to have a couple of dozen gods, who are, however, all regarded as aspects of the One God.) Then, before breakfast, he swims in the marble-lined pool in the courtyard of the palace's rear wing. Fifty laps. (Everything here seems to be made out of marble. There's a big stonequarry somewhere on the far side of Mount Balamoris, but also they bring finer grades of marble in by ship from Greece and Italy.)

Breakfast, then. Fruits, most of them strange tropical ones that I can't identify, followed by roast lamb. And a rich, sweet red wine. Wine for breakfast—well, that isn't anything I'd care to do. But the Prince is strong as an ox and it doesn't even make him a little bit tipsy. And these Athilantans, like all the Mediterranean peoples who I believe are descended from them, love their wine. There are vineyards all over the island. (All their wines are sweet. I know that real wine connoisseurs claim that the best wines are dry ones, but the Athilantans probably wouldn't care. They like it the way they like it. I suppose a Frenchman wouldn't approve, if there were any Frenchmen in existence. But there aren't any yet. Nor are there any vineyards right now, over there in the icebound land that will someday be France. And there aren't going to be for thousands of years.)

After breakfast Ram meets with the King. They go over all sorts of official documents and reports.

Most of what they deal with concerns the flow of raw materials that Athilantan ships bring in from Africa and southern Europe. These Athilantans are the world's first imperialists. They've colonized every part of the world within reach, importing things they need—minerals, mostly, but certain foodstuffs also—and giving not very much in return. Of course there isn't much that they could give, considering how primitive all the other humans of this era are. Your typical modern-era colonial power imports raw materials from backward countries and exports manufactured goods, but semi-nomadic Stone Age hunters don't have a lot of need for light bulbs, fancy plumbing fixtures, or rubber tires.

There's a tremendous cultural gulf between the Athilantans and the rest of the Stone Age world. It's incredible. They are so far beyond everybody else here in all ways that I can't even begin to explain it. A mutant race of supergeniuses that mysteriously arose out of nowhere during the late Paleolithic Era? That sounds too hokey to be believed. But what other explanation can there be?

The King and the Prince also discuss local matters at their morning conference. They decide which government officials deserve promotions and which need to be reprimanded for slacking off. They talk about street repair and new building construction. They make plans for upcoming religious festivals. None of this is very romantic. It's just their job—ruling the Athilantan Empire. And it's a lot of work, which never eases off.

Lunch is light: some grapes, some cheese, and the strange bread, hard as rock, that they make out of the wheat that grows here. Wheat is still in its early evolutionary stages and such wheat as they have isn't very different from grass seed. But even that is amazing, considering how far in the past we are. Still, it doesn't make remarkably good bread. The Prince drinks a light white wine with lunch, as sweet as perfume. Ugh.

Then a nap. And then he goes off for afternoon exercise: horseback riding, javelin throwing, another swim, and the like. He's a terrific athlete. You'd have to be, to ride the horses they have in this era—mean little guys, short legs, long manes, angry dispositions. They're wild animals and they don't pretend otherwise. The Athilantans understand the principle of the saddle but they don't know anything about bridles and bits, and their technique for controlling their horses is basically to grab them around the necks and wrestle them into submission.

After exercise, there's usually some ritual to perform. This is a very religious country, in its way. The place swarms with priests and priestesses of the various gods. All these gods constantly demand worship. The various rituals invariably involve the King and the Prince, because the King of Athilan is not only the monarch but also the high priest, and the Prince is his right-hand man. So they have to put in an hour or so in this temple or that one almost every day, presiding over these godly matters. The chants and prayers they utter are highly stylized and I don't have a clear idea of what they mean. A lot of animal sacrifice goes on, too. I still don't find that very easy to take.

In late afternoon the whole royal family gets together for a kind of relaxation hour, warm and affectionate, everybody funny and loving. Then they have dinner together, a terrific feast. The servants are mainlanders. (Slaves, I suppose. I have to keep reminding myself not to expect the Athilantans to abide by all our nice modern democratic institutions, like freedom. Like the Romans, like the Greeks, like a lot of advanced civilizations of antiquity, the Athilantans don't seem to see anything wrong with enslaving people. It's always a surprise, isn't it, when people who seem generally enlightened, like the Athilantans, turn out to practice something as cruel and wrong as slavery. But the past is the past, and things are different there, and no use expecting it to be otherwise. At least they seem to treat their slaves pretty well, for what that's worth.)

There's food galore at these royal feasts, a simply incredible amount of food, usually with a roasted ox as the main event, and amazing quantities of wine. (But everybody seems to stay sober. Is the wine very weak, or do these people have unusual tolerance for alcohol?)

Minstrels come in and sing when dinner is over. The favorite is a long historical epic, something like the Iliad and the Odyssey rolled into one. It sounds very stirring, but it also happens to be snug in some ancient version of the Athilantan language, and it's as hard for Prince Ram to understand as Chaucer's English would be for us. I can get only the vaguest drift of it, something about exile and wandering and the eventual building of this great city on the island of Athilan.

Listening to the minstrels gives me a wonderful feeling of what it must have been like to sit around the banquet hall in ancient Greece, listening to Homer strumming on his lyre and chanting the first editions of his poems. But then I have to tell myself that Greece isn't ancient yet–that it won't even exist as a concept for another 17,000 years and some–and that Homer, Achilles, Agamemnon, and the rest of that legendary crowd are unknown figures of the unimaginably misty future, so far as the Athilantans are concerned.

It gets dark early here. The Prince goes to sleep when the minstrels are finished, and sleeps like a marble statue until the first rays of dawn.

Or, at least, would sleep like a marble statue if I didn't insist on hauling him out of bed somewhere during the night so that he could write the letters for me. Of course he's completely unaware of that. I keep the letters hidden in a leather case underneath a stack of old togas that he doesn't seem to wear any more. Whenever I hear that a courier is about to set out for Naz Glesim, I put the Prince into trance and have him get the current letter and pack it up for shipment. I wonder, of course, if any of my letters will ever get to you. The distances are so great, the situation so tricky. But I have to keep on writing them. I need this contact with you so very much—even one-sided as it's been up till now.

I wish I had some way of dictating my impressions of this world into a recorder that I could take back to Home Era with me. The big trouble with being a disembodied web of electrical impulses, I keep thinking, is that you can't carry anything across time with you except the contents of your own mind. Better than nothing, but pretty frustrating all the same. I'd like to come home with bulging notebooks describing everything I've seen here, and maybe a suitcase or two of Athilantan artifacts. No way, though. No way at all.

Time to go. Ram's writing hand is cramping badly. He needs to rest. And, I think, so do I.

—Roy

6.

Day 5, Month of Western Wind, Year of Great River.

Almost a week since my last letter. I haven't wanted to write. Strange things have been going on in my mind and I didn't particularly care to talk about them, hoping they'd vanish of their own accord. But they haven't.

What's happening—not to be mysterious about it any longer—is that I've been feeling a powerful urge to let Prince Ram know I'm here.

I realize that this is a classic malady of time-travelers. The compulsion to stand up and shout, "Look at me! Look at me! I'm sitting right here inside your head!" There's even a name for it, isn't there? Observer Guilt Syndrome, I think. But knowing that I'm not the first one to experience this doesn't make it any easier for me.

The thing is that I have now spent several weeks observing Prince Ram at the closest possible range. I feel closer to him than any friend or wife could ever be. I know which side of his mouth he prefers to chew his food on, which god's name he takes in vain when he stubs his toe, and the details of the really nasty trick he pulled on his kid brother when he was nine years old. (And which he still feels guilty about, although Prince Caiminor was only four at the time and probably doesn't remember a thing.)

All this is producing the predictable Observer Guilt reactions in me. Maybe you're feeling a little of it yourself. I talked about this a few letters back—when I compared being an observer to being a spy, and said that it felt a little ugly. But it's starting to seem like something a lot worse than spying, now. It feels like being a Peeping Tom. A spy, at least, is serving his country. Peeping Toms are simply slimy.

I know, Lora, I know, I know. I'm serving the cause of knowledge by doing what I'm doing. And my training is supposed to help me get past these expectable feelings of guilt and shame.

But the longer I stay in Prince Ram's mind, the better I get to know him and the more I admire him. He is a strong, capable, intelligent, determined, disciplined, princely fellow. He has his flaws—who doesn't?—but he's basically a very good person who is going to be a great king some day. And the more I get to like him, the less I like myself for skulking here, invisible and imperceptible, inside his head. I'm coming to hate the sneakiness of it: eavesdropping on his conversations and even his most private thoughts, and putting him into trances that he doesn't in any way suspect so that I can use him to write these letters for me.

I want to let him know that I'm here—a visitor from the remote future who has come to study the great and glorious Athilantan empire in its heyday. I want to ask his permission, I guess, for continuing to occupy my hidden perch within his mind.

Don't worry. I haven't given him even the slightest hint so far. But in the past week I've come close, a couple of times, to making actual conscious-level contact with him. And the temptation isn't going away. If anything, it's getting stronger.

For the time being, I'm being very cautious about the degree of mind-entry I'm allowing myself with the Prince. Mostly I limit myself to low-level passive observation, simply monitoring minute-by-minute sensory information: what he sees, what he hears, and so forth.

I'm not trying to do any digging into the deeper stored data of his mind. That's the easiest way, of course, to make your host suspicious that something peculiar is going on in his head. And what I'm afraid of is that if he expresses any sort of suspicion that he has been possessed or inhabited or somehow taken over by an alien spirit, I'm going to blurt out the whole truth to him in a wild rush of confessional zeal. I don't dare risk that.

This is creating some serious disadvantages for me.

For example, without taking a deeper look into his mind, I have no way of understanding the significance of the unusual and apparently very important ritual that the Prince and his father performed last night.

In late afternoon a messenger came to the Prince and said, "It is the night of Romany Star."

I'm sure that's what he said: Romany Star.

The Prince, who had been relaxing after a strenuous workout on horseback, immediately called for his slaves, who bathed him, sprinkled him with some kind of aromatic oil, and clothed him in a shining scarlet robe (which looked very much like silk. Is the silkworm native to Athilan, or do their ships travel as far as China?) and a little silver coronet. Then he went to the uppermost floor of the palace, where there is a staircase leading to a roof-top garden.

King Harinamur was waiting for him up there in the garden, wearing a silken robe even showier than the

Prince's, and a beautifully worked golden coronet. There was nobody else present, no priests, no slaves.

Darkness began to fall. Father and son, working quickly, took long slender twigs and branches of some delicately colored aromatic wood from a storage chest against the wall, and arranged them on a little altar of green stone (jade?). Then they waited, standing stock still, staring rigidly at the sky. They were both looking at the same sector, almost directly overhead. I could feel Prince Ram slipping into a kind of trance of his own accord. His pulse rate rose, his eyes were dilated, his skin temperature dropped.

The stars were appearing, now. The unfamiliar constellations of the Paleolithic sky blazed above us. Ram's head was thrown back, his eyes were fixed. He scarcely even blinked.

"I see it," he said after a time, in a strange throaty voice, like a man talking in his sleep.

"Do you, so soon?" said the King. "Yes, young eyes would."

"Above the Great Whale. To the left of the Spear."

"Yes. Yes. I see it too. Hail, Romany Star!"

"Hail," murmured the Prince. "Romany Star!"

And then they began to chant, slowly, solemnly, in the ancient priestly language.

I was too awed—frightened, even—to try to penetrate Ram's mind and seek the meaning. They were like two statues, motionless but for their lips, staring up at that star and uttering their prayer to it. I think I know which star they were looking at: a brilliant one, a giant. It seemed to be of a reddish color. I'm no astronomer and I couldn't even begin to guess which star it was, and in any case the sky over Athilan is nothing like the sky we see back in Home Era.

Ram dropped deeper and deeper into trance. He seemed scarcely conscious now, and his father the same. The prayer went on and on, slow, somber, profoundly moving even though I couldn't comprehend a syllable of it. It was like some long, intricate poem. No: it was more like a prayer for the dead. Tears were quietly rolling down Ram's cheeks as he spoke.

Now they knelt and lit the twigs they had placed on the stone altar, and curling wisps of fragrant smoke rose above them. Calmly Ram began to rip his splendid silken gown to shreds; and calmly the King did likewise. They tore those gowns to ribbons, and cast the ribbons into the flame, so that they stood naked by the altar, wearing nothing but their coronets of gold and silver. And then they removed the coronets too, and crushed them in their bare hands, and tossed them on the fire.

The rite, whatever it was, was over.

Naked, still entranced, the King and the Prince turned and slowly made their way back into the palace. No one dared look at them. They parted, without a word, in the grand hallway, each going to his own suite. Ram went to his bedroom, lay down without bothering with the usual evening prayers, and fell instantly asleep. And that was the rite of Romany Star.

I don't have any idea what it was all about. But it was obviously more important than any of the other religious rites the Prince has taken part in since I've been here. He treated all the other ones simply as mere tasks, part of the job of being a prince. This one moved him deeply. This one shook him to his depths. I need to know why. If I were in better shape myself, I'd scout around in his mind until I found out. But right now I don't dare make any sort of contact with him at that level. I simply don't dare.

–Roy

7.

Day 11, Western Wind, Great River.

A big day for me.

The first letter from you in Naz Glesim came in today, with the regular diplomatic packet! I must have read it a dozen times. It was such an incredible joy, hearing from you after all this time, these weeks and weeks of being cooped up by myself inside Prince Ram's mind.

I have to confess it now; I was getting a little paranoid about not hearing from you. I know, I know, it takes forever for couriers to get from one end of the empire to the other. So I couldn't really have expected an answer from you any sooner than this. But here I was, sending off pages and pages of stuff to you and never getting even a postcard back, so to speak, and the time was passing—passing very slowly, let me tell you—and it seemed like years had gone by. I wondered if you were too busy to write. Or just didn't want to bother. And various other unworthy thoughts. It also occurred to me that something terrible might have happened to you. The time-travel process isn't absolutely safe, after all.

I kept all these worries to myself when writing to you. Or tried to, at least. But now none of it matters, because I know that you're all right, that you still care, that you've been answering my letters as soon as you could. And so on and so forth. And how glad I am!

The officials who sort through the stuff that Provincial Governor Sippurilayl sends to the capital from Naz Glesim must have been very puzzled indeed to unroll a scroll addressed to Prince Ram and discover that the whole thing was in some unknown kind of writing. But they came to the only logical conclusion—that it must be written in code, and therefore very important—and they brought it to the Prince right away.

Now came the ticklish part. The Prince glanced at it and thought it was all just some crazy scribble, and to my absolute horror he started to toss it in the fire. I had to override him and pull him back to his desk, right in front of the officials who had brought him the scroll. He stopped short, struggled against my override for a second, almost fell down.

God knows what they thought was happening to him—another "stroke," maybe. Ram didn't understand it either. But he waved them quickly out of his office, perhaps because he was embarrassed at having them see him staggering around like that and was afraid it might happen again in another minute.

The instant they were out of the room, I put him in trance and read your letter. And re-read it and re-read it, hungrily. It was so wonderful hearing from you at last that I came close to breaking into tears. (With Prince Ram's eyes!) Then when I knew your letter practically by heart I had the Prince roll it up and hide it away in the alcove where I keep letters waiting to go to you, and I awakened him, after trying to wipe from his memory all recollection of what had been taking place.

If I'm lucky, he won't recall a thing about the strange scroll with the peculiar writing on it. More likely he'll be left with some vague, misty impression of having been looking at a document that made no sense to him. My hope is that the Prince will think that he dreamed the whole thing—the way someone can dream of picking up a book in Greek or Arabic and is able, in his sleep, at least, to read it with complete understanding, even though he can't remember a word of it afterward.

At any rate, you sound happy and healthy and generally in great shape, and I'm glad for you. I'm relieved to hear that the weather isn't as awful as I feared. Cold, yes, but that's only to be expected in Ice Age Europe, and at least it hasn't been snowing much. The description you give of the house where you're living, made entirely of mammoth bones, is fascinating. The foundation of mammoth skulls, the wall of mammoth jawbones stacked crosswise like that, the huge thighbones forming an entranceway—I guess that's what passes for a grand mansion out Naz Glesim way. Naturally the Athilantan Provincial Governor would have the best accommodations, such as they are.

Very interesting about that ugly, shaggy-looking character with the receding chin and the sloping forehead who was seen skulking around outside the village. Do you think there's really any likelihood that he's a Neanderthal? My understanding of these things is that the Neanderthals have been extinct for a long time now, fifteen or twenty thousand years, at least. But I guess it's possible that a few of them still linger on in the back woods, drifting around like sad displaced outcasts.

(We keep finding out, don't we, how little we actually

knew about prehistoric man in the days before time exploration began! Of course all we had to go by was a little scattering of skeletons that had survived by flukes here and there, and an assortment of stone tools and weapons. And out of that we conjured up some kind of notion of hundreds of thousands of years of human life. It was a pretty good guess, I suppose, considering the data we had. But now that we're actually back here seeing it for ourselves, how different it all looks. Neanderthal Man isn't completely gone after all, if your idea is correct. And the Paleolithic Homo sapiens people have a much more elaborate culture than we ever imagined. And then, of course, there are these spectacular Athilantan folk, whose existence we never even remotely suspected, dominating everything, operating a modern technological civilization all the way back here. With electricity, no less.)

Now that I know you are in fact getting my letters, and are able to write back, I'll probably write more often. And I hope you will too. It was magical the way hearing from you dissolved the terrible sense of isolation I've been feeling, the miserable loneliness, the fidgety worrying about problems that didn't really need to be worried about. I can hardly wait for the next one from you.

Of course it's risky, isn't it? Not only because we have to take control of our host's body to write our letters, but because having all these bizarre scrolls in an unknown language traveling back and forth is eventually likely to make someone suspect sorcery, or espionage, or something else serious. There could be an investigation, I suppose. But it's worth it, despite the risks, don't you think? I'm absolutely convinced of that. Getting that letter from you this morning was one of the great moments of my life. To find out that you're okay, to hear about what you've been doing these past weeks, to read those words, "I love you." Now I want the next letter. And the next. And the one after that.

Got to stop now. More later.

And now it is later—a little before dawn.

Big trouble. The Prince knows I'm here.

Although I haven't been monitoring his mind deeply for some time now, for reasons which you already know, I can't help but be aware of the mental vibrations he gives off. When he's excited, I feel it. When he's angry. When he's tired. When he's tense. It's a constant broadcast that I automatically pick up.

Today, a couple of hours after the episode of the arrival of your letter and my overriding of his attempt to throw it on the fire, I began detecting a new and troublesome mood in him. It was somewhere between anxiety and anger, and it was growing stronger moment by moment, a slow, steady buildup of tension that had to be leading to some sort of explosion.

That was pretty scary, feeling him ticking away like a bomb. I was tempted to reach in and try to defuse him before he went off. But I didn't know where to reach or what to defuse. So I waited uneasily, wondering what was going to happen, while he went on working himself up.

Then at last he spoke—mentally, loud and clear—directly to me. It was like a bomb going off right in my face:

—Who are you, demon, and why are you within me?

Remember when I said that what we really are is demons, taking possession of the minds and bodies of our hosts? That's the way Prince Ram sees it too.

I was totally stunned. I didn't know what to say or do or think.

This was my chance, if ever there was one, to make direct contact with the Prince. As you know if my more recent letters have been getting through to you, I've been fighting that temptation for days. Successfully. This sudden shot in the dark from the Prince might easily have broken through my will to resist Observer Guilt Syndrome. But it didn't. When the chips were down, I found myself maintaining total silence after all, just as our training tells us to do. I kept myself sealed off, allowing just minimal contact with Prince Ram's mind.

But he kept after me.

–I know you are there. I feel you hiding in my mind.

I remained silent. What could I do? Tell him he was imagining things? Any contact I made would have the effect of revealing me, of confirming my presence.

–Who are you, demon? Why do you assail me?

He was growing more excited moment by moment. He trembled and shook. His heart was pounding and there was a throbbing like a hammerblow in his temples. He knelt and covered his face with his hands. Then he pressed his hands to the sides of his head with tremendous force, as if trying to drive me out by sheer pressure. He focused all his power of concentration on the task of expelling me from his mind.

Of course none of this had any effect on me. But the strain on the Prince was fearful. Every muscle of his body was writhing. His eyes bulged, his breath came in wild gasps, sweat broke from all his pores. Stress hormones flooded his system. There was such internal violence going on all over him that it was scary. Could he harm himself like this? I didn't know.

But I had only two choices, to reveal myself or to put him into trance and calm him down. I opted for the second choice, and he slumped and lay still.

For a time I was afraid to do anything else. Then, gradually, I began to explore the upper levels of his mind.

What I discovered was—as I suspected—that I hadn't done a complete enough job of editing out the memory of seeing your letter. He remembered just enough of it, and of the earlier letter of mine that he had seen that time when his steward had walked in on him aboard the ship. That led him to think about the odd stumble he had taken that afternoon, and the "stroke" he had suffered when I originally entered his mind weeks ago, and the strange sorenesses in his arm, and various other little curiosities directly related to my presence within him. And he had jumped to exactly the correct conclusion. The Prince is a highly intelligent man, you know.

I couldn't hope to cancel out all his justified suspicions by tinkering now with his mind. That would involve so much messing around that I'd certainly do great damage. I couldn't leave him conked out on the floor, either. So I settled for reaching in here and there and returning his hormonal flow to make him as calm as possible. And then I brought him out of trance.

He sat up, frowning, shaking his head. But he didn't try to communicate with me again. Simply arose, paced around the room a few times, put his head out the window, took three very deep breaths. And called his steward, and asked for a flagon of wine. Sipped a little of it. Sat staring at nothing in particular for a while, his mind almost blank. Finally said his prayers, got into bed, dropped into a deep sleep. Now it's almost morning. He hasn't awakened.

My whole mission's in danger now. I'm going to have to be extra careful about everything I do. I know he's still convinced that there's a demon in him. And he's right. The intensity of his reaction was truly frightening. I don't want him driving himself into seizures of some sort–or having a mental breakdown that could affect his position as heir to the throne. Probably I can take the risk of continuing to use him to write these letters while he's under trance, but otherwise I'll have to lay low. If worst comes to worst I may even have to abandon the whole project and return ahead of schedule to Home Era. We'll see. Keep your fingers crossed for me, love. More later, I hope.

Continued, the following day.

They have had a rite of exorcism to drive me out of the Prince's mind. Obviously, it didn't work. Even so, my position remains very precarious.

The first thing Ram did upon awakening was to summon the Counsellor Teneristis, who is a vizier of the realm and has been the Prince's special mentor for many years. Teneristis is a very short, brusque old man, businesslike and tough, with two thick tufts of wiry white hair that stick out comically from the sides of his head like horns. There's nothing in the least comic about him, though.

The Prince said, "There is a demon in me. It turns my mind dark and makes me see and do things I do not understand."

"You will go to the Labyrinth, then," Teneristis replied instantly. "You have sinned, or no demon could have entered you. And in the Labyrinth you will be purged of your sin."

The Labyrinth! Shades of Theseus and the Minotaur! But this isn't Crete and the myth of Theseus won't be invented for more thousands of years than I want to think about. The Labyrinth of Athilan isn't a prison for a monster, it's a holy sanctuary, located in a maze of dark musty caverns halfway up the flank of Mount Balamoris. My guess is that the caverns are natural ones, most likely part of the intricate geological plumbing that lies beneath most volcanos—all those tubes and vents and conduits and whatnot that a volcano creates as it rises. This volcano has been dormant for a long time and the Athilantans have honeycombed these warrens along its slopes with a network of sacred shrines.

It's a beautiful mountain. So peaceful, so lovely, that you tend to forget that one morning in the very near future it's going to come roaring back to life and destroy this whole fantastic civilization.

Alone, the Prince rode out in the early mists of morning through the white and glittering streets of Athilan, past temples and palaces, past villas and parks, up the glorious green slopes of the foothills of Mount Balamoris. And tethered his horse, and knelt, and prayed. And walked without hesitation toward the narrow mouth of the Labyrinth.

It was a bare slit, unmarked, unadorned, fairly high up the mountain. He stepped through it into an eight-sided chamber lined with white-and-blue tiles that led to a paved passageway heading inward and downward. The chamber was lit by three electrical lamps that gave off a rich golden glow. The passageway wasn't lit at all beyond the first twenty paces. Dimness engulfed him, and then even the dimness gave way to the complete absence of light. For what seemed like hours he spiraled down and down and down, far beyond the reach of the deepest beam of light, into a realm of terrifying darkness.

In that utter blackness your only guide is the sequence of smooth high-relief carvings on the walls. You grope your way, feeling for the age-old holy images, "reading" the walls with your hands. There is a logical pattern to the order of the images that makes sense to an Athilantan, though not to me, and so long as you can summon up the proper passages from the religious teachings you have studied, you'll be able to find your way. If you become confused even in the slightest detail, you get lost immediately and the chances of your being able to get out again are extremely small. So Teneristis was taking a considerable risk with the heir to the throne by sending him to the Labyrinth.

The Prince didn't seem worried. He moved along briskly, passing his hands over this carving and that one. He appeared to know what to expect as he went, and he always found it. There was only one moment—a bad one—when he paused after stroking one of the carvings and a jolt of uncertainty went through him like a spear, leaving a trail of jitter-hormones in his veins. But he halted, took a few deep breaths, forced himself to a state of icy calm, touched the carving again.

This time he found the clue that he had missed before, a double zigzag of lines to the left of the main image. Breathing more easily, he went onward.

And on and on, down and down.

The walls of the passageway were narrower here, and lower. He had to stoop and shuffle. The air grew warmer. He was wearing nothing but a loincloth, but even so, he became slippery with sweat. Though his mind was at ease—cool, confident—there was the awareness of danger not very far from the center of his soul. All he needed to do was take one wrong turn and he would lose himself beyond all hope. A terrible death, alone down there in the sweltering darkness, crying out for food, for water, for light.

Then I felt his heart thump with joy and he came suddenly around a sharp bend of the corridor into a place where he could actually see.

This was the end of the line, the core of the Labyrinth, the penitential chamber.

It was a circular room, dome-roofed, with an opening in

the floor at its very center. Light came up through that opening—red, flickering light, the flaming heart of the world glowing up through the bowels of the volcano. Peering over the edge, Ram could see, and I saw with him, rosy pools of fiery lava far below, sluggishly tossing and stirring. Gusts of hot wind rose from them. And, staring down into that distant churning furnace, I saw the death of Atlantis waiting to burst loose.

Here he crouched, head pressed against his knees. Here he prayed to be liberated from the spirit that had invaded him.

He named the names of gods. He named the names of kings—the secret names, the names they had worn as princes, before they became the newest Harinamur. He called upon all the forces of the universe to free him from—

Me.

The words came pouring out of him in a wild, keening howl, weird and strange-sounding. "I have strayed from the path of my fathers," he cried, sobbing. "I know not how, but I have sinned, and I have been punished for my sin, and now I am accursed. Tell me my penitence, O gods! Tell me how I can set myself free!"

And knelt there, shivering in the volcanic heat, waiting for the grace of his gods to descend upon him.

For one crazy instant I actually thought it was going to work—that I would be scraped from his mind and hurled into some unthinkable limbo. It was terrifying. Whirlwinds swooped and roared about me. The walls of the chamber seemed to be closing in on me. The mountain was pressing down.

Ram seemed completely in charge, Ram and his gods. I could feel him searching around for me, trying to get a grip on me and pry me loose.

I had to fight like a—well, like a demon. I pushed him

away from me, set up defense blocks around myself, fled down the corridors of his mind. There were moments when I felt him seizing me, prying me free, thrusting me out.

I suppose there must have been some way for me to take control of his mind and keep him at bay, but just then that didn't seem possible. I was on the run. For one long scary moment down there in that sweltering room in the belly of the mountain, he had the upper hand and I was helpless. I hunkered down tight and tried to make myself very small within him, invisible, unfindable.

And the moment passed. I reached out and linked myself to his mind again, and found the levers of control. I felt the pressure ease. I was the rider again, and he was the vehicle. I was safe.

The whirlwinds died away. Everything that had been crowding close upon me now retreated. After a time Ram rose from his crouch.

He was very calm—relaxed, even. Did he think he had succeeded in expelling me? Perhaps. Perhaps. Or maybe he was simply content to have come so close to victory over me. He swung his arms cheerfully, he stretched his legs, he filled his lungs, like an athlete who has just completed a grueling match and is beginning to unwind.

And started back up the winding passageway, feeling his way quickly, carving by carving, until in a surprisingly short time he had reached the mouth of the cavern.

As he stepped out into the bright afternoon sunlight he said—inwardly, speaking directly to me—

—So even the Labyrinth is of no avail.

His words hit me like blows.

You have not fooled me, demon! I know you are still there. But I will not let you rule me. I will not let you be my master.

There was a strange new strength flowing from him. He

was determined now to fight me to the finish, and I knew it.

Can he possibly do it?

He's strong and tough. But I know how to operate his mind, and he doesn't know how to operate mine. Not really. He was close, back there in the Labyrinth, but not close enough.

Still, I could feel him resisting me when I put him in trance to write this last section of this very long letter. I was able to win out, of course. But the next time it could be a lot harder. I have a real tiger on my hands.

The situation looks messy. I'll try to keep you posted. That may not be so easy, though.

—Roy

8.

Day 18, Western Wind, Great River.

Where I left things in the last letter, it all seemed pretty dire. But actually I've had a few days of respite. Much to my surprise, Prince Ram has been behaving as though the exorcism in the Labyrinth really did work and the evil spirit has been cast forth from his soul. At least, that's what he told Counsellor Teneristis when he returned to the palace later that day. And he hasn't tried to aim any more direct communications my way.

I have these four explanations for the way he's acting:

1) He really has convinced himself that the exorcism must have worked, despite what he said to me as we were coming out of the cavern.

2) He's trying to fake me out, so that he can blindside me when he thinks my guard is down.

3) He's afraid that Teneristis, upon hearing that the Labyrinth didn't do the job, will send him off on some even more dangerous and strenuous pilgrimage that he really doesn't want to undertake.

4) With the Rite of Anointing coming up very shortly—the grand ceremony by which Prince Ram becomes virtual co-monarch with his father—he simply doesn't want to have to deal with the distraction of thinking about the demon that may or may not be possessing him.

Any or all of these four may be correct. Or none.

If Ram really thinks I'm gone, why did he tell me that he knows I'm still here? Doesn't make sense. Nor can I easily believe that he's afraid of Teneristis, or of any new penitence that Teneristis might saddle him with. The Prince didn't seem at all hesitant about going into the Labyrinth. What could possibly be worse than that?

The theory about the Rite of Anointing has a little more substance. It's the biggest event of his life so far. What if it's dangerous in some way, or blasphemous, to try to undergo the rite while you're possessed by a demon? Maybe Ram's so eager for the Anointing that he doesn't want the rite postponed, which might happen if he let Teneristis know that he's still carrying that stubborn demon around in his head. On the other hand, Ram is honorable, above all else. Can he honorably conceal the fact that the exorcism didn't work, and let himself go through with this immensely significant ceremony while he's in a ritually impure state?

That leaves #2, which unfortunately seems all too plausible. Ram has been trained to be a king, and that involves being crafty. If there's a pesky enemy bothering you who won't go away, one way to handle him would be to lay low and clobber him when he's not expecting it.

There's also the possibility that Ram's worried that this whole demonic possession business could lead to his being disqualified to become king at all, that he might be passed over in favor of his younger brother, unless he sweeps the entire thing under the carpet as fast as he can.

Whatever the reason, the Prince is keeping quiet these days. And so am I.

Three hours later. And everything is completely different now. Just for starters, let me tell you that the Prince is not in a trance as I write this. He's completely conscious, aware of what's going on, though of course he has no idea of the meaning of the words that his hand is shaping under my control.

I may be making the worst mistake of my life. And the last mistake of my life, too. But somehow I think everything is going to be all right. Let me tell you what happened.

The thing that kicked it off was the arrival of the diplomatic pouch from Naz Glesim. It contained the second of your letters, the one in which you talk about the mammoth hunt. (I think they have to be nuts to go out hunting gigantic beasts like that in the middle of a driving snowstorm. Even if they do believe that warm weather will never come unless they do it.) As before, the scroll was packed as if it had come from Provincial Governor Sippurilayl and was addressed to Prince Ram, so the bureaucrats downstairs brought it straight to the Prince in his study.

This time the Prince waited until they were gone before opening it. I waited, too, figuring I'd pounce on him and put him in trance just as he started to unroll it, so that he wouldn't even have a phantom memory of once again having glimpsed something written in English. But he was way ahead of me.

Without unrolling it, he said, aiming the thought right at me, sharp and fierce as a lightning-bolt:

—Does this contain more of your demon-writing?

So he knew I was still there. I remained silent and tried to seem inconspicuous. Didn't help.

—Tell me. What is this all about? Is there a demon inside Provincial Governor Sippurilayl also? What do you two demons say to each other in your letters?

Then he opened the scroll and stared at it.

—Yes, he said. *As I thought. More demon-marks. Very well, demon. I am unable to expel you; therefore, I must attempt to know you. Tell me who and what you are, demon. I command you to reply. By all the gods do I command you!*

I was at a crossroads. I could have knocked him out then and there, and tried once more to edit from his mind all recollection of this latest scroll. Or I could admit the truth—despite everything that our training says—and see what would happen next.

Lora, I didn't hesitate more than a fraction of a second.

—I am not a demon, I said. *I am a visitor from a land that lies far away at the other end of time.*

I said it. I actually said it. I gave away the whole show.

I didn't feel that I had any other option, Lora. Probably we never should have started sending these letters back and forth; but we did—I take the blame for that—and so the Prince and most likely Provincial Governor Sippurilayl also have been exposed to the sight of documents written in English. And the Prince, at least, has managed to figure out that something peculiar is going on.

I suppose I could, even at this point, have gone into Prince Ram's mind and tried to carve out every bit of data having to do with my presence there and with the scrolls he had seen. But I hadn't done such a great job of editing his mind in my previous attempts, apparently, and there was so much now to remove that I didn't for a moment think I could do it without seriously damaging him.

I wasn't going to risk that.

Better to break all the rules, and tell him the full truth, and take the consequences, both here and in Home Era, for what I had done.

And what was the Prince's reaction, do you think? Bewilderment? Shock? Horror? Or a simple snort of anger and derision at the thought that the demon who was infesting him was a crazy demon, thus making a bad situation worse?

None of the above. He wasn't annoyed or upset. He was very calm, matter-of-fact, almost casual. I suppose that is one of the differences between ordinary mortals and princes who have been trained all their lives to be rulers of a great realm. Your basic prince needs to know how to stay cool and collected in the face of any sort of crisis, no matter how weird.

He said, *So you come from the time when the gods walked the earth? That golden time long ago?*

–No. I come from a time yet unborn.

–A future time, you mean?

–The future, yes. More than twenty thousand years from now.

–Ah. How very strange. And are you of our people?

I hesitated. *–I don't think so. No.*

He thought about that. *–Of the Dirt People, then?*

–Perhaps. I can't be certain.

–Because you come from such a distant time?

–Yes, I said. *In twenty thousand years many things change.*

His mental voice was silent a long while. I felt him pondering the information I had given him, examining it, mulling it, digesting it.

At last he said, *If you come from so far away, then you must be a great wizard.*

—Not really. But great wizards sent me here.

—You are no wizard? You are only a demon?

—Neither a demon nor a wizard, Prince Ram.

He said, after considering that a moment, *I think you are a wizard all the same. What is your name, wizard?*

—Roy Colton.

—That is a name only a wizard would have.

—It's a very ordinary name, I assure you.

—It is a wizard's name, the Prince replied firmly. *I have no doubt of that.* He was still completely calm. *And why have you entered my mind, wizard? What is it you seek there?*

The tone of his mental voice was casual, conversational. It unsettled me a little, the ease with which he seemed to be accepting my presence within him now. Knowing about it had upset him at first, sure, but he didn't appear to have any problem with it now. He seemed to find it pretty interesting. He was curious about the whys and wherefores.

Was he setting a trap for me?

It didn't look that way. I took a readout on his endocrine systems and saw that beneath his pose of calmness lay nothing but more calmness. You or I, discovering that some inexplicable phantom has taken residence in our heads, would never have been so calm. We'd have figured we were going psycho and checked ourselves into the nearest ward for a complete workover. But that's the value, I guess, of living in a world where the gods are still real and vivid and where you expect to run into the occasional demon or wizard now and then. It didn't occur to Prince Ram that he might have lost his sanity when he started hearing voices in his head. My being inside him was simply a challenge that had to be dealt with, a problem that had to be solved.

His openness and straightforwardness were tremendously appealing. He simply wanted to know who I was and what my being here was all about.

So I told him everything. I broke every rule in the book.

I told him how in the distant future land where I lived, we had developed the power to send our minds backward in time. I described the way time research had begun, the first experiments, the failures and the successes, the early short-hop attempts at going back a few hours, a few days, a few weeks. I went on to talk about how, as we mastered the technique, we'd begun to send volunteers back across the centuries in the form of disembodied consciousnesses—jumping a hundred years, five hundred, a thousand.

Whether he really understood very much of this is anybody's guess. But from the fluctuations of his hormone levels I could tell that he was spellbound, utterly fascinated, when I spoke of the way time explorers, reporting on their experiences, are able to recapture the past and make it seem to live again.

And then I spoke of Athilan—"Atlantis, as we call it," I said. I described how, as we pushed our research back and back and back, we began picking up sketchy details of the existence of Athilan, and I told him that of all the nations of the ancient world, the empire of Athilan was the greatest, and therefore was the one that we yearned most to know about.

I held my breath, afraid that I'd given away too much. I didn't want to have to tell him of the coming destruction of his land, the obliteration of all but the most hazy memory of the great empire that was Athilan. But I had tossed him a big hint, of course. If Athilan was all but forgotten in my time, what was I saying, if not that it had been destroyed somewhere along the way? But he was so interested in the idea of consciousnesses wandering back in time that we went right by that obvious point.

—Are you the first wizard of your people to visit Athilan? he asked.

—*The third,* I said. And I told him of Fletcher's pioneering trip, and Iversen's, and how the information they brought back was useful in its way but too limited, because Fletcher had landed in the mind of a slave, and Iversen in that of a not very bright shopkeeper, and neither one was capable of providing much insight into the details of Athilantan life. So a deliberate attempt was made, I said, to see to it that the next explorer who went back to Athilan entered the mind of a member of the ruling family.

—*And here you are,* Prince Ram said.

—*And here I am.*

We talked half the afternoon, through what would normally have been his exercise period. He overflowed with questions about the world I came from.

I described telephones for him, and television, and supersonic transports, and space satellites. I told him that we had mining camps on the Moon and three little scientific outposts on Mars, and were talking about sending a crew out for a close look at the moons of Jupiter. I made a stab at explaining what our system of government is like, and what it's like to live in a world that has several great nations instead of only one, and how we managed to survive the ferocious conflicts that almost finished us all off in the horrendous twentieth century.

He wasn't skeptical in the slightest. I guess he had no trouble believing that wizards capable of sending a man's mind back twenty thousand years could also make machines that could fly from Thibarak to Naz Glesim in a couple of hours, or send pictures halfway around the world in a moment.

The only thing he absolutely couldn't swallow was the notion of democratic elections. He wanted to know the name of our king, and how long he and his family had ruled.

–*It doesn't work that way any more,* I said. *In our land we choose a new ruler every four years. If he or she rules wisely, they are often given four years more. And then we choose someone else.*

That made no sense to him, no matter how many different ways I explained it.

The people choose the king? A stranger is allowed to replace an established ruler?

He was baffled. His body grew tense, his head began to throb. Only when I told him that there were other countries where the rulers held power for a great many years, sometimes for their whole lives, did he ease back a little.

But even the concept of dictatorship seemed bizarre and troublesome to him. To grab power and proclaim yourself the boss, and then to rule until the people grow tired of you and overthrow you, whereupon somebody else stands up and says he's boss–no, no, Prince Ram couldn't swallow that. It seemed like insanity to him. Our scientific wonders, our television and time travel and voyages to Mars, those he could accept without a quiver of doubt. But not our politics.

Wrapping it up, the next day.

Where it stands now is that Ram and I have become pals. The best of friends. He completely accepts my presence within him, is not at all spooked by it, thinks it's just terrific. A wizard from the far future living behind his forehead who can tell him all sorts of marvelous things. Doesn't intend to let anyone know about it, naturally. His little secret, to cherish and enjoy.

I realize that this violates all our training, for me to have let him in on the truth of the situation. It goes against everything that we're taught in the way of procedural tactics. My neck's going to be on the block for sure when I return to Home Era. So all this has big implications not just for my future, but for yours and mine together. Don't think I haven't been troubled by that. But I couldn't help doing what I've done. It was the only honorable choice. Either admit the truth, or risk destroying Prince Ram's sanity. Well, I made my choice, and now I have to stick with it, even though it certainly means the ruination of my career.

He knows that you're occupying the mind of Provincial Governor Sippurilayl. He knows that we communicate by means of these letters, and he will continue to oblige me by serving as my scribe. Whether you want to reveal yourself to Sippurilayl is entirely up to you. Personally I don't think you should. You have nothing to gain from it and everything to lose once you're back in Home Era. After all, you still have a career in time research to think about, regardless of the mess I've made of mine.

Will you go on writing to me, knowing what you know now?

I hope you will. I'll be devastated if you don't, Lora.

Please don't worry that by corresponding with me you'll be making yourself some kind of accomplice in my breach of the rules. I'm going to let it be known loud and clear, when we've returned to Home Era, that I chose to make my presence known to Ram entirely on my own, without consulting you and certainly without any suggestion from you that I do it.

As you know, I never intended to blow my cover this way. It was just something that happened. To do it was wrong, and I'm prepared to take the consequences, whatever they may be, when the time comes. I have to say, though, that I don't really see what harm it does, this far in the past, to let one clever prince know that we of the twenty-first century are capable of roving through time. His knowing that can't possibly change any aspect of history, can it?

Or can it?

Well, so be it, What I've done can't be undone. Ram kept himself up half the night talking with me, asking a million and one questions, the way you would with a new college roommate. All about my family, the place where I was born, my training as a "wizard," et cetera, et cetera, et cetera, until he was goofy with fatigue and I had to ease him to sleep without his knowing it, for his own sake.

Roommates is what we are, all right.

How strange this all is, Lora! How totally strange.

–Roy

9.

Day 22, Western Wind, Great River.

News. Big news. A flabbergasting, mind-blowing discovery, in fact. A completely unexpected discovery that makes everything that was impossible to explain about the Athilantan empire fall suddenly into place.

Now that I no longer need to conceal my presence from Ram, I can move about freely in his mind. That doesn't seem to bother him. He doesn't see it as an invasion of his privacy; he doesn't seem to understand the concept of privacy at all. Or care about it, if he does.

One thing I wanted to know about was the rite of Romany Star.

Remember that mysterious ceremony that Ram and his father performed one night last month? The Prince and the King staring at the sky, chanting solemn prayers to one particular star, shredding and burning their garments, destroying the coronets that they wore? Obviously an important rite. But what was its significance?

I slipped down into the depths of Ram's consciousness

to see what I could learn about it. And got a lot more than I was expecting.

As I hardly need to tell you, you can't do research in a human mind, whether it's your own or someone else's, the way you would in a public library. Minds have no indexes and you can't run a computer scan to find the particular data you want. Everything is arranged systematically inside the mind, I suppose, but the genius has not yet been born who is capable of figuring out what that system is. So the best you can do is poke around randomly and try to make the connections you need.

I touched here and there within Ram's mind, looking for the memories of the night of the Romany Star rite. I came up with all sorts of other things—the time in the Labyrinth, and a stroll along a spectacular beach, all white sands and sparkling water, and a wild horseback ride down some forest glade, and so on and so on—and then there it was, Ram and the King on the palace roof chanting their prayer.

That entry in Ram's memory file had a special feel to it, a distinct resonance, a tone all its own. It was like one of those haunting melodies that you couldn't possibly sing yourself, but which you'd recognize whenever you heard it. I can't describe it to you, but I know what it was like. And, now that I had experienced it, I had a reference point. I went darting off down this mental avenue and that one, hoping to pick that special tone up again somewhere else, another point of association with Romany Star.

And I found it. It came rising up toward me out of a part of his brain where history and myth lay sleeping. Intermingled with it was a strange bleak image: charred debris, bits of burned rope, twisted fragments of what looked like hammocks, rising out of a sea of ashes. I looked closer. I felt dry hot winds. I saw a great swollen red sun in the sky.

Closer. Deeper. The ashes rose and became an eerie city

made of woven reeds. Buildings, streets, bridges—everything light, delicate, insubstantial. Somber-faced people walked in silence through its narrow, interlacing lanes. Sometimes it was night, and a string of shining moons was hung across the sky. Then came day, and that gigantic menacing sun.

The people had the look of the people of Athilan: dark hair and eyes, dark complexions, stocky bodies, broad shoulders. I thought I saw Ram in those streets, and his father.

The sun grew larger. The air grew hotter. There was terror in the eyes of the people who walked in the streets. Their world was coming to an end. Soon fire would sweep through the sky; soon this delicate city of woven reeds would become the sea of ashes that I had been shown before.

I saw ships lifting off into space. Maybe a dozen or more of them, carrying the lucky few, chosen by lot, who would escape the explosion of the red sun.

And the rest—the rest—oh, Lora, I knew what would happen to them, and my heart ached for them! A whole world destroyed. Romany Star sending spears of flame across the gulf of space, and everything perishing, everything except what was aboard those twelve or sixteen starships.

The moment of devastation came. Terrible light, like the fury of a thousand nuclear bombs at once, burst overhead. But the starships were on their way, up and out, heading into the vast darkness that lay beyond the blazing sky.

Do you understand what I'm saying, Lora?

Lora, these Athilantans are aliens. Humanoid aliens, so much like humans that it's just about impossible to tell the difference. They came here aboard those starships, refugees from some other world lightyears away that died when its sun went nova.

No wonder they're head and shoulders above the real

natives of the Paleolithic world. Maybe a thousand years before the era that you and I are visiting now, maybe three thousand, they dropped down suddenly out of space, bringing to a world that didn't yet know the use of metals a culture that could build spaceships capable of traveling between the stars. That is, a culture that's advanced even beyond our own.

To the Cro-Magnons and their contemporaries, they must have seemed like gods. In a way they were gods. And they built a mighty city in the midst of Earth's frostbound Stone Age darkness.

Their descendants here in Athilan still look back in sorrow and anguish to their old lost home, which they call Romany Star. On a certain night each year they turn their eyes to the stars, and they chant the prayer for the dead, in remembrance of all that had been theirs before the red sun swelled in the sky, before their unstable home star flared up and destroyed their world.

Now I understand why the people of Athilan gave thanks for Ram's return to the human realm when he came back to the city from the mainland, and why they refer to the mainlanders as the Dirt People.

I suppose they could have found some more complimentary term for them than that, but the fact remains that the Athilantans see themselves as the only true humans, and the mainlanders, the natives of Earth, as some sort of inferior alien beings. It isn't really the sort of racism that used to be so common in our modern world. That involved one branch of the human species telling itself that it was superior to the other branches of the human race. There wasn't any justification for those feelings of superiority. All the different races of modern Earth are just minor variations of the same species, Homo sapiens. But these people really are superior. And they aren't simply a special branch of Homo sapiens. They aren't Homo sapiens at all, even though they look just like us, or nearly so. They're a different species entirely. I'm not saying it's admirable or pretty in any way for them to have such contempt for the mainlanders. But at least I can understand why they feel that way. And also I think that when we translate their words into ours the terms they use may come out sounding a little more contemptuous than the Athilantans actually intend.

Doesn't it all sound completely crazy? Refugees from the stars, traveling here on spaceborne arks, founding a glorious city on this balmy isle in the eastern Atlantic, and setting up a far-flung Paleolithic empire? But it's true. I've located Ram's memories of the historical chronicles that he studied when he was a boy. You can probably find the same stuff in Sippurilayl's mind if you look for it.

And now we know why these people are so improbably far ahead of everyone else who existed on Earth in prehistoric times. They had a tremendous head start.

The present-day Athilantan civilization isn't nearly as advanced as the one that died with Romany Star. They've lost a lot of their old technological knowledge over the centuries, perhaps through neglect, or maybe simply because they weren't able to reconstruct it on this new world. But they're still inconceivably superior in abilities and attainments to the primitive hunting folk over whom they rule.

It does sound too fantastic to be true. A myth, a legend, a poem, anything but the actual truth.

Well, it is the actual truth. I absolutely believe that. I've discussed it with Ram and he vehemently insists that it isn't any myth—that it all really happened, the solar flare that destroyed their world, the migration to Earth, the building of Athilan on an uninhabited island in the warmest part of the planet. They have detailed and reliable chronicles describing the whole thing. Every child studies the history of the calamity the way we study Christopher Columbus and George Washington.

Go check out Provincial Governor Sippurilayl's memories of his childhood history lessons. You'll find it all there. I know that you will.

And what a tremendous story it is, isn't it?

–Roy

10.

Day 4, Month of Golden Days, Year of Great River.

I hope you haven't been worried about me during my long silence. Everything's fine here. I just haven't felt much like writing letters.

The truth is I've been a little embarrassed about my last two letters, the one in which I confess that I've revealed my presence to Ram, and the one in which I tell you about my discovery of the extraterrestrial origin of the Athilantans. (Have you received that second one yet? You'll be awfully confused by what I've just said if you haven't.) I was afraid that one or the other of those letters would convince you that I'd gone loony–that you'd write back to me full of fury about my breaking of the time-travel rules, or that you'd tell me that the business about the Athilantans coming from a different solar system was the craziest nonsense you had ever heard. So I couldn't bring myself to send you any more letters until I saw what your reaction to those two was.

Well, now your reply to my I've-told-Ram-everything letter has come in. I'm immensely relieved that you aren't angry with me, Lora. It makes me realize all over again what a wonderful person you are. And why I love you so much.

No question, as you say, that I'm going to be in very hot water when I get back to Home Era. But you do recognize, as I hoped you would, that letting Ram know the truth was my only honorable course. I simply couldn't let the heir to the throne go on thinking he was possessed by a demon, and calling in all sorts of witch-doctors to exorcise him.

You don't comment on the other and bigger revelation, from which I conclude that you haven't seen my second letter yet, though you'll be able to figure out something of what it's about from what I've said here. In any case I can tell you that I've done a lot of further research—Ram has taken me through the royal archives, which contain extremely elaborate records of every event in Athilantan history—and I have no doubt at all that the interstellar-migration story is accurate. Ram and his people really do come from another world.

The Athilantans have been on Earth for 1143 years. Harinamur—the first one—was the captain of the space fleet that brought them here. The migration took them only thirty-one years, which means they must have traveled at the speed of light, or something pretty close to it. That implies a technology way beyond ours, at least so far as space travel goes, since we haven't managed yet to reach speeds anything like that and we're still limited to our own Solar System. For the time being, anyway.

Sixteen starships altogether made the trip. They don't exist any more—they were dismantled and totally recycled into other things during the early years of the colony, when metals were scarce. When they landed here, they knew they were here to stay: they weren't going to be journeying between the stars ever again.

It ought to be possible for the people up front to check

all this out by running an astronomical survey. There can't be many red stars within a 31-lightyear radius that have a history of instability, and maybe they can figure out which one of them went nova about 20,000 B.C. And then we'd know where Romany Star was. When we become capable of building spaceships fast enough to travel to other stars, which I guess is still another hundred years or so ahead for us, we can send an expedition out to look for the charred ruins of the civilization that once lived there, and confirm that whole thing.

On to other matters.

The Prince and I are getting along very well. He's completely comfortable with the idea that we share the same body. As he goes through his day's princely chores he keeps a running commentary going, explaining everything that he's doing. I've learned vast amounts about the trade routes of the Athilantan empire, about its history, about its religion. I hope I can keep it all straight in my head until I get back to Home Era. (Damn not having any way to take notes back with us! But at least they did a good job of training us to use our memories.)

The Prince questions me, too, about Home Era. Our time is like a fantasy to him—a time when billions of people occupy the Earth and all sorts of different cultures exist—and his appetite for details about it is tremendous. He wants to know about city planning, about our arts and religions, about sports, about automobiles and airplanes, about almost anything. I think he suspects that I'm making up some or even all of what I tell him. There are moments it almost feels like that to me: Home Era seems terribly far away, terribly unreal. After these months here I sometimes think that only Athilan is real and everything else is a fairy tale. Having no body of your own will do that to you, I've heard.

A big event lies just ahead: the Rite of Anointing. Preparations are already in full swing and the whole city is involved in them.

You will recall that this is the third of the four major rites that a prince must undergo, following the Rite of Designation and the Rite of Joining, before he is ready to become Grand Darionis of Athilan. Apparently in this one the heir to the throne receives certain great revelations that every king must know. What these revelations might be, Ram has no idea. But the prospect of finally finding out has him terrifically excited.

Me too, I have to say.

It's another few weeks, now. We're both going to have a tough time waiting for the days to pass.

The one thing I'm afraid of now is that the folks back at Home Year are going to give me the hook just before the rite. That really upsets me; knowing that the clock is ticking all the time. And then I'll never find out what the mysteries were.

How much more time here do I really have? That's the big question. I don't know. You remember in one of my first letters I told you that I had lost track of the count of Home Era days. The information you sent helped a little, but not enough. I may be as much as a week off in my count. On top of that, it's unclear to me what the exact day when they're supposed to pull me back is. "Six months," they said, but do they mean that right down to the day, or is it just a rough figure? So I might have another two weeks here, a month, maybe even six weeks. I can't tell. And I want to stay here as long as I can, Lora. For obvious reasons I'm not looking forward to going back there and facing the music. But aside from that I simply don't want to leave. Not yet. Not until I've learned everything I can possibly learn about this place.

And I have a feeling that the Rite of Anointing is going to tell me plenty.

Hope to hear from you soon.

With all my love–

–Roy

11.

Day 36, Golden Days, Great River.

Another long silence from me, I know. I was holding off, so I could describe the Rite of Anointing to you. Well, the Rite of Anointing has now taken place—it was three days ago. The mysteries have been revealed. It was a tremendous event—and also tremendously upsetting. A fantastic experience. Completely overwhelming, the kind of thing that takes absolute possession of you and won't let go. Both Prince Ram and I were pretty badly shaken up by it all. And so I've needed a few days just to think about what happened, to come to terms with it, to understand my own reactions and feelings. I'm not sure I really have a handle on it even now.

Let me see—where should I start?

At the beginning, I guess. The morning of the day of the Rite of Anointing. It was one of those magnificent spring-like Athilantan days, warm golden sunlight, clear crisp blue sky, that make the fact that we are actually living in the Ice Age seem like such a joke. (Every day is springtime in

Athilan. Something like the best days California can do, but even lovelier.)

The Prince had fasted all the previous day, and had stayed awake all through the night, praying and chanting. We had no contact with each other. I took care to keep myself well below the threshold of his consciousness. Obviously he didn't want to be disturbed, and I didn't want to disturb him.

At dawn, his personal slaves led him to the great marble bath chamber of the palace, and bathed and anointed him with perfumes and oils. They dressed him then, in a magnificent robe of pure white cotton bordered in purple richly brocaded and trimmed with cloth of gold. From the bath chamber he went to a small, very austere chapel on the ground floor, where for a time he prayed in front of column of shining black stone.

Now his family came to him: first his sister Princess Rayna, then his younger brother Prince Caiminor, and then his mother, Queen Aliralin, whom I hadn't encountered before. (A slender, stately, very queenly woman of great beauty. She had been on the north shore of the island, it seems, in a religious retreat.)

As they went before Prince Ram, each one knelt to him, even his mother, and with outstretched hands silently offered him a shallow cup of polished pink stone that contained a small quantity of some aromatic wine. He sipped very solemnly. One wine was ruby red, one was golden, one scarcely had any color at all. Each affected him in a slightly different way. The overall effect was not one of making him drunk—the wines of Athilan don't seem to make anybody drunk—but nevertheless transforming his spirit, giving it a glow, a radiance, that it had not had before.

Then his father came to him, bareheaded but clad in the most sumptuous royal robe imaginable, deep purple with great flaring shoulder-pieces of rich scarlet, and loomed before him like a god. He didn't speak a word, but simply extended his hand to Ram, drew him from the chapel, walked with him out of the palace and down those myriad steps to the great plaza out front. A chariot was waiting, drawn by two of the fierce, snorting little horses that the Athilantans use.

The entire population of the city, so it seemed, had turned out to see the royal procession go by. The route was a grand circle through the city. We went westward, first, down the Concourse of the Sky almost as far as the waterfront, then around to the north along a broad curving boulevard, paved with shining pink flagstones, called the Avenue of the Gods. There were cheering crowds everywhere, calling out to Ram.

"Thilayl!" they yelled. "Highness!"

And also: "Stolifar Blayl!" Which is part of his secret formal name, and means "Light of the Universe," and apparently is only spoken aloud on the Day of Anointing.

The purpose of the procession, which took hours, was simply to display Ram to the populace. By midday, we were back almost exactly where we had started, in the zone of temples and palaces at the center of the place. The sun was high and bright, now, glinting off the white stone facades of Athilan.

We went around to the eastern side of the sacred district, where the land starts to slope up toward the foothills of Mount Balamoris. Here, overlooking the entire city, is the glorious Plaza of a Thousand Columns, one of the most magnificent public spaces any city ever had. Just beyond the north side of the plaza stands an unassuming, windowless little building made of big blocks of black granite. This is the House of the Anointing, where royal powers are conferred on the members of the ruling family of Athilan.

Walking barefoot, side by side, Ram and his father went in. It was dark within except for a single shaft of noonday light that pierced a twelve-sided opening in the ceiling. The King formally touched fingertips with his son, and they embraced; and then, without a word, the King left the building.

Ram knelt beneath that shaft of light.

Three figures in priestly robes appeared from the darkness beyond. Smooth white masks, unbroken except for tiny eye-slits, completely hid their faces. They loomed above the kneeling Ram and lightly brushed his forehead with a thick, sweet oil. The Anointing, this was. Then they commenced a slow rhythmic chant, speaking in the ancient form of the Athilantan language which is used for epic poetry and religious scriptures, and which—like Latin in our own day—hardly anyone here really understands. Certainly Ram was able to comprehend just a few scattered phrases—all cliches, things about his high royal heritage, the grave responsibilities that were to be his, et cetera, et cetera.

Then, just as his sister and brother and mother had done much earlier that day, each priest in turn offered Ram a shallow bowl of polished stone to drink from. The wine, if wine it was, had a light, spicy taste, and it was giving off gentle fizzy bubbles.

The priests withdrew.

Ram knelt, head down, waiting.

Slowly, slowly, slowly, a dreamlike state began to take possession of his mind. A darkness, a dizziness, overtook him. The narrow golden beam from above grew dim. Swirls of color swept back and forth like waves, like billowing curtains, in the black depths of the House of Anointing.

Visions came to him.

Everything was turbulent and unclear at first. Then his mind became a screen, and he saw, and I saw with him, the night sky, the vastness of space, meteors rushing past, stars and galaxies, great surging comets.

The focus changed. Now his mind drifted down to the surface of the old world of Romany Star, as it had been before its destruction. The wickerwork houses, the streets of woven reeds, everything supple and pliant, shifting in the slightest breezes. And the people of Romany Star quietly going about their tasks, living busily, happily–

Until the sun began to swell, until that great red eye came to fill the heavens–

Motionless, impassive, Prince Ram and I watched once again the destruction of his people's original world. The prayers, the outcries, the dry wind, the scorching heat, the first pale puff of flame, the smoldering houses, and then the holocaust, a world afire, everything transformed into ashes in a moment, while the sixteen gleaming starships rose desperately into the heavens with their little load of lucky escapees–

The migration, then, we watched. The years of wandering through space, searching for a habitable planet. The first wondrous glimpse of Earth, blue and shining in the black bowl of night. The survey party landing, going forth across the bleak chilly continents to find a place where the Athilantans might live. The discovery of the warm lovely isle lapped by a kindly ocean. The sixteen ships plunging downward, bringing the wanderers at last to their new home.

Prince Ram and I were eye-witnesses, within a span of just moments, to the entire history of his race. The wine, the drug, whatever it was that had been in those shallow stone bowls, had cut him free from the bonds of the time-line, and he drifted untethered through the ages, roaming the whole past without restraint, without boundary.

We saw the city being built. Harinamur the One King, the original one, amidst his people, laying out the avenues and boulevards, selecting the sites for the temples, the palaces, the parks, the marketplaces. Workers using cunning devices swiftly carving slabs of marble from the hillsides. This city would be nothing like the old lost home on Romany Star. There, everything had been lithe, delicate, yielding. Here they would build of stone.

The city arose. And the people of Athilan went forth from it into the frosty hinterlands beyond, and made themselves known to the savage people who dwelled there, and built an empire linked by the first roads and the first ships this world had ever seen.

We watched the city grow. We watched it flourish. Brilliant sunlight glinting off the palaces of white stone. Magnificent villas climbing the green slopes of Mount Balamoris. The harbor crowded with ships, bearing goods from every quarter of this splendid untouched planet.

And then—then everything changed. In a moment. In the twinkling of an eye.

First came a darkening of the sky. Then a strand of black smoke rising from the summit of the mountain. A sudden tremor underfoot. I was caught without warning by the shift in the tone of the vision. Ram, deep in his dreams of the past, had no idea at all of what was coming. But, after a moment, I did.

I saw now that in the Anointing he was able to wander both forward and backward in time. He had had a vision of this great city's founding. And now he was going to be shown its doom.

Oh, Lora, if I could have spared him the sight! If I could have covered his eyes and kept him from seeing the death of Athilan, I tell you I would have done it! But I had no power. I was only an insignificant passenger crammed into a corner of his dreaming mind.

And so we watched it together.

The flames bursting from the mountain. The smoke staining the pure clear sky a dirty dingy gray. The sudden rainfall of small light pumice stones clattering down everywhere. Then the thick clouds of ash bursting forth. The mighty tremors running through the ground. Huge slabs of marble dropping from the facades of buildings. The columns of the Plaza of the Thousand Columns moving crazily from side to side, then tumbling as if struck by the side of a giant's hand.

The earth shaking–heaving–splitting open–streets cracking, houses falling, pavements vanishing into newly created abysses–

The sky turning black–

The sea rising–

A great terrifying groaning sound filling the air, coming not from the throats of the populace but from the earth itself. Flames everywhere. The roar of the water as it rushes forward onto the land. Lava spilling down the sides of the mountain and pouring into the city. Earthquake, flood, volcanic eruption, everything at once. Destruction on all sides. Doom. Doom. Doom.

A few ships putting out from the harbor, struggling against the fantastic heaving of the waves. A pitiful band of refugees, once again setting forth to save themselves as Athilan is brought down into ruin, just as Romany Star once had been.

The surface of the land subsides. It just drops downward into itself, as if everything that had been supporting it had gone up in the eruption. The sea comes pouring in, and nothing can hold it back. There's a different sound now, a strange taut high-pitched one, like the thrumming of some immense insect, growing louder, louder, louder, until it fills every space and there can be room for nothing else anywhere in the world. It's the sound of the city dying. And then it stops, with awful abruptness, with a crack of silence followed by a great stillness.

The stillness goes on and on.

The sky is clear again, blue with a golden sun, and the hugeness of the sea spreads before us.

Of the island of Athilan there is not the slightest sign. It has been devoured; it has been swallowed up; it has vanished beneath the surface of the water as though it had never existed.

The vision ended. Ram didn't move. He knelt there as though he'd been clubbed. Through his numbed mind there ran, again and again, ghastly scenes out of the last hour of Athilan.

Then the door of the House of Anointing opened, and the three masked priests returned. With them was the King. He wore no mask; and his face was stark and stern as he knelt over his son and drew him gently to his feet. From his look, I realized that the King knew what Ram had seen. He had seen it himself, years before, on the day of his own Anointing.

So this is the mystery that the princes of this empire are shown as they enter into full manhood. They are pulled loose from the framework of time—how, I can't even guess—and allowed to float freely, backward and then forward. And they are shown the fate that awaits this greatest of all cities.

What a shattering thing to learn! To discover that all striving is in vain, that discipline and ambition, hard work and planning, prayers and rituals, lead only to fiery doom and watery destruction! Why, then, bother to take on the burdens of being a king? Everything is pointless. Nothing you achieve can possibly withstand the coming fury. Your homeland will sink beneath the sea and be forgotten. What a devastating lesson that is!

No wonder Ram had crouched there in a stupor of shock and defeat.

When he left the House of Anointing with his father and the three priests he walked as a prince must walk, straight-backed, square-shouldered. But his eyes were bleak and his mind still lay locked in gloom and torment and cold despair. And that's how he has been, these three days past. A cloud of seemingly unbreakable depression hangs over him. He won't speak to anyone, he doesn't eat at all, he remains in his room.

I can't say I feel a lot better myself. The waves of sorrow and amazement and horror that come from Ram's mind have seeped into my own, and my mood is gray and chilly. There's no use trying to kid myself with cheery little uplifting cliches. I've been forced right up against the underlying truth of things. What a dark and cruel place the world is, for all its beauty, for all its wonder! We have miracles around us on every side—a spiderweb is a miracle, Lora!—but also we have violence, insanity, terrible disease, sudden death. The same Nature that brings us the mountains and the rivers and the green glistening meadows brings us the hurricane, the earthquake, the flood of red-hot lava rolling toward the city.

That Atlantis was one day to be destroyed was hardly any secret to me when I came here. But even so, it was a truly miserable experience to be forced to watch at close range as the news of the city's inevitable doom was brought to someone who has spent his entire life preparing to be its king.

I wish I could do something for him. But he doesn't want to talk even with me. My few attempts at making mental contact have been hurled back with furious snarls. He needs to work this thing through by himself, entirely by himself.

I suppose the Athilantans see the Anointing as a necessary part of the education of a future Grand Darionis. But to me, right now, it seems terribly cruel, a needless disillusionment. It utterly pulls the rug out from under you.

Everyone wants some way of seeing into the future, of course; but these people actually have one, and look at the damage it does. If I were going to become Grand Darionis of Athilan in a few years I'd just as soon be spared the knowledge that the whole place is fated eventually to go down the tubes regardless of anything anyone do.

I did, by the way, get your last letter just before all this happened.

I'm glad to hear you backing me up on the theory that the Athilantans came here from another world. Somebody else might just have shrugged and said that poor Roy has gone completely nuts. Instead you went and peered into Governor Sippurilayl's memories of his boyhood history lessons and found that he'd been taught the same story Ram had. Of course, that doesn't mean it's true; but I think it is, and apparently so do you. Thanks for your support. A good guy, you are. I don't need to tell you, do I, how much you mean to me, how deeply I miss you, how eager I am to see you again?

And thanks also for the revised calendar information. Using the data you sent, I was able to sit down finally and plot everything out the way I should have done a long while back. I see now that my stint in Atlantis is just about over. Six days more, maybe seven, and they'll be yanking us back to our sleeping bodies up there in Home Year. So we'll actually be together again soon. I feel good about that, you can bet. But I hate the idea of leaving Atlantis at a time like this.

My God, these have been an awful few days.

With much much love–

–Roy

12.

Day 42, Golden Days, Great River.

This is my last letter. We'll be home soon. In fact you won't even get to read this, because it can't possibly reach you out there in Naz Glesim before we leave. But I need to set all this down on paper anyway, just to get everything clear in my own mind. Let's pretend that you'll get it next week, although you won't, not here. But you'll be hearing it from me next week in person, up in Home Era.

The basic situation is this: I've been breaking rules again. In a big way. I'm beginning to think I'm suffering from some kind of compulsion to go against everything we were trained to do when we became time observers.

What happened was that I decided that since I've got very little time left to spend in Atlantis, I would save the city from the doom that's bearing down on it before I have to leave. That's right. All by myself I would spare this great civilization from destruction.

I don't mean that I came up with some way to defuse that volcano or to keep the earthquake from happening. All I did was go to work on Prince Ram, trying to convince him to order an evacuation to some safer place while there was still time.

I should tell you that Ram had come up out of his state of deep gloom by this point. On the fifth morning after the Rite of Anointing he awakened in a perfectly calm, cheerful mood. He prayed, he swam about eighty laps in the palace pool, he ate an enormous breakfast, he met with his father and tackled a colossal stack of official reports that needed to be scanned and approved. It was as thought the Rite of Anointing had never taken place. He was absolutely his old self again. No trace remained of the dark, bitter, agonized frame of mind that had gripped him since the day of that terrible revelation.

This is evidently a familiar pattern for the Prince. Remember how upset he was when he first found out that a "demon" was hiding in his mind? Trembling, shaking, pressing his hands violently against his head to drive me out? But then he calmed down completely. In the Labyrinth, again, he got pretty excited while he was trying to work that exorcism on me; but once he realized that he had failed to expel me, he became so cheerful and tranquil that I wasn't sure he knew I was still there. He's extremely tough and well balanced. Something strange can really get to him and shake him; but in his steady, determined way he works on it, gets control of it, regains his poise. And then everything's all right for him again.

He said to me, *–You've been very quiet lately, wizard.*

–I didn't think you needed to hear from me. You've had enough to handle.

–You saw what I saw? The destruction of the city?

—Yes.

—And what do you think, wizard? You know all that is to come. Was it a true vision? Or only a bad dream, a nightmare designed to test me?

I could have given him false consolation then, I suppose. I could have lied, and said that what he had seen was a fever dream, a fantasy, that Athilan would endure forever and a day. But I'm not much good at lying. And I knew that he wasn't looking for lies from me, or consolations, or anything else that might make him feel good for a moment at the expense of the truth.

So I said,—The city will be destroyed, Prince.

—Truly.

—Truly, yes. In my era nothing will be remembered of it except that it once existed. And many people will think that even that is only a foolish tale.

—Destroyed and forgotten.

—Yes, Prince Ram.

He was silent for a while. But I was monitoring the flow of his moods, and there was no return to the bleakness that had gripped him in the days just after the Rite of Anointing. He was calm. He was steady.

He said at last, *—How far in the future is the time of destruction, wizard? Ten thousand years? Five thousand?*

—Perhaps ten thousand years. Perhaps much less.

—Perhaps it will happen this year, even?

—I don't know, Prince.

—A wizard should know the future.

—But your calling me a wizard doesn't make me one, Prince. What you speak of as the future is the remote and misty past to me. I have no way of knowing when Athilan perished. Believe me, Prince.

Another period of silence. Then he said:

–I believe you–wizard.

And then I said, taking myself completely by surprise, *–Prince, you need to save your city while there's still time.*

–Save it? How could I possibly save it?

–Leave this island. Lead everyone across to the mainland. Build a new Athilan in some place that will be invulnerable. And it will endure forever.

I felt undertones of amazement coming from him. I tell you, I was amazed myself at what I was doing.

But I couldn't help it, Lora. I was caught up in the crazy rapture and wonder of my scheme.

I told him where to erect his New Atlantis. *–Go to North Africa,* I said. *It's warm there. There's a place called Egypt, where a mighty river flows out of the heart of the continent. Your ships can get there easily from here, by sailing east and south. The land is fertile. You'll have access to the sea. There's stone to build with. You can create a new empire ten times as great as this one, one that will spread around the world.*

–Or else, I said, *go further east, to a place known as Mesopotamia. There are two rivers there, and it's warm there too, and the land is perhaps even more fertile than in Egypt. And from there you can expand ever eastward, to a land called India, and one called China. You'll be better off there than in Europe–in the mainland right here. Europe will be locked in ice for many more thousands of years. But China–India–Egypt–*

I was berserk, Lora.

I was grossly interfering with the past. Not only had I opened direct contact with my own time-host, but here I was trying to get him to take a course of action that would beyond any doubt change the entire direction of history! Carried away by my own brilliance, I was telling him to go and found Egypt long before the Pharaohs would. Or better yet to create his new kingdom in Sumer or Babylon, and then to colonize the Orient, and—this part didn't even matter to me, so crazed was I, so eager was I to be helpful—set up a Second Athilantan Empire that might become so powerful it would last on and on right into what you and I think of as historical times!

How about that? A tremendous sprawling kingdom ruled by extraterrestrial aliens, dominating the world for the next twenty thousand years, while none of our "real" history gets a chance to occur! No Greece, no Rome, no England, no United States—only eternal Athilan, all-powerful, reaching out in every direction, controlling everything! What a vision! What lunacy, Lora!

I offered to draw maps for him. I offered to give him geographical lessons. I promised to ransack my brains for every detail of what I knew about the Paleolithic Near East.

He let me rave for a long time.

And then he said, finally, *—What a rare vision this is. What a wondrous scheme.*

—Yes, I said, sure that I had convinced him.

And then: *—But you know I would never do anything like this, wizard. Not even if I were Grand Darionis today, and I knew that the calamity would fall upon us in ten months' time, would I do such a thing.*

I was caught off balance.

—You wouldn't?

He laughed. *—Why do you think the princes of Athilan are shown the vision of the Rite of Anointing?*

I said, really flustered now *—Well—it's because—I would assume—that is, it seems to me that it's done in order to prepare you for the eruption. In case you happen to be the one who's King at the time when it actually takes place. So that* *you can plan to take protective measures, arrange a safe evacuation, things like that.*

–No. Not at all.

–Why is it done, then?

He paused a moment. Then he said, *–To teach us that even though we are kings, we are as nothing in the hands of the gods.*

–I don't understand.

–You are no wizard then.

–I have never pretended to be one.

He said, *–The gods have decreed that Athilan one day must perish, just as they decreed the fiery death of Romany Star. Don't you think that we were aware that that would happen, too? And this city came out of that one. New greatness flowers out of lost greatness. It is our destiny, wizard, from time to time to be chastised by the gods, to be driven forth in sorrow from our homes, to begin anew, to create that which never existed before to replace that which was taken from us. Do you think we dare defy the gods? Do you think we dare thwart their will? We must accept what comes to us. That is the lesson of the Rite of Anointing. That is the thing I had to learn, if I am to be Grand Darionis some day. The vision was a test, yes. And I have passed that test.*

–Your ancestors knew that Romany Star would be destroyed? And they did nothing to save themselves?

–They built sixteen starships, and loaded aboard them whatever they could. The rest they left behind to face the flames. And when the catastrophe comes to the isle of Athilan, we will have ships ready, and once again we will save what we can. The rest will be destroyed beyond recovery.

I said, bewildered, *–I can't believe that you'll just sit here like sheep and take no action, even though you can see* *the future and you know that the future holds destruction for you.*

—Tell me this, wizard. In your era, do people still die?

—Yes. Of course.

—And yet you go about your daily lives, doing your work and making plans for the future and seeking always to better yourselves, even though you know that in twenty or thirty or fifty years you will certainly be dead? You don't simply give up and lie down, the moment you discover that death is inevitable, and abandon all striving right at that point?

—It isn't the same thing, I said. *The individual has to die sooner or later, yes. But the family goes on, the nation goes on, the world goes on. Each one of us does his part in the time that's allotted. What other choice do we have?*

—And if you knew—you absolutely knew—that the world itself would perish on the day of your own death? Would you give up all striving because it seemed futile, wizard? Or would you continue to work and plan?

His argument seemed wrong to me. *—But this isn't a matter of the whole world being destroyed! It's a matter of one island being struck by catastrophe, and its people having advance warning of the fact, and being unwilling to move to a safer place despite everything they know. That makes no sense to me.*

—Only the kings know of the doom that is coming. Not any other soul.

—Even so. If the kings know, it's their duty to save their people.

—And shall the king then thwart the will of the gods? Ram asked. *We must take what comes. And fully learn the lesson the gods wish to teach.*

That was where I gave up. I understood, then: these people really are alien. Their minds don't work like ours. They see the steamroller coming, and they refuse to get out of the way. It's the will of the gods, they say. And for them that's all there is to it. Pure fatalism. A philosophy like that isn't easy for me to comprehend. But after all I'm only a visitor here.

And my visit's almost over. I feel the bond weakening; I feel Home Era starting to pull me back. In a little while I'll be up front there, giving my report, confessing my blatant errors of judgment, surrendering myself to the judgment that's waiting for me. If I'm lucky they'll go easy on me. I understand that I'm not the first time-traveler to give in to the temptation to help his host avoid serious trouble. We're only human, after all.

And what will happen here, I wonder?

Well, Atlantis will be destroyed. That was a given fact from the start. Perhaps it'll happen when Ram is king, perhaps in the reign of some grandchild of his—but it will happen. No question of it. Fire and brimstone will fall, and the sea will rise, and the island will be swallowed up. In that moment the empire will end.

But a few ships are going to escape. I'm certain of that.

Where will they go? Egypt? Mesopotamia?

Will they live to build still another civilization, which will eventually perish also, but manage to pass a few fragments onward, until our world, the world that we call "modern," has taken form? Somewhere in our own world today are the descendants of these Athilantans. Of that I'm certain too. These perpetual wanderers, these many-times-refugees—surely they endure, surely they still dwell among us. By now they've forgotten their own history, I suspect. They don't know that their ancestors came from another world to live among us Dirt People, and once built the greatest empire that ever was, of which not a trace remains. It's all forever lost, back here in the distant buried corridors of time.

But that's not important. Time devours everything. Entire histories vanish. What matters is endurance. The spirit survives and goes onward when the palaces crumble and the kings are forgotten.

And if I've learned anything from this fantastic journey in time, Lora, that's it. You too, out there among the mammoth-hunters in their houses of bone, have seen what it's like to struggle against hostile nature and prevail. I, here in glittering Athilan, have also discovered a thing or two about how harsh a place the universe can be, and how stubborn we mortals can be in fighting back.

Ram knows I'm leaving soon, disappearing into a distant future time that's not even a dream to him. I wonder if he'll miss his "demon," his "wizard." I suspect he will.

I know I'm going to miss him. He's the most noble guy I've ever known. And I think he's going to be the greatest Grand Darionis that the Empire of Athilan has ever had.

And that's the whole story. It's just about time to go now, love. I'll be seeing you in a little while, only twenty thousand years from here. I hope they have a pizza waiting for us when we get there.

PROJECT PENDULUM

1.

Eric
– 5 minutes

Displacement hit him like a punch in the gut. He had to fight to keep from doubling up, coughing and puking. He was dizzy, too, and his legs kept trying to float up toward the ceiling. But the sensation lasted only a fraction of a second, and then he felt fine.

He was still in the laboratory, standing right in front of himself. In front of Sean, too. Twin and twin. Sean and the other version of himself were sitting side by side on the shunt platform in their strange little three-legged metal chairs, waiting for it all to begin.

Five minutes from now the singularity coupling would come to life and the displacement force would take hold of them. And they would be shuttled at infinite speed between the black hole and the white hole until they were thrust out through the time gate. But right now they were staring in wonder and amazement at him—at the extra Eric, Eric$_2$, the one who had been conjured up out of the mysterious well of time. Who had been pulled five minutes out of the future to stand before them now.

Weird to be looking at yourself like this, Eric thought. Seeing yourself from the outside.

In a sense, of course, he had had a way of seeing himself from the outside all his life. He just needed to glance at his twin brother, Sean. Looking at Sean's eyes was almost like looking into a mirror. The same color, the same glinting alertness. The same quick motions, taking everything in.

But this was different. Sean was like a mirror image of him, and your mirror image is never what you are. Eric didn't feel he looked as much like Sean as everyone else seemed to think, anyway. But now he was looking at *himself*, not Sean. Seeing neither his twin brother nor his own mirror image, but seeing himself unreflected, as others saw him all the time.

Strange. His nose—the nose of the other Eric—didn't seem right and his smile turned the wrong way at the corners of his mouth. His eyebrows were reversed, with the one on the right side pointing up. His whole face looked out of balance.

Eric wandered around the lab like some sort of disembodied spirit, prowling here and there. Someone aimed a camera at him and he made faces into it, putting his hands to his ears and wiggling them.

Dr. Ludwig said, "Five minutes exactly. Perfect displacement. Perfect visibility."

"Paradox number one," Dr. White chimed in. "The duplication. The overlap of identity."

"And paradox number two, also. The cumulative and self-modifying aspects of the time-stream correction."

"Say that again?" Eric asked.

Ludwig didn't trouble to reply. He glowered and scowled and vanished into the flow of his own intricate thoughts. It seemed to bother him that Eric had spoken at all. As if Eric were nothing more than an irritating distraction at this very complicated moment.

All around the room, technicians were throwing switches and tapping commands into terminals. Everybody was tense. To all these people Time Zero, the moment of the initial shunt, was still four and a half minutes away. The final delicate calibrations and balances had to be made.

Some of the staff people were staring at him the way they might stare at a ghost. That puzzled him for a moment. They should be used to backward-going time travelers by now. After all, Sean had already come this way on the minus-fifty-minute shunt, hadn't he? And Eric would be doing the minus-five-hundred-minute one himself a few hours ago. Even though he hadn't experienced it yet, *they* had. Or should have.

But then Eric recalled what they had told him about these past-changing paradoxes. Each swing of the pendulum retroactively corrected everybody's memories and perceptions. That was how it had been in the earlier experiments with robots and animals and they expected it to work the same this time. Nobody remembered Sean's minus-fifty-minutes appearance, or any of the earlier ones, because they hadn't happened yet. But as the pendulum kept swinging, those appearances *would* happen, at times earlier than this, and the corrections would be made, and everyone would begin to remember a past that right now didn't yet exist. Or something like that. It made no sense if you tried to think of it in the old straight-line way. Now that time travel was a fact, no one could think that way ever again.

Warning lights were lit up on all the instrument panels now. Critical displacement momentum was nearly attained. Sean and that other Eric would be on their way in another few instants. And he'd be moving along, too. He couldn't stay here much longer. Any minute now the next $Eric_2$ would be making the journey from Time Zero back to minus-five-minutes, the journey that he himself had just taken. The mathematics of time wouldn't allow him still to be here when the loop began all over again. You could have an Eric and an $Eric_2$ in the same place at the same time, but not more than one $Eric_2$. He would have to be up and out, swinging toward his second stop, the plus-fifty-minute level.

He could feel the force pulling at him now.

Eric waved jauntily at the Eric and Sean on the platform. When shall we three meet again, he asked himself? Probably never. He'd see Sean again at the end of the experiment, sure. If all went well. But there was no reason why he should ever come face-to-face with himself a second time.

Which was just as well, he decided. There's something creepy about looking yourself in the eye.

"Have a good trip, guys!" he called out to them. And the force seized him and swept him away into the time-stream.

2.

Sean
+ 5 minutes

And then at long last they threw the final switch, the one that would send him spinning off into the vast distant reaches of time, and nothing happened. At least that was how it felt to Sean at first. No blinding flashes of light, no strangely glowing haloes, no sinister humming sounds, no sense of turbulent upheaval. Nothing. An odd calmness, even a numbness, seemed to envelop him. So far as he could tell, nothing had changed at all. He was still sitting right where he had been, on the left-hand focal point of the singularity coupling.

Maybe it was too soon. Only an instant had passed, after all. Maybe the displacement cone was still building up energy, still gathering the momentum it would need to hurl him across the centuries.

A moment later Sean started finding out how wrong he was.

That first moment of calm began to fade as bits of data came flooding into his mind: scattered and trivial bits at first, adding up very quickly into something overwhelming.

Subtle wrongnesses became apparent, little ones that quickly grew bigger and bigger in his mind:

–Dr. Ludwig, who had been over by Eric's side of the singularity coupling when the last switch was thrown, had moved to his left, barely outside the event horizon of the shunt field.

–Dr. White, who had been all the way across the big room in front of the bank of monitor screens frantically fidgeting with her thick curling hair, now was leaning against the frame of the lab door with her arms folded calmly.

–The computer printers, which had been standing silent in the moment before the throwing of the switch, were spewing copy like crazy. The frontmost one had an inch-thick stack of pages in its hopper.

–Half a dozen technicians who had been scattered here and there around the room were gathered in a tight cluster just beyond the gleaming nickel-jacketed hood of the field shield. They were staring in at Sean as though he had sprouted a second head–or had lost the one he used to have.

–And more. The pattern of lights on the instrument panels was different. Someone had restrung the tangle of drooping gray cables on the back wall. And the video camera dolly had been pushed about halfway down the track in his direction. It had been in front of Eric before. At least a dozen tiny changes of that sort had been made.

It was, he thought, very much like one of those before-and-after blackout tests they give you when you're a kid, when they want to measure your I.Q. They show you the image of a room, and then the screen goes dark, and a moment later it lights up and everything's been moved around. You have to note down as many of the changes as you can pick out, within thirty seconds or so. That was what had happened here. In the twinkling of an eye, *before* had turned into *after*. Five minutes after.

So he really had taken a leap through time.

After all the months and months of planning and training and doubting and hoping, he had finally embarked on this fantastic voyage into the remote past and the far-off unknown future, a voyage that would unfold in a series of jumps. Small jumps at first, and then unimaginably vast.

Jump number one. He was five minutes in his own future. All the little changes around the room told him that.

And now he noticed the biggest change of all, the one he had somehow managed to keep blocked from his awareness until this moment.

—Eric wasn't there anymore.

Eric's three-legged aluminum chair was still there, to the right of the singularity coupling. But Eric himself was gone.

Sean felt dazed. A thick oily fog was trying to wrap itself around his brain. It was like a delayed reaction coming on, the whole crushing weight of the knowledge that he had actually been ripped out of space and time and then had been thrust back into place somewhere else.

"How do you feel, Sean?" Dr. Ludwig asked.

The words were like rolling thunder in Sean's ears. He had to work hard to wring some sense from the blurred, booming sounds.

"Not bad," he said automatically. "Not bad at all."

He kept staring at the empty chair to his right, beyond the cone of the displacement torus. Eric wasn't there. Eric wasn't there. That was the only thought in his mind. Suddenly it had driven even the fact of the time voyage itself from the center of his consciousness.

For the entire twenty-three years of Sean's life, Eric had always been there. Somewhere. Maybe not close at hand but always in some way *there*. They could be on opposite sides of the continent and yet they always remained aware of each other's presence in some mysterious, indefinable way that neither of them tried to understand or explain. It had been like that for them all the way back to the beginning, to that time when they had shared the same womb, Eric lying beside him, jostling for space, poking his little arms and legs where they didn't belong.

Sean had never been alone like this before.

He had understood that the experiment was going to separate them in time, sending Eric one way, him another. But there is understanding and there is understanding. There are things you understand in your mind, and there are things you understand in your bones. Now that the contact between them had actually been severed, he was coming fully to realize what it meant to be separated from his twin by an enormous and uncrossable gulf of time. That was different. That was terrifying.

"Sean?" Dr. Ludwig said again, rumbling and strange as before. "I asked you how you were feeling."

"Not bad, I told you." He turned, stared, worked hard at focusing his eyes. He was getting some odd visual effects now. Streaks of colored lights, reds and blues and greens. Everything seemed too long and narrow. And there was some double vision. He was dimly aware that Dr. Ludwig was still talking to him. And Dr. White, too. Their words came to him from a million miles away. How are you feeling, how are you feeling, how are you feeling. What did that mean? Oh. It means how are you feeling, he thought. Is that any of their business? He was so terribly confused.

"Sean—"

"I'm all right!" he snapped. He didn't want them to think he couldn't take it.

They looked at him blankly. He tried to explain things, but he had the feeling his words were ricocheting around them like bullets. They turned to each other in bewilderment.

"What did he say?"

"What did he say?"

"What did he say?"

"Sean? Try to speak more slowly. You're all hypered up."

"Am I? You sound all slowed down."

It was getting worse. He felt that his own chair was melting and flowing beneath him. And he was starting to melt with it. A sense of chill and a sense of burning at the same time. A strangeness in his stomach. A rising and a falling in his chest. That first calm moment when nothing seemed to have changed seemed like a million years ago. Everything was changing now. Everything. He wondered if Eric was feeling anything like this. Wherever Eric was right now. *Whenever* Eric was.

"Maybe my voice will be easier for you to make out, Sean."

That was Dr. White. Speaking gently, softly, carefully. Her voice sounded deeper than it should have been, but not as strange as Dr. Ludwig's.

Sean tried to force himself to relax.

He said, making an effort to be understood, "What was the span of the jump, Dr. White?"

"Five minutes precisely. Right on target."

"And how long has it been since I got here?"

"Fifteen, twenty seconds."

That was all? It felt like half an hour. His mind was feeding him distorted information. Was this how it was going to be, on and on through time, everything blurred and confused? Like a nightmare. Stumbling across millions of years in a dopey fog, understanding nothing.

"What have you heard from my brother?" Sean asked.

"Your brother's fine." Dr. Ludwig's voice.

"You've heard from him?"

"We saw him. Five minutes before Time Zero."

Sean frowned and shook his head. Everything was so hard to follow.

"Five minutes before the shunt? Well, yes, but what I meant was—" He paused. He didn't know what he meant. "I know you saw my brother then. You saw both of us then, right here. But—"

"We saw him and we saw you." The soft voice of Dr. White. "But we saw an extra Eric also, Eric$_2$, the one traveling backward from Time Zero. Don't you remember that?"

"An extra Eric." He felt so *stupid.*

"Smiling at us. Winking. Happy and confident."

"Traveling backward," Sean murmured, struggling to cut through the fog in his brain. "An extra Eric."

So muddled, his mind. His fine mind, his outstanding mind. He wondered if he'd ever be able to do physics again. Or even simply to think straight. He shook his head again, slowly, heavily, like a wounded bear.

They had seen Ricky traveling backward in time. Saw him arrive five minutes before Time Zero, before the start of the experiment. In this very room. Why can't I remember seeing him? Or do I? I think I do, yes. Sean closed his eyes a moment. He tried to imagine the scene.

That ghostly figure, hovering in front of them, looking so very cheerful. Ricky always looked cheerful, even at crazy times. So there had been one Eric Gabrielson sitting in the right-hand chair on the shunt platform and another one, Eric$_2$, floating around the middle of the room. And that had been five minutes before Time Zero—the shunt that balanced this one that had carried him five minutes beyond Time Zero. The first swing of the giant pendulum that would cut across millions of years, carrying them backward and forward, backward and forward, backward and forward—

He wasn't sure if he could remember seeing that other Ricky or not.

Sean struggled to understand. His mind still felt doped. It was temporal shock, the effect of the shunt plus the effect of the change that had just taken place in the very recent past with Ricky's arrival there. The past would be constantly changing with each swing of the pendulum. The robot experiments had shown that. Each swing and they'd all have an entirely new set of memories, reaching back farther and farther, five minutes, fifty minutes, five hundred minutes, five thousand minutes–

Something was glowing now on the far wall.

The temporal energy must be building up again, creating displacement momentum for the next shunt. They had said the swings were going to be quick ones in the early stages of the journey, in and out of the past or the future in just a couple of minutes during the first few shunts, zip zip zip zip.

Dr. White said, "There's nothing to worry about, Sean. It's all going to work out all right."

Sean nodded and smiled. Suddenly his mind seemed to clear a little. He was beginning to feel like himself again. "Sure it will," he said. "I never doubted it." He became aware of strangeness beginning to enfold him. The field was taking him onward. "Say hello to Ricky for me," he said, and waved at them as they grew blurry around him. "I'll see you all a little later."

3.

Eric
+ 50 minutes

He was falling. Like Alice going down the rabbit hole, except that when she fell it was in a slow, stately way, with plenty of time to look around. He was plummeting crazily, a wild juggernaut zooming through the center of the earth. Down through the geological strata, past the Cretaceous and the Jurassic, past the Permian, the Silurian, the Cambrian. Choking and gasping, tumbling end over end, arms and legs flailing, his hair flying in the hot breeze that came blasting up from below.

He thought he was going to fall forever.

He had never imagined it was possible to feel so sick and dizzy.

All the worst stuff comes right at the beginning, Sean had told him. *And then it's okay.*

Had Sean really said that? Eric tried to remember. Yes. It was at the minus-fifty-minute level, just when he and Sean both were starting to get a little panicky about the crazy project they had committed themselves to. And then $Sean_2$, had come whistling out of the future looking cocky and cheerful. Engaging in a whole bunch of incomprehensible babble with Dr. Ludwig about how past tense and future tense lose their meanings when you travel in time. And then, jaunty as can be, coming over to Eric and Sean$_1$, to tell them not to worry about anything.

It's all going to be fine. Just let yourself go, and don't try to fight it.

Sure, Sean.

Down and down and down. Did *you* fall like this, Sean, when you made *your* first jump into the future? Down, down, down through the primordial rock of the earth into the bubbling volcanic magma at the core of the planet?

Eric wondered when it was going to stop. And what it was going to feel like when he hit bottom.

Then he realized that he was floating rather than dropping. And then that he wasn't even floating. He was still in the laboratory, not in some tunnel that passed through the bowels of the earth. That falling sensation had been just in his imagination, a side effect of the trip forward in time. In fact his feet were firmly planted on the floor of the shunt platform.

So he had arrived. He was fifty minutes in the future.

Everything was a blur. Eric was so dizzy that he thought his head would spin free from his shoulders. And the nausea that he was feeling was real star-quality nausea. It was so intense that he wanted to applaud it. As soon as he felt a little better.

"Somebody grab me or I'm going to fall," he managed to blurt.

They caught him just as he started to go over.

"Easy," someone said. "The disorientation lasts only a couple of moments. Going into the future seems to be more traumatic than going into the past."

"So I notice," Eric murmured.

But they were right: you did come out of it pretty fast. He was able to stand unaided now. He could focus his eyes again. The digital elapsed-time counter on the rear wall confirmed that he was exactly fifty minutes into the experiment. Right on schedule.

Sean must already have materialized here ahead of him, making the plus-five-minutes shunt. Eric wondered whether Sean had gone through the same hellacious rabbit-hole sensation then. He wondered whether Sean–

Sean–

Suddenly Eric felt with full force the impact of his twin brother's absence. The strangeness, the aloneness, the separateness.

It came rushing in like a roaring tsunami: the knowledge that time stood between him and his brother like a sword. He hadn't felt it on his first time-jump, because that had been a backward one, and when he arrived he had seen Sean right there in the lab, getting ready to begin the experiment. But at this very moment Sean was a hundred minutes away, back at the minus-fifty-minute level. The balancing swing of the pendulum, the equal and opposite displacement.

From here to Time Ultimate–the end of the experiment, some 95 million years out from the starting point–they were never going to be on the same side of the time-line again. One of them would always be in the minus-time level while the other one was an equal distance up ahead in plus-time.

Eric stepped down from the platform. Took a couple of uncertain steps.

"How do you feel now?" Dr. White asked.

He managed to smile at her. "Better." It was a lie. "Just a little wobbly. Just a little."

"It's a jolt, isn't it?"

He nodded. He wanted to ask Sean how *he* had felt on

his first forward jump. But of course Sean wasn't here. It was weird, not having him nearby. Not feeling that odd, almost telepathic bond. The sensation that said, *I am here, I am Sean, I am closer to you than anyone on this planet and always will be.* Almost as if they were Siamese twins and not the ordinary kind. Eric had never talked about that with Sean. It had always seemed, well, embarrassing–telling him what he felt, asking him if he felt it, too. But he was pretty sure that Sean felt it, too.

And right now Eric was feeling the lack of it. Intensely.

"Fifty minutes from Time Zero," he said. "I don't suppose much can have changed in the world yet."

Dr. White chuckled. "Not in fifty minutes. All the really interesting things are still ahead of you."

"Ahead of me?" Eric shook his head. "No, you've got it upside down. The way I look at it, all the really interesting stuff's *behind* me."

She looked baffled by that.

"You don't know what I mean?" he said.

"Well–"

"No, you don't, do you. I'm Eric, remember?"

"Yes, of course, but–" Her voice trailed off.

"The twin who's the paleontologist. The one who's a lot more interested in the past than the future." He made a broad, sweeping gesture. "I don't mind getting a peek at the future. But what I'm really waiting for is at the other end of the pendulum. The Mesozoic, back there at the end of the whole circus. The dinosaurs!" He felt heat rising in his cheeks. Excitement coursing through him, making his heart pound. "That's why I volunteered for this crazy ride, don't you know? To meet the dinosaurs, face-to-face. It's as simple as that. To walk up to a live dinosaur and say hello."

4.

Sean
– 50 minutes

It was different this time, the second shunt. Sean didn't feel that initial sense of dead calmness that had tricked him before into thinking he hadn't gone anywhere. Nor was there a rush of confusion and bewilderment and dismay right afterward. Instead he felt only a second or two of mild dizziness, and then everything seemed fine.

Maybe it's only the first shunt that's the bummer, he thought. Or maybe it's easier because this time I went backward in time instead of forward.

He looked around the lab.

They were all running back and forth like a bunch of lunatics, getting all the last-minute stuff ready. The experiment would happen in less than an hour. So there they were, hooking things up, checking circuits, crunching numbers. There was Dr. Ludwig, face shiny with sweat, yelling into a pocket telephone. And Dr. White, who was usually so calm and gentle, practically tearing at her hair. Harrell, the math man, working at two computers at once. Other scientific types frenziedly doing other final-hour things. And the technicians zipping around the way people did in the ancient silent movies, going much too fast and moving in a silly jerky way.

The only people who looked calm were Ricky and Sean, those intrepid Gabrielson boys. They were standing off to one side with a numbed, zonked look on their faces, waiting to be told to mount the shunt platform and sit down on either side of the displacement torus.

It all looked terribly familiar. Sean had lived through this scene once, after all, less than an hour ago. Now here he was again. Only this time he wasn't waiting around to be told to sit down on the platform. That was those two fellows over there; he was somebody else, $Sean_2$, the traveler in time, the man from fifty minutes in the future.

"Hey," he said. "Over here. Me. Anybody going to say hello to me?"

There was a sudden stunned silence in the room. They had all been so busy running through the final insane setting-up procedures that they hadn't even noticed him materialize. But they noticed him now.

"The second backswing!" someone cried. "Here he is!"

"Absolutely," Sean said. "The big surprise. The walking, talking paradox man. You've never seen anything like me, right? You don't remember seeing any of us heading backward before, is that it?"

"Not yet," replied Dr. Ludwig. His voice sounded thick and hoarse. He looked a little dazed, as though perhaps he hadn't been fully prepared for what was happening. Even he, who had spent years thinking about these concepts while he was planning the experiment. "You are the first, but of course not the last. Others will come before you, but we do not remember them yet. You are Sean, yes? Making your second shunt, the minus-fifty-minute swing. But soon there will be Eric at minus five hundred minutes, coming in yesterday evening."

Sean laughed. " 'There *will* be Eric, coming in yesterday evening'? I like the way you say that."

"We will come to remember his visit, yes, after he has made it. We will need an entirely new grammar to speak of these things. Past tense and future tense lose their meanings when cause and effect are broken free from all mooring. You understand what I am saying?"

"Absolutely," Sean said.

On this shunt all of it made perfect sense to him. How different from his experience at plus five minutes, when fog was so thick in his brain! Thank God his mind was working right again. It had been scary to think he might have been rendered stupid forever by his trip through time.

It wasn't logical, of course, that this retroactive rearrangement of the past should happen in stages. With everyone's memories of the hours and days just prior to Time Zero being altered again and again, each time a wider swing brought a new Eric or a Sean back to some point earlier than the last one.

Logically all such changes in the past should occur at once. From the moment the final switch was thrown, there *would always have been* Erics and Seans scattered all up and down the time-stream across the whole span of the experiment's 190 million years.

But there wasn't anything logical about time-travel in the first place, Sean knew. It gloriously defied all the laws of cause and effect. And so evidently each swing of the pendulum was going to produce a completely new version of the past. Reality would be fluid from now on, and no one within that shifting reality would ever be aware of the changes. They could never remember the past as it used to be. The moment the change was made, the past would always have been the way it was now.

Only he and Eric, the daring young men on the flying trapeze, moving as outside observers, would be able to comprehend the havoc they were wreaking as they flashed back and forth across the fabric of time, reweaving it as they went. And even they would start to lose track of the changes as the paradoxes mounted.

He walked over to Eric and $Sean_1$. God, they looked pale and sweaty! That was embarrassing. They were really nervous. He didn't remember having felt that nervous himself when it had been his turn to be $Sean_1$, fifty minutes ago. He thought of himself as having waited calmly, coolly, confidently for his launching into the time-shunt.

But he realized that he was probably kidding himself. The way $Sean_1$ looked now was the way he himself must have looked fifty minutes ago, because he had been $Sean_1$ then. There was no hiding from the truth of that. He had been scared stiff. Fifty minutes ago he had been sitting there waiting to be converted into a cluster of tachyons—particles that move faster than light and travel backward in time in an anti-time universe. What the singularity coupling did was turn him into a tachyonic replica of himself, throwing off showers of anti-time energy that would be exactly balanced by the time-force liberated in the opposite direction. At least that was what it was supposed to do. And he had been sitting there wondering if it would.

Well, it had. And here he was.

They were staring goggle-eyed at him. As though he had no business being there. As though he were some evil being who had come to haunt the place.

Sean smiled.

"Relax," he said. "It's all going to be fine. Just let yourself go, and don't try to fight it. You won't like it at first, but all the worst stuff comes right at the beginning, and then it's okay."

A little comfort, a little friendly cheer. It was the least he could do for them, he thought. For Ricky. And also for Sean, who was sitting there looking so pale and miserable. His brother and his other self. If there's anyone in the world who's closer and dearer to you than your twin brother, Sean thought, it's your other self.

5.

Eric
-5×10^2 minutes

The big room was oddly peaceful, here on the night before the experiment. It was about two in the morning. The overhead lights were turned off, and the only illumination came from a couple of green security lamps off to the side.

Nobody seemed to be there when Eric stepped off the shunt platform after a moment of arrival vertigo blessedly more brief than it had been the last time. He looked around. Nobody here at all? That was peculiar. They knew what time he'd be due to arrive on this swing. Even if most of them would be asleep at this hour, resting up for the big day ahead of them tomorrow, *somebody* should have been here to debrief him when he showed up.

Then he noticed one of the younger scientists—a quasiconductor man named John Terzunian—dozing in the darkness.

Eric went over to him. Touched him gently on the shoulder.

"Johnny? Johnny, wake up. It's me, Eric, making the minus-five-hundred-minute shunt."

"What? Who?" A look of sudden panic. "Oh, God, I must have slumped off."

"Happens to anyone," Eric said. The other man looked hardly older than he was, maybe twenty-five, twenty-six, barely past his doctorate. His hair was thinning already. His eyes were jet black and very bloodshot. "Don't worry. I won't tell. Everyone else is asleep, huh?"

Terzunian nodded. "The last one left an hour ago. We drew lots for who would stay till you came in."

"And you lost."

A sheepish smile. "Nobody's had much sleep for three or four nights in a row, now. I wouldn't mind being sacked out right this minute. But somebody had to be here to meet you."

"Sure," Eric said. "I understand."

He thought of $Sean_1$ and $Eric_1$, snoring away in the dorm section a couple of hundred yards from the lab. For them, he knew, edginess had fought a battle with exhaustion and exhaustion had won.

Well, it was a good idea for them to be sleeping. This would be the last chance they'd have to get a proper night's sleep in the year 2016 for a long time to come. Little more than eight hours from now they were going to set out on a journey that would carry them some 95 million years in each direction before they saw their own home year again. Adrift in the time-stream, swinging back and forth, swooping through the eons.

It was strange, thinking of $Sean_1$ and $Eric_1$ as *them* instead of *us*. But he had to. Those two guys sleeping down there in the dorm weren't Sean and Eric Gabrielson at all, not really. Not to him. They were two entirely other people: $Sean_1$ and $Eric_1$. Yesterday's selves. They hadn't yet begun to oscillate in time. They still had no real idea of what any of this was going to be like.

To them, if they thought of him at all, he would be $Eric_2$, an Eric of the future, tomorrow's Eric, an unreal Eric. That was all right. He didn't feel unreal. He wasn't living in tomorrow. He was living in *now*. It was a now that kept sliding around between past and future, but all the same it was the only now he had. He was real enough to himself: the true and authentic Eric. And the true and authentic Sean, for him, was the one who was nearly seventeen hours away just now, up there at the plus-500-minute level, at the opposite end of the time-travel seesaw that they were riding.

Everything in balance. Everything symmetrical.

It all had the intense bright clarity of a very powerful dream. Except it was actually happening to them, and it would go on happening for something like ninety-five million years.

Terzunian said, "Can I get you anything? A drink of water? Something to eat?"

"No, thanks," Eric said. "So far as subjective time goes, this is still just the beginning of the experiment for me. I've only experienced a few minutes of elapsed time since the whole thing started."

"All right," Terzunian said. "We'd better get down to work, then. I'm supposed to ask you questions about your psychological and physical state upon arrival. Here—the camera's on. Testing. Testing." He seemed twitchy, ill at ease, afraid of messing anything up. Well, Eric thought, he's been involved with this project for years, and now here it is, actually happening.

Actually happening. Yes.

There were times when he had trouble believing that he and Sean had really agreed to do it. Of course they had known about the experiment for years—Project Pendulum had gotten underway when they were still in high school, as soon as the development of artificially produced mini-singularities had provided the technological basis for traveling in time.

Sean had brought home a pile of theoretical papers about it. Explaining how the phase-linkage coupling of a minute black hole, identical to those that are found all over interstellar space, and its mathematical opposite, a "white hole," created an incredibly powerful force that ripped right through the fabric of space-time—and how that force could be contained and controlled, like a bomb in a basket, so that it could be used as a transit tube for making two-way movements in time.

Eric's first reaction on hearing that was to imagine himself running backward along the earth's geological history as if seeing a film from back to front—soaring through the epochs, past the Pleistocene and the Pliocene into the days of the dinosaurs, the early amphibians, the trilobites, back even to the primordial days when there was nothing on the surface of the world except a bare granite shield rising above a steaming sea. Tremendous! To see it all. Not to have to reconstruct it from compressed strata and scattered fossils, but to look at everything with your own eyes while it still existed.

His second reaction was to think that the whole notion was completely crazy, a fantastic pipe dream.

No, Sean had said. It really can work. Here, let me show you the equations—

And Sean had scribbled equations for him until he begged for mercy. Math on Sean's level was a mysterious language to him, as remote and inaccessible as the language the ancient Egyptians spoke in their dreams. The more Sean explained of it, the less Eric understood—or cared. But Sean was convinced that the theory of time-shunting was correct, and Sean was usually right about anything he investigated with such passion. At least in the world of physics.

That's extraordinary, Eric had said, figuring that fifty or sixty years of heavy-duty work would be necessary, at the very least, before time travel was anything more than a set of fascinating equations. And then he put it all totally out of his mind. He had other things to think about that seemed more urgent, like going to college, and his graduate work in paleontology after that.

But then came news that the first displacement machine had actually been built and tested. Eric paid some mild attention to that. Robots equipped with data-recording gear and cameras went off, so it was claimed, on safaris in time. The robots made their journey and returned to the same instant from which they had been sent off. To the watching scientists the elapsed time of the experiment was zero. So there was no way of telling that anything had happened, except for the power drain that the instrument measured—and except for the paradoxes.

The paradoxes! Even though the robots hadn't seemed to go anywhere, they turned up in the laboratory hours and days and weeks before they had been sent out. That gave everyone headaches, thinking about it. The past kept flowing and shifting around, and nobody's memory was a safe place: things were always getting different from what you thought you remembered.

And the robots also turned up an equal number of hours and days and weeks *after* the experiment, flashing suddenly into existence in the laboratory and staying around for a few minutes, maybe an hour or two, before vanishing again.

The robots seemed to have suffered no ill effects from their mysterious journeys. They appeared still to be in fine working order. But the cameras they carried yielded nothing but fogged film. Sean explained that film emulsion was evidently unable to withstand the tachyon storms to which it was exposed during the time shunts. The data-recording gear had produced scrambled digital readouts, just static, probably for the same reason.

Oh, Eric had said. Tachyon storms, is that it?

He didn't bother asking for more elaborate explanations. Not then.

They sent living creatures through the machine, too—turtles, frogs, rabbits. The usual nature organizations complained about that, but the animals all came back safely. Back from where? Who could say? No question that they had gone *somewhere*. The usual time-displacement paradoxes had been observed: rabbits popping out of nowhere in the laboratory three days before the start of the experiment, and doing the same thing three days after the experiment, too.

That was interesting, a remarkable achievement. If the rabbits could be sent three days backward and forward in time, they might well have gone a million years, or fifty million. Still, what could a turtle or a rabbit tell anybody about the way the Mesozoic really looks, or the world of A.D. One Million? You could send a turtle to the end of time and back, and it wouldn't give you one syllable of useful information about its trip.

So of course they called for volunteers.

Human time-travelers would have to go through the machine in order to get any significant results. Only a lunatic, Eric figured, would volunteer for a deal like that.

The word went out that they wanted to use a pair of identical twins, because there had to be an exact balance of momentum down to the last milligram. Twins, because they had the same bone structure and pretty much the same distribution of body fat, would make it that much easier to attain that balance.

That's nice, Eric thought. And went back to his doctoral thesis on Arctic amphibian life in the Mesozoic period.

They're looking for twins with scientific background, someone told him.

Eric simply shrugged.

Ideally they want one twin who's a physicist and one who's a paleontologist, someone else told him. In order to maximize the value of their observations.

Right. Eric was a paleontologist. Sean was a physicist.

That's very interesting, Eric said, still showing no interest at all. I suppose we're not the only twins who meet that requirement. They'll find someone sooner or later who'll be willing to risk the trip.

Then one day Sean turned up and said, "Don't you think it could help your research a little if you got a look at some *living* Mesozoic critters, Ricky?"

And now here he was five hundred minutes in his own past, locked into an unstoppable series of ever-widening swings in time, back and forth, back and forth, minutes and hours and months and years and centuries and eons. Like a dream, a very strange and intense dream, a dream brighter and sharper than any reality he had ever experienced.

"Go ahead," Terzunian said. "This is the minus-five-hundred minute level, John Terzunian speaking. Eric Gabrielson has just arrived right on schedule: the third backswing." He pointed at Eric to give him his cue. "Okay. Make your report."

"There's not a lot to tell. Easy arrival, none of the queasiness I felt when I made the minus-five-minute shunt. Just a fast flicker of discomfort, then everything normal. Some minor spatial displacement: I came in a couple of feet to the left of my departure point. No fatigue so far. Maybe some mild uneasiness—no, uneasiness is too strong a word, a little edginess, maybe—"

Terzunian was staring at him. There was a peculiar expression on his face, what seemed to be a mixture of fascination and envy and what might have been something like pity.

"Well, look," Eric said, "there really isn't anything to report yet. Give me another few shunts and I'll have plenty to say. *Plenty.*"

But who will I say it to, he wondered? When I'm nine and a half years in the past? Or 950,000 years in the future?

6.

Sean
+ 5×10^2 minutes

This time it felt as if some giant had scooped him up, popped him into a slingshot and whirled him around, and tossed him with all his might. When he landed, the sides of the laboratory were circling around him like the rim of a big centrifuge and the floor was rocking wildly from side to side. The place might just as well have been a carnival funhouse. Sean flung himself down flat, hanging on for all he was worth.

But the effect lasted only a moment or two. The wild funhouse gyrations slowed down and then they stopped altogether. He patted the floor to make certain it had finished moving. Apparently it had. He got carefully to his feet, steadying himself with his outstretched arms. He took two or three cautious steps. Everything was holding still, now. Fine. Fine.

"It takes a little getting used to," he said to nobody in particular.

He looked around. There were new changes in the laboratory. He was five hundred minutes in the future: eight hours and twenty minutes since the start of the experiment. Night had fallen. The fluorescent lights seemed harsher and brighter. The big room was weirdly quiet, almost ominous.

"Tell us what you experienced," Dr. Ludwig said.

Dr. Ludwig and Dr. White were the only people in the room. The technicians must have been sent home. The shunt platform was strangely forlorn and abandoned with no one around it. The two metal seats that flanked the displacement cone might have been nothing more than a couple of classroom chairs. The cone itself seemed trivial, a mere chunk of inactive machinery.

Staring at it, Sean had trouble believing that under that glossy lump of shielding lurked a symmetrical pair of laboratory-generated collapsed stars: a miniature black hole and its mirror image, a so-called white hole. Together they made up a pair of perfectly balanced singularities—zones of strangeness where nothing behaved according to the rules of the ordinary universe—held in an unbreakable coupling. Infinite energy forever circled in a loop between the interlocked event horizons of those singularities. Energy that had opened the time gate through which Sean and Eric had been shunted to begin their immense voyage through time and antitime.

Dr. Ludwig's eyes looked bleary and his plump cheeks were dark with stubble. It was the look of a man who has been in the office too long. When Sean had made his last trip through here at plus five minutes—hardly any time at all ago for Sean, eight hours and twenty minutes for them—Dr. Ludwig had been pink and freshly shaven.

"The first time," Sean said, "I thought I was losing my mind. The first forward swing, the plus-five-minutes one. Let me tell you, it was a truly hideous experience."

"The forward swings are worse than the backward ones?" Dr. White asked.

"So it seems. All that disorientation and mental fog, the sheer *stupidity* that I felt. The first backward swing, the minus-fifty-minutes one, was a little jarring, but nothing like that. And the disturbance only lasted for a moment."

"And this time? The second forward swing?"

"Dizziness, really serious dizziness, everything whirling like mad. But not as strong as the first time and it didn't last nearly as long."

"Yet it was stronger than what you felt on the one back-swing you've made so far."

Sean nodded. "It's as though there's some real effort in making the forward swings, something that demands a lot from you in breaking free of the time fabric. Whereas when you go the other way you slide along the track pretty easily, and there's just the slightest little shimmy of disturbance."

"Perhaps so," Dr. Ludwig said. "But we have reason to think that the shunt effects in both directions will diminish the farther you get from Time Zero."

Sean grinned. "They'd better. We're not going to be landing in this nice safe lab many more times, are we?" The pendulum swings were going to be getting wider and wider. Sudden visions blazed in his mind: the dark steamy past, the shimmering unimaginable future. "It'll be nice not to get an attack of the dizzies every time we arrive," he said. "In some of the places where we're going to turn up we may need to hit the ground running."

7.

Eric
$+ 5 \times 10^3$ minutes

"If nobody minds very much," Eric said, "I'd like to have a quick look at today's newspaper before I shuffle along toward last month."

The elapsed-time counter in front of him read 83.33 hours. Which was just short of three and a half days since Time Zero. And so this ought to be Friday night, the twenty-second of April.

He saw them exchanging glances. Was it okay to give him a paper? They weren't sure. Someone on the psych staff went off to ask Dr. Ludwig, and apparently the answer was yes, because he came back with a newspaper in his hands.

It was a fresh printout. It had that brand-new smell that papers have when they first come from the wall slot. Eric stared at the date.

Friday, April 22, 2016.

So it really was true. He was actually traveling in time.

Unless this was all some crazy hoax—some kind of psychological experiment, maybe? And they had given him a paper with a phony date, so that he'd be fooled into believing–

That's mighty paranoid thinking, Ricky-boy, he told himself. *All this is real. You'd better believe it.*

He glanced quickly over the front-page stories. Tenth anniversary of lunar settlement celebrated here and on the moon. The President's visit to Antarctica. An earthquake in Turkey, 6.3 on the Richter scale, exactly as predicted last month. A big feature at the bottom of the page about the Robot Pride Day parade in Detroit, fifty thousand mechanical workers taking part.

He didn't see any story about the time-travel experiment now underway at Cal Tech.

But it would have surprised him if he had. The whole project was classified data, partly because the government wanted it that way and partly because a lot of people were scared stiff of the whole idea of time travel. The response to the earliest announcements of the project had been unexpectedly heated. Certain historians and philosophers had argued that there might be irreparable damage to contemporary life if the past were changed in any way by time travelers. One small alteration–the plucking of a flower, the squashing of a bug–might wipe out whole empires, for all anyone knew. Then too some religious leaders were troubled by the possibility that visitors to the past might discover that scriptural history was inaccurate in some way. And there were always those people who feared any new development in science, especially one as startling and magical as this. So it had been decided on the highest levels not to release any details of Project Pendulum until there had been a chance to study the effects of the first few shunts.

Turning to the sports pages, Eric saw that the Dodgers had just dropped their third straight game in Osaka after losing two out of three in Honolulu. The new baseball season wasn't starting off very promisingly. Things were doing a little better for the local basketball team: the Lakers had won their playoff series against Buenos Aires and were going on now to play Nairobi for the championship.

The weather for the Pasadena area was going to be fair and warm. It had rained in San Francisco yesterday but the storm wasn't expected to reach Southern California. The stock market had had a good day, the Dow Jones averages rising 112 points to 7786. Eric felt curiously superstitious about looking at the obituary page and went past it quickly, averting his eyes.

"Here," he said, handing the paper back. "Thanks."

"How does it feel?"

Eric grinned. "I always like to see Friday's newspaper on Tuesday," he said. "You get a good jump on things that way."

8.

Sean
-5×10^3 minutes

Four of them were waiting for him on the next swing: Dr. White and Dr. Thomas representing the psychological side of the experiment, Dr. Mukherji and Dr. Camminella representing the theoretical mathematicians.

This was his fourth shunt. It was beginning to mount up now. The swings were calibrated in logarithmically increasing intervals, each one ten times wider than the one before. So he had gone five minutes into the future, then fifty minutes into the past, five hundred minutes into the future, five thousand minutes into the past–

Five thousand minutes. Five times 10^3 minutes. Five thousand minutes was 83 hours and 20 minutes, which was 3.46 days. Time Zero for the experiment, the point from which all the shunting began, was Tuesday, the nineteenth of April, 2016, at half past ten in the morning. And here he was, stepping down from the shunt platform three and a half days before that.

The reception committee seemed to be having a little trouble coming to terms with that. They were all trying hard to look cool and collected. Sean could see them working at it.

But they didn't even come close to being able to hide their amazement. Their eyes were wide, their faces were flushed, their tongues kept licking back and forth over dry lips. It was the look of people who knew that they were experiencing something miraculous.

"Nice of you all to be here to greet me," he said cheerfully. "I'm Sean, in case you weren't quite certain. It's last Friday night, isn't it?"

"Friday, yes," Dr. White said. Her voice was thick and husky, choked with emotion. "The fifteenth of April."

"At eleven-ten P.M.," said Sean. "On the button."

"On the button," Dr. White said.

Why did they seem so stunned? After all, this was his fourth shunt, two forward and now two back. They ought to be getting used to it by now.

Then he scowled at his own idiocy. *He* was getting used to it. But it was all new to these people. They were living three and a half days ago, back there before the start of the experiment. This was the first time they were seeing a shunter.

Maybe they had never truly believed the experiment would work. Or maybe they accepted it on a theoretical level but hadn't properly prepared themselves for the real thing—for having him come dropping right out of next Tuesday like this. Despite all the years they had put in, working toward this moment, thinking about what it was going to be like to make time travel an actuality, his arrival must be an overpowering, almost shattering event for them.

Dr. Thomas said, "We have a few tests that we'd like you to take."

Sean gave him a sour look. "Tests?"

Dr. Thomas was the team's head psychologist, and he

was *always* saying "We have a few tests we'd like you to take." Sean had never cared much for the trim, smug little psychologist, who sometimes seemed more like a computerized simulation of a human being than an actual flesh-and-blood person.

In the planning stages of the project he had subjected Sean and Eric to multiphasic electronic devices that buzzed and flashed and screeched maddeningly as they probed the twins' minds. The ordeal was necessary, they were told, to find out whether they were stable enough to withstand the stress of time-shunting. Apparently they were.

All right. What more did Thomas need to know now? The biggest test of all was underway this very minute: the experiment itself. Wasn't that enough for him? Sean hadn't been expecting another bout with those instruments of torture.

"Over here, please," Dr. Thomas said. "Can you walk unaided?"

"Of course I can walk unaided. You think I've become brain-damaged?"

"Please. There isn't much time."

"I simply wonder why it's necessary to inflict even more of these idiotic—"

"What we wish to determine," Dr. Thomas said frostily, "is whether retrograde motion through time has deleterious effects on the human nervous system. Or, if you prefer me to put it in words of a single syllable—"

"You wouldn't know how to," Sean said. "But I assure you that my mind is still working properly. I could even spell 'retrograde' for you. Maybe even 'deleterious'. How about 'retrograde' backward? That would be E-D-A-R-G—"

Dr. White put her hand lightly over Sean's and said very quietly, "We don't have any doubt that you're taking the shunt beautifully, Sean. But we do need quantitative data.

We have to know things about your pulse rate, your reaction times, your automatic reflexes, et cetera, et cetera. It really is important. And this is practically our only chance to get it. The testing machines are set up to record everything quickly and automatically. We've only got fifteen minutes, you know, before you go shunting off again into the future."

Throughout the entire life of the project Dr. White had been the cool, gentle voice of reason. Whenever anyone had started yelling—and there had been plenty of that, as deadlines neared and everybody's nerves grew taut—she had always been the one to restore peace.

Once again Sean found it impossible to resist her calm, easy manner. With a sigh he said, "All right, go ahead and test me."

He waited grimly for the onslaught of the blinking screens and whirling patterns and screaming sirens.

Might as well humor them, he thought. Dr. White was right that they wouldn't have many more chances to do this to him. The next time he came pastward, it would be at the minus-5×10^5-minutes level. That would be nearly a year ago. They probably would be expecting him then, and they'd have more tests ready. But the swing after that would bring him into the past at minus 5×10^7 minutes. That would be the year 1921. Dr. Thomas wouldn't even have been born yet, nor even his parents. Maybe not even Dr. Thomas's grandparents. He wasn't going to have to worry about Dr. Thomas or anybody else sitting him down in front of multiphasic testing machines in the year 1921.

9.

Eric
-5×10^4 minutes

It was raining. Eric could hear the drumbeat of the drops hitting the roof of the single-story laboratory building.

So this had to be March. The month before the experiment. It had rained practically every day in March, a torrential climax to the wettest winter Southern California had had in years, causing mudslides and other calamities all over the place. Then at the end of the month the sun had reappeared, and the weather had been dry and warm ever since, as it probably was going to be until the fall. There is hardly ever any rain in Southern California between April and November. But plenty of it was coming down right now.

The sound of the rain was beautiful in his ears. Maybe hillsides were turning to muck and goo out there and houses were floating off their foundations, but to Eric the pounding of those pelting drops was the sweetest music he could imagine. It told him that everything was still going according to plan.

He was fifty thousand minutes in the past. That was 833.3 hours. Or 34.72 days. They had drilled the arithmetic of the time journey into him until he could recite it in his sleep.

You jumped ten times as far on each shunt as on the one before. But you alternated a swing to the future with one to the past, so each time you returned to the past you landed a hundred times farther back than you had on the last jump. The same with the future. The early swings were very close together, but the hundred-fold factor kept multiplying.

So it was 8.33 hours back, and 83.3 hours forward, and then 833.3 hours back, and 8333.3 hours forward, and then 83,333.3 hours back, which worked out to 9.51 years into the past. Then 95.13 years forward. And then 951.3 years back. Then 9,513 years forward. And then 95,129.3 years back. And then 951,293.7 years forward. Then 9,512,937.5 years back. And then–

And then the top of the pendulum swing, the swing to Time Ultimate, the effective limit of the experiment, at which point he would have been carried some 95 million years into the future and then an equal distance back–back to the Cretaceous Period–back to the time of the dinosaurs–

He listened joyfully to the beat of the rain. Thinking, *Yes, carry me back, carry me back, let me look upon the dawn of time.*

"Eric?" a voice said.

"Right the first try."

"Do you know what day this is?"

"Wednesday, March 16, 2016."

"Yes. Yes, that's right. And what day is it for you?"

"Just a little bit past Time Zero. Tuesday, the nineteenth of April. At not quite eleven A.M."

They were staring at him that way that was getting to be so tiresomely familiar to him–staring as if they were looking at a ghost. Dr. Ludwig, Dr. White, Dr. Thomas, Dr. Mukherji, Dr. Camminella, and half a dozen more. The whole crew. They had a pale winter-time look about them and they were wearing heavier clothes than they had on when he had seen them a little while ago at Time Zero.

The lab was different, too. Everything was raw and half finished. Electrical conduits dangled in midair. The displacement cone was unshielded and the singularity cradles lay open and empty. Crates and cartons were scattered all about, still unpacked. A month and three days to go and they still had a ton of work to do, getting everything set up. But of course they were going to finish the job on schedule. There wasn't any doubt of that. His being here now was the proof of that.

The March rain drummed down in double time.

"If you don't mind," Dr. Thomas said. "There are some tests that we'd like to administer—"

10.

Sean
+ 5×10^4 minutes

"I know you're all waiting to stick the electrodes on my head and measure everything that's going on inside it," Sean said. "But would it be okay if I stepped out into the fresh air for a moment? I've still got a headache from the *last* batch of tests."

"Still?" Dr. Thomas asked. "That was a month ago!"

"A month ago for you people, yes. For me the lights and bells are still blasting away."

"Well, I suppose—for just a few minutes."

"Don't worry. I won't try to escape."

There was a little forced laughter at that. Even so, Terzunian and Mukherji went with him on his little excursion outside the lab. To look after him? Or to make sure he didn't bolt off into the night, fleeing Thomas and his dreaded multiphasic machines to enjoy a couple of hours of solitary jogging through the darkness?

It was gorgeous outside. The air was warm and sweet and gentle, and very clear. The moon was bright and the stars were sparkling. The vines on the laboratory's west wall were in bloom, great yellow flowers filling the air with wondrous fragrance. This was late May, one of the best months of the year, before the worst of the summer heat and the summer smog descended on the San Gabriel Valley.

He thought of poor Eric, back there in rainy March right at this moment, and smiled.

"Okay," he said, filling his lungs as deeply as he could. "I guess I can face those tests now."

11.

Eric
$+ 5 \times 10^5$ minutes

The drumbeat sound of the rain ceased between one moment and the next. It was cut off sharply and suddenly, as if an audio tape had been abruptly sliced. Now Eric heard the chirping of birds and the chattering of grasshoppers instead. The warm golden brightness of a perfect Southern California afternoon came bursting in upon him with startling impact.

He realized that he had made another jump. He must be almost a year in the future this time. Half a million minutes beyond Time Zero–347.2 days. This was March also, but March of a different year, March of 2017.

And he had landed outside the laboratory, on a broad lawn at the far west side of the campus. The time displacement was big enough now that some spatial displacement was occurring also. There were students all around him but nobody seemed to notice his arrival. Or care. Maybe by March of 2017 it was a common thing for time travelers to pop into being here and there around the campus.

Eric felt a heady sense of freedom. He was outdoors in

the fresh air, away from Dr. Ludwig and the rest of the Project Pendulum crowd, for the first time in—what? Weeks? Months? All that endless training, testing, rehearsing—he had felt like a rat in a cage, going around and around and around. But there were no Project Pendulum people anywhere in sight now. For however many hours it was until his next shunt, he could go where he pleased, do as he liked.

"Watch it!" someone yelled.

A gravity rotor came skimming by, zigzagging wildly up and down just above eye level. A tall, skinny undergraduate was running alongside it, trying to catch a ride. Eric got out of the way just in time. The student made a desperate lunge and grabbed the rotor just before it went lurching out of reach. It carried him a hundred yards or so through the air until it lost its spin and fluttered to the ground.

A pang of nostalgia went through him. It seemed like a million years since he had played with gravity rotors as a student on this same campus: though actually it was no more than three or four years ago.

Soon, he thought with a little shiver, he *would* be almost a million years away from his college days. And then a great deal more than that.

A slender blond girl keyed up the rotor again and let it fly. As it began to circle the lawn, Eric found himself suddenly loping after it. There were half a dozen students chasing it too, but he brushed them aside with a quick gesture. Easily, gracefully, he reached up and slipped his hands into the rotor's holdfasts and let it spin him upward and outward across the campus. He had always been good with gravity rotors. He knew how to play into their axis of rotation so they would take him on a maximum glide.

Up—up—

"Eric! Eric, have you gone crazy?" a hoarse angry voice was shouting, far below.

He laughed and waved.

"Come down from there, you lunatic! What do you think you're doing?"

"Having–some–fun–" he called, breathless with laughter.

Then he looked down. Half a dozen grim-faced Project members were wigwagging their arms wildly at him. As he went spinning past them, fifteen feet over their heads, he caught sight of Dr. Thomas, Dr. Mukherji, Terzunian, and a few others, staring at him in shock. Dr. Ludwig was running toward them from the general direction of the laboratory.

Regretfully he guided the gravity rotor into a down-spin and rode it to a landing.

"What kind of absurd stunt was that?" Dr. Ludwig blurted. "Suppose you had broken your neck! What would happen to the project then?"

Eric smiled. "I wouldn't have gotten hurt," he said serenely. "It's impossible. How could anything happen to me? I'm not really here, remember? I'm still back there at Time Zero sitting on the shunt platform. And at an infinite number of other places between there and Time Ultimate, all at once. So what's the harm in my taking a little ride?"

"Idiot!" Dr. Ludwig blazed. "Imbecile!" Eric had never seen him so furious. " *'I'm not really here'?* what are you talking about? Who put such nonsense into your head?"

"The mathematical model–" Eric stammered. "Sean explained to me that–"

"Sean! That other maniac!" Dr. Ludwig clenched his fists and shook them in frustration. In a tightly controlled voice he said, "Listen to me, Eric, and listen carefully. You are on a pendulum, yes, and you do occupy every point between Time Zero and Time Ultimate. But you can still be harmed at any point in that entire sequence of nearly two hundred million years. And if you are–if you are–" He looked ready to explode. "The past is fluid! The future is yet unborn! Anything can be changed! Anything! Who knows what will befall the entire history of the world, if anything happens to you? Who knows?"

12.

Sean
-5×10^5 minutes

Without warning the mild May night gave way to a glorious May morning–May of the year before. Sean was back in 2015, 347.2 days before the beginning of the experiment.

He stood blinking in the sudden sunlight. The shunts were coming much more easily now, causing little or no sense of transition as he shuttled between past and future. He was outside the laboratory. Outside the campus, in fact, half a mile or so east of it in downtown Pasadena. The first significant spatial displacement, he realized. The early shunts had moved him no more than a few inches from his Time Zero position on the shunt platform, but by now the jumps were getting big enough to carry him a fair distance.

Casually he strolled down Colorado Boulevard, heading east.

It surprised him that nobody from the lab was waiting here to meet him when he arrived. Up till now they hadn't allowed him to be alone for a moment. At each of his previous shunts–plus five minutes, minus fifty minutes, plus five hundred minutes, minus five thousand minutes, plus fifty thousand minutes—they had clustered around him as soon as he showed up. Now here he was half a million minutes in the past and they had left him completely on his own. Why weren't they here?

Then he realized that at this stage of the project, back in May of 2015, he and Eric hadn't even been selected yet to be the experimental subjects. The preliminary screening interviews were still going on, all that interminable testing and questioning and checking.

So as of this moment the Project Pendulum people didn't even know who they were going to be sending on the shunt, let alone what time of day or month their time-travelers were going to be turning up in the past. How could they? Time Zero itself had kept getting postponed again and again. The choice of April 19 at half past ten in the morning as the final-final day and hour and minute for the departure point hadn't been nailed down until the third of March, just six weeks before the day of the experiment.

And even after they had picked it, the Project people would still have had somehow to send information back to themselves of the year before, notifying themselves that experimental subject Sean Gabrielson was due to be popping out of nowhere in downtown Pasadena at such-and-such a time of the morning on such-and-such a day in May, 2015, which would be precisely 347.2 days prior to the beginning of the great time-travel event.

Probably they could have done it by sending off a preliminary shunt carrying a robot with the schedule. Maybe they *should* have done it, on the theory that it was best not to let their time-traveler have to fend for himself back here. But Project Pendulum's funds had been running pretty low in the final few weeks. Most likely there hadn't been any slack in the budget for extras like that. So they hadn't been able to send the word to anyone back here in 2015 that he'd be coming this way.

But he could.

Sean grinned slyly. He was tempted to saunter over to the Cal Tech campus right now and drop in at the laboratory.

"Hi," he would say. "I'm Sean Gabrielson. You're going to pick me next month for the shunt. Let's all take an hour off and go out for some pizza, okay?"

He could do that, sure. But suppose they didn't like his dropping in like that. Suppose it struck them as a cocky smartass sort of thing to do. Suppose they decided to dispense with the Gabrielson twins entirely, and pick a different pair of candidates for the shunt. What then? What would happen to him, back here in 2015? Out like a snuffed candle, that's what. He'd never get to see the far future or the distant past, or anything else. He'd go right back to being a graduate physics student in the year 2016 and he'd have no memory of any of the shunts he'd already experienced, let alone the ones that were still to come.

He didn't want to risk that.

But there *was* something he *could* do. It carried some paradox risk also, but he thought it was relatively safe. And useful, in a manner of speaking. And fun.

He thought back to last year, to the final few weeks before the names of the successful candidates for the shunt were announced. Six different pairs of twins had been in the running. Sean had figured all along that he and Eric had the best shot, because they wanted a physicist and a paleontologist, and he and Eric were the only ones who really fulfilled that requirement. But toward the end he had begun to think that the choice might land on one of the other sets of twins. Those shy Bengali girls, the Chakravarti sisters, maybe. They were mathematicians, but one had some sort of a background in archaeology. They were very, very bright. And, most important of all, they had the backing of their countryman, the Project Pendulum theoretician Dr. Mukherji.

Right before the choice was due to be announced, Sean had absolutely convinced himself that it was going to be the Chakravartis. He could already feel the disappointment seeping into his soul, and knew that it would embitter him for the rest of his life. A chance to travel to the ends of time, and it had slipped away from him! For days he could hardly sleep or eat. He was half crazy with tension most of the time, snapping and snarling at everybody.

Well, now that he was back here again at the time when that had been going on, he could spare himself all that anguish, couldn't he? Tell himself not to worry, let himself know that everything was going to turn out fine?

A phone booth loomed before him at the corner of Colorado and Fair Oaks. He stepped inside and pressed his thumb to the identification plate. The telephone asked him for the number he wanted and he gave his own.

"The line is busy," the telephone told him.

"Break in on him. This is an emergency."

"One moment, please."

Then his own voice said irritably, "All right, but if this is any kind of sales pitch–"

"Don't worry, fellow. It's a legitimate call," Sean said.

"Who's there?"

"You mean you don't recognize my voice?"

A pause. "Ricky?"

"Close. Try again."

"Look, I've got no time for guessing games. I happen to be in the midst of very important–"

"Sure you are. I know that. Listen, dope, you're talking to Sean Gabrielson."

"What?"

"Sean$_2$, let's say. I'm just passing through."

"What?"

"On my way to the year 2025. And then back to 1921."

"What? What?"

"Maybe you aren't as bright as they say you are, buddy. If all you can do is honk like a duck."

"Hey, I don't have to listen to this kind of crazy—" came the angry voice from the speaker grille, and then the CONNECTION INTERRUPTED light went on.

"Call him back," Sean told the phone.

"The line is busy."

"Break in on him, then."

"The line is under privacy seal," said the telephone.

Sean swore and shook his head. "Tell him it's a family emergency."

"The line is under privacy seal," the phone repeated.

"I know that. Doesn't family emergency take priority?"

"The line is under privacy seal," said the phone once more.

"All right," Sean grunted. "Forget it."

For a moment he considered grabbing a cab and going out to his place near the beach to confront himself face to face. But he decided against it. If Sean, was so twitchy and strung out that he couldn't figure out who had been calling him, he deserved to go on sweating a little while longer about who was going to get the nod for Project Pendulum. Sure, Sean thought. The hell with him. Let him keep on worrying another few weeks. The dummy. Let him just keep right on worrying.

13.

Eric
-5×10^6 minutes

He could see the house, halfway down the block on the other side of the street. It looked smaller than he recalled, and the pink stucco badly needed repainting. The big palm tree in front was leaning way over, with its roots pulled halfway out of the ground. The earthquake had done that, he remembered. He could see the earthquake crack along the front wall of the house, too. A raw gully like an open trench ran for a hundred yards down the middle of the street. The quake must have come just a couple of days before. They hadn't had a chance to do much cleaning up yet.

The quake, the big Santa Monica earthquake, had happened right at the beginning of October, 2006, his freshman year in high school. So once again the shunt had brought him in smack on target, carrying him back exactly 9.51 years. From April of 2016 to October of 2006—yes, just right. Here he was. Nine and a half years in the past. And actually in his own teenage neighborhood.

That part of it was hard to believe. The shunt had

dumped him down in the middle of Santa Monica, at the corner of Wilshire and Eighteenth. His old territory. No more than a five-minute walk from the house where he and Sean had lived from the time they were ten until they went to college. So of course he had to go over to have a look at it. And maybe to catch a glimpse of his own younger self. Of course.

Now, standing across the street from the pink stucco house, Eric found himself wondering if it was such a hot idea to be poking around in his own past like this. Suddenly it didn't feel really good.

Not just stirring up the earthquake memories—the jolt in the middle of the night, dogs barking, the sound of dishes breaking, frightened people running out into the streets. He would have expected that bringing it all vividly back to mind would be disturbing, and it was.

But what was even more troublesome was simply revisiting the ordinary memories, the routine day-by-day stuff. The world of 2006 looked a lot less glamorous than Eric remembered, earthquake damage aside. Everything seemed shabbier and more seedy than he expected. The shops out on Wilshire, the cars in the streets, the advertising billboards—it all was run-down, everything had a dreary, old-fashioned look.

Would things really be so much sleeker and shinier nine and a half years down the line? Maybe so. Or maybe over the years he had simply polished up his memories until the past had a much brighter gloss in his mind than it ever had had in reality.

And then there was all the other stuff to think about again, the adolescent stuff, the business of crossing the line from boyhood into manhood. The changes happening in his body. The conflicts with Sean—he and Sean were always battling like fiends in those days, the good old sibling rivalry, five times as fierce because they were identical twins. Sean was fifteen minutes older and he liked to make a big deal about that. And then too the unfocused ambitions, wanting to do something great when he grew up but not having any idea what it would be. The shy, hesitant encounters with girls. Eric had filed all those things away deep within himself. Now, at twenty-three, he wasn't at all sure he wanted to come face-to-face with them again. It might be better, he thought, to turn around right now and walk quickly the other way.

But he stayed where he was, watching the little pink house across the street and hoping that nobody was watching him.

The upstairs room on the left: that one was his. A poster was taped in the window, probably the dinosaur poster from the County Museum. There was a big plaster-of-paris triceratops on the front lawn too, a pretty crude job but not really awful. The summer he was twelve he had spent a messy few days making that. As far back as he could remember, he had been absolutely nuts about dinosaurs. His ambition was to go out to Wyoming and dig up the biggest one ever found. Sean had laughed at that. "Sure," he said. "They'll call it *Ericosaurus supergigantus.*"

Everybody said it was a phase he was bound to grow out of when he was a little older, but he didn't. Instead he got deeper into it, paleontology and geology, too. He studied the folds and strata of the rocks in which fossils were found, though it was always the fossils themselves that fascinated him the most. He could remember feverishly packing his little collection of trilobites and ammonites into a suitcase in the first terrifying minutes after the earthquake, back here when he was thirteen, so that he wouldn't lose them in case a second shock struck and destroyed the house. And then—

Who's that?

A boy had come out of the house and was standing on the little porch, looking around in wonder and dismay at the earthquake debris in the street. Eric stepped back into the shadows. The boy was short and thin, with straight sandy hair going off wildly in all directions. He had to be thirteen and a half, but to Eric he seemed much younger. His face was smooth and bland-looking and had a strange unfinished look about it.

That must be Sean, Eric thought.

No—wait—

He wasn't sure. Of all the strange things that had happened to him since the pendulum had begun to swing, this was the strangest, that he should be staring at this boy and not know whether he was seeing his brother or himself. It was absolutely impossible to tell. Time had not yet carved the adult face of this boy out of the raw material of early adolescence. His nose was just a snub and his mouth and lower jaw had that unfinished look. And at this age he and Sean must have looked much more alike than they would later. Perhaps if both twins were standing side by side on the porch, he might be able to guess which one was Eric and which Sean. But as it was he was baffled.

It was almost frightening to have time swallow his identity like that. Simply being a twin is complicated enough. But when you start losing track of which twin you are—

Then the boy came down the three cracked steps to the lawn. Pausing by the plaster-of-paris triceratops, he grinned and stroked its long crooked horns for a moment in an unmistakably affectionate way. Eric, watching from a distance, grinned also.

No doubt of it now. That boy had to be his own younger self. He felt a shiver go sliding down his spine.

Go on, he told himself. Walk across the street. Introduce yourself to him.

He imagined half a dozen impossible things that he could say.

"Hi, there. You're not going to believe this, but I'm you of the year 2016, taking part in the first time-travel experiment ever."

Or: "I'm here to tell you not to worry about a thing. I know you're uneasy about all sorts of stuff that you know lies ahead of you, but I can guarantee that everything's going to turn out just fine for you when you grow up."

Or maybe: "There's going to be a girl named Carla in your junior year of high school that likes you a whole lot better than she does Sean, but you're going to convince yourself that it's the other way around. You'll be wrong about that. Invite her to the prom before he does."

Or: "The winner of this year's World Series will be–"

Or: "Your friend Charlie Graham is going to invite you to fly to Phoenix for Christmas with him and his family in his father's plane this year. Dad won't let you go. Be absolutely sure you don't do anything to change his mind, because that plane's going to get caught in a freak lightning storm, and–"

Or: "You and Sean are both going to go to Cal Tech four years from now. People are going to try to talk you into going to Harvard or Stanford instead, because they think you and Sean shouldn't go to the same college. Don't listen to them. Go to Cal Tech, or else you may change your entire future and miss out on the best thing that's ever going to happen to you."

Or–

But he didn't say any of those things. Instead he stayed on his side of the street and hung back in the shadows, watching his younger self emerge from the yard of the little pink house, peer into the mailbox for a moment, pause to pull a huge red flower from the hibiscus bush on the front walk, and go running off toward Wilshire. Eric smiled. He waved at the small retreating figure. And thought: *You don't need any special tips on the future, boy. Just do whatever feels right to you. You'll make some mistakes, but that's no crime. And one of these days you'll grow up and you'll be me, and you'll go off on the damndest wild trip that anybody in the whole history of the human race ever took.*

14.

Sean
+ 5×10^6 minutes

He guessed he must be somewhere out to the east of Pasadena, at least twenty-five miles, maybe more—around Azusa, Glendora, Claremont, one of those towns. Definitely east: he could see big mountains off to the north, and he was pretty sure that that was Mount Baldy over there. Certainly there weren't any mountains that size west of Pasadena. And the air had that hot, dry inland quality to it.

Sean wasn't surprised to find himself this far from the laboratory. A time displacement of nine and a half years was bound to move him a sizable distance in space. But going *east* puzzled him. After all, his last jump had been a backshunt and it had brought him out west of the laboratory. It stood to reason that shunting in the opposite direction in time ought to move him in the opposite direction spatially, too. But maybe not. Expecting anything about time travel to stand to reason was probably dumb.

For a moment he wondered whether he had actually

gone backward in time, not forward, on this shunt. Which might explain the eastward displacement.

No. Impossible. Dumb dumb dumb. The one thing that did make sense in all this shunting was the mathematics of reciprocity. Everything had to balance. You swung back, then you swung forward, while your brother at the opposite end of the seesaw made an equal and opposite journey. The last place Sean had been was the minus-5 $\times$ 10^5-minutes level. Now he had to be at the plus–5 $\times$ 10^6-minutes level. There were no two ways about that. Beyond any doubt, he must have gone forward. His location in time right now, he knew, had to be late November of the year 2025.

In any case he didn't need a computer to tell him that he had moved into the future. One quick look at his surroundings was all that it took.

This place was *strange.*

A lot of it looked like any Southern California town of the early twenty-first century, of course. But there were a good many new high-rise buildings too, twenty or thirty stories high. Sean didn't remember high rises being so common out here. And they were buildings of an astonishing weirdness of design.

One had twin curving spikes on its roof, like gigantic horns. Another had a strip of mirrors a yard wide running down its front from top to bottom. A number of buildings had large eye-shaped glass ovals above their entrances, and some had additional eyes higher up on the facade. Decorations? Or mysterious electronic devices? And the architects had apparently hated straight lines. All of the buildings had odd wriggling edges, sinuous and fluted and swirly. Sean couldn't look for long at any one of them without feeling that he was being pulled around the corner into some other dimension.

The newer cars in the streets had the same twisting,

looping lines. They were low and long and somehow sinister-looking, with single bands of grillwork across their fronts where headlights should be, and peculiar arching ornaments–or antennas?–rising in startling curves from their roofs. Some were carrying hornlike spikes similar to those on the building down the street. So a whole new kind of design would come into fashion in the years just ahead. He couldn't say that he admired it much.

The strangest thing of all was that there was no one in the streets.

No one. No one at all. He was all alone. He might have been the only human being in the whole world. He stood in the middle of the wide street under a warm midday sun, looking this way and that. No people in sight. No cars moved, no horns honked. Not a sound anywhere.

What had happened here?

Where was everybody?

This was starting to feel creepy. Frowning, Sean began to walk toward the building with the mirrored facade. Looking up, he saw his own image, broken and refracted a dozen times over. The entrance of the building was a wall of glass three times as tall as he was, decorated only by a jutting blue sphere that he assumed was some kind of doorknob. Hesitantly he put his hand to it.

The moment he touched it, music filled the air.

It came from everywhere at once, a hundred electronic brass bands blaring a hundred marching tunes. He whirled around, astonished, and saw lights suddenly blazing in every building, dazzling fireworks exploding overhead–fireworks in *daytime!*–banners unfolding from gravity-rotor platforms that had come spinning out from invisible hiding places.

He stared in amazement, trying to read all the banners at once.

WELCOME, SEAN!
THE CITY OF GLENDORA GREETS THE MAN FROM TIME!
GREATER LOS ANGELES CHAMBER OF COMMERCE SAYS
HELLO, SEAN!
THE YEAR 2025 IS GLAD TO SEE YOU!
SAN BERNARDINO COUNTY, CALIFORNIA'S GREATEST,
IS ALL YOURS!
HERE'S TO YOU—THE FIRST AND FINEST
TIME-TRAVELER!

He glanced up the wide street and saw the marchers advancing toward him now. What seemed like thousands of people, stretching off into the distance as far as he could see.

Of course. This was probably the biggest day in the history of this little town. And they had had better than nine years to prepare for it.

"Good God," Sean murmured. "I'm famous! And here comes the parade!"

15.

Eric
$+ 5 \times 10^7$ minutes

It was hot and steamy here, a dense, lush, tropical heat. Just drawing a breath was hard work. The humid air wrapped itself around him like a heavy cloak. The thick sweet perfume of a billion flowers lay upon the air. The sky had a curious greenish color, beautiful in its way, but strange and oddly troubling.

This time, Eric thought, the spatial displacement must have moved him clear out to Hawaii, or one of the South Pacific isles.

But something didn't seem right. Tropical isles were always warm but never this hot. The temperature must be well over a hundred here. *Well* over. He had sometimes experienced heat like this, or almost like this, on field trips out in the desert. But that had been dry heat, torrid yet bearable. This stuff was something else, like being in a steam room. Or worse. Not even the desert got this hot very often.

Where am I, he wondered?

He looked around. There was a wide beach in front of

him, crowded with sunbathers. It didn't have the exotic look of a tropical beach—crystalline water, white powdery sand. It looked very much like a California beach. Turning, he could see a town or small city a little way inland, and, behind the town, a steeply rising wall of rugged, heavily forested mountains.

It all seemed very familiar.

It definitely had the look of the California coast—up by Santa Barbara, say, where the mountains come down close to the shore. Though these mountains seemed a little closer to the shore than he remembered from his last visit to Santa Barbara.

But what about this sweltering tropical heat? You almost never got temperatures like this along the California coast. And this stifling humidity? Never. Where were the cooling sea breezes? Puzzled, he walked up toward the promenade separating the beach from the town. Here the vegetation seemed wrong. The slim, graceful palm trees that were growing everywhere didn't look like the ones he had known all his life. They were some kind of more tropical species, most likely—coconut palms or royal palms or something else, something too tender to grow in California's mild but sometimes chilly climate. And these vines, these creepers, these odd ferns, these riotously blossoming shrubs with glistening leaves—no, no, Eric thought, none of this is California stuff. California is dry all summer long. These plants must come from some moist jungle.

He paused to catch his breath. Moving around was a real struggle in this greenhouse environment.

Where am I? he wondered again.

He had to be fifty million minutes in the future—a little more than ninety-five years. So this was the summer of the year 2111. If he was still alive in this year, he'd be 118 years old. Stretching his luck a little, maybe.

So he knew *when* he was. But *where–where–?*

And suddenly he knew. *This greenhouse environment.* That was what he had called it a moment ago. He trembled with fear and shock as full understanding hit him. He was in California, all right. But a California that had been utterly transformed–in a world that had undergone what must have been a colossal calamity–

"You savah, mister?" asked someone at his elbow.

A girl, about thirteen, fourteen. She was wearing only the tiniest of bathing suits and she had a small metallic pack strapped to her back. A flexible tube ran from the backpack to her mouth. A tall boy stood behind her. He had a similar backpack on.

"Savah?" Eric repeated. "I don't understand."

"Are you savah?" she said again. "Are you all right? Are you okay?" She said "okay" as if it were a word from some foreign language. "You don't have your breather on."

"No," he said. "I don't have one."

"You lose it? You look bad mal, savvy? Tray mal."

She was speaking a sort of French, he realized. French and English, mixed. He leaned on the railing of the promenade. She was telling him that he looked sick. And he felt sick.

"The air," he said. "So thick–so humid here, so hot–"

"Not the heat," said the girl. "It's the see-oh. It'll plonk you in a quick."

See-oh. C-O, he thought. CO_2. Carbon dioxide.

"Lend him your breather, Slowjoe," the girl said impatiently, gesturing at her companion. "Can't you see he's going to plonk?"

Eric was feeling dizzier and dizzier. Vaguely he was aware of the boy unstrapping the device from his back and handing it to him. The girl put the tube in his mouth and told him to breathe deeply. Almost at once his head began to clear. Oxygen? They were watching him worriedly. Nice kids, he thought. Lucky for me.

"Savah?" she asked. "Better now?"

"Much," he said.

"Bien. Go on. Put it on your back."

"But I can't let him give me his breather."

"He'll go and get another one. Five minutes without won't mort him. We're used to this stuff, you know."

Eric nodded. *This stuff.* So it had really happened, he thought. The greenhouse effect that the environmental scientists had worried about all those years. The buildup of carbon dioxide in the atmosphere through the centuries of industrial development, until a thick mantle of heat-retaining gas surrounded the Earth and temperatures everywhere started to climb. And the polar ice caps melted, and the seas rose, and the air turned into chemical soup, and the temperate lands turned into steaming tropics, and God only knew what had become of the places that had been tropical before.

Now Sean understood why the mountains here seemed closer to the shore than he thought they ought to be. The mountains hadn't moved. The rising seas had come up onto the land. If sea levels have risen twenty-five or fifty feet, he thought, what has become of Santa Monica? Of New York? The hills of San Francisco must be islands now.

"What's the name of this town?" he asked the girl.

"Santa Barbara," she said.

"Santa Barbara, California?"

"No, Santa Barbara on the moon." And she laughed. "Where do you think you are?"

"I thought it might be Santa Barbara," he said. "But everything's so different from what I—" He paused.

"Go on," she said. "Different from what you remember, right?"

"You know who I am?"

"You're a voyageur, yes? A time traveler? You come from the cool years, right?"

"The cool years, yes. From the year 2016, matter of fact."

The girl smiled. She didn't seem notably startled by what he had just said. Time-travelers must be commonplace items by now, he thought. People dropping in from the past all the time. "I knew it toot sweet, right away. You talk like the vieux-time people. You must have been one of the first, no?"

"The first," he said. "The very first."

"No blague!" she said admiringly. "Imagine that!" But she still didn't sound enormously impressed. "Well, enjoy yourself here. If you can. Don't forget to use your breather. You'll plonk real fast without it, you know. *Real* fast."

16.

Sean
-5×10^7 minutes

"Well, here comes the parade, finally," said the short red-faced man just to Sean's left.

What, again? The parade was over. Was time backing up on him? Had the pendulum slipped a cog? Yes, he could hear the sounds of parade music all over again. Had he somehow been taken a shunt within a shunt, going back to the start of his stay in 2025 to live through an experience he had already had?

"Yes, sir, that's what I call a parade!" the red-faced man said.

Sean stared. It was a parade, all right, but not the one he had just been in. He could see the prancing drum major now, far down the street. The half-built, dinky-looking, antiquated street. And he could hear the music. Not electronic sounds, no, but an old-fashioned brass band making a joyous blaring uproar. A real bass drum sending out vast booming sounds.

This wasn't Glendora in the year 2025. And this wasn't

any parade in honor of Sean Gabrielson, the visitor from out of time. Not at all.

He was in a small town, but it was a much older one. There weren't any futuristic high-rise buildings with horns and eyes on them. There weren't any high-rises at all, just little wooden or stucco one- and two-story buildings with scrawny young palm trees standing in front of them. And the sign on the street corner—an old-fashioned sign, white letters on blue metal, no infoglow, no shimmerglass—said that this was Wilshire Boulevard.

So the name of this small town was Los Angeles. There wasn't much to it, back here in this year that he realized now must be 1921. The hills to the north were bare. The lofty roadbeds of the freeways were nowhere to be seen. The street was paved, but it looked like a country lane, hardly fit for heavy traffic. Everything had a raw, new look to it.

Boom—boom—boom—

The red-faced man pointed, waved, clapped his hands in glee. He didn't seem to be bothered by the fact that Sean had just materialized out of nowhere beside him. Or that Sean was dressed in the strange clothes of another era, an era yet unborn. Well, this was Hollywood, after all. The man probably thought that Sean was in costume for some science-fiction movie and had just stepped out of the studio to see the parade.

It was a fine spring day. The air was fresh and clean. They haven't even invented smog yet, Sean thought in astonishment.

It all looked so peculiar here. And yet not as peculiar as he had expected. In a way he was surprised to see that 1921 was in actual living color, not in black and white, and that the people moved at a normal pace, not in some herkyjerk frenzy. He had seen ancient movies and he realized that he really had imagined that everything in reality would look the way it did in those movies. Quaint, musty, unreal. Well, it was quaint and musty, yes. But not unreal.

Sean turned to the red-faced man. He was wearing a stiff, uncomfortable dark suit, a necktie, a vest. On a warm spring day like this. But everybody else nearby along the parade route was dressed the same way. So formal, so elaborate. Neckties! Vests! The women all had hats on. And gloves. They were the ones who seemed to be in movie costumes, not he. But this was no movie, for these people. This was the real world of 1921; and in that world, this was how people dressed.

"What's the parade all about?" Sean asked.

The man frowned at him. "Why, in honor of the President!"

"The President," Sean said. "Ah–is the President here?"

"The President's in Washington, getting sworn in. Don't you know that? But even if we're three thousand miles away, we can celebrate. Yes, sirree! We're having a parade to honor the new President. Can't you see the banners?"

Sean turned and looked. The main float was passing by right now. Real orange trees, laden with fruit, atop a horse-drawn platform. And banners, painted on canvas:

WARREN GAMALIEL HARDING, PRESIDENT OF THE UNITED STATES
CALVIN COOLIDGE, VICE PRESIDENT
INAUGURATION DAY MARCH 4, 1921

"Three cheers for President Harding!" the red-faced man shouted, waving his hat in the air. "He's my man! America first! No more wars! Back to normal! Harding! Harding! Harding!" He nudged Sean in the ribs. "What's the matter, are you a Democrat? Let's hear you cheer!"

Sean nodded. Why not?

When in Rome, do as the Romans do. When in 1921, give a cheer for the new President, if that's what everybody all around you is doing.

"Harding!" he yelled. "Harding! Harding! Three cheers for President Harding!"

17.

Eric
-5×10^8 minutes

Eric felt a rush of cool sweet air, almost dizzying. After the dank, moist, thick soup that was the air of Santa Barbara in the year 2111, this was like fresh new wine. He was in a forest of towering redwood trees so tall their tops were lost in the mist high overhead. He reached up to take the breathing device from his mouth.

But the breather was gone. Of course. It was impossible to carry any physical object from one shunt to the next except the things he had had with him when the trip began. The laws of conservation of energy were very strict about that. Whatever gear he had set out with from Time Zero would stay with him throughout the journey, but nothing that he picked up along the way could be transported. There wasn't any possibility of returning from the past with a lost painting of Leonardo da Vinci under your arm, or coming back from the future with some fantastic device that would change the whole world.

Well, he didn't need any gadgets to help him breathe

here. This air was the purest he had ever known. He couldn't even imagine how air could be cleaner or fresher than this.

He checked his instruments. Longitude 121 degrees W. He was still in California, then. Latitude a little more than 36 degrees N. That would put him a bit north of the midway line between Los Angeles and San Francisco—somewhere around Monterey, Eric guessed. A pretty hefty spatial displacement this time. But he was 500 million minutes in the past, now. That was 951.3 years. By his best calculation this was a mild, misty January morning in the year A.D. 1065.

The forest was beautiful. He had never seen a lovelier place than this.

The mighty chocolate-red redwood trunks were like the columns of a vast cathedral. Far above him, nearly four hundred feet up, the treetops met in a roof of foliage. A pearly twilight glow was all that broke through to brighten the forest floor. The stillness was fantastic. He could hear no sound except the gentle patter of the droplets of condensed fog that fell to the soft needle-carpeted floor, and the distant murmur of a brook. The fronds of huge glistening ferns were everywhere about him.

The year 1065! In Europe now, the man who would be called William the Conqueror was laying his plans for the invasion of England. The Crusades would soon be beginning. There were great native American empires in Mexico and Peru. And at this moment, who knew what was happening in the palaces of China, Africa, the Baghdad of the Arabian Nights—?

He felt a moment of something very like regret at finding himself in this place.

If the spatial displacement had been greater, this shunt might have dropped him down in the hectic midst of history—in Rome, say, or Constantinople, or Venice, or perhaps one of the stone cities of the Mayas. But here—here in this peaceful redwood forest on the California coast—Eric was as alone as though this were the dawn of time. There was no trace here of whatever sparse and scattered Indian population California had at this time. All was silence. All was peace.

That pang of regret vanished as suddenly as it had come.

To be allowed to see such beauty as this was a privilege beyond measure. How could he yearn for some other place?

Quietly, struck by wonder, Eric wandered through the stupendous groves of trees. He thought of the California he had left behind, the roar of the freeways, the droning of the planes overhead, the immense sprawl of the cities. They had saved a few little redwood forests, sure, somewhere far up north of San Francisco. Like museum exhibits. But everywhere else the hand of man had left its mark.

And this was how it all had looked before we came, he thought.

Here, in this awesome solitude, in this place where perhaps no human being had walked before, he felt himself suddenly swept by an emotion that was completely new to him. He wanted to drop to his knees and give thanks—to whom, to what, he wasn't really certain—for the beauty he beheld. He had never done such a thing before. Even now he hesitated, embarrassed, self-conscious.

Go on, he thought. Nobody's watching. And even if somebody were, so what?

But it was too late. The moment had passed. It would be forced, artificial, unreal, for him to do it now. Instead he stood quietly, resting his hand lightly on the giant trunk of a tree by the edge of the little stream.

He felt the strength of it, the immensity. This tree, he thought, had made a great voyage through time, of a sort, itself. It must have been living when Jesus was born. Or even earlier. And on and on through the centuries to this year of 1065, and on beyond. Probably it would still be here in 1865 or 1875 or 1885 or whenever it was that men would come along with their saws and hatchets to cut it down. It might have lived on into the twenty-first century, the twenty-second, even the thirty-second, if it had been left to finish its long journey undisturbed.

After a while he walked onward. He had no regret now that the shunt had brought him here, instead of to some busy capital of the medieval world. This moment out of time, this quiet interlude in the strange fantastic journey that the swinging pendulum had launched him on, was worth a thousand Constantinoples.

He smiled. And then he dropped to his knees after all, and bowed his head, and gave thanks and praise, not knowing to whom, to what. For this beauty, for this moment of peace: thanks and praise. Thanks and praise.

18.

Sean
+ 5×10^8 minutes

Alt! No podo pasari! Todos tempuus vorbudt aqui!"

"Are you speaking to me?" Sean asked the huge mechanical creature that loomed before him.

"Anglic!" the great gleaming robot cried. "Du spikke Anglic! Yis u no?"

"Yis," Sean said, bluffing for all he was worth. "Ik spikke Anglic. Yis."

The thing was at least nine feet high, and it was all eyes and mouth. Half a dozen huge sparkling eyes ran around its upper end, some kind of band of sensors that flickered restlessly up and down the whole spectrum and probably beyond it into the infrared and the ultraviolet. And an ugly gaping slot of a mouth, big as the top of a garbage can, in its belly. The better to swallow you with, my little time-traveler. *Du spikke Anglic? Answer yis u no, or I'll gobble you up!*

Sean looked around uneasily. He was standing on some rubbery catwalk suspended about twenty feet above what might have been a street. The street looked rubbery too, with purple pumpkin-shaped growths sprouting from it at intervals of eight or ten feet. To his right was what looked like a wall of ice, a smooth glacial face rising to an enormous height. He could see people moving around freely within the ice. So it wasn't ice and not a glacier, but a building of some sort. On the other side of him the street was lined with giant metallic needles the size of telephone poles. They were glowing pale purple and giving off soft twanging sounds.

So this is the year A.D. 2967, Sean thought. Well, it sure looks like the year A.D. 2967.

"Anglic," the huge robot said. "Du spikke Anglic." Something was rumbling in its interior, making a cement-mixer sound. The eye-band turned a blazing yellow, then slowly subsided into orange and red. Small portholes on the robot's sides opened and swiveled. Projections like the feet of insects came poking out of them, waving and wriggling about.

It means to swallow me, Sean thought. As soon as it can figure out what I am. I'm going to be a tin can's afternoon snack.

He wondered what would happen to him if he turned and tried to make a run for it. Probably a bad idea. He imagined jets of gluey liquid squirting from those portholes and lassoing him at fifty paces.

"Anglic," said the robot again. "You are a speaker of Anglic. Yes. Yes. Mode adjustment made. Comprendus? You are a tempuu and Anglic is your sprak. Comprendus? Comprendus? Rispondim! Do you comprendan?"

"You don't quite have it right yet," Sean said. "But keep trying."

"No comprendus?"

"No comprendus, right."

"Correction mode. Correction mode." The robot began

sputtering and mumbling to itself. Cautiously Sean started to back away, moving very slowly. Maybe it won't notice that I'm leaving. The sounds from the metallic poles to his left grew higher in pitch. People were pointing at him through the glassy walls of the artificial glacier. "You will cease departing," the robot said. "Correction has been made. We use your mode now. You are Anglic-speaking time-traveler, unauthorized. You will us show your documentuus."

"Documents," Sean said. "That's better Anglic. English, we call it. But I don't have any documents. I'm too early for that. I come from the year–"

"No documentuus! No documentuus!" The robot's eyeband flashed vivid scarlet. "Illicitimu! Tempuu vorbudtu! No podo pasari!" It was getting really excited. The enormous froglike mouth was opening and closing. Sean saw lights flashing inside, and gears moving about. It began to move toward him in a slow, ponderous way.

It *is* going to gobble me up, he thought. Because I'm an unregistered time-traveler and I don't have the right passport. Or something.

He turned and started to run.

"No!" a voice cried behind him. "Alt! No flikken! Is safe! Is okay! I to do, you will safe!"

A girl, a woman–he couldn't tell which, he couldn't begin to guess her age–emerged out of nowhere. She was very slender and she was taller than he was. She had glistening silver hair and silver eyes too, and her skin was bright red, the color of a ripe apple. She looked strange, but she looked beautiful, too.

She might have been the most beautiful woman he had ever seen.

Darting swiftly around him, she ran right up to the giant robot and slapped the palm of her hand against its midsection. A panel opened at once. She reached in and pressed a key. Instantly the robot's eye-band color shifted toward blue. "Podo pasari," the robot muttered. "Tempuu licitimu. Validimu. Propriu." And it moved off, still muttering to itself.

The woman smiled. Her silver eyes dazzled him.

"You will forgive," she said. "My Anglic. Is not big good. But you will safe now." Her voice was deep and rich and warm, with an odd little crack in it. It was like no voice he had ever heard, but very beautiful. Her hand reached toward his. "They do not like tempuus, this year. Time-travelers. Too many come, too much confuse. But I will protect. My people will. How is your name?"

"Sean," he said. "Sean Gabrielson. From the year 2016."

"I bin Hepta-Noni-Acanta-Leela-Quintu-Quintu," she said.

"Is all that your name?"

"I am to you Quintu-Leela," she said, and laughed. Her laughter was magical. From the humming telephone poles came an answering sound, delicate, eerie. Her hand tightened on his. "Come with me. You will safe with me. I will show the world." Again the laugh. "Everything. You and me, we bin amicuus. Friends, you say? Friends. We bin very warm friends. Comprendus?"

Sean nodded. He felt as though an electric current were passing from her hand into his. Perhaps it was. Quintu-Leela, he thought. The sound of her voice was marvelously strange and strangely marvelous. And those silver eyes. He imagined her name and his entwined within a heart, blazing in purple fire in the sky.

Love at first sight, that was what it was.

He had heard about such things but he had never really believed they happened. Especially to him. Love at first sight! Was that too crazy? Quintu-Leela and Sean. Sean and Quintu-Leela. God, she was beautiful! And fascinating! That voice! Those eyes!

Yes, I do believe I'm falling in love, he thought.

With a woman who lives in the time of my own great-great-great-great-great-great-great-granddaughter. Who for all I know could *be* my own great-great-great-great-great-great-great granddaughter. The woman of my dreams, an incredible woman, a phenomenal woman, and any hour now, maybe any minute now, the displacement force is going to sweep me away from her forever.

19.

Eric
$+ 5 \times 10^9$ minutes

The tunnels went on and on, an endless maze, one smooth shining onyx-walled corridor after another. Eric had no idea where he was or where he had been or where he was heading. All he knew was that he was somewhere below the surface of the Earth, plodding through corridor after corridor after corridor, never once getting a glimpse of the sun, the sky, the stars. And never once seeing another human being.

He wondered how far underground he was.

He wondered whether any life, human or otherwise, still existed on Earth's surface, here in the 116th century A.D.

He wondered if he was still on Earth at all.

This was his third day in the tunnels now. At least that was what the chronometer said. But his mind and body both were hopelessly confused down here, where there was no day, no night, only the unending onyx walls lit by some mysterious radiance deep within the stone. He felt almost no need for sleep. When he did, he simply slouched up against the tunnel wall and closed his eyes for half an hour or so. He ate just as sparsely. Now and then he remembered to consume one of the food tablets from his utility belt. Most of the time he was content to coast along on the slow-release nutrient additives that the Project Pendulum medics had pumped into his bloodstream a few hours before Time Zero.

It had been a fantastic experience at first, roaming this mystifying underground world of the far future. None of his previous shunts had shown him anything remotely as strange as this. But the fascination was beginning to wear thin for him.

He had arrived in a glow of dense emerald light. It was all around, engulfing everything, so that he could almost believe he was at the bottom of the sea. The light was so deep and so strong that it was impossible for him to make out any features whatever of his surroundings.

Then the light vanished as though a hood had been thrown over his head, and he found himself in a zone of the deepest blackness he had ever known. For a long while after that nothing happened. He stood in complete silence, mystified, uncertain.

"Hello?" he said. "Anybody there?"

Nothing. No one. Silence.

He took a step. Another. Another. He was unable to see a thing. For all he knew, there was a pit a mile deep right in front of him. But he couldn't just stand here forever, waiting for things to happen. He went on, step by uneasy step.

There was a sweetness in the air, and something else, a touch of lemon, perhaps, or sage, or both at once. He wasn't surprised. Each era he had visited so far had had a distinct and characteristic flavor. He hadn't expected that, that every time would smell different from all other times. This is the smell of the 116th century, he thought. It was a likable odor, but unreal, synthetic.

Perhaps they make their own air in the year A.D., 11529,

he thought. He imagined giant air-making machines on the borders of every city, releasing flavors of every desired sort into the atmosphere. Maybe that was how they had coped with the buildup of carbon dioxide that had turned the whole world into a giant greenhouse in the twenty-second century. Just thinking about the time he had spent in that sweltering tropical world made him feel sweaty and weak. The air is a lot better here, he thought. Of course the greenhouse-effect problems were ancient history to the people of this era. Nine thousand years in the past, in fact.

That was before he realized that he wasn't breathing surface air at all. He was underground.

He put out his hand and touched smoothness to his left: highly polished stone. The moment he touched it, it lit up, and he saw that he was in a long cavern or corridor that stretched far in front of him, disappearing into dimness hundreds of yards away. The walls curved gently up to meet the rounded arch of the ceiling. He recognized the glossy brown stone as onyx, though it was astonishing to think of a corridor this size wholly lined with that rare and beautiful mineral. Synthetic onyx, maybe, he thought. This is the 116th century. They can do anything. There was pale light pulsing within the walls, an inexplicable inner radiance, cool and beautiful.

In awe and wonder he walked onward. After a little while he saw figures moving slowly toward him and he halted, narrowing his eyes to peer into the distance. He felt curiously unafraid. This was too much like a dream to seem real. And in any case he was confident that the beings of this future age would be too civilized to offer him any harm.

They came closer, within the range of his vision now. They weren't human.

They were cone-shaped beings eight or nine feet high, with brilliant orange eyes the size of platters and rubbery blue bodies. Clusters of scarlet tentacles dangled like nests of snakes from their shoulders. They walked in an odd gliding, lurching way on suction pads that made a peculiar slurping sound as they clamped down and pulled free again.

No way could evolution have transformed the human race into creatures like this, Eric thought. Not in 9500 years, not ever. These had to be aliens of some sort. There were half a dozen of them moving in a solemn procession along the opposite side of the corridor wall. He stared up at them. They were gigantic looming presences, massive, menacing.

He felt the first pricklings of fear. Being a traveler out of time gave him no invulnerability, only the illusion of it. This might be dreamlike but it was no dream, and those creatures were twice his size. Would they try to harm him? He stood poised on the balls of his feet, ready to bolt and dart past them at the first hostile sign.

But they paid no attention to him. Like a procession of mourners they shuffled toward him and past him, not giving him so much as a glance. They seemed completely preoccupied with their own ponderous thoughts.

Eric stared at them in amazement.

Was he so insignificant to them? No more important than a squirrel by the side of the road? Had he come 9500 years to be totally ignored?

Sudden crazy fury blossomed in him.

"Hey!" he called. "Wait! Aren't you even going to stop and ask the time of day? Don't you wonder what I am?"

They kept on going without looking back at him.

Eric shook his head. Anger gave way to bewilderment.

"I sure as hell wonder what you are," he muttered lamely.

The huge creatures continued to shuffle onward down the corridor. They dwindled in the dimness until he could barely see them, far down the way. And then, at a place where the corridor seemed to curve slightly to the right, all at once they disappeared, vanishing like soap bubbles in the air.

Frowning, Eric struggled to understand. Had they found some passage?

Maybe they had never been there at all. Maybe they had simply been hallucinations. Maybe this all *was* a dream.

He ran back after them.

When he came to the place where the giant creatures had disappeared he could find no trace of doorways or side passages. The walls of the corridor were as smooth and unbroken here as they had been from the start.

He shrugged, turned back in the other direction, and marched on.

After what seemed like hours more of plodding along the same empty hallway Eric reached a place where the corridor swelled and split into nine apparently identical tunnels. At random he entered the third tunnel from the left. It too seemed to be empty. But then once again he saw a procession of strange beings coming toward him.

These looked like giant purple starfish with rough pebbly skins. Each had a globe of brilliant white flame glowing at the center of its body and fifteen or twenty rigid tentacles radiating stiffly outward. The way that they moved was to roll along with weird grace on the tips of their tentacles, like acrobats turning cartwheels.

"Excuse, me," Eric said at once. "I'm Eric Gabrielson. I'm a time-traveler from the twenty-first century A.D., and—"

No use. They weren't any more interested in him than the suction-footed giants had been.

He watched in dismay as the starfish went rolling onward and beyond. When they were a hundred yards or so past him they all abruptly turned to the left and pressed themselves against the corridor wall, which emitted a painful blue glow the moment they touched it. Eric covered his eyes.

When it seemed safe to open them again, there was no sign of the starfish creatures. Had they stepped right through the corridor wall?

Puzzled, he backtracked and studied the wall. It looked no different from any other section of the wall. After a moment's hesitation he touched it with the palm of his hand. Nothing happened. No blinding blue glow, nothing.

He went onward.

He slept a little while. He nibbled a couple of food tablets.

He came to another place where the tunnel forked once more, branching into seventeen passages this time. He chose the rightmost branch. The tunnel was the same as before, smooth, glossy, bright with that inexplicable inner radiance.

More beings appeared, seemingly floating in the air. They were elongated transparent creatures filled with churning misty organs. They looked like the sort of things you might see under the microscope in a drop of water, blown up to giant size—huge protozoa, a tribe of colossal paramecia.

"Hello?" he ventured. "Does anybody here know what a human being is? Or was?"

The giant protozoa didn't seem to be interested in conversation, either.

Nor were the next creatures that he met, nor the next, nor the ones after those. Branch after branch, tunnel after tunnel, and it was always the same: silence, gleaming walls stretching far out before him, occasional bands of grotesque beings traversing the infinite corridors bound on unimaginable mysterious migrations. Sometimes they seemed to disappear into the corridor walls, as the starfish had done.

Sometimes they seemed to emerge from the walls just as mysteriously.

Eric might just as well have been invisible.

What had begun as an eerily fascinating experience was becoming maddening and frustrating. He found himself wondering how long it was going to be before the displacement force seized him and carried him out of here to his next shunt, 95,000 years deep in the past. At least the past was a place that he felt he understood.

Then, late on the third day, two beings that might almost have been human stepped suddenly out of the corridor wall no more than twenty feet in front of him.

Eric realized after the first startled moment that they weren't human, not at all. Their bodies were impossibly long and narrow and their arms and legs were thin as whips, with elbows every twelve inches. Their hands had more than five fingers. Their lips were nothing but slits, their bare waxy-looking skins were greenish-yellow, and their golden eyes seemed to be set on end, much longer than they were broad.

There might have been some evolutionary changes in the human race since his own time, but a mere ninety-five centuries could never have produced a transformation like this. They had to be some sort of aliens.

Strange as they were, they were humanoid, at any rate. Not giant paramecia or walking starfish or great shambling blue-and-orange monsters. And, unlike all the others, they hadn't simply walked past him without a glance and kept on going. They had actually stopped and were studying him with some interest. That gave him hope.

"Please," he said. "I'm lost. I don't have any idea where I am. Won't you help me?"

The two eerie humanoids exchanged a quick glance. Another positive sign. It was the first reaction he had managed to get from any of the beings he had encountered in these corridors. But they remained silent.

"Talk to me," he said. "Somehow. There's got to be a way that you can communicate with me. I know there is."

For a moment more they remained motionless. Then one of them made a gesture with its many fingers. In Eric's own time that gesture meant *come closer.* He had no notion what it might mean here. He decided to risk it.

When he was just a few paces from them they reached their long ropy arms toward him and touched their soft cool fingers to his. It was like touching an electric socket. A sudden tingling shock burst through him.

"No—wait—"

He tried to pull back, but he was unable to break the contact.

And then, amazingly, he felt intelligible words taking form in his mind.

There is no reason for you to fear us. Why would we want to harm you?

"I didn't know what was happening to me. Or what to expect. I—I—" He took a deep breath. "I'm Eric Gabrielson. I come from the twenty-first century. There's been this experiment, you see, in time displacement, and—"

We know that. We are the anterstrin thelerimane.

They said it as though that explained everything.

"Oh," he said. "And this is Earth, isn't it? In the year A.D. 11529?"

This is Earth, yes. You are in the quarantine section.

"Quarantine?"

All new arrivals are placed in quarantine until their clearances come through. It is the law. Visitors from time must undergo clearance just as visitors from space do. Once you are cleared you will be permitted to visit Upper Earth.

"I see," Eric said. "And how long does it take to get a clearance?"

The anterstrin thelerimane said, *In some cases, no more than ten or twenty days. In others, perhaps fifty to a hundred years, or even longer. Centuries, sometimes.*

Eric thought of the displacement force, gathering its irresistible momentum now, almost ready perhaps to sweep him away from this place.

"Can't it ever be done faster?" he asked.

There is much that must be determined before strangers can be released into Upper Earth. We ourselves have been here sixteen years, and our case is by no means settled. You may have to wait just as long.

"But I can't," Eric protested. "I'm shunting in time on pendulum swings. Do you understand what I'm saying? The next swing could carry me away in an hour, or a minute, or a day. And then I'd never get to see what Earth is like in this era."

Oh, no, the quiet mental voice of the anterstrin thelerimane. *You will not be suddenly carried away, we assure you. The rules are never broken. No one leaves quarantine until the galithismon permits it. You will stay here until your clearance comes. We promise you that. Even if you must remain in the quarantine tunnels for five hundred years.*

20.

Sean
-5×10^9 minutes

It was almost noon by the time Sean came to the eastern rim of the broad mesa that he had been crossing since dawn. He peered over the edge and what he beheld in the dark valley below made him gasp with wonder.

Bison. Thousands of them, maybe millions, great shaggy brown beasts with their heavy heads down close to the ground.

They were ripping fiercely at the thick lush grass of the valley as if trying to turn the place into a barren desert in a single day. The vast herd filled the valley as far as Sean could see. The cold, biting wind out of the east carried their odor to him, rank and musky and sharp.

At last. After three days of solitary wandering in this cool wet land that was supposed to be Arizona, seeing nothing bigger than a ground squirrel and feeling tension rising within him as silent emptiness gave way only to more emptiness, he was staring at more animals than he had ever seen in one place in his life. Giant animals. What he saw out there was probably one of the last of the great big-game herds that had survived from the Ice Age and still roamed the Southwest here in the paleolithic past.

"Hey!" he called. "Hey, all you bison! You're extinct, do you know that? You hear what I'm telling you? Lie down and roll over! You're extinct!"

Sean didn't expect the bison to pay any attention to him, and they didn't. They went right on grazing, tearing out enormous clumps of grass, shaking their huge heads almost angrily from side to side as they fed. He had simply needed to hear the sound of his own voice again.

The three days that he had spent trekking through this forlorn world of 5×10^9 minutes ago had been the loneliest days he had ever known. Especially after the shunt that had preceded this one. Lovely Quintu-Leela, his woman with silver eyes. How he missed her now! What pain that had been, seeing her waver and vanish before him as the displacement force pulled him onward in time! She was like something half-remembered from a vivid dream, now. She was up there in the future, in bewildering, incomprehensible A.D. 2967. And he was back here, five billion minutes in his own past.

Five billion minutes! That was some 9,513 years. This was the world of 7500 B.C., more or less. These bison belonged here. He was the intruder.

Everything was different here, everything was unfamiliar. The air, when it didn't reek of bison fur, had an odd crisp iron quality, a metallic harshness that Sean knew was simply its purity. He had never breathed truly fresh air before. The sky looked bigger and bluer, the horizon farther away than it ought to be. The light was more intense. The water that flowed in the many streams that crossed these plains seemed to have a strange electric tingle to it because it was so clean.

This was a world without automobiles, without airplanes, without chemical factories, without anything that belched fumes into the air. Strange huge animals roamed it freely, and human beings scarcely existed. Over on the other side of the world in the Near East and maybe China the first little towns were being founded, but even there the world must still be unspoiled. It was almost impossible to comprehend how far he was from his own time. The pyramids of Egypt would not be built for another five thousand years.

And yet Sean knew he had only begun his voyage across the eons. By the time he reached the outer limits of the pendulum swing, this era would seem like the day before yesterday to him.

He looked out into the sea of bison before him.

Now he noticed other animals down there too, moving on the edges of the great bison herd. To his left he saw a pack of large long-legged wolflike creatures with broad, heavy-looking heads and dense blue-black fur. They looked frightening, but there was something curiously unferocious about their movements: they were sniffling and snuffling around like scavengers hoping to find an easy meal, and even when a lost bison calf wandered past them they made no move to attack.

Farther to the left were three peculiar-looking massive creatures squatting down on their haunches in front of a slender pine tree. Even squatting like that, they were taller than the tree. They were methodically pulling it apart, stripping the bark from its branches and cramming it into their mouths. Sean remembered seeing pictures of them on the orientation tape for this period: giant ground sloths. Deeper into the distance, so far across the valley that he could barely make them out, were mastodons. Their elephantlike forms were unmistakable. He saw some things that might have been camels out there, too. And closer at hand was a pair of heavyset creatures that seemed midway between an elephant and a pig in shape. Giant tapirs, he supposed.

The experts had thought these creatures of the late Ice Age might be just about extinct, here in the Arizona of 7500 B.C. But there was some uncertainty about the date of the great extinction and they had asked Sean to keep an eye out for them as he passed through this level of the shunt. And there they were. Beginning their decline, maybe, but far from extinct.

Mastodons! Bison! Giant ground sloths!

What a fantastic sight!

As Sean stared out toward the far reaches of the valley, a sudden flash of activity closer at hand caught his attention. He looked down and to his left. The bison calf had strayed just a little too far. From a dense clump of bushes at the base of the mesa came now a quick and savage killer, long and low-slung, with a compact, powerful tigerlike body and two astounding gleaming fangs almost a foot in length.

The calf never had a chance.

Swiftly the saber-tooth pounced, rising from the ground with a fierce thrust of its strong back and loins and clamping its heavy forearms against the bison's shaggy hump. In the same instant those two great daggers rose and sank deep into the flesh of the bison. The calf shivered under the assault and sank to its knees, and then tumbled over, pushing desperately at the saber-tooth with its hooves as though trying to shoo away an annoying fly.

It was all over in moments. Somberly Sean watched the killer-cat feed; and then the wolves came forth, snarling with sudden fury, demanding their share. The saber-tooth glared at them coldly as if ready to take on the whole pack. Then it wriggled its heavy neck in something remarkably like a shrug, and slowly moved off. It had eaten its fill, and now it was abandoning its prey to the hungry wolves. They were scavengers after all, terrifying though they might look.

Eventually the wolves too vanished into the thickets, leaving the bloody carcass for smaller beasts to devour.

Sean now began warily to make his way down the mesa's steeply sloping eastern face. He wanted a closer look at all these animals. Now that the most dangerous predator down there had had its lunch, the risks he faced were probably not great. And in any case he had an anesthetic dart gun strapped in the utility belt around his waist, and a laser, too. The dart gun ought to be able to take care of most problems. He wasn't supposed to use the laser as a weapon except in the most desperate of circumstances. If he went around killing things with his laser in the remote past, he might be making significant changes in the fabric of time by removing this critter or that which hadn't originally been destined to die at the hands of a man of the far future. But his surviving the mission was important, too. He had to calculate the trade-offs before going for the weapon.

The soil was damp and soggy from the rain that had drenched these plains, and him, last night. As he descended he sank in almost an inch with every step, coming up with moist, sticky mud on his boots. Mud wasn't something he associated with Arizona. Or valleys rich with thick lush grass. The Arizona he knew was a place of parched wastelands, dry brittle soil, twisted thorny scrub vegetation. But his instrument reading showed that he was somewhere just to the north of the place where Phoenix would be in another nine thousand-odd years.

He had started out from Los Angeles, up there at Time Zero in A.D. 2016. Not only had the shunt displaced him in time, though, it had also moved him some four hundred miles in space. No surprise there. The preshunt calculations had predicted that. The longer the time-shunt, the farther the spatial displacement.

This was Arizona, all right. But it was prehistoric Arizona

at the tail end of the Pleistocene Ice Age. The great chill that had brought so much moisture to this part of the continent had already begun to retreat; the lakes and meadows were starting to dry out, the big game animals were becoming sparse. During his increasingly depressing three-day trek through the utter silence of this land he had begun to fear that they were already extinct. Now Sean knew that that was not so.

Slipping and sliding and stumbling, he made his way the last twenty feet to the valley floor and found himself about a hundred yards from the nearest bison.

This close, he realized that they had little in common with the bison he had seen in zoos except the shagginess of their hides. These animals were gigantic, each one as big as a truck. They were colossal. They were immense. Their horns, instead of curving back to lose themselves in the heavy fur, jutted out three feet or more on each side. And the sound they made as they grazed was a mighty throbbing growl like the sound a fire makes as it roars through a dry forest.

He edged sideways, keeping his back to the mesa wall. A few of the bison closest to him eyed him without curiosity for a moment, but most did not even bother looking up. Why should they? They had no reason to fear him. They might never have seen a human being before. The whole human population of North America at this time was probably no more than twenty or thirty thousand widely scattered nomads. And to these bison he must seem utterly harmless, a flimsy little two-legged thing with no teeth or muscles worth worrying about and no claws at all.

Seeing that the bison were ignoring him, Sean moved out a little more boldly into the valley. The hugeness of the animals filled him with awe. They were like mountains. Even the calves seemed immense. He had all the more respect now for the strength of that saber-tooth.

He saw other animals now, smaller ones, animals he could not name. They were almost familiar—something that could almost have been a badger, and waddling birds that were somewhat like turkeys, and little scrambling rodents not much unlike guinea pigs. But they were all somehow different from their modern counterparts.

He wished he knew more about prehistoric zoology. This was an amazing place. Evidently this valley was a rich and fertile location that was particularly attractive to beasts great and small from all over central Arizona. What an amazing privilege it was to be allowed to see this congregation of great creatures!

Then he realized that he was not the only person here.

Shouts came from a fold in the valley floor a few hundred yards away. Glancing up in surprise, Sean was startled to see eight or ten tall, slender men in loincloths pelting one of the bison calves with rocks to drive it into a small box canyon. They were armed with spears tipped with tapering stone points, and as they pursued the angry, frightened calf they jabbed at it again and again, barely penetrating its thick furry hide. Killing it was going to be a difficult job.

Sean had been so concerned with the animals that he hadn't heard the hunters approach. Now, struck with wonder and amazement, he stepped back behind a tree to watch them in action. They were long-limbed, graceful men. They seemed almost to be floating as they ran along behind the calf. Though they had dark skins of a deep coppery hue, they looked very little like the Indians of his own time. Their heads were narrow and tapering, their shoulders sloped, their features were small, almost delicate. The chilly air seemed to bother them not at all, practically naked though they were.

He leaned forward, peering intently, fascinated by the sight of these prehistoric hunters at their task.

Then he felt a sudden stiff jab between his shoulder blades.

He whirled. And found himself looking at another of the hunters, who had come up silently behind him. His eyes were dark and shining, almost glowing with a light of their own. They were fixed on Sean in absolute concentration. The hunter grasped a spear lightly in his left hand, balancing it easily by the middle of its shaft.

He must have used the wooden end of the spear to poke Sean in the back. But now he had swung it around the other way. Sean stared. The long, sharp, elegantly carved stone point of the spear came into close focus just in front of him. It was aimed at the center of his chest, hovering just a couple of inches over his heart.

21.

Eric
-5×10^{10} minutes

The rules are never broken. That was the last thing that he remembered the anterstin thelerimane saying, back in the tunnels that ran beneath the world of A.D. 11529. Those two spooky humanoids with the long whiplike limbs had seemed to be telling him that he was going to dwell in the tunnels forever. *No one leaves quarantine until the galithismon permits it. You will stay here until your clearance comes, we promise you that. Even if you must remain in the quarantine tunnels for five hundred years.*

And then he felt the familiar swooping dizzying sensation that let him know he was making a shunt, and the anterstin thelerimane disappeared. The weird glistening tunnel with the onyx wall disappeared. The whole world of A.D. 11529 disappeared.

So much for the quarantine powers of the galithismon, Eric thought. Whoever or whatever the galithismon might be, it had been unable to withstand the power of the great pendulum that was carrying Eric back and forth across time.

What now? he wondered.

He found himself on an icy windswept plain, bleak and desolate. Leafless trees with dark crooked trunks rose here and there above the snowfields. The air was harsh and sharp, with howling gusts cutting deep. He touched his utility belt to give himself a little protection against the cold.

This was the minus-fifty-billion-minute level. Fifty billion minutes! He was 95,129 years into the past now–the Pleistocene period, the last Ice Age, the Fourth Glacial. Eric took his bearings. Latitude 41 degrees north. Longitude 6 degrees east. *East?* He was in Europe, then. Right in the middle of Spain. A whopping spatial displacement, clear across the whole United States and the Atlantic, too. Halfway around the world and smack into the teeth of an Ice-Age gale.

And there were tracks in the fresh snow in front of him.

Human tracks.

No question about it. The tracks had been made by someone with a wide foot, very wide. Probably a short person, because the prints were fairly close together.

But human, without a doubt. Because the feet that had left those tracks in the snow had been clad in sandals of some sort. The imprint was unmistakable: no sign of toes or claws, only the rounded front end of the sandal and the tapering heel.

Human? In Pleistocene Spain?

Neanderthals, Eric thought in sudden wonder. And he began to follow the trail.

It led up and over a hummock of rock that jutted from the snowfield, and down the other side through a region of loose and annoyingly deep snow that gave him much trouble, and then up the side of a steep hill. Climbing it was real work. For one bad moment he thought he had lost the trail altogether; but then he picked it up again, midway up the hill. Behind him, the winds grew wilder and snow began to fall. He scrambled upward.

A cave. A fire burning within.

He stared. Eight, ten people inside, close together by the campfire. Wearing shaggy fur robes, though some were bare to the waist. Short people, stocky and squat, with big heads and thick necks and barrel chests and broad, low-bridged noses. They weren't pretty, no. But they weren't apes, either. They were human beings. Different from us, but not by much. Cousins. Our Neanderthal cousins. Eric shivered, and not just from the cold.

One of them was singing, and the others were gathered around, nodding and clapping their hands in time. A slow, rhythmic chant, which suddenly speeded up, then slowed again, speeded again: an intricate rhythm, constantly changing. Almost like a poem. Almost? It *was* a poem! Those complex rhythms, the solemnity of the chanter's voice, the rapt attention of the listeners. The *Iliad* of the Neanderthals, maybe, a tale of heroic battle deeds. Or the *Odyssey*, the story of a man who had gone to war across the sea and had had a hard time getting home. A tribal poet, telling the great old stories around the campfire. Stories that would fall into the deepest sort of oblivion when these rugged people of the Ice Age were swept away into extinction, thirty or forty thousand years from now.

Neanderthal poetry! The idea stunned and dazzled him.

He leaned forward as far as he dared, peering into the mouth of the cave, straining to hear the words, hoping with an impossible hope to understand the meaning.

Abruptly the chanting stopped. There was silence in the cave.

They knew he was there. How? He had crouched down

behind a great rock partly blocking the entrance. But they were looking his way. Sniffing. Those big noses, those wide nostrils. They could smell him. They were murmuring to each other. Suddenly these people seemed less like ancient cousins, more like hairy ogres or trolls.

The storm was lashing the plain now: wild winds, flailing the falling snow into thick white curtains. Eric backed away from the mouth of the cave. He heard a shout from within, then another, another. Desperately now he began to run down the hill, slipping and stumbling in the loosely packed snow.

And they were coming after him.

Don't try to run, he thought. Slide for it! Slide!

He dropped down flat and gave himself a shove. And went wildly tobogganing away, moving at an ever accelerating speed with his knees drawn up tight against his chest and his arms pulled in over them. A couple of times he fetched up against some upjutting snag of a tree, or some hunk of rock, and gave himself a nasty whack; but then he pushed on, down and down and down the hill.

After a time he looked back. The Neanderthals had stopped pursuing him. They were standing some distance above him on a snowy ridge, staring at him in what looked like openmouthed astonishment.

They probably think I'm crazy, Eric thought. Crazy skinny peculiar-looking guy with a strange outfit on, who can't find any better way to amuse himself than go sliding down a bumpy hill in the middle of a snowstorm. Obviously a low-I.Q. type, a real moron.

Or maybe not. Maybe they think I'm having a good time.

He stood up, waved, shouted to them.

"Come on!" he called. "You try it, too! It's fun, guys! It's fun!"

He saw them muttering to each other. Maybe they were considering it. Maybe they were seriously thinking about taking up body-sledding, now that I've shown them the way.

I may have started something here, he thought. The Neanderthal Winter Olympics!

He brushed snow from his clothes and trudged on down the hillside, feeling a little creaky and battered. When he looked back next, the Neanderthal conference was still going on, and two of them were lying in the snow, trying to shove themselves downhill.

22.

Sean
+ 5×10^{10} minutes

The point of the spear just barely grazed Sean's chest. The other man held it there. Sean froze, not even breathing. He looked down, eyes bugging, at the sharp stone tip against his breastbone. This is it, he thought. The end of Sean, nine thousand years ago in Arizona. The archaeologists will be real confused when they find the bones of a white man in the ancient strata here.

You have to do something, he told himself.

Go for the dart gun? Or even the laser? No. It took a little time to get the anesthetic darts armed and primed. He didn't have that much time. As for the laser, he knew he was supposed to avoid using the weapon unless he had absolutely no other option. Besides, he suspected that the moment he made any movement toward his utility belt that spear would be sticking out his back.

Do something. Anything.

He began to sing.

He had no idea what good it would do. He just opened his mouth and let melody come flowing out.

Oh, say, can you see
By the dawn's early light . . .

The hunter looked astounded. He stepped back, one pace, two, three, without taking his eyes off Sean.

Reprieve. Somehow.

. . . what so proudly we hailed
by the twilight's last gleaming . . .

The hunter spoke: a single stream of words punctuated by explosive little bursts of breath.

"Sorry," Sean said. "I don't speak Prehistoric Hopi, or whatever you're talking." He managed a smile. It wasn't easy. It must have looked more like a tense grimace. Every culture understands smiling, he knew. Show your teeth. It's a sign of good will. "You are a Hopi or something, right? An Indian, anyway. An early version. An ancestor. My name is Sean. I come here in peace from the year 2016. Do you want me to sing some more? 'God rest ye merry gentlemen, let nothing you dismay—' "

The hunter spoke again, the same speech, faster this time. To Sean his words sounded blunt, cruel, harsh.

Sean responded with another smile, a little on the edgy side. And came out with:

California, here I come
Right back where I started from . . .

It was hard to tell what the other was planning to do. The hunter's eyelids were fluttering now. His nostrils flared wide. He grasped his spear at both ends and pulled it back tightly against his chest. He spoke once more, slowly and in a deeper voice. As if he were sinking into some sort of trance.

Keep on singing, Sean thought.

I am the captain of the Pinafore
And a right good captain too.
De deedle deedle dee and deedle deedle dee
With chimpanzees for my crew.

They weren't quite the right words, but he doubted that the hunter would know that. And at least the tune was there.

The other hunters were approaching now. Their faces were smeared with bison blood. One of them prodded Sean with the business end of his spear, pushing against the close-knit fabric of his jumpsuit. It was just the lightest of touches, but Sean shivered as he felt the keen tip of the stone point. He tried singing the "Hallelujah" chorus. It didn't sound so good solo. They came in closer now, pinching and poking him. He switched to "Silent Night" thinking it might calm them some. The first one, the one who seemed to have gone into a trance, made a low rumbling sound far back in his throat.

I'd like to get out of here, Sean thought.

Somehow. Any way at all.

Just let it be right now.

He smiled again, the widest smile he could manage. "I know you can't understand a thing that I'm saying, but I'm saying it calmly and reasonably. I'm not here to cause any trouble. I'm simply a visitor. My name is Sean Gabrielson and I'm twenty-three years old and I have a degree in physics from Cal Tech, and I mean to keep right on speaking quietly and reasonably to you until you decide that I'm no threat. I'm also willing to sing anything you request. I can do some nice old rock numbers, I know a couple of hymns, I can do patriotic songs. And I can keep it up until the next shunt comes and gets me, if I have to. Just stand there and listen peacefully, okay?" He started in on "Rock of Ages." They all looked almost hypnotized now. Eyes wide, staring. They didn't know what to make of him. "I can tell you all sorts of useful things, too. For example, I can advise you to start thinking about migrating north, because these animals here that you hunt are going to clear out of this territory in another few hundred years, once things start getting really warm and dry, and—"

They were looking at him in what looked like awe. Maybe they're beginning to think I'm a god, he thought. Or maybe they just love the sound of my voice.

"You see, this is the late Pleistocene, but eventually this is going to be known as the state of Arizona, and I can prophesy that there's going to be a freeway right down the middle of this valley, running from Flagstaff down to Phoenix or Tucson—"

They were down on their knees. Yes. Worshipping me, Sean thought. He grinned. They *do* think I'm a god. Unless they're just begging me to stop talking and start singing again.

Old Man River, that Old Man River . . .

This is going to be fun, he told himself.

Then he felt the displacement force tugging at him.

Not now, he thought in annoyance. Not just when it's getting good! But there was nothing he could do about it. The force had pulled him away from Quintu-Leela and now it was yanking him away from his first good shot at being a god, or at least being a star singer. One moment he was staring at a bunch of awed prehistoric bison hunters, and the next he was floating in a globe of green light, somewhere very far away.

So long, fellows. Onward to—what?

This was serious future now, a truly heavy distance. He was 95,129 years down the line, an enormous jump. His last forward swing had taken him a mere 951 years ahead. Even that world, Quintu-Leela's world of A.D. 2967, was utterly unlike anything he knew or could understand. That was how vast the changes had been between his own time and Quintu-Leela's.

Now he was a hundred times as far from Time Zero. 95,129 years! The transformations in human life during such an immense span must have been incredible. It had taken only five thousand years to go from the first civilizations in Egypt and Mesopotamia to the age of travel through time and space. Now he had covered twenty times as many years. Did the human race even exist any more? Or had it evolved into something unimaginably strange?

Where was he? What was this globe of green light? What was going to happen to him?

Many questions, no answers.

Then a deep gentle voice said, "Hey, it's good to see you again, Sean. Been a long time, boy."

A very familiar voice. His grandfather's voice, rich and warm. Grandpa Gabrielson who lived in San Diego.

Sean blinked into the greenness. "Is that you, Grandpa?"

"Who else, boy?"

Unmistakable, that voice. The voice of the wise, loving old man who had spent so many holiday weekends with them, who liked to tell all those stories of the first television sets, the first jet planes, the first trip to the moon, the first flights of the space shuttle. Grandpa Gabrielson had worked as an engineer for the Apollo space program when he was a young man, and later he had been involved in the shuttle project. He had seen the whole modern world take shape in his lifetime.

But Grandpa Gabrielson had no business being here in the 932nd century. Grandpa Gabrielson had lived to a good old age, well past eighty. But he had died last year, just before Sean and Eric had been chosen for Project Pendulum.

"I'm here too, son. It really *has* been a long time!"

His grandmother's voice. She had died when he was ten. And then his father was in the green globe with him, clapping him on the back, laughing, asking him if he was managing to keep up with the baseball scores while he was shunting around. And his mother, glowing with pride. And his mother's parents, Grandfather and Grandmother Weiss. He hardly knew them, because they lived in Belgium.

And Eric was there also.

It was Thanksgiving Day, and there was a huge turkey on the table, and mounds of cranberry sauce, and mountains of candied yams and turkey stuffing and everything else, and the whole family was there. His father was busy carving, as he always did. And he and Eric were side by side for the first time in 95,129 years.

Sean looked at his brother. He could feel the strange force, the brother-force, that had bound him to his twin all his life. The force which he had not felt since the moment they had gone their separate ways at Time Zero on the shunt platform.

"Are you really here?" he asked.

Eric grinned. "What do you think? That I'm just some sleazy illusion?"

"But this can't be happening," Sean said. "Thanksgiving Day in the year 95,129? Grandpa and Grandma here? Mom and Dad? No. I'm in some kind of green globe and this is just some hallucination that who knows what kind of creatures are pulling out of the memories they find in my brain. Right? Right?"

Eric gave him a pitying look. "You must have lost your mind. Or misplaced it, at the very least. I'm as real as you are, and probably a lot hungrier. Shut up and pass the turkey, turkey!"

23.

Eric
$+ 5 \times 10^{11}$ minutes

Scrambling down an icy hillside through a blinding snowstorm was bad enough. But every breath was agony. Breathing this fierce Fourth Ice Age atmosphere was like inhaling icicles. And to have a pack of angry Neanderthals coming after him, besides–

Eric felt the shunt take him and sweep him mercifully into some far-off warmer place. He landed on all fours, gasping and coughing, and crouched there a moment until he had recovered. At last he looked up.

A Neanderthal face was looking back at him. Sloping forehead, rounded chin, broad nose, mouth like a jutting muzzle. Shrewd dark eyes studying him intently.

"Huh? Did I bring you along with me somehow?"

The Neanderthal knelt beside him and said something in an unknown language. His voice was deep and the way he spoke seemed oddly musical, though very strange. He didn't seem hostile. Behind him, Eric saw softly rounded green hills, a wide valley broken by a chain of lakes, a forest in the distance.

There were prehistoric hominids wandering about wherever he looked.

He had landed in a group of ten or fifteen Neanderthals. Off to his left a hundred yards away were some slender little creatures looking a bit like apes but walking confidently upright. Eric recognized them as australopithecines from the early Pleistocene, creatures that occupied a place somewhere midway on the evolutionary path that had led to *Homo sapiens.* And over there, that awesome monster of an ape, as massive as a grizzly bear? Wasn't that Gigantopithecus, from a million years B.C.? And those, in the middle distance? Sturdy-looking people who seemed almost human but for their strangely apelike faces: could those be *Homo erectus,* the ancestors of mankind whose fossil remains had been found in Java and China?

And those–

And those–

And those–

Wherever he looked, some not-quite-human creatures could be seen in the valley. The whole history of the evolution of humanity seemed to be here, all the extinct forms that he had studied in school and a good many that he was unable to identify at all.

What was this place? Unless he had lost count of the shunts, he was at the plus-500-billion-minute level now. 951,000 years in the future. What were all these creatures doing here, all wandering around at random like this?

"You have just arrived, I suppose?" a pleasant voice said behind him. Eric whirled. The speaker was a bearded man of about fifty, elegant and amiable-looking, wearing what looked like riding clothes of the late eighteenth or early nineteenth century. He might have been some English gentleman out for a stroll in the woods. "Bathurst," he said. "Benjamin Bathurst. Former Minister Plenipotentiary of His

Britannic Majesty George III to the court of Franz I, Emperor of Austria. Of course, I'm nothing very much any more."

"Eric Gabrielson," Eric said shakily. "From Los Angeles, California, the—the United States."

"Very pleased to make your acquaintance," Bathurst said. "Always charming to see another human face. There are forty of us now, I think. Of course, we're greatly outnumbered by the apes, but everyone's friendly enough. You're a million years in the future, you know. The United States, you say? Of America? The former Colonies? California was never one of the Colonies, as I recall. But I suppose—"

"We got it from Mexico," Eric said. "Somewhere around 1849. And yes, I know we're a million years in the future. Approximately. But you—George III—"

He was having trouble speaking clearly. An overdose of confusion was making his voice husky. The Neanderthal, muttering to himself, began to fondle Bathurst's intricately carved walking stick. The Englishman smiled and gently drew it away.

"What year are you from?" he asked Eric.

"2016 is when I set out from."

"Ah. 2016. The fabulous future, indeed. Well, well, we will have much to talk about, then. No one else here comes from any year later than 1853, I believe. Most are much earlier. We have a Roman couple, do you know, and several Greeks, and an Egyptian or two. And some who speak no language any of us can fathom. They must be quite ancient. I myself was seized in 1809."

"Seized?"

"Oh, yes, of course, boy! How did you think we all got here?"

Eric moistened his lips. "I'm here as a result of an experiment in travel through time carried out at the California Institute of Technology," he said. "But you—"

Bathurst shrugged. "A victim of kidnapping. Forced transport. Seized unawares. The same fate that has befallen all the creatures here, both human and otherwise. Except you, it would seem, if you indeed have come voluntarily. The rest of us are captives. It is a very comfortable captivity, I must say, but it is captivity all the same. And it is imprisonment for life, I grieve to say. Yet it is a very comfortable imprisonment, for all that."

Kidnapped from 1809? Romans? Greeks? Neanderthals? Australopithecines?

"But who—who—"

"Who is responsible for bringing us here, you mean to ask? Why, the demigods who inhabit this distant eon, boy! Our own remote descendants! Perhaps you'll meet them someday. I myself have seen them on three occasions thus far. Quite remarkable, you'll find. True demigods, as far beyond us as we are beyond these shaggy apelike fellows here. We've been collected, do you see? All manner of historical specimens, and prehistorical specimens too, I dare say. It's a kind of zoological garden here. An exhibit, do you see, of the people of ages gone by, collected by mysterious magical means from every era of antiquity. I'm one of the items on display, boy, for the amusement and edification of our remote descendants. And now so are you, do you see? So are you."

24.

Sean
-5×10^{11} minutes

He was almost coming to believe that it was real. The tender succulent turkey meat, the sweet rich cranberry sauce, the hot steaming rolls–it was all so much like the family feasts of his boyhood that after a while he simply accepted it and let it engulf him like a warm bath. Mom, Dad, his grandparents, Eric–

But then it all turned misty and insubstantial. He had a final glimpse of the sphere of green light once again, and he thought he saw a row of faces behind the light, faces that might have been human and might have been something else. Then everything went black and the shunt took him and swept him away.

He was in heavy jungle terrain now. The air was thick and close, the trees were tall and slender and set close together with their crowns meeting overhead to form a canopy. Here and there, through a break in the foliage, he saw pale sugarloaf-shaped mountains on the horizon. This, he knew, was the world of 951,293 years before Time Zero.

And there was the biggest gorilla anyone had ever seen, standing twenty feet in front of him.

Actually he doubted that it was a gorilla. Perhaps it was more like an orangutan, with that deep chest and short neck. Or something midway between the two. But it was colossal. It was supporting itself on all fours, but he suspected that when it stood upright it would be close to nine feet tall.

It was watching him with a who-the-devil-are-*you?* look in its beady yellow eyes, and it was making a low growling sound, very ominous. Gorillas and orangutans, Sean told himself, eat fruits and vegetables. This guy doesn't look like a hunter to me. But he's big. Very big. And not friendly looking. Absolutely not friendly. And I'm on his personal turf, and he doesn't like it.

"Listen," Sean said, "I don't want you to get annoyed about anything, okay? Just as I was telling those Indians a little while ago, it's not my plan to bother you in the slightest. I'm only a visitor here. I'm simply passing through, and I'm not going to be here very long, let me assure you of that."

The giant ape appeared to frown. It seemed to consider what Sean was telling it.

It didn't seem to like what it had heard, though.

It began to snort and growl. It raised itself to its full unbelievable height and pounded itself on its chest like King Kong in a feisty mood. It made unmistakably angry sounds. Sean wondered if it was going to charge him. He wasn't sure. The ape didn't seem quite sure, either. For a long moment it rocked back and forth in place, growling, beating its chest, glaring at the intruder.

Then it leaned forward on its knuckles and made a different sound, deep and ominous.

Yes, Sean thought. It *is* going to charge. It very definitely is going to charge.

And I'm going to die, back here in the umptieth century B.C.

Or else I'll get shunted out of here in the nick of time and it's Eric who'll die when he shows up right in front of a crazed charging ape. It's just as bad either way.

Damn! Damn! *Damn!*

25.

Eric
-5×10^{12} minutes

The shunts were coming too fast, too close together. Eric was drowning in a torrent of wonders. To be given a glimpse of Neanderthals in their own time, chanting by their own campfire, and then to be swept far onward to a magical place where pithecanthropi and australopithecines and Romans and Greeks and nineteenth-century Englishmen lived all jumbled together in some kind of far-future zoo, and to be pulled away from that much too soon, before he had even begun to learn the things he wanted to know—

And now this. Nine and a half million years in the past. Paradise for the sort of dreamer who once built fossil dinosaurs out of papier-mâché. Not that there were any dinosaurs here, of course. Not in the Pliocene period, no. Dinosaurs were much earlier than that: this was mammal time, here. But, dinosaurs or no, he had been let loose in a garden of zoological wonders and he would gladly have spent a year here, five years, ten. There was so much to see. Paleozoology wasn't even his field—he barely knew the names of half the creatures who were parading before his astounded eyes—and even so he would have given anything to be allowed to remain.

Another month—another week—

But he knew that the irresistible force of the shunt soon would surround him and tear him free of this place and sweep him onward.

That giant piglike thing with the fantastic bristly face and the terrifying teeth, a creature bigger than any rhinoceros, snorting and snuffling in the underbrush—

That hairy elephant with the short trunk and the long outthrust jaw, and the second pair of tusks jutting down over the other ones—

That skittish yellow animal with a camel's silly face and a gazelle's agile body, running in frantic herds across the plains—

That one that had a camel's body and a camel's head, but a neck like a giraffe's, reaching up easily to graze on treetops close to twenty-five feet high—

The deer with its horns on its nose, and the one with fangs like a tiger's, and the one whose head was all knobs and crests and other strangenesses—

The giant ground sloth with the long weird drooping snout, almost like a little trunk—

The armadillo as big as a tank, angrily lashing its spiked tail against the ground—

Dream-animals. Nightmare-animals. They were everywhere on this wondrous plain, grazing, creeping, crawling, climbing, hunting, sleeping. He wanted to see every one, to commit them all to memory, to come home with mind-pictures of this Pliocene wonderland that would keep paleozoologists busy for decades. Unique discoveries, animals unknown to science. But already he felt the force tugging at him.

No–wait–

Another day, he begged. Half a day. Another three hours.

No chance. The equations were inexorable. Forces had to balance.

Now–now–onward–

26.

Sean
+ 5×10^{12} minutes

He was five trillion minutes from home and the giant ape was no longer his immediate problem. Because the pendulum had swung and the iron fist of the displacement force had grabbed him and converted him into a shower of tachyons and sent him rocketing off toward the other end of time. So it was Eric who was destined to show up right in the path of the ape's charge, when they started down the homeward slope of the voyage.

I have to do something to warn him, Sean thought. But what?

He looked around. He was standing in a fragrant bower of blossoming plants that sprouted on shining crystalline stalks three feet high, plants that looked like nothing he had ever seen before. And a great blue world was shining overhead like a dazzling beacon, filling half the sky.

It looked a little like the Earth, that huge world floating up there. There was one great bulging land mass that was very much like Africa, though it seemed too far to the south, and he couldn't find Europe where it ought to be, only a broad ocean occupying what might have been the place of the Mediterranean Sea. To the west Sean could make out something similar to the curve of North America's eastern seaboard, though the shape wasn't a perfect match with what he remembered, and the West Indies weren't there. Far down to the side was an enormous round hump of an island, vaguely in the position that South America once had had.

If that was Earth, then, that loomed above him in the sky, it was an Earth vastly transformed.

Earth? Up there in the sky? Then where was he? On the moon?

A garden of fragrant green and gold flowers rising on stalks of crystal–on the moon?

Flowers on the moon? Sweet fresh air on the moon?

Nine and a half million years. Anything was possible.

He took a few steps. The pull of gravity seemed normal enough. It should feel almost like floating, he knew, to walk on the moon. Unless they had changed that, too. If they could give the moon an atmosphere and make gardens grow on it, they could give it Earth-like gravitation also.

Should the Earth look this close, though? He wasn't sure. He wished his astronomy was a little sharper. And his knowledge of geology, too. He knew that the continents drifted around, over the course of many millions of years, but could they have rearranged themselves so drastically in just nine and a half million? Eric would know, of course. But Eric wasn't here.

The people of this era, Sean decided, can do anything they feel like doing. They can move the moon closer to the Earth. They can move South America farther from North America. Anything. Anything.

An age of miracles is what it must be.

He felt like an apeman suddenly swept millions of years forward into a world of telephones, television, computers, spaceships. Miracles. Miracles everywhere. And that was really what he was, he knew: a primitive creature, a prehistoric ape, a hairy shambling ancient man who needed to shave his face every day and who still carried an appendix around in his belly. How they must pity him, the unseen watchers who—he was entirely sure—were studying him now! Were they human at all? Did the human race still exist? Or had it died out long ago, and given way to some race of superbeings?

He reached down and let his fingers caress one of the lovely crystalline flowers.

It wriggled with pleasure like a cat being stroked, and began to sing, a slow, sinuous, sensuous melody. Immediately the others nearby started to preen and sway as if trying to get Sean's attention. *Touch me,* they were telling him. *Touch me, touch me, touch me! Make me sing!*

He was reminded of the garden of talking flowers that Alice had found in Looking-Glass Land: the vain and haughty Tiger-lily, and Rose, and Violet. How many times had he read that book, he and Eric! Eric had always liked Wonderland better; Sean had preferred the world beyond the looking-glass. And now here he was in Looking-Glass Land himself, where the flowers sang, and the blue Earth hung in the sky instead of the moon.

"You like that, do you?" he asked the flowers.

And he stroked this one and that, reaching out toward them, going on down the garden row until hundreds of them were swaying and singing. The sweetness of their song was dreamlike on the thick perfumed air. He had never heard anything so beautiful.

A great strange peace came over him. He felt a Presence in his spirit. Something magical, something almost divine. Slowly he walked between the rows of flowers, savoring the mild night air, pausing often to stare up at the blue world that seemed so close overhead. It was an overwhelming privilege, being here in this place so many millions of years beyond his own time. He knew he would never see more of it than this garden, and that he would never understand any of it at all, but none of that mattered. He was here. He had been touched by Something that was as far beyond him as he was beyond the apes of the forests of humanity's dawn. Something magnificent. Something all-powerful. And yet, small as he was, splendid and mighty as It was, he felt a kinship with It. He was part of It; It was a part of him.

Then he thought of Eric, and the snarling, roaring, maddened giant ape that he was fated to meet head-on when it was his turn to arrive back there in that prehistoric jungle. And his mood of harmony and tranquility shattered.

At once the flowers began to sing a soothing song. He stared at them a long while, not soothed, brooding about his brother. That ape looked really murderous. What if he kills Ricky, Sean thought? What happens to the experiment? What happens to the world? What happens to *me*? It was the big risk that they had all tried to make believe would not be a factor. But Sean had seen the look in that ape's eye.

If only I could warn him, he thought. But how? How?

To the flowers he said, "I have to save my brother."

They made a gentle humming sound.

He sat quietly, staring at a smooth flat white rock, like a gleaming slab of marble, just in front of him in the garden.

An idea came to him.

"Forgive me," he said. "I've got to mess up this beautiful place a little. But it may be that the whole structure of the past and the future depends on it."

He took out his laser and turned it to high beam. And began to write, carving a message on that flawless stone slab in ugly black charred letters.

As concisely as he could, he told his brother when and where the ape was waiting for him in the time stream. And suggested in the strongest possible way that he had better have his anesthetic dart gun primed and ready the moment he arrived.

"Do you think that'll do it?" he asked the flowers. "Will he turn up here in this exact spot? Will he see the message? Will he be able to nail the ape in time?"

The flowers were singing again. Soothing, comforting sounds. Everything will be all right, they were saying. Everything will be fine.

I hope that's true, Sean thought, trying to relax.

Gradually the magic returned. This was too beautiful a place to be tangled up in fears and fretfulness for long.

He felt that celestial harmony again. He felt that peace, he felt that Presence.

Then the flowers fell silent. He stared up at the shining Earth with trembling wonder.

27.

Eric
+ 5×10^{13} minutes

Onward–

–onward, unimaginably far–

He hovered in space, midway between somewhere and anywhere. There was golden light all about him. Comets left dazzling trails in the void. Suns whirled and danced. He filled his hands with the stuff of space, warm and soft.

He felt like a god.

He *was* a god.

This was Time Ultimate. The power of the singularities that had propelled him through time reached its limit here. The world he knew lay 95 million years behind him. Here in this realm of light everything was utterly strange. He was drifting among the stars, far from Earth. Earth? He could barely remember Earth. He could barely remember himself, who he was, why and how he had come here. So far away now, so faint in his mind. All that noisy striving, all that energy, all that restless seeking. The boiling cauldron that had been Earth and its billions of people.

He knew that they had found whatever it was they had

been seeking, those restless questing people, back in that time when Earth still was. They had gained their answers long ago and they had become like gods. And Earth was gone now, and they were gone with it, gone forth into the universe, into this shining kingdom.

They had touched the stars, and the stars had accepted them into their company. As they would accept him, pilgrim out of time that he was.

How can it be, he wondered, that I'm out here in space and still able to breathe?

And a quiet voice out of nowhere said, *While you are here, you will be as we are. And when you leave we will restore you to what you were.*

Who are you, he asked? Where are you? What are you?

We are everyone. And we are everywhere. We are those for whom you prepared the way. And we protect you now and cherish you and welcome you among us.

I see, Eric said, and almost thought he did.

His long journey now seemed almost like a dream. Fragments of strange scenes floated through his mind: endlessly branching tunnels through which strange silent creatures marched, and a boy coming out of a small house on an earthquake-jumbled street, and vines flourishing in tropical heat, and squat shaggy creatures gathered around a fire in a cave on a snowy hillside, and giant redwood trees rising like the columns of a cathedral, and an Englishman in riding clothes pointing to a hominid ape that had been extinct four million years, and a camel with the neck of a giraffe, and more, much more. A torrent of images. He had made a voyage beyond all belief; and it was not over yet, for soon the pendulum would be carrying him back down the eons, taking him to new wonders as he descended through time. But that was yet to come. He was here now, in the great stillness of the world beyond the world, dwelling among people who had touched the stars.

He, too, could touch the stars. He could reach out and embrace them and engulf them, and be engulfed by them. Here blazed a blue star, and here a white one, and here a giant red one in the forehead of the night, and he touched them all. And felt the throbbing weight of the billions of years of Creation upon him. And heard the soaring song of those who had gone forth before him into this realm of light. And drifted on the bosom of the firmament. And gave thanks. And joined in that great song.

28.

Sean
-5×10^{13} minutes

There were dinosaurs all over the place. You walked around a bush and there was a dragon the size of a school bus eating its breakfast. You came over a hill and there was something that looked like an armored tank taking its babies for a stroll. You looked up and a flotilla of pterodactyls went zooming by, flapping their long leathery wings.

It was a real zoo here. A Cretaceous zoo, fantastic monsters lumbering around everywhere. You had to look lively to keep from getting trampled on, of course. And there was always that itchy feeling between your shoulder blades that made you think a tyrannosaurus was coming up behind you, thinking about a snack.

The air was hot and dank. Gigantic ferns, big as palm trees, formed dark close forests. Dragonflies the size of hawks fluttered around terrifyingly, buzzing and droning.

"Ricky?" Sean said out loud. "Ricky, you ought to see this! Man, you'd go *crazy*! This stuff is really wasted on me. But you, you old dinosaur freak—"

Well, Eric would be seeing all this soon enough, he knew. Unless something had happened to him during his zigzag voyage across the immensity of time. Sean didn't want to think about that possibility. Eric was all right. Eric *had* to be all right. And he'd be showing up here in a little while so that they could begin the homeward leg of their incredible journey.

This was Time Ultimate, the farthest swing of the pendulum. They had gone as far as they could go.

Right now Eric was somewhere out in the unthinkably remote future, 95 million years on the other side of Time Zero. And he, Sean, was here in the Cretaceous period, with a triceratops family grazing at the edge of the marsh and something that looked like a brontosaurus, but probably wasn't, rearing its snaky head high over the surface of the lake down there. But at any moment the force of the pendulum would be fully extended and he and Eric would start their downward swing, back toward Time Zero and the scientists waiting for them in the laboratory.

Sean had a pretty good idea of what it would be like. For an instant, time would seem to stand still. Then there would be a breathtaking plunge across the whole span of the displacement as he and Eric changed places. Eric would land here, among his beloved dinosaurs, and Sean would go swinging outward into whatever unimaginable place the world of A.D. 95 million might be.

And then from there, it would be down the line for them. He would shoot into the world of nine and a half million years ago, and then to the one of 951,000 years in the future, and then to 95,000 years in the past, and so on all the way back, changing places with Eric at each level, one brother replacing the other without an instant of transition.

So Eric would visit the garden of miracles on the moon, Eric would have to cope with the charging giant ape, Eric would turn up at the Thanksgiving dinner that never was. Eric would have to deal with those bison-hunters back in Arizona. Eric would take his place in Quintu-Leela's arms and probably he too would be swept off into time too fast for it to matter. Eric would cheer at President Harding's inauguration parade. Eric would show up for the tail end of his own parade in Glendora.

And meanwhile–

Sean stood leaning against a tree fern that was four times his own height, watching the parade of giant reptiles, and thinking of everything that had befallen him on this whirlwind trip through past and future. The world would never be the same, now that the gates of time stood wide open. And neither would he. His mind was full of such strangenesses as no other mortal being had ever experienced. None except Eric, at any rate.

Sean wondered what was in store for him in all those eras where Eric had already been.

Perils, thrills, bewilderments galore–no doubt of that. And perhaps some burst of sudden ecstasy to match or even surpass that mystical moment among the singing flowers that glowed by the light of the full Earth in the sky.

He'd know, soon enough. He could feel the force tugging at him now, starting to take him onward.

He smiled. He slapped the tree fern fondly, as if saying goodbye to an old friend, and went strolling down toward the lake. His boots made sucking noises. It was all wet, spongy swampland here. The dinosaurs all around him snorted and mooed and grunted as they went about their business.

They didn't know what he was, and they didn't care. They were lords of the world and they could look forward to millions of years more of snorting and mooing and grunting in this warm, leafy kingdom of theirs. Eric was going to have the time of his life when he got here. How he would hate it, when the force pulled him away. As it was pulling Sean, now.

The pull was getting stronger.

So long, triceratops. So long, pterodactyls. So long, whatever-you-are with the spikes on your back. I'm moving along. But Eric's coming to take my place. He's okay, Ricky is. You and he will get along pretty well.

Going away, now. Moving up and out. Heading for the downswing, starting the journey back, everything running in reverse.

Until at last it all came winding down to the starting point, and he and Eric would step off the shunt platform in the very moment of their departures. Or so it would seem to everyone else. But the strangeness wouldn't end there. Five minutes later, $Sean_2$, would materialize in that lab, and $Eric_2$ also. And again, eight hours after that. And again in three days. And again and again and again, throughout all the rest of their lives and far beyond. He and Ricky were destined to appear like comets, he knew, showing up at fixed intervals across the 95 million years that followed Time Zero. While at the same time they would be trying to live their ordinary lives through to their normal spans, doing whatever it was that they were destined to do until the time came to grow old and die. With 95 million years of life still waiting for them.

That was going to be really strange. To know in 2025 that yourself of nine and a half years earlier was going to show up out of time. And then ninety-five years later to have it happen again, if they were lucky enough to live to that kind of an age—and probably many people would, by then—

Going away now. Time to be starting for home, by way of the year A.D. 95 million.

Sean saw the dinosaurs fade and grow misty.

Time seemed to stand still for a billion billion years. The pendulum had reached the balance point.

And he saw Ricky.

His twin brother hovered in the air just in front of him, shimmering like a vision. Sean realized that he was probably shimmering just the same way. This was the moment of turnaround, when all the forces were equaling out, and it was like no other moment in the trip.

"Ricky?" he said. "Ricky, can you hear me?"

Sean saw his brother's lips move. He was saying something, asking something. But he was unable to hear Ricky's voice. They were still cut off from each other by the barrier of time. And yet not really cut off, for he could look straight into his brother's eyes. He knew now that Ricky had come through everything okay. And that they were going to make it back to the starting point at Time Zero, too.

And he saw the look of wonder shining in Ricky's eyes.

He has seen miracles, Sean thought. Different miracles from the ones I've seen, but miracles all the same. The ones that I'm heading for now.

"Ricky?" Sean said again. "Hey, Ricky. Look! Here come your dinosaurs, man! Here come your dinosaurs at last!"

He waved and smiled. And Eric smiled and waved back at him.

"See you back at Time Zero!" Sean called. "And watch out for that oversized monkey!" But he knew that the ape wasn't going to be a problem. Ricky would see the message in the garden on the moon. Ricky would be quick on the draw with the anesthetic darts. His shimmering presence here left Sean with no doubts that the experiment was going to go successfully right to the end.

Eric was vanishing now. Growing faint, growing insubstantial.

No, Sean thought. I'm the one who's vanishing. He's coming, I'm going. So long, dinosaurs! Here I go!

The moment at the balance point was over. The pendulum was moving again. Carrying him off into the mists of time to come.

Sean didn't want the voyage ever to end, not really. But at the same time he knew that he did. So that he could get back to Time Zero, and Eric. To tell him about everything he had seen. And to hear about what had happened to him. He needed to share every detail of the voyage, and he knew that Ricky did, too. No one else could possibly understand.

They were going to have plenty to tell each other, Sean knew. Enough to last them for the rest of their lives.

THE TIME HOPPERS

One can conceive of Heaven having a Telephone Directory, but it would have to be gigantic, for it would include the Proper Name and address of every electron in the universe. But Hell could not have one, for in Hell, as in prison and the army, its inhabitants are identified not by name but by number. They do not *have* numbers, they *are* numbers.

—W. H. Auden, *Infernal Science*

That Time should be a length travelled over is, all said and done, a rather elaborate conception; yet that this is the way we do habitually think of Time is agreed to by everyone, both educated and—which is much more curious—uneducated . . . How did we arrive at this remarkable piece of knowledge?

—J. W. Dunne, *An Experiment with Time*

1.

There was a beauty in the crowded world, so they said. The crystalline city towers in serried ranks assembled, the patterned rhythms of a surging mob at a quickboat ramp, the dance of sunlight on a million iridescent tunics in one of the great plazas—in such things, the esthetes said, was the abode of beauty.

Quellen was no esthete. He was a minor bureaucrat, a humble civil servant of decent intelligence and normal proclivities. He looked at the world as it presented itself in A.D. 2490, and found it hellish. Quellen was unable to perform the intricate inner dance by which hideous overcrowding could be written off as modern beauty. He hated it. If he had been Class One or even Class Two, Quellen might have been in a better position to appreciate the new esthetics, because he would not have been required to live right in the middle of them. But Quellen was Class Seven. The world does not look quite the same to a man in Class Seven as it does to a man in Class Two.

And yet, all things considered, Quellen was not too

badly off. He had his comforts. Illegal comforts, true, obtained by bribery and cajolery. Strictly speaking, what Quellen had done was shameful, for he had taken possession of that to which he was not entitled. He had pocketed a private corner of the world, just as though he were a member of the High Government—that is to say, Class One or Class Two. Since Quellen had none of the responsibilities of the High Government, he deserved none of the privileges.

He had taken those privileges though. It was wrong, criminal, a betrayal of integrity. But a man is entitled to a fatal flaw of character somewhere. Like everyone else, Quellen had begun with high dreams of rectitude. Like nearly everyone else, he had learned to abandon them.

Pong.

That was the warning bell. Someone wanted him, back in the miserable warrens of Appalachia. Quellen left the bell alone. He was in a tranquil mood, and he didn't care to puncture it simply to answer the bell.

Pong. Pong. Pong.

It was not an insistent sound, merely an obtrusive one, low and mellow, the sound of a bronze dish struck with a felt-covered hammer. Quellen, ignoring the sound, continued to rock uneasily back and forth in his pneumochair, watching the sleepy crocodiles paddling gently through the murky waters of the stream that ran below his porch. *Pong. Pong.* After a while the bell stopped ringing. He sat there, joyously passive, sensing about him the warm smell of green growing things and the buzzing insect noises in the air.

That was the only part of Eden that Quellen did not like, the constant hum of the ugly insects that whizzed through the calm, muggy air. In a way they represented an invasion; they were symbols to him of the life he had led before moving up to Class Seven. The noise in the air then had been the steady buzz of people, people swarming around in a vast

hive of a city, and Quellen detested that. There were no real insects in Appalachia, of course. Merely that symbolic buzz.

He stood and walked to the rail, looking out over the water. He was a man just short of middle years and just above middle height, leaner than he once had been, with unruly brown hair, a wide, sweat-flecked forehead, and mild eyes of a shade not quite green and not quite blue. His lips were thin and tautly compressed, giving him a look of determination instantly belied by a less than affirmative chin.

Idly he flipped a stone into the water. "Get it!" he called, as two crocs glided noiselessly toward the disturbance in hopes of nabbing a fat gobbet of meat. But the stone sank, sending up black bubbles, and the crocs bumped their pointed noses lightly together and drifted apart. Quellen smiled.

It was a good life here at the heart of darkness, here in tropical Africa. Insects and all, black mud and all, humid solitude and all. Even the fear of discovery was supportable.

Quellen rehearsed the catalog of his blessings. *Marok,* he thought? *No Marok here. No Koll, no Spanner, no Brogg, no Leeward. None of them. But especially no Marok. I miss him the least.*

What a relief it was to be able to stay out here and not suffer their buzzing voices, not shudder when they burst into his office! Of course, it was wanton and immoral of him to set up shop as an *übermensch* this way, a modern Raskolnikov transcending all laws. Quellen admitted that. Yet, he often told himself, life's journey was a trip he'd take only once, and at the end what would matter but that he had traveled First Class part of the way?

This was the only freedom, out here.

And being far from Marok, the hated roommate, was best of all. No more to worry over his piles of undone dishes, his heaps of books scattered all over the tiny room they shared, his dry, deep voice endlessly talking on the visiphone when Quellen was trying to concentrate.

No. No Marok here.

But yet, Quellen thought sadly, yet, the peace he had anticipated when he built his new home had somehow not materialized. That was the way of the world: satisfaction draining off into nowhere at the moment of attainment. For years he had waited with remarkable patience for the day he reached Class Seven and was entitled to live alone. That day had come; but it had not been enough. So he had purloined Africa for himself. And now that he had encompassed even that, life was simply one uneasy fear after another.

Restlessly, he shied another stone into the water.

Pong.

As he watched the concentric circles of ripples fanning out on the dark surface of the stream, Quellen became conscious again of the warning bell ringing again at the other end of the house. *Pong. Pong. Pong.* The uneasiness within him turned to sullen foreboding. He eased himself out of his chair and headed hurriedly toward the phone. *Pong.*

Quellen switched it on, leaving the vision off. It hadn't been easy to arrange things so that any calls coming to his home, back in Appalachia half a world away, were automatically relayed to him here.

"Quellen," he said, eyeing the gray blank screen.

"Koll speaking," came the crackling reply. "Couldn't reach you before. Why don't you turn on your visi, Quellen?"

"It's not working," Quellen said. He hoped sharp-nosed Koll, his immediate superior at the Secretariat of Crime, would not smell the lie in his voice.

"Get over here quickly, will you, Quellen? Spanner and I have something urgent to take up with you. Got it, Quellen?

Urgent. It's a High Government matter. They're treading us hard."

"Yes sir. Anything else, sir?"

"No. We'll fill in the details for you when you get here. Which will be at once." Koll decisively snapped the contact.

Quellen stared at the blank screen for a while, chewing at his lip. Terror clawed his soul. Was this it, the summons to headquarters to discuss his highly illegal, criminally selfish hideaway? Had the downfall come at last? No. No. They *couldn't* have found out. It was impossible. He had everything squared.

But, came Quellen's insistent thought, they must have discovered his secret. Why else would Koll send for him so urgently, with the whiplash tone in his voice? Quellen began to perspire despite the air conditioning, which kept away most of the fierce Congo heat.

They would put him back in Class Eight if they found out. Or, much more likely, they would bounce him all the way back to Twelve or Thirteen, and slap a perpetual hold on him. He would be doomed to spend the rest of his life in a tiny room inhabited by two or three other people, the biggest, smelliest, most unpleasant people the clicking computers could find for him.

Quellen calmed himself. Perhaps he was taking alarm for no reason. Koll had said it was High Government business, hadn't he? A directive from above, not any private arrest. When they really found him out, Quellen knew, they wouldn't simply summon him. They would *come* for him. So this was some affair of work. He had a momentary vision of the members of the High Government, shadowy demigods at least eleven feet high, pausing in their incomprehensible labors to drop a minislip memo down the chute to Koll.

Quellen took a long look at the green overhanging trees,

bowed under the weight of their leaves and glistening with the beaded drops of the morning's rain. He let his eyes rove regretfully over the two spacious rooms, his luxurious porch, the uncluttered view. Each time he left here, it was as though for the last time. For a moment, now that everything might well be just about lost, Quellen almost relished the buzzing of the flies. He gulped in a final sweeping look and stepped toward the stat. The purple field enveloped him. He was sucked into the machine.

Quellen was devoured. The hidden power generators of the stat were connected by direct link to the central generator that spun endlessly on its poles at the bottom of the Atlantic, condensing the theta force that made the stat travel possible. What was theta force? Quellen could not say. He could barely explain electricity, and that had been around for a longer time. He took it for granted and gave himself to the stat field. If someone had introduced a minor abscissa distortion, Quellen's atoms would be broadcast to the universe and never reassembled, but one did not think about such things.

The effect was instantaneous. The lean, lanky form of Quellen was shattered, a stream of tagged wavicles was relayed halfway across the planet, and Quellen was reconstituted. It happened so fast—molecule ripped from molecule in a fragment of a nanosecond—that his neural system could not pick up the pain of total dissolution. The restoration of life came just as swiftly.

One did not think about the realities of stat travel. One simply traveled. To do otherwise was to ask for the miseries.

Quellen emerged in the tiny apartment for Class Seven citizens of Appalachia that everyone thought he inhabited. Some messages awaited him. He glanced at them: they were advertising blares mainly, although a note told him that his sister Helaine had come calling. Quellen felt a twitch of guilt. Helaine and her husband were prolets of the prole, ground under by the harsh realities. He had often wished he could do something for them, since their unhappiness added prongs to his own sense of conscience. Yet what could he do? He preferred not to get involved.

In a series of swift motions he slipped out of his lounging clothes and into his crisp business uniform, and removed the *Privacy* radion from the door. Thus he transformed himself from Joe Quellen, owner of an illegal privacy-nest in the heart of an unreported reservation in Africa, into Joseph Quellen, CrimeSec, staunch defender of law and order. He left the house. The elevator tumbled him endless stories to the tenth-floor quickboat landing. Stat transmission within a city was technically impossible; more's the pity, Quellen felt.

A quickboat slid onto its ramp. Quellen joined the multitudes pressing into it. He felt the thrum of power as it moved outward. Aching humbly from fear, Quellen headed downtown to meet Koll.

The building of Secretariat of Crime was considered an architectural masterpiece, Quellen had been told. Eighty stories, topped by spiked towers, and the crimson curtain-walls were rough and sandy in texture, so that they sparkled like a beacon when illuminated. The building had roots; Quellen had never learned how many underlevels there were, and he suspected that no one really knew, save certain members of the High Government. Surely there were twenty levels of computer down there, and a crypt for dead storage below that, and a further eight levels of interrogation rooms even deeper. Of that much, Quellen had sure knowledge. Some said that there was another computer, forty levels thick, underneath the interrogation rooms, and there were those who maintained that this was the true computer, while the one above was only for decoration and camouflage. Perhaps. Quellen did not try to probe too deeply into such things. For all he knew, the High Government itself met in secret councils a hundred levels below street level in this very building. He kept his curiosity under check. He did not wish to invite the curiosity of others, and that meant placing a limit on his own.

Clerical workers nodded respectfully to Quellen as he passed between their close-packed rows. He smiled. He could afford to be gracious; here he had status, the *mana* of Class Seven. They were Fourteens, Fifteens, the boy emptying the disposal basket was probably a Twenty. To them, he was a lofty figure, virtually a confidant of High Government people, a personal associate of Danton and Kloofman themselves. All a matter of perspective, Quellen thought. Actually he had glimpsed Danton—or someone said to be Danton—only once. He had no real reason to think that Kloofman actually existed, though probably he did.

Clamping his hand vigorously on the doorknob, Quellen waited to be scanned. The door of the inner office opened. He entered and found unfriendly figures hunched at desks within. Little sharp-nosed Martin Koll, looking for all the world like some huge rodent, sat facing the door, sifting through a sheaf of minislips. Leon Spanner, Quellen's other boss, sat opposite him at the glistening table, his great bull neck hunching over still more memoranda. As Quellen came into the room, Koll reached to the wall with a quick nervous gesture and flipped up the oxy vent, admitting a supply for three.

"Took you long enough," Koll said, without looking up.

Quellen glowered at him. Koll was gray-haired, gray-faced, gray of soul. Quellen hated him. "Sorry," he said. "I had to change. I was off duty."

"Whatever we do won't alter anything," rumbled Spanner,

as if no one had entered and nothing had been said. "What's happened has happened, and nothing we do will have the slightest effect. Do you see? It makes me want to smash things! To pound and break!"

"Sit down, Quellen," Koll said offhandedly. He turned to Spanner, a big, beefy man with a furrowed forehead and thick features. "I thought we'd been through this all before," Koll said. "If we meddle it's going to mix up everything. With about five hundred years to cover, we'll scramble the whole framework. That much is clear."

Quellen silently breathed relief. Whatever it was they were concerned about, it wasn't his illegal African hideaway. From the way it sounded, they were talking about the time-hoppers. Good. He looked at his two superiors more carefully, now that his eyes were no longer blurred by fear and the anticipation of humiliating punishment. They had obviously been arguing quite a while, Koll and Spanner. Koll was the deep one, with his agile mind and nervous, birdlike energy. But Spanner had more power. They said he had connections in high places, even High places.

"All right, Koll," Spanner grunted. "I'll even grant that it will mix up the past. I'll concede that much."

"Well, that's something," the small man said.

"Don't interrupt me. I still think we've got to put a stop to it. We can't undo what's done, but we can cut it short this year. In fact, we must."

Koll glared balefully at Spanner. Quellen could see that his own presence was the only reason Koll was concealing the anger lying just behind his eyes. They would be spewing curses at one another if the underling Quellen did not happen to be in the room.

"Why, Spanner, why?" Koll demanded in what passed for measured tones. "If we keep the process going we maintain things as they are. Four thousand of them went in '86, nine thousand in '87, fifty thousand in '88. And when we get last year's figures, they'll be even higher. Look—here it says that over a million hoppers arrived in the first eighty years, and after that the figures kept rising. Think of the population we're losing! It's wonderful! We can't *afford* to let these people stay here, when we have a chance to get rid of them. And when history says that we did get rid of them."

"History also says that they stopped going back to the past after 2491. Which means that we caught them next year," Spanner said. "I mean, that we *will* catch them next year. It's ordained. We've got no choice but to obey. The past's a closed book."

"Is it?" Koll laughed; it was almost a bark. "What if we don't solve it? What if the hoppers keep on going back?"

"It didn't happen that way, though. We *know* it. All the hoppers who reached the past came from the years 2486 to 2491. That's a matter of record," said Spanner doggedly.

"Records can be falsified."

"The High Government wants this traffic stopped. Why must I argue with you, Koll? You want to defy history, that's your business, but defying Them as well? No. We don't have that option."

"But to clear away millions of prolets—"

Spanner grunted and tightened his grasp on the minislips he was holding. Quellen, feeling like an intruder, let his eyes flick back from one man to the other.

"All right," Spanner said slowly. "I'll agree with you that it's nice to keep losing all those prolets. Even though on the face of things it appears that we won't go on losing them much longer. You say we have to let it keep going on, or else it'll alter the past. I take the opposite view. But let that pass. I won't argue the point, since you seem so positive. Furthermore, you think that it's a good thing to use this time-hopper business as a method of reducing population.

I'm with you on that too, Koll. I don't like overcrowding any more than you do, and I'll admit things have reached a ridiculous state nowadays. But consider: we're being hoodwinked. For someone to be running a time-travel business behind our backs is illegal and unethical and a lot of other things, and he ought to be stopped. What do you say, Quellen? Ultimately this is going to be the responsibility of your department, you know."

The sudden reference to him came as a jolt. Quellen was still struggling to get his bearings in this debate, and he was not entirely sure what they were talking about. He smiled weakly and shook his head.

"No opinion?" Koll asked abrasively.

Quellen looked at him. He was unable to stare straight into Koll's hard, colorless eyes, and so he let his gaze rest on the bureau manager's cheekbones instead. He remained silent.

"No opinion, Quellen? That's too bad indeed. It doesn't speak well of you."

Quellen repressed a shudder. "I'm afraid that I haven't been keeping up with the latest developments in the time-hopper case. As you know, I've been very busy on certain projects that–"

He let his voice trail off, feeling like a fool. His eager assistants probably knew all about this situation, he thought. He wondered why he had never bothered to check with Brogg. But how could he anticipate everything?

Koll said, "Are you aware that thousands of prolets have vanished into nowhere since the beginning of the year, Quellen?"

"No, sir. Ah, I mean, of course, sir. Certainly. It's just that we haven't really had a chance to take action on it," Quellen said.

The footling sound of his own voice appalled him. *Very*

lame, Quellen, very lame, he told himself. *Of course you don't know anything about it, when you spend all your free time in that pretty little hideaway across the ocean. But Stanley Brogg probably knows every detail. Brogg is very efficient.*

"Well, just where do you think they've gone?" Koll asked. "Maybe you think they've all hopped into stats and gone off somewhere to look for work? To Africa, maybe?"

The barb had poison on it. Quellen came close to gasping in shock before he could convince himself that Koll was stabbing in the dark. He hid his reaction as well as he could and replied evenly, "I have no idea, sir."

"You haven't been reading your history books very well, then, Quellen. Think, man: what was the most important historical development of the past five centuries?"

Quellen thought. What, indeed? The Entente? The coming of the High Government? The breakdown of the nations? The stat? He hated the way Koll could turn him into an idiotic schoolboy. Quellen knew he was no fool, however inane he might seem when hauled on the carpet. He was competent enough. But at the core of his being was his vulnerability, his hidden crime, and that meant he was jelly at the core. He began to sweat. He said, "I'm not sure how to evaluate that question, sir."

Koll casually flipped the oxy up a little higher, in an almost insulting gesture of friendliness. The sweet gas purred into the room. Softly Koll said, "I'll tell you, then. It's the arrival of the hoppers. And *this* is the era they're starting out from."

"Of course," Quellen said. Everyone knew about the hoppers, and he was annoyed with himself for not simply offering the obvious to Koll.

"Someone's developed time travel in the past few years," Spanner said. "He's beginning to siphon the time-hoppers back to the past. Thousands of unemployed prolets are gone already, and if we don't catch him soon he'll clutter up the past with every wandering workingman in the country."

"So? That's just my point," Koll said impatiently. "We know they've already arrived in the past; our history books say so. Now we can sit back and let this fellow distribute our refuse all over the previous five centuries."

Spanner swiveled round and confronted Quellen. "What do you think?" he demanded. "Should we follow the order of the High Government, round up this fellow, and stop the departure of the hoppers? Or should we do as Koll says and let everything go on, which defies not only Them but also incidentally the information of history?"

"I'll need time to study the case," Quellen said suspiciously. The last thing that he wanted to have happen to him was to be forced into making a judgement in favor of one superior over another.

"Let me show you your path right now," Spanner said, with a side glance at Koll. "We have our instructions from the High Government, and it's futile to debate them. As Koll here knows quite well, Kloofman himself has taken an interest in this case. Our task is to locate the illegal nexus of time-travel activity and bring it under official control. Koll, if you object, you'd better appeal to the High Government."

"No objections," said Koll. "Quellen?"

Quellen stiffened. "Yes, sir?"

"You heard Mr. Spanner. Get on it, fast. Track down this fellow who's shipping the hoppers and put him away, but not before you get his secret out of him. The High Government wants control of the process. And a halt to this illegal activity. It's all yours, Quellen."

He was dismissed.

2.

Norman Pomrath looked coldly at his wife and said, "When is your brother going to do something for us, Helaine?"

"I've told you. He can't."

"He won't, you mean."

"He *can't.* Who do you think he is, Danton? And will you please get out of my way? I need a shower."

"At least you said please," Pomrath grumbled. "I'm grateful for small mercies."

He stepped to one side. Out of some tatter of modesty he did not watch as his wife stripped off her green tunic. She crumpled the garment, tossed it aside, and got under the molecular bath. Since she stood with her back to him while she washed, he let himself watch her. Modesty was an important thing, Pomrath thought. Even when you've been married eleven years, you've got to give the other person some privacy in these stinking one-room lives. Otherwise you'll click your gyros. He gnawed a fingernail and stole furtive glances at his wife's lean buttocks.

The air in the Pomrath apartment was foul, but he didn't dare turn up the oxy. He had drawn this week's supply, and if he nudged the stud, the utility computer somewhere in the bowels of the earth would say unpleasant things to him. Pomrath didn't think his nerves could stand much garbage from a utility computer just now. His nerves couldn't stand much of anything. He was Class Fourteen, which was bad enough, and he hadn't had any work in three months, which was worse, and he had a brother-in-law in Class Seven, which really cut into him. What good did Joe Quellen do him though? The damned guy was never around. Ducking out on his family responsibilities.

Helaine was finished with her shower. The molecular bath used no water; only Class Ten and up was entitled to use water for purposes of bodily cleaning. Since most people in the world were Class Eleven and down, the planet would stink halfway across the universe but for the handy molecular baths. You stripped down, stood in front of the nozzle, and ultrasonic waves cunningly separated the grime from your skin and gave you the illusion of being clean. Pomrath did not bother to avert his eyes as Helaine's nude white form crossed in front of him. She wriggled into her tunic. Once, he remembered, he had thought she was voluptuous. He had been much younger then. Later, it had seemed to him that she had begun to lose weight. Now she was thin. There were times—especially at night—when she hardly looked female to him.

He slid down into the webfoam cradle along one windowless wall and said, "When do the kids get home?"

"Fifteen minutes. That's why I showered now. Are you staying here, Norm?"

"I'm going out in five minutes."

"To the sniffer palace?"

He scowled at her. His face, creased and pleated by

defeat, was well designed for scowling. “No,” he said, “not to the sniffer palace. To the job machine.”

“But you know the job machine will contact you here if there’s any work, so—”

“I want to go to *it*,” Pomrath said with icy dignity. “I do not want it to come to *me*. I will go to the job machine. And then, most likely to the sniffer palace afterward. Perhaps to celebrate and perhaps to drown my sorrow.”

“I knew it.”

“Damn you, Helaine, why don’t you get off me? Is it my fault I’m between jobs? I rank high in skills. I ought to be working. But there’s a cosmic injustice in the universe that keeps me unemployed.”

She laughed harshly. The harshness was a new note, something of the last few years. “You’ve had work exactly twenty-three weeks in eleven years,” she told him. “The rest of the time we’ve collected doles. You’ve moved up from Class Twenty to Class Fourteen, and there you stick, year after year, and we’re getting nowhere, and the walls of this damned apartment are like a cage to me, and when those two kids are in it with me I feel like tearing their heads off, and—”

“Helaine,” he said quietly. “Stop it.”

To his considerable surprise, she did. A muscle knotted in her jaw as she caught herself headlong in her stream of protest. Much more calmly she said, “I’m sorry, Norm. It’s not your fault we’re prolets. There are only so many jobs to be had. Even with your skills—”

“Yes. I know.”

“It’s the way things are. I didn’t mean to screech, Norm. I love you, do you know that? For better, for worse, like they say.”

“Sure, Helaine. All right.”

"Maybe I'll go to the sniffer palace with you, this time. Let me get the kids programmed and–"

He shook his head. It was very touching, this sudden display of affection, but he saw enough of Helaine in the apartment, day and night. He didn't want her following him around as he took his pitiful pleasures. "Not this time, sweeting," he said quickly. "Remember, I've got to go punch the job machine first. You'd better stay here. Go visit Beth Wisnack, or somebody."

"Her husband's still gone."

"Who, Wisnack? Haven't they traced him?"

"They think he–he hopped. I mean, they've had a televector on him and everything," Helaine said. "No trace. He's really gone."

"You believe in this hopper business?" Pomrath asked.

"Of course."

"Traveling in time? It doesn't make any sense. I mean, as a matter of teleology, if you start turning the universe upside down, if you confuse the direction in which events flow, Helaine, I mean–"

Her eyes were very wide. "The faxtapes say there's such a thing. The High Government is investigating it. Joe's own department. Norm, how can you say there are no time-hoppers, when people are disappearing every day? When Bud Wisnack right on the next level–"

"There's no proof he did that."

"Where else is he, then?"

"Antarctica, maybe. Poland. Mars. A televector can slip up just like anybody else. I can't swallow this time-travel deal, Helaine. It has no thingness for me, do you follow? It's unreal, a fantasy, something out of a sniffer dream." Pomrath coughed. He was doing a lot of vociferous talking lately. He thought about Bud Wisnack, small and bald, with an eternal blue stubble on his cheeks, and wondered if he had really jumped a hoop in time and gone off to 1999 or whenever.

The Pomraths looked at each other in awkward silence for a moment. Then Helaine said, "Tell me something hypothetical, Norm. If you went outside now and a man came up to you and said he was running the hopper business, and did you want to go back in time and get away from it all, what would you say to him?"

Pomrath considered. "I'd tell him no. I mean, would it be honorable to skip out on my wife and family? It's all right for a Bud Wisnack, but I couldn't duck all my responsibilities, Helaine."

Her gray-blue eyes sparked. She smiled her don't-fool-me-kiddo smile. "That's very nobly said, Norm. But I think you'd go, all the same."

"You're entitled to think what you want to think. Since it's all a fantasy anyway, it doesn't really matter. I'm going to have a look at the job machine now. I'll give it a real punch. Who knows? I might find myself twitched right up to Class Seven with Joe."

"Could be," Helaine said. "What time will you be back?"

"Later."

"Norm, don't spend too much time at the sniffer palace. I hate it when you get high on that stuff."

"I'm the masses," he told her. "I need my opium."

He palmed the door. It slid open with a little whickering sound, and he went out. The hall light was burning feebly. Cursing, Pomrath groped his way toward the elevator. The hall lights weren't like this in Class Seven places, he knew. He had visited Joe Quellen. Not often, true; his brother-in-law didn't mingle much with the prolets, even when they were his own kin. But he had seen. Quellen led a damned good life. And what was he, anyway? What were his skills?

He was a bureaucrat, a papershuffler. There was nothing Joe Quellen could do that a computer couldn't do better. But he had a job. Tenure.

Gloomily Pomrath stared at his distorted reflection in the burnished framework of the elevator oval. He was a squat, broadshouldered man just past forty, with heavy eyebrows and tired, sad eyes. The reflection made him look older, with much flesh at his throat. Give me time, he thought. He stepped through the oval and was sped upward toward the surface level of the huge apartment house.

I made my choices of my own free will, he insisted. I married the voluptuous Helaine Quellen. I had my permitted two children. I opted for my kind of work. And here I am in one room for four people, and my wife is skinny and I don't look at her when she's naked because I have to spare her nerves, and the oxy quota is used up, and here I am going to punch the job machine and find out the old, old story, and then to drop a lousy few pieces at the sniffer palace, and—

Pomrath wondered what exactly he would do if some agent of the time-hopper people came up to him and offered to peddle him a ticket into a quieter yesterday. Would he do a Bud Wisnack and grab at the chance?

This is nonsense, Pomrath told himself. Such an option doesn't exist. The time-hoppers are imaginary. A fraud perpetrated by the High Government. You can't travel backward in time. All you can do is go relentlessly forward, at a rate of one second per second.

But if that's the case, Norm Pomrath asked himself, where did Bud Wisnack really go?

When the apartment door closed, and Helaine found herself alone, she slumped down wearily on the edge of the all-purpose table in the middle of the room and bit down hard on her lower lip to keep back the tears.

He didn't even notice me, she thought. I took a shower right in front of him and he didn't even notice.

Actually, Helaine had to admit, that wasn't true. She had watched his reflection in the coppery wall-plate that was their substitute for a window, and she had seen him covertly looking at her body as she stood with her back to him under the shower. And then, when she had walked naked across the room to pick up her tunic, he had looked at her again, the front view.

But he hadn't *done* anything. That was the essential thing. If he felt some spark of sexual feeling for her, he would have showed it. With a caress, a smile, a hasty hand slammed against the button that would bring the hidden bed sliding out of the wall. He had looked at her body, and it hadn't had any effect on him at all. Helaine suffered more from that than from all the rest.

She was thirty-seven, almost. That wasn't really old. She had seventy or eighty years of actuarial lifespan ahead of her. Yet she felt middle-aged. She had lost a great deal of weight lately, so that her hip-bones jutted out like misplaced shoulderblades. She no longer wore her off-the-bosom dresses. She knew that she had ceased to have much sensual appeal for her husband, and it pained her.

Was it true, the stories going around that the High Government was promoting special anti-sex measures? That by order of Danton the men were getting impotence pills and the women were receiving desensualizers? That was what the women were whispering. Noelle Kalmuck said that the laundry-room computer had told her so. You had to believe what a computer told you, didn't you? Presumably the machine was plugged right into the high Government itself.

But it made no sense. Helaine was no genius, but she had common sense. Why would the High Government want to meddle with the sex drive? Surely not as a birth-control measure. They controlled birth more humanely, by interfering with fertility, not with potency. Two children per married couple, that was *it.* If they allowed only one, they might be making some headway with the population problem, but unfortunately there were substantial pressure groups who insisted on the two-child family, and even the High Government had bowed. So population was stabilized, and even reduced a little—taking into account the bachelors, like Helaine's brother Joe, and the couples who had sworn the Sterility Pledge, and such—but no real headway was made.

Still, with fertility controlled, it was illogical for the High Government to take away sex as well. Sex was the sport of the prolets. It was free. You didn't need to have a job in order to enjoy sex. It passed the time. Helaine decided that the rumors she had heard were sheer foolishness, and she doubted that the laundry computer had said anything on the subject to Noelle Kalmuck. Why should the computer talk to Noelle at all? She was just a giggly little fool.

Of course, you could never tell. The High Government could be devious. This time-hopper business, for example: was there any truth in it, Helaine wondered? Well, there were all the accredited documents of time-hoppers who had arrived in previous centuries, but suppose they were all frauds inserted in the history books simply to baffle and confuse? What was the real and what was imagined?

Helaine sighed. "What time is it?" she asked.

Her earwatch said gently, "Ten minutes to fifteen."

The children would be arriving home from school soon. Little Joseph was seven, Marina was nine. At this age they still had some shreds of innocence, as much as any children could have who spent all their lives in the same room as their parents. Helaine turned to the foodbox and programmed their afternoon snack with furious jabs of her knuckles. She had just finished the job when the children appeared.

They greeted her. Helaine shrugged. "Plug in and have your snacks," she said.

Joseph grinned angelically at her. "We saw Kloofman in school today. He looks like Daddy."

"Sure," Helaine said. "The High Government has nothing better to do than visit schoolrooms, I know. And the reason why Kloofman looks like Daddy is–" She cut herself short. She had been about to say something untrue, but Joseph had a literal mind. He'd repeat it, and the next day the investigators would come around to know why the class Fourteen Pomrath family was claiming to be related to one of Them.

Marina broke in, "It wasn't really Kloofman anyway. Not himself. They just showed pictures of him on the wall." She nudged her brother. "Kloofman wouldn't come to your grade, silly. He's much too busy."

"Marina's right," Helaine said. "Listen, children, I've programmed you. Have your snack and start your homework right away."

"Where's Daddy?" Joseph asked.

"He went to punch the job machine."

"Will he get a job today?" Marina wanted to know.

"It's hard to say." Helaine smiled evasively. "I'm going to visit Mrs. Wisnack."

The children ate. Helaine stepped through the door and went uplevel to the Wisnack apartment. The door told her that Beth was home, so Helaine announced herself and was admitted. Beth Wisnack nodded to her wordlessly. She looked terribly tired. She was a small woman, just about forty, with dark, trusting eyes and dull-green hair pulled back in a tight grip to a bun. Her two children, the usual boy and girl, sat with their backs to the door, snacking.

"Any news?" Helaine asked.

"None. None. He's gone, Helaine. They won't admit it yet, but he's hopped, and he won't ever come back. I'm a widow."

"What about the televector search?"

The little woman shrugged. "According to law they've got to keep it going eight days. Then that's all. They've searched the registered list of hoppers, but there's nobody named Wisnack on it. Which doesn't mean a thing, of course. Very few of them used their real names when they arrived in the past. And the early ones, they didn't even record the physical descriptions. So there'll be no proof. But he's gone. I'm applying for my pension next week."

Helaine felt the weight of Beth Wisnack's misery like some kind of additional humidity in the room. Her heart went out to her. Life wasn't very attractive here in Class Fourteen, but at least you had your family structure to cling to in times of stress. Beth didn't even have that, now. Her husband had put thumb to nose and disappeared on a one-way journey to the past. "Good-by, Beth, good-by, kids, good-by, lousy twenty-fifth century," he might have said, as he vanished down the time tunnel. The coward couldn't face responsibility, Helaine thought. And who was going to marry Beth Wisnack now?

"I feel so sorry for you," Helaine murmured.

"Save it. There'll be troubles for you, too. All the men will run away. You'll see. Norm will go too. They talk big about obligations, but then they run. Bud swore he'd never go, either. But he was out of work two years, you know, and even with the check every week he couldn't stand it any more. So he went."

Helaine didn't like the implication that her own husband was about to check out. It seemed ungracious of Beth to hurl such a wish at her, even in her own grief. After all, Helaine thought, I came on a simple neighborly mission of consolation. Beth's words hadn't been kind.

Beth seemed to realize it.

"Sit down," she said. "Rest. Talk to me. I tell you, Helaine, I hardly know what's real any more, since the night Bud didn't come back. I only wish you're spared this kind of torture."

"You mustn't give up hope yet," Helaine said gently.

Empty words, Helaine knew. Beth Wisnack knew it too.

Maybe I'll talk to my brother Joe, she thought. See him again. Maybe there's something he can do for us. He's Class Seven, an important man.

God, I don't want Norm to become a hopper!

3.

Quellen was glad to escape from Koll and Spanner. Once he was back in his own office, behind his own small but private desk, Quellen could feel his status again. He was something more than a flunky, no matter how Koll chose to push him around.

He rang for Brogg and Leeward, and the two UnderSecs appeared almost instantly.

"Good to see you again," Stanley Brogg said sourly. He was a large man, somber-looking, with a heavy face and thick, hairy-backed fingers. Quellen nodded to him and reached out to open the oxy vent, letting the stuff flow into the office and trying to capture the patronizing look Koll had flashed at him while doing the same thing fifteen minutes before. Brogg did not look awed. He was only Class Nine, but he had power over Quellen, and both of them knew it.

Leeward did not look awed either, for different reasons. Leeward simply was not sensitive to small gestures. He was a towering, cadaverous, undemonstrative man who went about his work in a routinely methodical way. Not a dolt, but destined never to get out of Class Nine, either.

Quellen surveyed his two assistants. He could not bear the silent scrutiny he was getting from Brogg. Brogg was the one who knew the secret of the African hideaway; a third of Quellen's substantial salary was the price that kept Brogg quiet about Quellen's second, secret home. Big Leeward did not know and did not care; he took his orders directly from Brogg, not from Quellen, and blackmail was not his specialty.

"I suppose you've been informed of our assignment to handle the recent prolet disappearances," Quellen began. "The so-called time-hoppers have become the problem of the Secretariat of Crime, as we have anticipated for several years now."

Brogg produced a thick stack of minislips. "As a matter of fact, I was going to get in touch with you about the situation just now. The High Government's taken quite an interest. Koll no doubt has told you that Kloofman himself is involved. I have the new statistics. In the first four months of this year sixty-eight thousand prolets have vanished."

"But you're on the case?"

"Of course," Brogg said.

"Progress report?"

"Well," Brogg said, pacing up and down the little room and wiping the sweat from his heavy jowls, "you know the theory, though it's been occasionally controverted. That the hoppers are starting out from our proximate timenexus. I've plotted it all. Tell him, Leeward."

Leeward said, "A statistical distribution shows that the theory is correct. The present disappearances of prolets are linked directly to historical records of the appearance of the so-called hoppers in the late twentieth century and succeeding years."

Brogg pointed to a blue-covered volume lying on Quellen's desk. "History spool. I put it there for you. It confirms my findings. The theory's sound."

Quellen ran a finger along his jawline and wondered what it was like to carry around as much fat on one's face as Brogg did. Brogg was perspiring heavily, and his expression was a sad one; he was virtually begging Quellen with his eyes to open the oxy vent wider. The moment of superiority pleased the harried CrimeSec, and he made no move toward the wall.

Crisply Quellen said, "All you've done is to confirm the obvious. We know the hoppers have been taking off from this approximate era. That's been a fact of record since roughly 1979. The High Government directive orders us to isolate the distribution vector. I've developed an immediate course of action."

"Which has been approved by Koll and Spanner, of course," Brogg said insolently. His jowls quivered as his voice rumbled through them.

"It has," Quellen said with as much force as he could muster. It angered him that Brogg could so easily deflate him. Koll, yes, Spanner, yes—but Brogg was supposed to be his assistant. Brogg knew too much about him, though. Quellen said, "I want you to track down the slyster who's shipping these hoppers back. Do anything within the codes to halt his illegal activity. Bring him here. I want him caught before he sends anyone else into the past."

"Yes, sir," Brogg said with unaccustomed humility. "We'll work on it. Which is to say, we'll continue our already established line of exploration. We have tracers out in various prolet strata. We're doing all we can to pull in a lead. We think it's only a matter of time now. A few days. A week. The High Government will be satisfied."

"Let's hope so," Quellen snapped, and dismissed them.

He activated a view-window and peered at the street far below. It seemed to him that he could make out the distant figures of Brogg and Leeward as they appeared on the street, jostled their way to a belt, and disappeared among the multitudes that thronged the outdoor environment. Turning away, Quellen reached for the oxy vent with almost savage joy and flipped it to its widest. He leaned back. Hidden fingers in his chair massaged him. He looked at the book Brogg had left for him, and thumbed his eyeballs wearily.

Hoppers!

It was inevitable, he realized, that this would be dumped on him. All the odd things were, the scrawny conspiracies against law and order. Four years ago, it had been that syndicate of bootlegged artificial organs. Quellen shuddered. Defective pancreases peddled in pestilent alleyways, throbbing blood-filled hearts, endless coils of gleaming intestines, marketed by shady slysters who flitted noiselessly from zone to zone. And then it had been the fertility bank and the grubby business of the sperm withdrawals. And then the alleged creatures from the adjoining universe who had run through the streets of Appalachia clashing hideous red mandibles and clutching at children with scaly claws. Quellen had handled those things, not brilliantly, for brilliance was not his style, but competently, at least.

And now hoppers.

The assignment unsettled him. He had haggled for secondhand kidneys and he had quibbled over the price of ova, all in a day's work, but he did not like this business of coping with illegal time-travel. The framework of the cosmos seemed to warp a little, once you admitted the possibility that such a thing could occur. It was bad enough that time kept flowing relentlessly forward; a man could understand that, though he did not necessarily have to like it. Backward, though? A reversal of all logic, a denial of all reason?

Quellen was a reasonable man. Time paradoxes troubled him. How easy it would be, he knew, to step into the seat and leave Appalachia behind, return to the tranquil humidity of his African hideaway, shrug off all responsibility.

He conquered the creeping apathy that beset him and snapped on the projector. Stereoscopic Julesz figures flashed on the screen while his eyes adjusted to undifferentiated blacks and whites. The Julesz edge kept the screen perpetually in focus, no matter what the degree of optical distortion. The history spool began to unroll. Quellen watched the words, sharp as blades, stream by:

> *The first sign of invasion from the future came about the year 1979, when several men in strange costumes appeared in the district of Appalachia then known as Manhattan. Records show they appeared with increasing frequency throughout the next decade, and when interrogated all ultimately admitted that they had come from the future. The pressure of repeated evidence eventually forced the people of the twentieth century to accept the disturbing conclusion that they were in truth being subjected to a peaceful but annoying invasion by time-travelers.*

There was more, a whole reel more, but Quellen had had enough for the moment. He cut the projector off. The heat of the little room was oppressive, despite the air conditioning and the oxy vent. He could smell his own acrid sweat and didn't like the sensation. Quellen looked despairingly at the confining walls, thinking with longing of the murky stream that ran by the front porch of his African retreat.

He nudged the pedal stud of the minislip dictator and delivered himself of a few memos:

"1. Can we catch a live hopper? That is, a man from our own time who went back, say, ten or twenty years and has lived on back through his own lifespan a second time? Are there such men? What would happen if one met himself of pre-hop existence?

"2. Assuming capture of a live hopper, apply interrogation techniques to discover source of original backward momentum.

"3. Current indications are that hopper phenomenon ceases as of year 2491. Does this indicate success in our prevention attempts or merely lacunae in the records?"

"4. Is it true that no hoppers were recorded prior to A.D. 1979? Why?

"5. Consider possibility of masquerading as Class Fifteen prolet in order to experience solicitation by hopper-transport agents. Would such an arrest be considered entrapment? Check with legal machines.

"6. Take depositions from families of recently departed prolet hoppers. Sociological index, reliability rating, etc. Also attempt to retrace events leading up to disappearance of hopper.

"7. Perhaps–"

Quellen rejected the last memo in unfinished form and kicked over the pedal. The dictator thrust minislips at him. He let them lie on his desk and started the projector again, reeling out some more of the history spool.

> *Analysis of the time-hopper records indicates that all reported arrivals took place within the years 1979 and 2106* A.D.*–that is, an era prior to the establishment of the High Government.* (Quellen made a mental note. Possibly it was significant.) *Those hoppers who upon interrogation were willing to admit to a year of departure listed the same as*

lying between 2486 and 2491 A.D., without exception. Of course, this does not foreclose the possibility of unreported hoppers departing from a time other than that, just as it does not eliminate all possibility that arrivals were not confined wholly to the aforementioned period of 127 years. Nonetheless—

There was an interruption in the text. Brogg had inserted his own memo here:

See Exhibits A, B. Examine possibility of time-travel outside recorded temporal zones. Occult phenomena. Worth study.

Quellen found Exhibits A and B on his desk: two more spools. He did not put them into the projector. Nor did he run the history spool any further just yet. He paused and considered.

All the hoppers seemed to be coming from a single five-year period, of which this was the fourth year. All the hoppers had landed within a temporal spectrum of about a century and a quarter. Naturally, some hoppers had escaped detection, slipping smoothly into the life-patterns of their new era and never showing up on the charts of time-travel. Methods of persona-detection had been fairly primitive three and four hundred years ago, Quellen knew, and it was surprising that so many of the hoppers had actually been found and recorded. Low-order prolets, though, weren't likely to be subtle about concealing themselves in an era to which they were unaccustomed. But surely the syndicate running the hopper business was not sending back only prolets!

Removing the history spool from the projector, Quellen slipped Brogg's Exhibit A into its place and switched the machine on. Exhibit A was uninspiring: nothing less nor more than a census roll of the recorded hoppers. Quellen tuned in on the data in a random way as it flowed past.

> BACCALON, ELLIOT V. Detected 4 April 2007, Trenton, New Jersey. Interrogated eleven hours. Declared date of birth 17 May 2464. Skill classification: computer technician fifth grade. Assigned to Camden Hopper Rehabilitation Zone. Transferred to Westvale Polyclinic District 30 February 2011 for therapy. Discharged 11 April 2013. Employed as switching technician 2013–22. Died 7 March 2022, pleurisy and complications.
>
> BACKHOUSE, MARTIN D. Detected 18 August 2102, Harrisburg, Pennsylvania. Interrogated fourteen minutes. Declared date of birth 10 July 2470, declared date of departure 1 November 2488. Skill classification: computer technician seventh grade. Assigned to West Baltimore Rehabilitation Zone. Released in full capacity 27 October 2102. Employed as computer technician, Internal Revenue Service, 2102–67. Married Lona Walk (q.v.) 22 June 2104. Died 16 May 2187, pneumonia.
>
> BAGROWSKI, EMANUEL. Detected–

Quellen halted the roster as ideas flooded his mind. He ran ahead to Lona Walk, *q.v.*, and made the interesting discovery that she was a hopper who had landed in 2098, claiming to have been born in 2471 and to have shipped out for the past on 1 November 2488. This, obviously, had been a prearranged rendezvous, boy of eighteen, girl of seventeen, chucking the twenty-fifth century and heading for the past to start a new life together. Yet Martin Backhouse had landed in 2102, and his girlfriend 2098. Clearly they hadn't planned it that way. Which told Quellen that the hopper-transporting process was not exact in its attainment of destinations. Or, at least, had not been exact a few years ago. That must have been uncomfortable for poor Lona Walk, Quellen thought: to land in the past and then to find that her heart's desire hadn't made it to the same year.

Quellen was quick to devise some grievous hopper tragedies of this sort. Romeo lands in 2100. Juliet in 2025. Heartbroken Romeo comes upon decades-old gravestone of Juliet. Worse yet, youthful Romeo encounters ninety-year-old Juliet. How did Lona Walk spend the four years while waiting for Martin Backhouse to drop into her era? How could she be sure that he would arrive at all? What if she lost faith and married someone else the year before he showed up? What if the four-year gulf had destroyed their love—for by the time he reached the past, she was objectively twenty-one years old, and he was still only eighteen?

Interesting, Quellen thought. No doubt the playwrights of the twenty-second century had a rich time mining this lode of imaginative material. Bombarded with emigrants out of the future, bedeviled by paradoxes, how those ancient ones must have wrinkled their foreheads over these hoppers!

But of course it was nearly four hundred years since any known hoppers had turned up. The whole phenomenon had been forgotten for generations. Only the fact that the hoppers were coming from *now* had revived it. More's the pity, Quellen thought dourly, that it had to be my time in office.

He pondered other aspects of the problem.

Suppose, he speculated, some hoppers had made a good adaptation, settled down, married people of their new era. Not, like Martin Backhouse, marrying other hoppers, but marrying people whose time-lines began four or five hundred years before their own. That way they might well have married their own great-great-great-great-grandmothers. And thus become their own great-great-great-great-grandfathers. What did that do to genetic flow and continuity of the germ plasm?

Then, too, how about the hopper who lands in 2050, gets into a fist-fight with the first man he meets, knocks him to the pavement, kills him—only to discover that he's slain one of his own direct ancestors and broken his own line of descent? Quellen's head ached. Presumably, any hopper who did that would wink out of existence instantly, never having been born in the first place. Were there any records of such occurrences? Make a note, he said to himself. Check every angle of this thing.

He did not think that such paradoxes were possible. He clung firmly to the idea that it was impossible to change the past, because the past was a sealed book, unchangeable. It had already happened. Any manipulation done by a time-traveler was already in the record. Which makes puppets out of us all, Quellen thought gloomily, finding himself down the dead end of determinism. Suppose I went back in time and killed George Washington in 1772? But Washington, we know, lived till 1799. Would that make it impossible for me to kill him in 1772? He scowled. Such inquiries made his mind spin. Brusquely he ordered himself to return to the business at hand, which was to find some way to halt the further flow of hoppers, thus fulfilling the implied deterministic prophecy that there would be no more hoppers going back after 2491 anyway.

Here's a point to consider, he realized:

Many of these hopper records listed the actual date on which a man took off for the past. This Martin Backhouse, for instance; he had skipped out on November 1, 2488. Too late to do anything about that one now, but what if the records listed a hopper who had taken his departure on April 4, 2490? That was next week. If such a person could be put under surveillance, tracked to the hopper-transporting agent, even prevented from going–

Quellen's heart sank. How could someone be prevented from going back in time, if documents hundreds of years old said that he had made it safely to the past? Paradox, again. It might undermine the structure of the universe. If I interfere, Quellen thought, and pull a man out of the matrix just as he's setting forth–

He scanned the endless roster of hoppers that Brogg had compiled for him. With the furtive pleasure of a man who knows he is doing something quite dangerous, Quellen searched for the information he desired. It took him a while. Brogg had arranged the hopper data alphabetically by name, and had not sorted for date of departure or date of arrival. Besides, many of the hoppers had simply refused or neglected to reveal their date of departure except in the most approximate way. And, with the series of dates nearly four-fifths expired by now, Quellen did not have much leeway.

Half an hour of patient searching, though, turned up the man he wanted:

> RADANT, CLARK R. Detected 12 May 1987, Brooklyn, New York. Interrogated eight days. Declared date of birth 14 May 2458, declared date of departure? May 2490 . . .

It didn't give the exact date, but it would do. A close watch would be kept on Clark Radant during the month to come, Quellen resolved. Let's see if he can slip back to 1987 while we watch him!

He punched for Master Files.

"Get me documents on Clark Radant, born May 14, 2458." Quellen snapped.

The huge computer somewhere below the building was designed to give instant response. It did not necessarily give instant satisfaction, however, and the response that Quellen got was less than useful.

"NO RECORD OF CLARK RADANT BORN 14 MAY 2458," came the reply.

"No record? You mean there's no such person?"

"AFFIRMATIVE."

"That's impossible. He's in the hopper records. Check them. He turned up in Brooklyn on May 12, 1987. See if he didn't."

"AFFIRMATIVE. CLARK RADANT LISTED AMONG 1987 ARRIVALS AND 2490 DEPARTURES."

"You see? So you must have some information on him! Why did you tell me there was no record of him, when—"

"POSSIBLY FRAUDULENT HOPPER LISTING IS ONLY ENTRY. NAME ON LIST DOES NOT IMPLY LEGITIMATE EXISTENCE, EXPLORE POSSIBILITY THAT RADANT NAME IS PSEUDONYM."

Quellen nibbled his lower lip. Yes, no doubt of it! "Radant," whoever he might be, had given a phony name when he landed in 1987. Perhaps all the hopper names on the list were pseudonyms. Maybe they were individually instructed to conceal their real names when they arrived, or possibly indoctrinated so that they could not reveal them, even after interrogation. The enigmatic Clark Radant had been interrogated eight days, it said, and he still hadn't offered a name that corresponded to anything in the birth records.

Quellen saw his bold plan fluttering into the discard. He tried again, though. Expecting to search another half hour, he was rewarded with a new lead after only five minutes:

MORTENSEN, DONALD G. Detected 25 December 2088, Boston, Massachusetts. Interrogated four hours. Declared date of birth 11 June 2462, declared date of departure 4 May 2490 . . .

He hoped it had been a merry Christmas in Boston for Donald Mortensen four hundred two years ago. Quellen punched for Master Files again and demanded to know what there was to be known about Donald Mortensen, born 11 June 2462. He was prepared to learn that no such individual was recorded in the voluminous birth annals of that year.

Instead, the computer began to chatter to him about Donald Mortensen—his skill classification, his marital status, his address, his physical description, his health record. Quellen at length had to silence the machine.

Very well. There *was* a Donald Mortensen. He had not—*would* not—bother to use a pseudonym when he showed up in Boston on Christmas Day forty decades ago. *If* he showed up. Quellen consulted the hopper records again and learned that Mortensen had found employment as an automobile service technician (how prehistoric, Quellen thought!) and had married one Donna Brewer in 2091, fathering five children on her (even more prehistoric!) and living on until 2149, when he expired of an unrecorded disease.

Those five children no doubt had had multitudes of offspring themselves, Quellen realized. Thousands of modern-day human beings might be descended from them, including Quellen himself, or some leader of the High Government. Now, if Quellen's minions closed in on Donald Mortensen as the critical day of May 4 arrived, and prevented him from taking off for the year 2088—

He felt hesitant. The sensation of bold determination that had gripped him a few moments before evaporated completely as he considered the consequences of altering Donald Mortensen's chosen path of action.

Perhaps, Quellen thought, I should have a talk with Koll and Spanner about this, first.

4.

The job machine—more formally, the Central Employment Register—was located in the grand lobby of a geodesic dome six hundred feet wide. The dome was surfaced with a platinum spray three molecules thick. Within, along the walls of the dome, were the external manifestations of the computer banks, which were located somewhere else. A busy inanimate mind worked unsleepingly to tally employment opportunities and to match them with qualifications.

Norm Pomrath took a quickboat to the job machine. He could have walked, and saved a piece of change at the expense of an hour of his time, but he chose not to do so. It was a deliberate squandering. His time was almost infinite; his cash supply, despite the generosity of the High Government, was limited. The weekly dole checks that reached him through the courtesy of Danton and Kloofman and the other members of the ruling elite covered all basic expenses for the Pomrath family of four, but they did not go much beyond those basic expenses. Pomrath usually conserved his cash. He hated the dole, of course; but there was little likelihood of his ever getting regular work, so he accepted the impersonal benevolence like everyone else. No one starved except through free will in this world, and even then it took some doing.

There was really no need for Pomrath to have gone to the machine. Telephone lines linked every apartment with any computer to which there should be public access. He could phone to learn of his status; and in any event if there had been some upward twitch in his job profile, the machine would have been in contact with him by this time. He preferred to get out of the house, though. He knew the job machine's answer in advance, so this was merely a ritual, one of the many sustaining rituals that enabled him to cope with the numbing fact that he was a wholly useless human being.

Subfloor scanners hummed as Pomrath stepped into the building. He was checked, monitored, and identified. If he had been on one of the registers of known anarchists, he would not have been permitted to cross the threshold. Clamps emerging from the marble floor would painlessly have secured his limbs until he could be disarmed and removed from the premises. Pomrath meant no harm to the job machine, however. He harbored hostilities, but they were directed against the universe in general. He was too intelligent a man to waste his wrath on computers.

The benevolent faces of Benjamin Danton and Peter Kloofman beamed down on him from the lofty reaches of the geodesic dome. Giant tridim simulacra dangled from the gleaming struts of the huge building. Danton managed to look severe even while he was smiling; Kloofman, who was reputed to be a man of great humanitarian warmth, was a more inviting figure. Pomrath remembered a time about twenty years ago when the public representatives of the

High Government had constituted a triumvirate, with Kloofman and two others whose names he had begun to forget. Then one day Danton had appeared and the pictures of the other two were taken down. Doubtless one day Kloofman and Danton both would vanish, and there would be two—or three—or four new faces on the public buildings. Pomrath did not concern himself too deeply with changes in the personnel of the High Government. Like most people, he had some fundamental doubts about the existence of Kloofman and Danton. There was good reason to believe that the computers were running the whole show, and had been for at least a century now. Yet he did not fail to nod his head reverently to the tridims as he entered the job machine building. For all he knew, Danton might actually be watching him out of the cold eyes of that big simulacrum.

The place was crowded. Pomrath walked to the center of the marble floor, and stood for a moment enjoying the buzz and clamor of the machine. To his left was Bank Red, for job transfers. Pomrath had no dealings there; you needed to have a job before you could start negotiating for a transfer. Straight ahead of him was Bank Green, for members of the hard-core unemployed like himself. To his right was Bank Blue, where new members of the labor force filed applications for work. Each of the three banks had a long line in wait. Kids to the right; a bunch of eager-beaver Class Tens to the left, looking for advancement; straight ahead, the dismal legions of the jobless. Pomrath joined the line at Bank Green.

It moved swiftly. No one spoke to him. Wrapped in a cocoon of privacy in the midst of this crowd, Pomrath wondered, as he often did, where his life had been derailed. He had a high I.Q., he knew. Good reflexes. Determination and ambition and flexibility. Why, he could have been Class Eight by now, if the breaks had gone his way.

They hadn't. They never would. He had trained as a

medical technician, thinking that illness was a constant even in a well-ordered world, and so there would always be a job for him. Unfortunately, many other young men of his generation had arrived at the same conclusion. As in the arthropod races, Pomrath thought. You picked your favorite lobster with care, judging his abilities and aggressiveness with all the shrewdness at your command. The factors were there to be assessed. The trouble was a lot of other men were just as shrewd as you; if you could isolate a really superior racer, so could they, and the odds had a way of being 11-10 or worse when you got your bet down. If you won, you were just about breaking even. The secret was to find the 50-to-1 shot who could win. But if he could win, he would not carry such fat odds. The universe, thought Pomrath, is not unfair; it simply is not interested.

He had backed the sure thing, and so his reward had been correspondingly slim: a few weeks of work, many months of unemployment. Pomrath was a good technician. He had his skills, and they were at least the equal of those of a genuine doctor of a few centuries ago. Today, real doctors–there weren't many of them–rated Class Three, just below the lower echelon of the High Government. Pomrath, though, as a mere technician, was bogged down in Class Fourteen and all the attendant discomforts, and the only way he could gain slope on the rating curve was to add to his work-experience rating, but there was no work. Or not very much.

What irony, he thought. Joe Quellen, with no skills at all, is a big-deal Class Seven. Private apartment, no less. And here I am twice as far down the curve. But Quellen was a member of the government–not the High Government, of course, not the policy-making group, just the government–and so Quellen had to have status. They had to put Quellen in one of the higher classes simply so he'd be able to enforce his authority. Pomrath chewed at a ragged fingernail and wondered why he had not had the good sense to think of going into government service.

Then he answered himself: the odds were even worse there. Quellen had had luck. Maybe a little ability too, Pomrath conceded grudgingly. If I had gone into government instead of becoming a medic, I'd probably be a Class Fourteen clerk today, with regular work but no other advantages that I don't have at the present. The universe is not unfair. But it can be terribly consistent sometimes.

Pomrath was at the head of the line, now.

He was confronted by a blank aluminum plate, some two feet square, in the center of whose shiny surface was mounted a circular scanning shield made of pebbled glass. The shield glowed green and Pomrath clasped his hand over it in the old, familiar ritual.

It was not necessary to talk to the job machine. The job machine knew why Pomrath had come, and who he was, and what fate was in store for him. Nevertheless, Pomrath said in his deep, husky voice, "How about a little work, maybe?" and punched the activating stud.

He got his answer speedily.

Something in the wall behind the shiny aluminum plate made a whirring, chittering sound. Probably strictly for effect, Pomrath thought. To make the prolets believe that that machine is really doing something. A little slot opened in the plate and a minislip came rolling out. Pomrath ripped it off and studied it without much interest.

It bore his name, his job classification rating, and the rest of the identifying gibberish that had accreted to him in his journey through the world. Below that in neat block letters was the verdict:

EMPLOYMENT PROGNOSIS CURRENTLY UNFAVORABLE. WE WILL INFORM YOU AS OPPORTUNITIES FOR GAINFUL EMPLOY DEVELOP. WE URGE PATIENCE AND UNDERSTANDING. TEMPORARY PRESSURES PREVENT THE ATTAINMENT OF THE HIGH GOVERNMENT'S FULL EMPLOYMENT QUOTA.

"Too bad," Pomrath murmured. "My sympathy to the High Government."

He placed the minislip in the disposal slot and turned away, shouldering a path through the swarm of emotionless men waiting to get their share of the bad news. So much for the visit to the job machine.

"What time is it?" he asked.

"Half past sixteen," said his earwatch.

"I think I'll drop in at my friendly sniffer palace. Do you think that's a good idea?"

The earwatch wasn't programmed for such responses. For twice the money, you could get one that would really talk to you, would tell you things other than the time. Pomrath did not think he rated such a luxury in these troubled times. He was also not so hungry for companionship that he yearned for the conversation of an earwatch. Still, he knew, there were those who took consolation from such things.

He stepped outside, into the pale sunlight of the spring afternoon.

The sniffer palace he particularly favored was four blocks away. There were plenty of them, dozens within a ten-block radius of the job-machine building, but Pomrath always went to the same one. Why not? They dispensed the same poisons at each one, so the only commodity that distinguished one from the next was personal service. Even an unemployed Class Fourteen likes to know that he's a valued regular client of something, if only a sniffer palace.

Pomrath walked quickly. The streets were crowded; pedestrianism was in fashion again lately. The short, heavy-set Pomrath had little patience for the obstacles in his way. In fifteen minutes he was at the sniffer palace. It was on the fortieth underlevel of a commercial tank building; by law, all such places of illusion-peddling had to be underground, so that impressionable children at street level would not be prematurely corrupted. Pomrath entered the tank and took the express drop-shaft. With great dignity he descended five hundred feet. The tank had eighty levels, terminating in an undertract that linked it to several adjoining buildings, but Pomrath had never been down that deep to see. He left such subterranean adventures to the members of the High Government, and had no wish to come face to face with Danton somewhere in the depths of the earth.

The sniffer palace had gaudy, somewhat defective argon lights out front. Most such establishments were all-mechanical, but this one had human attendants. That was why Pomrath liked it. He walked in, and there was good old Jerry just within the door, scanning him out of authentic, bloodshot human eyes.

"Norm. Good to see."

"I'm not so sure about that. Business?"

"Lousy. Have a mask."

"Glad to," Pomrath said. "The wife? You got her pregnant yet?"

The plump man behind the counter smiled. "Would I do a crazy thing like that? In Class Fourteen, do I need a house full of kids? I took the Sterility Pledge, Norm. You forget that?"

"I guess I did," Pomrath said. "Well, okay. There are times I wish I'd done the same. Give me the mask."

"What are you sniffing?"

"Butyl mercaptan," he said at random.

"Come off it. You know we don't–"

"Pyruvic acid, then. With a jolt of lactate dehydrogenase 5 as a spike."

Pomrath drew laughter, but it was mechanical, the laughter of an entrepreneur humoring a valued if slightly embittered customer. "Here, Norm. Stop contaminating my brain and take this. And sweet dreams. You got couch nine, and you owe me a piece and a half."

Taking the mask, Pomrath dropped a few coins into the fleshy palm and retreated to a vacant couch. He kicked his shoes off. He stretched out. He clasped the mask to his face and inhaled. A harmless pastime, a mild hallucinatory gas, a quick illusion to enliven the day. As he went under, Pomrath felt electrodes sliding into place against his skull. To serve as wardens for his alpha rhythms, was the official explanation; if his illusion got too violent, he could be awakened by the management before he did some harm to himself. Pomrath had heard that the electrodes served another, more sinister purpose: to record the hallucinations, to tape them for the benefit of Class Two millionaires who liked the vicarious kick of sitting inside a prolet's mind for a while. Pomrath had asked Jerry about that, but Jerry denied it. As well he might do. It hardly mattered, Pomrath thought, if the sniffer palace chose to peddle second-hand hallucinations. They were free to loot his alphas, if they cared to. So long as he got some decent entertainment for his piece and a half, his proprietary interests ended there.

He went under.

Abruptly he was Class Two, the occupant of a villa on an artificial island in the Mediterranean. Wearing nothing but a strip of green cloth about his waist, he lay restfully on a fat pneumochair at the edge of the sea. A girl paddled back and forth in the crystal water, her tanned skin gleaming when she broke the surface. She smiled at him. Pomrath acknowledged her with a negligent wave of his hand. She looked quite lovely in the water, he told himself.

He was viceroy for interpersonal relations in Moslem East, a nicé soft Class Two sinecure that involved nothing more than an occasional visit to Mecca and a few conferences each winter in Cairo. He had a pleasant home near Fargo, North Dakota, and a decent apartment in the New York zone of Appalachia, and of course this island in the Mediterranean. He firmly expected to reach Class One in the next personnel kickover of the High Government. Danton consulted with him frequently. Kloofman had invited him to dinner several times down on Level One Hundred. They had discussed wines. Kloofman was something of a connoisseur; he and Pomrath had spent a splendid evening analyzing the virtues of a Chambertin that the synthesizers had produced back in '74. That was a good year, '74. Especially for the bigger Burgundies.

Helaine crawled up out of the water and stood incandescently bare before him, her tanned, full-blown body shimmering in the warm sunlight.

"Darling, why didn't you come swimming?" she asked.

"I was thinking. Very delicate plans."

"You know that that gives you a headache! Isn't there a government to do the thinking for you?"

"Underlings like your brother Joe? Don't be foolish, love. There's the government, and there's the High Government, and the two are quite distinct. I have my responsibilities. I have to sit here and think."

"What are you thinking about?"

"Helping Kloofman assassinate Danton."

"Really, love? But I thought you were in the Danton faction!"

Pomrath smiled. "I was. Kloofman, though, is a connoisseur of fine wines. He tempted me. Do you know what he's devised for Danton? It's magnificent. An autonomic laser programmed to put a beam through him at the exact moment when he—"

"Don't tell me," Helaine said. "I might give away the secret!" She turned, presenting her back to him. Pomrath let his eyes rove up and down the succulent voluptuousness of her. She had never looked more delightful, he thought. He wondered if he should participate in Kloofman's assassination scheme. Danton might reward him well for information. It was worth further thought.

The butler came rolling out of the villa and planted itself on four stubby telescoping legs beside Pomrath's lounge chair. Pomrath regarded the gray metal box with affection. What could be better than a homeostatic butler, programmed to its master's cycle of alcohol consumption?

"A filtered rum," Pomrath said.

He accepted the drink, which was extended toward him by a spidery arm of crosshatched titanium fibers. He sipped it. A hundred yards off shore, the sea abruptly began to bubble and boil, as though something monstrous were churning upward from the depths. A vast corkscrew-shaped nose broke the surface. A metal kraken, paying a visit. Pomrath gestured in the defense-motion, and instantly the guardian cells of the island threw up a picket fense of evenly spaced copper wire, each strand eight feet high and a sixteenth of an inch thick. The defense screen glowed between the strands.

The kraken lumbered toward the shore. It did not challenge the defensive screen. Rearing twenty feet out of the water, the bulky grayish-green object cast a long shadow across Pomrath and Helaine. It had large yellow eyes. A lid opened in the tubular skull, and a panel slid forward, out of which a human figure descended. So the kraken was merely a means of transportation, Pomrath observed. He recognized the figure who was coming ashore, and ordered the screen to drop.

It was Danton.

Cold eyes, sharply beaked nose, thin lips, swarthy skin betokening a more than usually mixed ancestry: Danton. As he stepped ashore, the Class One potentate nodded courteously to the nude Helaine and held both palms out to the apprehensive Pomrath. Pomrath tapped the butler's control panel; the metal box scuttled off to fetch a pneumochair for the newcomer. Danton settled into it. Pomrath procured a drink for him. Danton thanked him kindly. Helaine sprawled out on her belly to sunbathe.

Danton said quietly, "About Kloofman, now. The time has come–"

Pomrath woke, the taste of old rags in his mouth.

It was always like that, he thought sadly. Just as the hallucination got really exciting, the effect wore off. Now and then, experimentally, he had paid for a double-strength jolt so he could enjoy the fantasy longer. Even then, though, the mid-hallucination interruption was the rule. TO BE CONTINUED, the mask always said, ringing down the curtain. But what did he expect? A neatly rounded episode, beginning, middle, climax, resolution? Since when did the universe work that way? He elbowed up from the couch and headed back to the front desk to drop off the mask.

"You have a good one, Norm?" Jerry asked.

"Terrific," Pomrath said. "I was demoted to Class Twenty and put in maximum confinement. Then they found work for me as assistant to a sanitation robot. I was the one who worked the squeegee. After that I started to get cancer of the inner ear, and–"

"Hey, don't fool me. You got a dream like that here?"

"Sure," said Pomrath. "Not bad for a piece and a half, was it? Some fun!"

"You got a hell of a sense of humor, Norm. I don't know, a guy like you, where you think up the jokes."

Pomrath smiled thinly. "It's a gift from heaven. I don't question a thing like that. It comes to you out of the blue, like cancer of the inner ear. See you, Jerry."

He walked out and took the shaft to the top of the tank. It was late, close to dinnertime. He was in the mood for walking, but he knew Helaine would bend the walls if he dawdled like that on the way home, so he made for the nearest quickboat ramp. As he approached it, Pomrath saw a seedy figure coming toward him at a rapid clip. Pomrath tensed. I'm ready for anything, he thought. Just let him try some funny stuff.

"Read this," the man said, and jammed a crumpled minislip into Pomrath's hand.

Pomrath unfolded the tough, yellowish synthetic fiber. The message was simple, printed in purple letters right in the center of the slip:

OUT OF WORK?
SEE LANOY

That's interesting, Pomrath thought. I must have the look of the hard-core unemployed in my eyes, by now. Out of work? Sure!

But who the hell is this Lanoy?

5.

Martin Koll made a great show of rearranging the papers on his desk, to cover a confusion that he was scarcely eager to let Quellen see. The CrimeSec had just brought Koll a very disturbing proposition, as full of ricocheting implications as an image trapped between two mirrors. Koll, in turn, would have to refer it to the High Government for a judgment. He would gladly have impaled Quellen on a rusty spike for having caused such trouble for him. Agreed, it was a clever proposal. But cleverness was out of character for Quellen. The man was dogged, methodical, reasonably adept, but that was no reason for him to present his superior with a treacherous proposition like this.

"Let me see if I grasp it," said Koll, who grasped it all too perfectly. "Your search of the hopper records has produced an authentic individual named Mortensen who is listed as having departed for the past from next month. It's your suggestion to monitor him, track him to his contact point, and if necessary prevent him forcibly from completing his trip to the past by arresting those who have agreed to send him there."

Quellen nodded. "That's it."

"You realize that it would be a direct interference with the past, in a deliberate way that's never been tried before, so far as I know?"

"I realize it," said Quellen. "That's why I came to you for authorization. I'm caught between two imperatives: catch the time-travel slyster, and preserve the orderly structure of history. Obviously this Mortensen is in contact with the slyster, or will be, if May 4 is his actual departure date. So if we slap a tracer on him—"

"Yes," Koll said drily. "You've said that already. I appreciate the difficulty."

"Do you have an instruction for me?"

Koll fidgeted with his papers again. He suspected that Quellen was doing this intentionally, putting his boss on the spot in a rare display of temperament. Koll was cognizant of the niceties of the situation. For ten years now he had made Quellen dance to *his* tune, compelling him to catch one hot assignment after another and then watching with some amusement as Quellen brought his limited capacities into play to deal with the problem. Koll admitted that there had been a element of sadism in his treatment of Quellen. It was fair enough; Koll was entitled to his personality faults, just like everyone else, and it seemed justifiable to him to release his aggressions through hostility toward the uncomplaining Quellen. All the same, it was a bother to have Quellen concoct a mess like this by way of revenge.

After a long moment of awkward silence Koll said, "I can't give you an instruction just yet. I'll have to consult with Spanner, of course. And most likely we'll need to get an advisory view from the other quarters."

Meaning the High Government. Koll did not fail to

observe the small smile of triumph that passed rapidly over Quellen's amiable features. Quellen was enjoying this, there could be no doubt of it.

"I'll hold off taking critical action until further word, sir," the CrimeSec said.

"You'd better," Koll replied.

Quellen went out. Koll dug his fingernails into his palms until his hands throbbed with pain. Then, with quick, disgusted taps of his fingers, he punched the autosec buttons until the machine disgorged a spool of his conversation with Quellen. That was for Spanner to study. And after that—

Spanner was out, just now. Checking on some complaint in another department. Koll, perspiring badly, wished that Quellen had waited until a time when Spanner was in the office before presenting this Mortensen nonsense. But no doubt that was part of Quellen's devilish plan, too. Koll bitterly resented being persecuted by the underling. He closed his eyes and saw Quellen's face on the inside of the lids: long straight nose, pale blue eyes, cleft chin. An ordinary face, a forgettable face. Some might even say a handsome face. No one had ever called Martin Koll handsome. On the other hand, he was clever. Far cleverer than the hapless Quellen, or so Koll had always thought, until this afternoon.

An hour later, Spanner came back. As he settled into his desk like a beast returning from a gorging meal, Koll slid the spool over to him.

"Play this. Then tell me what you think."

"Can't you give me a précis?"

"Play it. It's simpler," Koll said.

Spanner played it, mercifully using his earphone so Koll would not have to listen to the conversation again. When the spool had run its course, Spanner looked up. He tugged at the flesh of his throat and said, "It's a good chance to catch our man, isn't it?"

Koll closed his eyes. "Follow my train of thought. We tag Mortensen. He does not go back in time. He does not have the five children he is credited with fathering. Three of those five children, let us say, carry significant historical vectors. One of them grows up to be the father of the assassin of Secretary-General Tze. One of them becomes the grandfather of the unknown girl who carried the cholera to San Francisco. One of them is responsible for the line of descent that culminates in Flaming Bess. Now, since Mortensen never actually reaches his destination in the past, none of those three are born."

"Look at it another way," said Spanner. "Mortenson goes back and has five children. Two of them remain spinster girls. The third is killed falling through thin ice. The fourth becomes a common laborer and has some children who never amount to anything. The fifth—"

"How do you know," asked Koll quietly, "what the consequences of removing a single common laborer from the matrix of the past would be? How do you know what incalculable changes would be worked by removing even a spinster? *Do you want to risk it, Spanner?* Do you want the responsibility?"

"No."

"Neither do I. It's been possible to intercept hoppers for four years, now, simply by going through the records and catching them before they take off. No one's done it. No one's even suggested it, so far as I know, until the fiendish idea was hatched in the mind of our friend Quellen."

"I doubt that," said Spanner. "As a matter of fact, I've thought of it myself."

"And kept the idea to yourself."

"Well, yes. I hadn't had the time to work out the implications. But I'm sure it's occurred to others in the government who have been working on the hopper problem. Perhaps it's already been done, eh, Koll?"

"Very well," said Koll. "Call Quellen and ask him to file a formal request for approval of his plan. Then you sign it."

"No. We'll both sign it."

"I refuse to take the responsibility."

"In that case, so do I," Spanner said.

They smiled at each other in non-amusement. The obvious conclusion was all that was left.

"In that case," said Koll, "we must take it to Them for a decision."

"I agree. You handle it."

"Coward!" Koll snorted.

"Not really. Quellen brought the matter to you. You discussed it with me and got an advisory opinion that confirmed your own feelings. Now it's back to you, and you're the one who's riding it. Ride it right up to Them." Spanner smiled cordially. "You aren't afraid of Them, are you?"

Koll shifted uncomfortably in his seat. At his level of authority and responsibility, he had the right of access to the High Government. He had used it several times in the past, never with any degree of pleasure. Not *direct* access, of course; he had spoken face to face with a few Class Two people, but his only contacts with Class One had been on the screen. On one occasion Koll had spoken with Danton, and three times with Kloofman, but he had no way of being certain that the images on the screen were in fact those of authentic human beings. If something said it was Kloofman, and spoke in Kloofman's voice, and looked like the tridims of Kloofman that hung in public places, that still did not necessarily mean that there now was or ever had been such an actual person as Peter Kloofman.

"I'll call and see what happens," said Koll.

He did not want to make the call from his own desk. The need for physical motion was suddenly great in him. Koll rose, too abruptly, and scuttled out, down the hall, into a darkened communicator booth. The screen brightened as he keyed in the console.

One hardly dared to pick up the phone and call Kloofman, naturally. One went through channels. Koll's route to the top was through David Giacomin, Class Two, the viceroy for internal criminal affairs. Giacomin existed. Koll had seen him in the flesh, had touched his hand on one instance, had even spent a numbing two hours at Giacomin's private domain in East Africa, one of the most memorable and harrowing experiences in Koll's entire life.

He put through the call to Giacomin. In less than fifteen minutes the viceroy was on screen, smiling pleasantly at Koll with that easy benevolence that a Class Two man of secure ego could afford to display. Giacomin was a man of about fifty, Koll thought, with close-cropped iron-gray hair, lips that ran lopsidedly across his face, and a furrowed forehead. His left eye had been damaged irreparably some time in the past; in its place he wore a stubby fiber-receptor whose glass rods were plugged directly into his brain.

"What is it, Koll?" he asked amiably.

"Sir, one of my subordinates has proposed an unusual method of obtaining information about the hopper phenomenon. There's some controversy about whether we should proceed along the suggested path of action."

"Why don't you tell me all about it?" Giacomin said, his voice as warm and comforting as that of a frood begging to know about your most severe neurosis.

An hour later, toward the end of his working day, Quellen learned from Koll that nothing had been settled concerning Mortensen. Koll had talked to Spanner, and then he had talked to Giacomin, and now Giacomin was talking to Kloofman, and no doubt one of Them would be handing down The Word on the Mortensen project in a few days. Meanwhile, Quellen was to sit tight and take no provacative action. There was still plenty of time between now and Mortensen's documented May 4 departure date.

Quellen did not feel any sense of delight at the trouble he was causing. Tagging Mortensen was a clever idea, yes; but it was dangerous sometimes to be too clever. Quellen knew that he had made Koll uncomfortable. That never paid. For all he could tell; Koll had made Giacomin uncomfortable too, and now Giacomin was troubling Kloofman, which meant that Quellen's clever proposal was stirring eddies of annoyance all the way to the very top of the global power structure. When Quellen had been younger, and seething with ambitions to rise to Class Seven eminence, he would have liked nothing better than to win such attention to himself. Now, though, he *was* Class Seven, so he had attained the private apartment that was his dream, and further promotions would gain him little. Besides, his highly illegal nest in Africa weighed on his conscience. The last thing he wanted was to have a member of the High Government say, "This man Quellen is very clever—find out all you can about him." Quellen wished to remain inconspicuous, these days.

Still, he could not have let himself suppress the Mortensen idea. He had official responsibilities to fulfill, and the extent of his private deviation from the residence laws made him all the more conscientious about doing his public duties.

Before going home for the day, Quellen sent for Stanley Brogg.

The beefy assistant said at once, "We've got a wide net out for the slyster, CrimeSec. It's only a matter of days or even hours before we know his identity."

"Good," said Quellen. "I've got another line of approach for you to begin on. But this has to be handled with care, because it hasn't been officially approved yet. There's a man named Donald Mortensen planning to take his time-hop on May 4. Check him in the records you gave me; that's where I found out about him. I want tracers put on him. Check his activities and contacts. But it's got to be done with extreme delicacy. I can't stress that too highly, Brogg."

"All right. Mortensen."

"*Delicately.* If this man finds out we're tracing him, it could lead to a gigantic mess for all of us. Demotions or even worse. So get it straight: work around him, but don't even graze him. Otherwise it'll go hard for you."

Brogg smiled slyly. "You mean you'll drop me a couple of classes if I bungle?"

"Quite likely."

"I don't think you'd do that, CrimeSec. Not to *me.*"

Quellen met the fat man's eyes steadily. Brogg was becoming offensive lately, taking too keen a relish in the power he held over Quellen. His accidental discovery of Quellen's African villa was the great torment of the CrimeSec's life.

"Get out of here," Quellen said. "And remember to be careful about Mortensen. It's very possible that this line of investigation will be quashed by the High Government, and if it is we'll all be frying if They find out we've alerted Mortensen."

"I understand," said Brogg. He left.

Quellen wondered if he should have done that. What if word came down via Giacomin that Mortensen was to be left alone? Well, Brogg was competent enough—too competent, sometimes. And there was really not much time to handle the Mortensen situation if approval did come through. Quellen had to initiate the project in advance. On a speculative basis, so to speak.

He had done all he could for now. Fleetingly he considered the idea of getting Brogg to handle the whole filthy case while he went back to Africa, but he decided that that would be inviting disaster. He shut up his office and went outside to catch the nearest quickboat back to his little Class Seven apartment. In the next few weeks, he knew, he might be able to slip off to Africa for an hour or two at a time, but no more than that. He was mired in Appalachia until the hopper crisis was over.

Returning to his apartment, Quellen discovered that he had neglected to keep his foodstocks in good supply. Since his stay in Appalachia threatened to be long or possibly permanent, he decided to replenish his stores. Sometimes Quellen ordered by phone, but not today. He fastened the *Privacy* radion to his door again and went down the twisting flyramp to the supply shop, intending to stock up for a long siege.

As he made his way down, he noticed a sallow-looking man in a loose-fitting purple tunic heading in the opposite direction up the ramp. Quellen did not recognize him, but that was unsurprising; in the crowded turmoil of Appalachia, one never got to know very many people, just a handful of neighbors and relatives, and a few service employees like the keeper of the local supply shop.

The sallow-looking man stared curiously at Quellen. He seemed to be saying something with his eyes. Quellen felt profoundly uncomfortable about the contact. In his departmental work, he had learned a good deal about the various classes of molesters one could encounter on the streets. The ordinary sexual kind, of course; but also the ones who sidled up to you and punctured your veins to inject the addictive dose of some infernal drug like helidone, or the sinster sorts given to jamming carcinogens against your skin in a crowd, or perhaps the secret agents who subtly stuck a molecular probe into your flesh that would transmit every word of your conversation to a distant pickup point. Such things happened all the time.

"Take it and read it," the sallow-faced man muttered.

He brushed against Quellen and shoved a wadded minislip into his hand. There was no way Quellen could have avoided the contact. The stranger could have done anything to him in that brief instant; right now Quellen's bone calcium might be turning to jelly, or his brain sloughing off through his nostrils, all to satisfy the gratuitous needs of some bump-killer. But it seemed that all the man had done was to put some kind of advertisement into Quellen's palm. Quellen unfolded the minislip after the other had disappeared up the flyramp, and read it:

OUT OF WORK?
SEE LANOY

That was all. Instantly Quellen's CrimeSec facet came into play. Like most lawbreakers in public office, he was vigorous in prosecution of other lawbreakers, and there was something in Lanoy's handbill that smacked of illegality, not just the offensive means of person-to-person transmission but also the offer itself. Was Lanoy running some kind of job placement operation? But that was a government responsibility! Quellen swung hastily around with the thought of pursuing the rapidly retreating sallow-faced man. He caught one last glimpse of the loose purple tunic, and then the man was gone. He could have gone almost anywhere after leaving the flyramp.

Out of work? See Lanoy.

Quellen wondered who Lanoy was and what his magic remedy might be. He made up his mind that he would have Leeward or Brogg look into the matter.

Carefully stowing the minislip in his pocket, Quellen entered the supply shop. The lead-lined door swung back to admit him. Robot merchandise-pickers were scuttling down the shelves, taking inventories, filling orders. The red-faced little man who ran the shop—as a front for the computers, naturally; what housewife wanted to gossip with a computer?—greeted Quellen with an unusual display of heartiness.

"Oh, it's the CrimeSec! We haven't been honored by you in a long time, CrimeSec," the rotund shopkeeper said. "I was beginning to think you'd moved. But that's impossible, isn't it? You'd have notified me if you had gotten a promotion."

"Yes, Greevy, that's true. I've just not been around lately. Very busy these days. Investigations." Quellen frowned. He did not want the news of his frequent absences noised all around the community. Quickly, edgily, he grabbed up the greasy gray binding of the basic catalog and began to call off numbers. Canned foods, powdered concentrates, staples, all the components of a basic diet. He scrawled his list and jammed it before the sensors while the shopkeeper looked on benignly.

Greevy said, "Your sister was in yesterday."

"Helaine? I haven't seen much of her lately."

"She looks poorly, CrimeSec. Terribly thin. I programmed some Calfill for her, but she didn't want it. Has she been to the medics?"

"I really don't know," said Quellen. "Her husband's had some medical training. Not a doctor, just a technician, but if there's anything wrong with her he ought to be able to diagnose it. If he's got his wits still working. The rest of him certainly isn't."

"That's a trifle unfair, CrimeSec. I'm sure Mr. Pomrath would be happy to work more often. Why, I *know* it. No one likes to be idle. Your sister says he's really suffering. In fact—" the shopkeeper leaned close to whisper conspiratorially "—I shouldn't be telling you this, maybe, but there's some bitterness about you in that family. They think that perhaps, with your political influence—"

"I can't do a thing for them! Not a thing!" Quellen realized he was shouting. What business was it of this damned shopkeeper's that Norman Pomrath was out of work? How dare he meddle like this? Quellen struggled for calm. He found it, somehow, apologized for his outburst, quickly left the supply shop.

He stepped out into the street for a moment and stood watching as the multitudes streamed past. Their clothes were of all designs and colors. They talked incessantly. The world was a beehive, vastly overpopulated and getting more so daily, despite all the restrictions on childbirth. Quellen longed for the quiet retreat he had built at such great cost and with so much trepidation. The more he saw of crocodiles, the less he cared for the company of the mobs who swarmed the crowded cities.

It was an orderly world, of course. Everybody numbered, labelled, registered, and tagged, not to say constantly monitored. How else could you govern a world of eleven or twelve or maybe thirty billion people without imposing a construct of order on them? Yet Quellen was in a fine position to know that within that superficial appearance of order, all sorts of shamelessly illegal things went on—not, as in Quellen's case, justifiable efforts to escape an intolerable existence, but shady, vicious, unpardonable things. Take the drug addictions, he thought. There were laboratories in five continents grinding out new drugs as fast as the old addictions were abolished. Right now they were pushing some kind of deathly alkaloids, and they pushed them in the most flagrant ways. A man walks into a sniffer palace hoping to buy half an hour of innocent hallucinatory amusement, and buys a hellish addiction instead. Or, aboard a quickboat, a man's hand traverses a woman's body in what seems like something no more deplorable than an indecent caress, but two days later the woman discovers she has developed an addiction, and must seek medical help to find out what it is she's addicted to.

Things like that, thought Quellen. Ugly, inhuman things. We are a dehumanized people. We injure one another without any need but the simple need to do injury. And when we turn to each other for help, we get no response but fear and withdrawal. Stay away, stay away! Let me alone!

And consider this Lanoy, Quellen ruminated, fingering the minislip in his pocket. Some kind of crookedness going on there, yet it was concealed well enough to have avoided the attention of the Secretariat of Crime. What did the computer files say about Lanoy? How did this Lanoy manage to hide his illegal activities from his family or roommates? Surely he did not live alone. Such an outlaw could not be Class Seven. Lanoy must be some shrewd prolet, running a free-enterprise swindle for his own private benefit.

Quellen felt a strange kinship with the unknown Lanoy, much as it repelled him to admit it. Lanoy, too, was beating the game. He was a wily one, possibly worth knowing. Quellen frowned. Quickly he moved on, back to his apartment.

6.

Peter Kloofman lay sprawled out in a huge tube of nutrient fluid while the technicians changed his left lung. His chest panel was open on its hinges, exactly as though Kloofman were some sort of robot undergoing repair. He was no robot. He was mere mortal flesh and blood, but not very mortal. At the age of a hundred thirty-two, Kloofman had undergone organ replacements so frequently that there was very little left of his original persona except for the gray slab of his wily brain itself, and even that was no stranger to the surgeon's beam. Kloofman was willing to submit to such things gladly, for the sake of preserving his existence, which is to say his infinite power. He was real. Danton was not. Kloofman preferred to keep things that way.

"David Giacomin is here to see you," purred a voice from the probe riveted just within his skull.

"Admit him," said Kloofman.

Some twenty years ago he had had himself reconstructed so that he could carry on the business of the state even while undergoing regenerative surgery. It would have been impossible to remain in power, otherwise. Kloofman was the only flesh-and-blood member of Class One, which meant that all power lines converged toward him. He delegated as much as he could to the assortment of cams and relays that went by the name of Benjamin Danton; but Danton, after all, was unreal, and in the long run even he was only an extension of the tireless Kloofman. It had not always been this way. Before the Flaming Bess affair there had been three members of Class One, and still further back Kloofman had been but one of five.

He carried on satisfactorily this way, however. And there was no reason why he could not continue to bear his unique burden for another six or seven hundred years. No man in all the history of the world had held the power Peter Kloofman held. In his occasional moments of fatigue he found that a comforting thing upon which to reflect.

Giacomin entered. He stood in a position of relaxed attentiveness beside the nutrient tub in which Kloofman lay. Kloofman valued Giacomin highly. He was one of perhaps two hundred Class Two individuals who provided the indispensable underpinning for the High Government. Between Class Two and Class Three was a qualitative gulf. Class Two understood the way the world was run; Class Three, on the other hand, enjoyed great comforts, but no true understanding. To a Class Three surgeon or administrator, Danton was probably real, and other unnamed Class Ones existed as well. Giacomin, privy to the knowledge a Class Two man had, was aware of the truth.

"Well?" Kloofman asked, watching with detached interest as the surgeons lifted the gray, foamy mass of the replacement lung and inserted it in his gaping chest cavity. "What's the story for today, David?"

"Hoppers."

"Have they located the process yet?"

"Not yet," said Giacomin. "They're taking steps, though. It won't be long."

"Good, good," murmured Kloofman. This enterprise of illicit time travel troubled him more than he cared to admit. For one thing, it went on despite the best efforts of the government to track it to its source, and that was bothersome. But of course it was only a few days since Kloofman had requested a detect on the operation, anyway. Much more annoying was the fact that for all his power he could not reach out instantly, seize this temporal process, and put it to his own uses. It had been developed independently of the instrumentalities of the High Government. Thus it was a conspicuous reminder to Kloofman that not even he was omnipotent.

Giacomin said, "There's a problem. They've thought of isolating a potential hopper and keeping him from making the jump."

Kloofman moved convulsively in his bath. Fluid splashed into his chest cavity. Homeostatic pumps imperturbably removed it, and a surgeon clamped his lips together and went about the job of stapling the new lung in place without comment. The world leader said, "A listed hopper? One who's been recorded?"

"Yes."

"Have you permitted this?"

"I brought it to you. I've got a hold on it until The Word comes down."

"Kill it," said Kloofman decisively. "Beyond a doubt. I go further: make absolutely certain that there's no interference with any listed hoppers. Take that as a flat rule. Anyone who has left must leave. Yes? That's The Word, David. It goes out to all departments that are even remotely connected with the hopper business."

As he spoke, Kloofman felt a faint stinging sensation in the fleshy part of his left thigh. Sedation; he must be getting too excited. The automatic monitoring system was compensating by chemical means, dilating arteries, flooding his system with useful enzymes. He could do better than that. Consciously, he willed himself to be calm even in the face of this threat. Giacomin looked concerned.

Kloofman grew tranquil. Giacomin said, "That was all I wanted to report. I'll pass your instructions along."

"Yes. And notify the Danton programmers. Anything going through his office should carry the same notification. This is something too important to let slide. I don't understand how I failed to anticipate the possibility."

Giacomin departed, making his way carefully around the tank and out of the faintly clammy atmosphere of the chamber. Kloofman eyed the green vitreous walls with displeasure. He realized that he should have been forewarned. It was the job of those in Class Two to plot the pitfalls for him in advance, and they had been cognizant of the hopper problem for some time now. As far back as '83, contingency schedules had been drawn to deal with the hopper problem. Why had they not included *this?* Of all things to forget!

Kloofman forgave himself for overlooking it. The others, though—they were in for a declassing.

Out loud he said, "Imagine what could have happened if anybody had begun meddling with the registered and documented hoppers. Pulling chunks out of the past—why, it might have turned the world upside-down!"

The surgeons did not reply. It would be worth their classifications if they ever spoke to Kloofman except on matters of their own sphere of professional competence. They closed his chest and ran anemostats over it. The instant healing process began. The temperature in the nutrient bath began to descend as the automatic regulators prepared Kloofman for his return to independent motility.

He was badly shaken, not by postoperative shock—that was unknown these days—but by the implications of what had almost happened. Meddling with the past! Pulling hoppers from the matrix! Suppose, he thought fretfully, some bureaucrat in Class Seven or Nine or thereabouts had gone ahead on his own authority, trying to win a quick uptwitch by dynamic action, and had rounded up a few known hoppers in advance of their departure. Thereby completely snarling the fabric of the time-line and irrevocably altering the past.

Everything might have been different, Kloofman thought.

I might have become a janitor, a technician, a peddler of fever pills. I might never have been born. Or I might have landed in Class Seven with Danton real and in charge. Or there might have been total anarchy, no High Government whatsoever. Anything. Anything. A wholly different world. The transformation would have come like a thief in the night, and the editing of the past would naturally be indetectable, so that I would never know there had been a change in my status. Perhaps there had already been several changes, Kloofman thought suddenly.

Was it possible?

Had two or three hoppers already been thwarted in their documented escapes by some zealous official? And had fundamental changes in the historical patterns of the past five centuries resulted, changes that could never be observed? Kloofman felt an abrupt and fatiguing sense of the instability of the universe. Here he was, two thousand feet down in the solid earth, living as always at the bottom of civilization, for the High Government was the lowest level occupied, and he had known absolute power for decades of a kind never remotely comprehended by Attila or Genghis Khan or Napoleon or Hitler, and yet he could feel the roots of the past ripping loose like torn strings about him. It sickened him. Some faceless individual, a mere government man, could wreck everything in a harmless blunder, and there was nothing Kloofman could do to prevent it from happening. It might already have begun to happen.

I should never have embarked on this hopper enterprise, Kloofman thought.

But that was wrongheaded, he knew. He had done the right thing, but he had done it carelessly, without full consideration of the danger factors. Before turning his bureaucracy loose on catching the shipper of time-hoppers, he should have issued strict orders concerning interference with the past. He trembled at the thought of the vulnerability he had opened for himself. At any time since 2486, his entire edifice of power, so laboriously constructed over so many years, could have been wrecked by the blind whim of an underling.

The stabs of a dozen homeostatic injections reminded Kloofman that he was losing his calmness again.

"Get me Giacomin," he said.

The viceroy entered a few moments later, looking puzzled at the peremptory recall. Kloofman leaned heavily forward, straining himself half out of the tank, causing the servomechanisms within his body to whine in tinny protest. "I just wanted to make certain," he said, "that there was full understanding of my instruction. *No* interference with hopper departures. None. None whatever. Clear?"

"Of course."

"Do I worry you, David? Do you think I'm a garrulous old man who ought to have his brain scraped? Let me tell you why I worry about this thing. I control the present and to some extent the future, right? Right. But not the past.

How can I control the past? I see a whole segment of time that's beyond my authority. I admit to being frightened. Maintain my authority over the past, David. See that it remains inviolate. What has happened must happen."

"I've already taken steps to see that it will," said Giacomin.

Kloofman dismissed him a second time, feeling reassured but not sufficiently so. He summoned Mauberley, the Class Two man in charge of running the Danton operation. As one who considered himself a quasi-immortal, Kloofman did not spend much time designating heirs apparent, but he had high respect for Mauberley, and regarded him as a possible eventual successor. Mauberley entered. He was sixty years old, vigorous and muscular, with a flat-featured face and wiry, thick hair. Kloofman briefed him on the new development. "Giacomin is already at work on the problem," he said. "You work on it too. Redundancy, that's the secret of effective government. Get Danton to make an official proclamation. Circulate it downward through Class Seven. This is an emergency!"

Mauberley said, "Do you believe there have already been changes in the past as a result of contra-hopper activity?"

"No. But there could be. We'd never know."

"I'll deal with it," he said, and left.

Kloofman rested. After a while, he had himself withdrawn from his nutrient bath and taken to his office. He had not been to the surface in sixteen years. The upper world had become slightly unreal to him; but he saw no harm in that, since he was well aware that to most of the inhabitants of the upper world *he* was slightly unreal, or more than slightly. Reciprocity, he thought. The secret of effective government. Kloofman lived in a complex of interlocking tunnels spreading out for hundreds of miles. At any given time, machines with glittering claws were energetically at work extending his domain. He hoped to have the world girdled with a continuous network of High Government access routes in another ten years or so. His personal Midgard Serpent of transportation. Strictly speaking, there was no need for it; he could govern just as effectively from a single room as from any point along a world-rimming tunnel. But he had his whims. What was the use of being the supreme leader of the entire world, Kloofman wondered, if he could not occasionally indulge a small whim?

He moved on purring rollers to the master control room and allowed his attendants to attach him to contact leads. It bored him to depend on words for his knowledge of external events. One of the many surgical reconstructs that had been performed on him over the years allowed a direct neural cut-in; Kloofman could and did enter directly into the data stream, becoming a relay facet of the computer web itself. Then, only then, did a kind of ecstasy overwhelm him.

He nodded, and the flow of data began.

Facts. Births and deaths, disease statistics, transportation correlations, power levels, crime rates. Synapse after synapse clenched tight as Kloofman absorbed it all. Far above him, billions of people went through their daily routines, and he entered in some way into the life of each of them, and they entered into his. His perceptions were limited, of course. He could not detect individual fluctuations in the data except as momentary surges. Yet he could extrapolate them. At this very instant, he knew, a hopper was departing for the past. A life subtracted from the present. What about mass? Was it conserved? The possibility of a sudden and total subtraction. Two hundred pounds abruptly removed from now and thrust into yesterday—how could it be possible, Kloofman wondered? It was done, though. The records showed it. Thousands of hoppers thrust out of his time and into the time of his predecessors. How? How?

Peter Kloofman brushed the thought from his throbbing mind. It was an irrelevancy. What was relevant was the sudden, unthinkable possibility that the past might be altered, that all this might be taken away from him in a random fluctuation against which no defense existed. That struck horror into him. He filled his brain with data to drown out the possibility of total loss. He felt the onset of his delight.

Caesar, did you ever have the whole world running through your brain at once?

Napoleon, could you so much as imagine what it might be like to be plugged right into the master computers?

Sardanapalus, were there joys like this in Nineveh?

Kloofman's bulky body quivered. The mesh of fine capillary wires just beneath his skin glowed. He ceased to be Peter Kloofman, world leader, lone human member of Class One, benevolent despot, sublime planner, the accidental inheritor of the ages. Now he was everyone who existed. A flux of cosmic power surged in him. This was the true Nirvana! This was the ultimate Oneness! This was the moment of full rapture!

At such a time, it was not possible to brood on how easily it could all be taken away from him.

7.

Helaine Pomrath said, "Norm, who's Lanoy?"

"Who?"

"Lanoy. L–A–N–"

"Where did you hear that name?"

She showed him the minislip and watched his face carefully. His eyes flickered. He was off balance.

"I found this in your tunic last night," she said. " *'Out of work, see Lanoy,'* it says. I just wondered who he was, what he could do for you."

"He—uh—runs some kind of employment bureau, I think. I'm not sure." Pomrath looked thoroughly uncomfortable. "Somebody slipped that to me as I was coming out of the sniffer palace."

"What good is it, if there's no address on it?"

"I guess you're supposed to follow it up," Pomrath said. "Hunt around, do some detective work. I don't know. Actually, I had forgotten all about it, to tell you the truth. Give it here."

She surrendered it. He took it quickly, and thrust it into

his pocket. Helaine did not like the speed with which he got the incriminating document out of sight. Although she hadn't even a remote notion of its implications, she was easily able to detect her husband's guilt and general embarrassment.

Maybe he's planning a surprise for me, she thought. Maybe he's already been to this Lanoy and done something about getting a job, but he was saving it to tell me next week when it's our anniversary. And I bungled it by asking him questions. I should have let it go a while.

Her son Joseph, stark naked, stepped down from the platform of the molecular bath. His sister, equally naked, got under it. Helaine busied herself with programming breakfast. Joseph said, "We're going to learn geography in school today."

"How lovely," Helaine said vaguely.

"Where's Africa?" the boy asked.

"Far away. Across the ocean somewhere."

"Can I go to Africa when I grow up?" Joseph persisted.

There was a shrill giggle from the bath. Marina whirled around and said, "Africa's where the Class Twos live! Are you going to be Class Two, Jo-Jo?"

The boy glowered at his sister. "Maybe. Maybe I'll be Class One. How do you know? *You* won't be anything. I got something you don't have already."

Marina made a face at him. All the same, she turned around to hide her undeveloped nine-year-old body from his beady eyes. From his corner of the room, Pomrath looked up from the morning faxtape and grunted, "Cut it out, both of you! Jo-Jo, get dressed! Marina, finish your bath!"

"I just said I wanted to go to Africa," the boy muttered.

"Don't speak back to your father," said Helaine. "Breakfast's ready, anyhow. Get dressed."

She sighed. Her head felt as though someone had poured powdered glass into it. The children always bickering, Norm sitting in the corner like a guest at his own wake, mysterious minislips popping up in the wash, four windowless walls hemming her in—no, it was too much. She didn't understand how she could tolerate it. Eat, sleep, bathe, make love, all in one little room. Thousands of grubby neighbors mired in the same bog. Picnic once a year, via stat to some faraway place that wasn't all built up yet—bread and circuses, keep the prolets happy. But it hurt to see a tree and then come back to Appalachia. There was actual pain in it, Helaine thought miserably. She had not bargained for this when she married Norm Pomrath. He had been full of plans.

The children ate and left for school. Norm remained where he was, turning and twisting the fax-tape in his stubby fingers. Now and then he shared an item of news with her. "Danton's dedicating a new hospital in Pacifica next Tuesday. Totally automated, one big homeostat and no technicians at all. Isn't that nice? It reduces government expenditures when no employees are required. And here's a good one, too. Effective the first of May, oxy quotas in all commercial buildings are reduced by ten per cent. They say it's to enable additional gas supplies to reach householders. You remember that, Helaine, when they cut the home quota too around August. It always goes down. When it gets to the point where they're rationing air—"

"Norm, don't get worked up."

He ignored her. "How did all this happen to us? We've got a right to something better. Four million people per square inch, that's where we're heading. Build the houses a thousand stories high so there's room for everyone, and it takes a month to get down to street level or up to the quickboat ramp, but what of it? It's progress. And—"

"Do you think you'll be able to locate this Lanoy and get a job through him?" she asked.

"What we need," he went on, "is a first-class bacterial plague. Selective, of course. Wipe out all those who are lacking in functional job skills. That cuts the dole roll by a few billion units a day. Devote the tax money to makework programs for the rest. If that doesn't work, start a war. Extraterrestrial enemies, the Crab People from the Crab Nebula, everything for patriotism. Start a *losing* war. Cannonfodder."

He's cracking up, Helaine thought as her husband went on talking. It was an endless monologue these days, a spewing fountain of bitterness. She tried not to listen. Since he showed no sign of leaving the apartment, she did. She hurled the dishes into the disposal unit and said to him, "I'm going to visit the neighbors," and walked out just as he launched into an exposition of the virtues of controlled nuclear warfare as a means of population check. Random spasms of noise, that was what Norm Pomrath was producing these days. He had to hear himself talk, so that he did not forget he was still there.

Where shall I go, Helaine wondered?

Beth Wisnack, widowed by her time-hopping husband, looked smaller, grayer, sadder today than she had looked on Helaine's last visit. Beth's mouth was tightly drawn back in the quirk of suppressed rage. Behind the look of feminine resignation that she wore was inward fury: *how dare he do this to me, how could he abandon me like this?*

Courteously Beth offered an alcohol tube to her guest. Helaine smiled pleasantly, took the snub-ended red plastic tube, thrust it against the fleshy part of her arm. Beth did the same. The ultrasonic snouts whirred; the stimulant spurted into their blood-streams. An easy drunk, for those who did not like the taste of modern liquors. Helaine flickered her eyes, relaxing. She listened for a while to Beth's song of complaint, pitched all on one note.

Then Helaine said, "Beth, do you know about someone called Lanoy?"

Beth was at instant attention. "Who Lanoy? What Lanoy? Where did you hear of him? What do you know of him?"

"Not much. That's why I asked you."

"I heard the name, yes." Her pale eyes were agitated. "Bud mentioned it. I heard him talking, telling some other man, Lanoy this, Lanoy that . . . It was the week before he ran out on me. Lanoy, he said. Lanoy will fix it."

Helaine reached for a second alcohol tube without waiting to be invited. There was a sudden chill inside her that needed to be thawed.

"Lanoy will fix what?" she asked.

Beth Wisnack subsided defeatedly. "I don't know. Bud never discussed things with me. But I heard him talking about this Lanoy, anyway. A lot of whispering going on. Just before he left, he was talking Lanoy all the time. I've got a theory about Lanoy. You want to hear?"

"Of course!"

Smiling, Beth said, "I think Lanoy's the one who runs the hopper business."

Helaine had thought so too. But she had come here to learn otherwise, not to have her worst fears confirmed. Tense, her hands trembling a little, she smoothed her tunic, shifted her position, and said, "You really think so?"

"Bud talked Lanoy all week. Then he disappeared. He was hatching something and it had to do with Lanoy. I should know what? But I've got my theories. Bud met this Lanoy somewhere. They struck a deal. And–and–" The pain and rage welled too close to the surface. "And Bud left," Beth Wisnack said breathily. She popped another tube. Then she said, "Why do you ask?"

"I found a slip in Norman's clothes," Helaine said. "It was some kind of advert. *'Out of work? See Lanoy.'* I asked him about it. He got very embarrassed. Took the slip away from me, tried to tell me it was an employment agency, something like that. I could see he was lying. Hiding something. The trouble is, I don't know what."

"You better start worrying hard, Helaine."

"You think it's bad?"

"I think it's just the same as with Bud. Norm's in contact with them. He's probably trying to raise the money now. And they send him out. *Poof!* Gone. No husband. The widow Pomrath. Two kids, shift for yourself." Beth Wisnack's eyes were glittering strangely now. She did not look unhappy at the prospect that Helaine's husband might go hopper. It was the misery that craves company, Helaine knew. Let every husband in the world vanish into the maw of the past and perhaps Beth Wisnack would feel some delight.

Helaine fought to stay calm.

"When the police investigated Bud's disappearance," she said, "did you mention this Lanoy to them?"

"I named him, yes. They wanted to know if Bud had been seeing anyone unusual just before he vanished, and I said I didn't know, but there was this name he had mentioned a few times, Lanoy, that I didn't know. They took it down. I don't know what they did about it. It isn't going to bring Bud back. You can only go one direction in time, you know. Backward. They don't have any machines back there to send people ahead again, and in any case I understand it isn't possible. You go back, you're stranded there for keeps. So when Norm goes–"

"He's not going," said Helaine.

"He's seeing Lanoy, isn't he?" Beth asked.

"All he had was the minislip. It didn't even have an address on it. He said he didn't know where to find Lanoy. And we aren't sure that Lanoy is connected with the hopper business, anyhow."

Beth's eyes sparkled. "The Lanoy mob is in contact with him," she said. "That means they can reach him any time. So he can reach them. And they'll send him back. He's going to be a hopper, Helaine. He's going to go."

Q.E.D.

A quickboat took her to the flamboyant skyscraper that housed the Secretariat of Crime. Some persistent work at the front desk yielded Helaine the information that her brother was at the office today, and if she cared to wait a while perhaps he would see her. She requisitioned an appointment with him. The machine asked for her thumbprint, and she gave it, and then sat down to wait in an anteroom draped with somber purplish fabrics.

Helaine was not accustomed to venturing out into the world of office buildings and walking servomechanisms. She stayed close to home, and did her shopping by remote contact. "Downtown"—the world at the end of the quickboat routes—was a frightening place to her. She forced herself to remain cool. On a matter as serious as this, she had to see her brother face to face across a desk, so that he could not escape from her at the flick of a switch. She was terrified.

"The CrimeSec will see you," a flat impersonal vocoder voice told her.

She was ushered into the presence of her brother. Quellen stood up, flashed a quick, uncomfortable smile, beckoned her into a chair. The chair grabbed her and began to knead the muscles of her back. Helaine shuddered at the sensation, and pulled away in alarm as the invisible hands within the chair started to go to work on her thighs and buttocks. The delicate feedback sensors of the chair caught her mood, and the attentions ceased.

She looked uncertainly at her brother. Quellen seemed to be as ill at ease with her as she was with him; he tugged at his ear, clenched his jaws, popped his knuckles. They were practically strangers. They met on family occasions, but there had been no real communication between them for a long time. He was a few years older than she was. Once, they had been quite close, two devoted siblings bantering and heckling one another just as her Joseph and Marina did today. Helaine could remember her brother as a boy, stealing his peeks at her body in their one-room apartment, pulling her hair, helping her with her homework. Then he had begun his training for government service, and after that he had not been part of her world in any meaningful way. Now she was an edgy housewife and he was a busy public officer, and she was somewhat afraid of him.

For perhaps three minutes they exchanged friendly pleasantries about domestic matters. Helaine talked about her children, her social conscience unit in the apartment, her personal reading program. Quellen said very little. He was a bachelor, which set him further apart from her. Helaine knew that her brother kept company with some woman, somebody named Judith, but he rarely talked about her and seemed hardly ever even to think of her. There were times when Helaine suspected that Judith did not exist—that Quellen had invented her as camouflage for some solitary vice he preferred, or, worse, for some homosexual involvement. Sodomy was acceptable socially these days; it helped to keep the birth rate low. But Helaine did not like to think of her brother Joe taking part in such practices.

She brought the chatter to a deliberate end by asking

about Judith. "Is she well? You've never kept your promise to bring her to visit us, Joe."

Quellen looked as uncomfortable at the mention of Judith as Norm Pomrath had looked while Helaine was questioning him about the Lanoy minislip. He said evasively, "I've mentioned the idea to her. She thinks it would be fine to meet you and Norm, but not just yet. Judith's a little disturbed by having to meet your children. Children unsettle her. But I'm sure we'll work something out." He flashed the quick, hollow smile again. Then he dismissed the touchy subject of Judith by getting down to the business at hand. "I'm sure this wasn't just a social call, Helaine."

"No. It's business, Joe. I see by the faxtapes that you're conducting an investigation of the hoppers."

"Yes. True."

"Norm's going to hop."

Quellen sat stiffly upright, his left shoulder rising higher than the right one. "What gives you that idea? Has he told you so himself?"

"No, of course not. But I suspect it. He's been very depressed lately, about not working and all that."

"Nothing new with him."

"More so than usual. You should hear the way he talks. He's so bitter, Joe! He talks absolute nonsense, just a stream of angry words that don't make any sense. I wish I could quote him for you. He's building up to some kind of psychological explosion, I know it. I can feel the steam gathering inside him." She winced. The chair was starting to massage her again. "He hasn't worked for months now, Joe."

Quellen said, "I'm aware of that. You know, the High Government is furthering a whole sequence of plans designed to alleviate the unemployment problem."

"That's fine. But in the meanwhile Norm isn't working,

and I don't think it'll matter much longer. He's in contact with the hopper people and he's going to hop. Even while I'm sitting here telling you this, he might be getting into the machine!"

Her voice had risen to a tinny screech. She could hear the echoes of it go bouncing around in her brother's office. It seemed to her that the ends of her nerves had burst through her skin all over her body, and were jutting out like quills.

Quellen's manner changed. He seemed to make a conscious effort to relax, and he leaned forward benevolently, giving her a froodlike smile. Helaine expected him to ask, "Shall we now attempt to get to the bottom of this delusion of yours?" What he actually said, in honeyed, humoring tones, was, "Maybe you're getting overwrought for no real reason, Helaine. What makes you think he's having dealings with the hopper criminals?"

She told him about the Lanoy minislip, and about Norm's exaggerated reaction of unconcern when she had queried him on Lanoy. As she quoted the five-word slogan on the slip, Helaine was startled to see her brother's beaming look of phony solicitude give way for a moment to a blank expression betokening some sudden absolute terror within. Then Quellen recovered; but he had already betrayed himself. Helaine was sharp to detect such momentary flickers of the inner persona.

She said, "You know about Lanoy?"

"It happens that I've seen one of those slips, Helaine. They're being circulated pretty widely. You go up a quickboat ramp and somebody comes up to you and hands one out. No doubt that's how Norm got his."

"And it's advertising for the hopper people, isn't it?"

"I've got no reason to think so," Quellen drawled, his eyes proclaiming his lie to her.

"Are you investigating Lanoy, though? I mean, if there's reason to suspect—"

"We're investigating, yes. And I repeat, Helaine, there's no necessary cause to feel that this person Lanoy is in any way connected with the hopper problem."

"But Beth Wisnack said that her husband Bud talked about Lanoy all week before he went."

"Who?"

"Wisnack. A recent hopper. When I asked her about Lanoy, Beth told me point-blank that he was responsible for Bud's disappearance, and she also said that it was a sure thing that Norm would be going too." Agitated, Helaine crossed and uncrossed her legs. The chair's dull brain picked up the evidence of her restlessness, and after having been quiescent for a few minutes began to fondle her again.

Quellen said, "We can check this business of Norm's going hopper very easily." He swung around and produced a spool. "I have here the complete listing of all the documented hoppers who were recorded as they arrived in the past. This list was compiled recently for me and of course I haven't studied it completely, because it contains hundreds of thousands of names. But if Norm did hop, we'll find him here."

He activated the spool and began to search it, explaining in a half-mumble that the listings were alphabetical. Helaine sat rigidly as the search continued through the alphabet at a rate of thousands of bits per second. It would not take long for Quellen to reach the "P" entries. And then—

If Norm had gone, he would be entered here. His fate would be plain for her to see—his fate and hers, inscribed in this Doomsday Book of thermoplastic tape. She would learn that her marriage had been doomed three hundred years before she contracted it. She would find that her husband's name had been inscribed centuries ago on a roster of fugitives from this century. Why had that roster not been a matter of public record all this time? Because, she knew, it would lie like a dead hand across the souls of those who had hopped, would hop, must hop. What would it be like to grow up under the shadow of the knowledge that you were destined to leap from your own era?

"You see?" Quellen said triumphantly. "He isn't on the list."

"Does that mean he didn't hop?"

"I'd say so."

"But how can you be sure that all the hoppers are really listed?" Helaine demanded. "What if a lot of them slipped through?"

"It's possible."

"And the names," she went on. "If Norm gave a different name when he got to the past, he wouldn't be on your list either. Right?"

Quellen looked glum. "There's always the possibility that he adopted a pseudonym," he admitted.

"You're hedging, Joe. You can't be sure he didn't hop. Even with the list."

"So what do you want me to do, Helaine?"

She took a deep breath. "You could arrest Lanoy before he sends Norm back in time."

"I've got to find Lanoy," Quellen observed. "And then I've got to have some proof that he's involved. So far there isn't even any circumstantial evidence, just a lot of conclusion-jumping on your part."

"Then arrest Norm."

"What?"

"Find him guilty of something and lock him up. Give him a year or two of corrective therapy. That'll keep him out of circulation until the hopper crisis is over. Call it protective custody."

"Helaine, I can't use the law as a private plaything for members of my family!"

"He's my husband, Joe. I want to keep him. If he goes back in time, I've lost him forever." Helaine stood up. She swayed, and had to grip Quellen's desk. How could she make him understand that she stood at the edge of an abyss? To hop was effectively the same as to die. She was fighting to keep her husband. And there sat her brother in the cloak of his righteousness, doing nothing while precious seconds ticked away.

"I'll do what I can," Quellen promised. "I'll look into this Lanoy. If you'd like to send Norm here, I'll talk to him and try to find out what's on his mind. Yes. Perhaps that's best. Get him to come to see me."

"If he's planning to hop," said Helaine, "he's not likely to tell you about it. He won't come within five miles of this building."

"Why don't you tell him that I want to talk to him about a job opportunity? He's been complaining that I haven't been doing anything for him, yes? All right. He'll come to me, thinking that I've got an opening for him. And I'll pump him about hopping. Subtly. If he knows anything, I'll get it out of him. We'll smash the hopper ring and there'll be no danger of his taking off. How does that sound, Helaine?"

"Encouraging. I'll talk to him. I'll send him to you. If he hasn't already taken off."

She moved toward the door. Her brother smiled once again. Helaine winced. She was fearful that Norm had already vanished irretrievably, while she sat here talking. She had to get back to him in a hurry. Until this crisis was over, she knew she must keep close watch.

"Remember me to Judith," Helaine said, and went out.

8.

Quellen had not enjoyed the interview with his sister. Helaine always left him feeling flayed. She was so visibly unhappy that it pained him to see her at all. Now she looked five or six years older than he was. He remembered Helaine at thirteen or so, virginal and radiant, naive enough to think that life held something wonderful for her. Here she was a few years short of forty, marooned within four walls, clawing like a demon to hang on to her morose, embittered husband, because he was just about all that she had.

Still, she had given him some useful information. Lanoy had been on Quellen's mind ever since the sallow-faced stranger had pressed the wadded minislip into his hand on the flyramp. The next day, Quellen had initiated a routine check, but it had turned up nothing tangible. A mere last name was useless to the computer. There were thousands of Lanoys in the world, and Quellen could scarcely investigate every one of them for possible criminal activities. A random scoop had yielded no information. Now, though, came Helaine with her intuitive conviction that Lanoy was behind the hopper business. And this woman she had mentioned, this Beth Wisnack—Quellen made a note to send a man around to talk to her again. No doubt Beth Wisnack had already been interrogated about her husband's disappearance, but she would have to be approached from the direction of Lanoy information this time.

Quellen considered the possibility of posting a guard on Norm Pomrath to prevent any untimely departure. He had been ordered in no ambiguous terms to leave Donald Mortensen alone and to do no meddling with any of the listed hoppers. Koll had received The Word from Giacomin, who had it from the lips of Kloofman himself: "Hands off Mortensen."

They were afraid of changing the past. Quellen could feel the fear in them running right up to the High Government. It was within his power to shake the underpinnings of the universe. Pick up Donald Mortensen for questioning and put a laser bolt through his skull, for example.

"Sorry. Resisted arrest and had to be destroyed."

Yes. And then Donald Mortensen would never take off for the past on May 4. Which would upset the entire structure of the last few centuries. At the moment I shoot Mortensen, Quellen thought, everything will shift and it will turn out that we were conquered by an army of slimy centipedes from the Magellanic Clouds in A.D. 2257—a conquest that would have been prevented by one of the descendants of Donald Mortensen, if I hadn't been so thoughtless as to shoot him down.

Quellen had no intention of inviting the wrath of the High Government by interfering with the departure of Donald Mortensen. But Norm Pomrath was not on the hopper list. Was he covered by Kloofman's directive, then? Was Quellen required to abstain from any action that could possibly lead to the time-departure of any person whatever?

That made no sense. Therefore Quellen agreed with himself that he could without compromising himself keep watch on his brother-in-law and take steps to prevent Norm from going hopper. That would make Helaine happy. It might also, Quellen thought, contribute to an ultimate solution to this entire worrisome assignment.

"Get me Brogg," he said into his communicator mouthpiece.

Brogg turned out to be conducting an investigation outside the building. The other UnderSec, Leeward, entered Quellen's office.

The CrimeSec said, "I've got a possible lead. My brother-in-law Norm Pomrath is allegedly on the verge of seeking out a contact who'll help him become a hopper. I'm not sure there's any truth in it, but I want it checked. Slap an Ear on Pomrath and have him monitored on a twenty-four-hour, round-the-clock basis. If he utters so much as a syllable about hopping, we'll make our move."

"Yes, sir," said Leeward stolidly.

"There's also this matter of a certain Lanoy. Did anything new turn up?"

"Not yet, sir."

"I've learned that Pomrath's supposed contact man is this Lanoy. So that's our key syllable. Make sure that the monitors are triggered to flash if Pomrath mentions the name. I'm to be summoned immediately."

Leeward went off to take care of things. There was the end to Norm Pomrath's privacy, of course. From now until Quellen withdrew the Ear, Pomrath could not embrace his wife, relieve his bowels, scratch his armpit, or denounce the High Government without having some omniscient monitoring system making a record of it. Too bad. Quellen himself had been victimized by an Ear, and he knew the anguish of it, because that was how the treacherous Brogg had learned of the CrimeSec's illegal home in Africa. Yet Quellen had no real regrets about what he was doing to Pomrath. It was for Helaine's sake. She had asked to have Norm put in jail, hadn't she? This would be far less inconvenient to him. He'd never even know, most likely. And he might just lead Quellen to the source of the hopper enterprise. In any event it would be extremely difficult for Pomrath to take leave of the present century while he was being monitored.

Quellen dismissed the Pomrath problem from his mind, for the moment, and turned his attention to other matters of urgency.

The day's general crime reports had landed on his desk. Obsessed as he was with hoppers, Quellen still had responsibilities in other sectors. He was required to examine the details of all crimes committed within his zone of Appalachia, and to make recommendations for dispensation. The new stack was about the same size as yesterday's—crime was a statistical constant—and, Quellen knew, today's atrocities would be neither less nor more imaginative than yesterday's.

He leafed through the documents.

The roster of crimes no longer chilled Quellen, and that was the worst part of the job. A creeping loss of sensitivity was overtaking him year by year. When he had been young and new at this game, a fledging Class Eleven just finding out what it was all about, the extent of man's capacity to do injury to man had numbed him. Now it was all statistics and coded tapes, divorced from reality.

The crimes tended to be motiveless. The benign High Government had removed most of the archaic causes for crime, such as hunger, want, and physical frustration.

Everyone received a paycheck, whether he worked or not, and there was enough food for all, nutritious if not particularly tasty. No one was driven into banditry to support a starving family. Most addictive drugs were easily available. Sex of all varieties could be had cheaply at government-regulated cubicles. These measures were signs of maturity, so it was said. By making most things legal, the High Government had removed the need to commit illegalities.

True. The motives for crime were largely extinct. Crime itself, though, remained. Quellen had had ample proof of that melancholy sociological fact. Theft, murder, rape–these were amusements, now, not matters of need. The middle classes were shot through with criminality. Respectable Class Six burghers did the most hideous things. Plump matrons from Class Five households waylaid strangers in dark alleyways. Bright-eyed children took part in abominations. Even the officers of the law themselves, Quellen knew, circumvented authority by illegal acts, such as establishing second homes for themselves in reservations supposedly limited to Class Two personnel. Yet at least Quellen's own crime did no direct injury to other human beings. Whereas–

Here was the account of a Class Eight hydroponics man who was accused of a biological crime: unlawful insertion of living matter in the body of another human being. It was alleged that he had anesthetized a fellow technician, made a surgical opening in his body with an ultrasonic probe, and placed within it a lethal quantity of a newly developed Asian carniphage that proceeded to devour the circulatory system of the victim, rampaging up one artery and down the next vein, flowing like flame through the web of vessels. Why? "To see his reactions," was the explanation. "It was quite instructive."

Here was a Class Six instructor in advanced hermeneutics at a large Appalachian university who had invited a nubile young student to his luxurious two-room apartment and upon her refusal to participate in sexual relations with him did inflict on her a short-circuit of the pain centers, after which he raped her and turned her loose, minus all sensory reactions. Why? "A matter of masculine pride," he told the arresting officer. "The Latin-American concept of *machismo*–"

He had his pride. But the girl would never feel sensation again. Neither pain nor pleasure, unless the damage could be undone by surgery.

And here, Quellen saw, was the seamy account of a gathering of believers in the cult of social regurgitation, which had ended in tragedy instead of mystical experience. One of the worshippers, impelled by fathomless motives of cruelty, had covertly intruded three crystals of pseudoliving glass in his cud before turning it over to his companions. The glass, expanding in a congenial environment, had penetrated the internal organs of the victims in a fatal fashion. "It was all a terrible error," the criminal declared. "My intention was to swallow one of the crystals myself, and so share with them the torment and the ultimate release. Unfortunately–"

The story touched a chord of shock in Quellen. Most of these daily nightmare tales left him unmoved; but it happened that his Judith was a member of this very cult, and Judith had been on his mind since Helaine's visit. Quellen hadn't seen Judith or even been in touch with her since his last return from Africa. And it might just as easily have been Judith who swallowed these devilish crystals of pseudoliving glass as the unknown victims listed here. It might even have been me, Quellen thought in distaste. I should call Judith soon. I've been ignoring her.

He looked on through the reports.

Not all of the current crimes had been so imaginative.

There was the customary quota of bludgeonings, knifings, laserings, and other conventional assaults. But the scope for criminality was infinitely great, and fanciful atrocities were the hallmark of the era. Quellen turned page after page, jotting down his observations and recommendations. Then he pushed all the troublesome material aside.

He had not yet had a chance to look at the spool that Brogg had labeled Exhibit B in the hopper investigation. Brogg had said that it represented some tangential evidence of timetravel outside the recorded 1979–2106 zone. Quellen put the spool on and settled back to watch.

It consisted of Brogg's scholarly cullings of the annals of occultism. The UnderSec had compiled hundreds of accounts of mysterious appearances and apparitions, evidently under the assumption that they might represent time travelers of a prehopper phase. "I wish to suggest," Brogg's memorandum asserted, "that while the normal range of the time-transport apparatus lies within five hundred years of the present time, there have been instances when an overshoot resulted in transportation to a much earlier period."

Maybe so, Quellen mused. He examined the evidence in a mood of detached curiosity.

Exhibit: the testimony of Giraldus Cambrensis, chronicler, born at the castle of Manorbier in Pembrokeshire, circa A.D. 1146. Giraldus offered the tale of a red-haired young man who turned up unexpectedly in the house of a knight known as Eliodore de Stakepole in western Wales:

> This strange man said his name was Simon. He took the keys from the seneschal, and took over, also, the seneschal's job; but he was so clever and finished a manager that nothing was ever lost or wanting in the house, which ever more became prosperous. If

> the master or mistress thought of something they would like, and did not even speak their thought, he read their minds and, hey presto, he got it, and no orders given him! He knew where they cached their gold and jewels. He would say to them: 'Why this niggard care of your gold and silver? Is not life short? Then enjoy it, spend your gold or you will die without enjoying life and the money you so cautiously hoard will do you no service.' He had an eye for the good opinion of menials and rustics, and he gave them the choicest food and drink . . . This strange red-haired man set foot in no church, used no breviary, and uttered no Catholic word or religious sentiment. He did not sleep in the manor house; but was always on hand to serve and spring forward to give what was wanted.

The chronicler related that the Stakepole children were curious about this mysterious Simon, and took to spying on him around the grounds of the manor house:

> And, one night, peering out from behind a holly bush, when the strange man was, by chance, gazing hard into the waters of a still mill dam, they saw him moving his lips as if in converse with something unseen.

Which was duly reported to the elder Stakepole, and that virtuous knight instantly summoned Simon to his private chamber and gave him the sack:

> As they took the keys from him, the lady of the manor asked him: 'Who art thou?'

> He replied: 'I am begotten of the wife of a yokel of the parish by a demon who lay upon her in the shape of her own husband.'
>
> He named the man who was so cuckolded, who was lately dead. The mother was still alive, and when strict inquiry was made of her, the thing was certified to be true by her public confession.

Interesting, Quellen thought. Where did Brogg get these things? It could very well have been that the red-haired "demon" was a hopper accidentally hurled too far in time. So, too, these other monkish accounts. The twelfth and thirteenth centuries, according to Brogg's researches, had been a fertile era for the arrival of inexplicable strangers. Not all of them had arrived in human form, either. Quellen observed an extract from the *Eulogium Historiarum* prepared at Malmesbury Abbey, under the rubric A.D. 1171:

> On the night of the birthday of the Lord, there were thunderings and lightnings of which the like had not been heard before. And at Andover, a certain priest, at midnight, in the presence of the whole congregation, was cast down by lightning, with no other injuries . . . but what looked like a pig was seen to run to and fro between his feet . . .

Brogg had ferreted out a parallel case in the *Annales Francorum Regium* of the monk Bertin, inscribed circa A.D. 1160. The entry for A.D. 856 declared:

> In August, Teotogaudus, Bishop of Trier, with clerics and people was celebrating the office when a very dreadful cloud, with thunderstorms and lightning, terrified the whole congregation in the church, and

> deadened the sound of the bells ringing in the tower. The whole building was filled with such dense darkness that one and another could hardly see or recognize his or her neighbor. On a sudden, there was seen a dog of immense size in a sudden opening of the floor or earth, and it ran to and fro around the altar.

Pigs? Dogs? Trial runs, perhaps, in the early days of the time-travel enterprise, Quellen wondered? The machine was still new and unreliable, he imagined, and hapless beasts had been placed within its field, and then had been spurted into the past to the consternation of the devout, devil-dreading citizens of the middle ages. A deplorable overshoot had taken the unhappy creatures back beyond the industrial revolution, but of course the operators of the machine could not have known the ultimate destinations of their passengers, unless they had had knowledge of these same records that Brogg had unearthed.

Nor did all Brogg's cases involve medieval episodes. A good many sections of Exhibit B dealt with instances more recent, though still well outside the 1979 date that had been considered the extreme limit of pastward travel. Quellen gave heed to the case of a girl who appeared at the door of a cottage near Bristol, England, on the evening of April 3, 1817, and begged for food in what was described as "an unknown language."

How did they know what she was begging for, then, Quellen asked himself? The spool did not answer. It informed him instead that the girl who spoke unintelligibly was brought before a magistrate, one Samuel Worral, who instead of arresting her on a vagrancy charge took her to his home. (Suspicious, Quellen thought!) He questioned her. She wrote replies in an unknown script whose characters looked like combs, birdcages, and frying pans. Linguists came to analyze her words. At length came one who described himself as "a gentleman from the East Indies." He interrogated her in the Malay language and received comprehensible replies.

She was, he declared, the Princess Caraboo, kidnapped by pirates from her Javan home and carried off to sea, involving her in many adventures before at length she made her escape on the English shore. Through the medium of the "gentleman from the East Indies," Princess Caraboo imparted many details of life in Java. Then a woman of Devonshire, a Mrs. Wilcocks, came forward and announced that the Princess was actually her own daughter Mary, born in 1791. Mary Wilcocks confessed her imposture and emigrated to America.

Brogg had appended the following speculation to the case of the Princess Caraboo:

"According to some authorities a multiple imposture was practiced here. A girl mysteriously appeared. A man stepped forward and claimed to understand her language. An older woman declared that it was all a fraud. But the records are faulty. What if the girl was a visitor from the future, and the 'gentleman from the East Indies' another hopper who shrewdly tried to pass her off as a Javan princess in order to keep her true origin from coming out, and the pretended mother yet another hopper who moved in to protect the girl when it looked likely that the Javan hoax would be exposed? *How many time-travelers were living in England in 1817, anyway?*"

It seemed to Quellen that Brogg was being too credulous. He passed on to the next instance.

Cagliostro: appeared in London, then in Paris, speaking with an accent of an unidentifiable kind. Supernal powers. Aggressive, gifted, unconventional. Accused of being in actuality one Joseph Balsamo, a Sicilian criminal. The same never proven. Earned a good living in eighteenth-century Europe peddling alchemistic powders, love philtres, elixirs of youth, and other useful compounds. Grew careless, was imprisoned in the Bastille in 1785, escaped, visited other countries, was arrested again, died in prison, 1795. Fraud? Impostor? Time-traveler? It was wholly possible. Anything, thought Quellen sadly, was possible once you began giving credence to such evidence.

Kaspar Hauser: staggered into the town of Nuremberg, Germany, on an afternoon in May, 1828. Apparently sixteen or seventeen years old. (A trifle young for becoming a hopper, Quellen thought. Perhaps deceptive in appearance.) Capable of speaking only two sentences in German. Given a pencil and paper, he wrote a name: "Kaspar Hauser." Assumption made that that was his name. He was unacquainted with the commonest objects and experiences of everyday affairs of human beings. Dropped down out of a time fault, no doubt.

A quick learner, though. Detained for a while in prison as a vagrant, then turned over to a schoolmaster, Professor Daumer. Mastered German and wrote an autobiographical essay, declaring that he had lived all his life in a small, dark cell, living on bread and water. Yet a policeman who had found him declared, "He had a very healthy color: he did not appear pale or delicate, like one who had been some time in confinement."

Many contradictions. Universal fascination in Europe; everyone speculating on the mysterious origin of Kaspar Hauser. Some said he was the crown prince of Baden, kidnapped in 1812 by the agents of the morganatic wife of his postulated father, the grand duke. Denied. Subsequently disproven. Others said he was sleepwalker, amnesiac. October 17, 1829: Kaspar Hauser found with a wound in forehead, allegedly inflicted by a man in a black mask. Policemen assigned to guard him. Several further purported assaults. December 14, 1833: Kaspar Hauser found dying in a park, with deep stab wound on his left breast. Claimed that a stranger had inflicted the wound. No sign of weapon in the park, no footprints in vicinity except Hauser's own. Suggestion that the wound was self-inflicted. Died several days afterward after exclaiming, "My God! that I should so die in shame and disgrace!"

Quellen disconnected the spool. Pigs, dogs, the Princess Caraboo, Kaspar Hauser—it was all quite entertaining. It might even support a belief that the whole of human history was besprinkled with time-travelers, and not simply the period from 1979 to 2106. Fine. But such facts did little to solve Quellen's immediate problems, however much the gathering of them had gratified the beefy Brogg's taste for scholarship. Quellen put the spool away.

He dialed Judith's number. Her face appeared on the screen, pale, somber, austere. She fell short of being beautiful by quite a good deal. The bridge of her nose was too high, her forehead was somewhat domed, her lips were thin, her chin was long. Her eyes were disquietingly far apart, with the right one slightly higher than the left. Yet she was not unattractive. Quellen had toyed with the temptation of allowing himself to fall in love with her. It was awkward, though; he could not let her get too far within his emotional defenses without telling her about the place in Africa, and he did not want to share that fact with her. She had a streak of righteousness; she might inform on him.

She said, "Have you been hiding from me, Joe?"

"I've been busy. Submerged in work. I'm sorry, Judith."

"Don't let your guilts overflow. I've been getting along quite well."

"I'm sure you have. How's your frood?"

"Dr. Galuber? He's fine. He'd like to have the chance to meet you, Joe."

Quellen bristled. "I've got no plans for entering therapy, Judith. I'm sorry."

"That's the second time you've said you were sorry in the last three sentences."

"I'm sor—" Quellen began, and then they both laughed.

Judith said, "I meant for you to meet Dr. Galuber socially. He'll be at our next communion."

"Which is?"

"Tonight, as a matter of fact. Will you come?"

"You know that social regurgitation has never delighted me very much, Judith."

She smiled in a wintry way. "I know that. But it's time you got out of your shell a little. You live too much to yourself, Joe. If you want to be a bachelor, that's your business, but you don't have to be a hermit too."

"I can put a piece in the slot of a frood machine and get advice just as profound as that."

"Maybe so. Will you come to the communion, though?"

Quellen thought of the case he had studied only an hour or so back, of the earnest communicant who had slipped pseudoliving glass into the alimentary canals of his fellow worshippers and then had watched them die in agony. He pictured himself writhing in torment while a weeping Judith clung to him and tried to extract the last vestige of empathic sorrow from his sufferings, after the manner of her cult.

He sighed. She was right: he had been living too much to himself these days. He needed to get out, away from his official responsibilities.

"Yes," he said. "Yes, Judith, I'll come to the communion. Are you happy?"

9.

Stanley Brogg had had a busy day.

The UnderSec was juggling a lot of Quellen's hot potatoes at once, but it did not trouble him, for Brogg had a good capacity for work. He privately felt that he and Spanner between them kept the whole department going. They were two of a kind, both big men, massive and methodical, with a reserve of flesh to draw extra energy from in times of crisis. Of course, Spanner was in the administrative end, and Brogg a lowly legworker. Spanner was Class Six, Brogg Class Nine. Yet Brogg saw himself as Spanner's comrade-in-arms.

Those other two, Koll and Quellen—they were excrescences on the department. Koll was full of hatred and mischief, seething with wrath simply because he was small and ugly. He had ability, of course, but his basically neurotic orientation made him dangerous and useless. If ever there was a case for compulsory frooding, it was Koll. Brogg often compared him to Tiberius Caesar: a baleful man full of menace, not insane but badly askew and so to be avoided.

If Koll were Tiberius, Quellen was Claudius: amiable, intelligent, weak to the core. Brogg despised his immediate superior. Quellen struck him as a ditherer, unfit for his post. Now and then Quellen could act with vigor and determination, but it didn't come naturally to him. Brogg had been doing the legwork for Quellen for years; otherwise, the department would long since have fallen apart.

A surprising thing about Quellen, though: he was capable of criminality. That had startled Brogg. He didn't think the man had it in him. To obtain a plot of land in Africa by diligently falsifying records, to apply and receive illegal stat service from a Class Seven apartment to the Congo, to live a secret life of ease and even luxury—why, it was an achievement so monstrously bold that Brogg still couldn't see how Quellen had carried it off. Unless the explanation was that Quellen was so repelled by the harshness of life all about him that he was willing to take any risk to escape from it. Even a coward could rise to what looked like moral grandeur in the interests of his own cowardice. In the same way, a soft, flabby man like the Emperor Nero could transform himself into a demon simply to preserve his own flabbiness. Nero, thought Brogg, hadn't been innately demonic after the fashion of Caligula; he had drifted into monstrosity in easy stages. In a way it was out of character for him, just as Quellen's surprising act of boldness jarred with the image of the man that Brogg had constructed.

Brogg had found out Quellen's great secret purely by accident, though there was some degree of treachery mixed into it. He had suspected for quite a while that Quellen was up to something peculiar, but he had no idea what it was. Deviant religious activity, perhaps; maybe Quellen belonged to one of the proscribed cults, a chaos group perhaps, or one of the rumored bands that gathered in dark corners to pray to the vicious pyrotic assassin, Flaming Bess.

Not knowing the details, but sensing the defensive wariness in Quellen's recent behavior, Brogg sought to turn the situation to his personal profit. He had high expenses. Brogg was a man with pretensions to scholarship; immersed as he was in the study of ancient Romans, he had surrounded himself with books, authentic Roman coins, scraps of history. It took money to buy anything authentic. Brogg was living to the hilt of his salary now. It had struck him that Quellen might be a fruitful victim for extortion.

First Brogg had spoken to Quellen's roommate of the time, Bruce Marok—for Quellen had not yet been promoted to Class Seven, and like any unmarried male of his class he was required to share an apartment. Marok, while confirming that something odd was going on, did not offer any details. He didn't seem to know much. Then came Quellen's promotion, and with the uptwitch Marok dropped out of the picture.

Brogg slapped an Ear on his boss and sat back to listen.

The truth came out soon enough. Quellen had connived to get a chunk of Africa registered under a blind name for which he was the nominee. Much of Africa had been set aside as a private reserve for members of the High Government—the tropical part, particularly, which had been generally depopulated during the Spore War a century and a half back. Quellen had his slice. He had arranged for a house to be built there, and for unauthorized stat service so that he could pop back and forth across the Atlantic in a twinkling. Of course, Quellen's little scheme was certain to be exposed eventually by one of the resurvey squads. But that part of the world was not due for a resurvey for some fifty years, by which time Quellen would be in little danger.

Brogg spent a fascinated few weeks tracking Quellen's movements. He had thought at first that Quellen must take women to the hideaway for participation in illicit cultist activities, but no, Quellen went alone. He simply sought peace and solitude. In a way, Brogg sympathized with Quellen's need. However, Brogg had needs of his own, and he was not a sentimental man. He went to Quellen.

"The next time you stat to Africa," he said blandly, "think of me. I envy you, CrimeSec."

Quellen gasped in shock. Then he recovered. "Africa? What are you talking about, Brogg? Why would I go to Africa?"

"To get away from it all. Yes?"

"I deny all your accusations."

"I've got proof," said Brogg. "Want to hear?"

In the end, they reached an accommodation. For a generous cash payment, Brogg would keep silent. That had been several months ago, and Quellen had paid regularly. So long as he did, Brogg observed the bargain. He was not really interested in informing on Quellen, who was much more useful to him as a source of money than he would be in an institution for corrective rehabilitation. Pursuing his studies more easily on Quellen's hush money, Brogg hoped earnestly that no one else would unmask the CrimeSec's secret. That would mean the loss of his extra income, and might even send him to jail too, as an accomplice after the fact. These days, Brogg watched over Quellen like a guardian angel, protecting him from the prying eyes of others.

Brogg knew that Quellen feared and hated him, of course. It didn't trouble him. Secreted in various places throughout the vicinity were taped accounts of Quellen's iniquity, programmed to deliver themselves to High Government authorities in the event of Brogg's sudden death or disappearance. Quellen knew that. Quellen wasn't about to do anything. He was well aware that the moment sensors of those devilish little boxes ceased to pick up the alpha rhythms of Stanley Brogg, autonomic legs would come forth and the telltales would march down to headquarters to pour forth their accusations. So Quellen and Brogg were at a standstill of mutual benefit.

Neither of them ever mentioned the situation. In the office, work proceeded serenely, though Brogg occasionally allowed himself a veiled reminder to keep Quellen uncomfortable. Generally Brogg took orders and carried them out.

As, for example, on this hopper business.

He had spent the last few days tracking Donald Mortensen, the potential hopper who was due to skip out on May 4. Quellen had asked Brogg to handle the Mortensen case with the greatest delicacy. Brogg knew why. He was clever enough to foresee the time-paradox consequences that might result if somebody interfered with the departure of Mortensen, who was on the documented hopper list. Brogg had gone over those old lists himself to compile the spool he had labeled Exhibit A. Subtract a man from the old records and the whole world might totter. Brogg knew that. Undoubtedly Quellen knew that too. Why, most likely Kloofman and Danton would have a dozen aneurysms pop in their aging arteries when they found out that Quellen's department was monkeying with the structure of the past. Such monkeying jeopardized everybody's status in the present, and those who had the most status to lose—the Class Ones—were the ones who would get most agitated over the investigation.

So Brogg was careful. He was pretty sure that the High Government would quash the Mortensen investigation once word of it got to Them. In the meanwhile, though, Brogg was merely carrying out his assignment. He could fry Quellen by botching the work and tipping off Mortensen; but Brogg had powerful motives for preserving Quellen from harm.

He found Mortensen easily: a lean, blonde man of

twenty-eight, with pale blue eyes and eyebrows so white they were virtually invisible. Brushing against him at a quickboat ramp, Brogg managed to affix an Ear to the man, hanging the hooked patch of transponding equipment neatly in Mortensen's flesh. Brogg used a splinter model, working it into a callus in Mortensen's palm. The man would never feel it. In a few days it would dissolve, but meanwhile it would transmit a world of information. Brogg was expert at such things.

He tuned in on Mortensen and recorded his activities.

The man was involved with a person named Lanoy. Brogg picked up things like:

"—at the station with Lanoy on the hop day—"

"—Lanoy's fee is on deposit—"

"—you tell Lanoy that I'll be going out the first week in May—"

"—yes, at the lake, the place I met him the last time—"

Mortensen was married. Class Ten. Didn't like his wife. Hopping provided instant divorce, Brogg thought with amusement. The Ear gave him Sidna Mortensen's shrill complaints, and he couldn't help but agree that the best thing Mortensen could do was hop. Brogg compiled a considerable dossier on the potential hopper.

Then came The Word, from Kloofman via Giacomin via Koll to Quellen and thence to Brogg:

"Leave Mortensen alone. He's not to be tampered with. That's The Word."

Brogg looked questioningly at Quellen. "What should I do? We're learning a lot from Mortensen."

"Discontinue the investigation."

"We could chance carrying it on quietly," Brogg suggested. "So long as Mortensen takes no alarm, we'd continue to get data from him. I'm not suggesting that we actually interfere with his departure, but until—"

"No."

Coward, Brogg thought. Afraid the High Government will flay you!

In a moment of anarchy Brogg saw himself deliberately destroying Donald Mortensen, flying in the face of the High Government, possibly smashing everything like Samson putting his shoulders to the pillars of the temple. It would have amused Brogg to learn that the supposedly meek Quellen had had the same rebellious thought. There was tremendous power in knowing that the minor act of a minor official could threaten the security of the High Government. Yet Brogg did not give way to the impulse, any more than Quellen had. He obediently discontinued the Mortensen investigation. Mortensen would depart for the past on May 4, and the continuum would be preserved.

Anyway, Brogg had a new lead on Lanoy.

It had come to light today. A prolet named Brand, Class Fifteen, had had too much to drink in a common saloon. Leeward, refreshing himself in the drinker, had listened to Brand running off at the mouth about Lanoy and his hopper business. Without benefit of modern technology, Leeward thus picked up a vital clue and brought it to Brogg.

"Let's have Brand in for interrogation," Brogg said when he heard what Leeward had done. "Get him here. No—wait. I'll get him. You cover the office."

Brogg went out for a reconnaissance. He scouted the drinker, saw Brand, calculated the imponderables. After some hesitation he cut Brand out from the herd, identified himself as a government man, and remanded the prisoner for interrogation. Brand looked frightened. "I didn't do nothing," he insisted. "I didn't do *nothing*!"

"There'll be no harm to you," Brogg promised. "We simply want to question you."

He took Brand into custody. When he reached the Secretariat building with the prolet, Brogg learned that Quellen had issued a new instruction.

"He wants an Ear put on his brother-in-law," Leeward said.

Brogg grinned. "Nepotism even in criminal investigations? Doesn't the man have any shame?"

"I couldn't answer that," said Leeward stolidly. "But he says that the brother-in-law is thinking of making a hop. He wants it checked. He wants an Ear on the fellow and round-the-clock monitoring, right away. Norman Pomrath's the name. I've already got the data on him."

"Good. We'll take care of Pomrath at once."

"Pomrath's supposed to be in contact with Lanoy. Quellen said."

"Looks like everybody's in contact with Lanoy. Even Quellen's been approached, did you know that?" Brogg laughed. "I haven't had a chance to tell him that Mortensen was dealing with Lanoy too, but I doubt that it'll surprise him. And this prolet here, this Brand you found–there's another lead to Lanoy. We're bound to trace one of them back to the source in another day or so."

"Do you want me to put the Ear on Pomrath?" Leeward asked.

"I'll do it," said Brogg. "I've got a gift for that kind of thing. You have to admit it."

Brogg certainly did. He could move gracefully for a man of his bulk. As sinuously as any dedicated *frotteur*, Brogg could approach a victim in a quickboat and gently introduce an Ear to the unlikeliest of places. It was a gift that had stood him in good stead when he set out to spy on Quellen; he had handled the Mortensen situation equally skillfully. Now Pomrath. Brogg went down to the laboratory and rummaged about for the most advanced model Ear that was available.

"Here's a beauty," the lab technician told him with pride. "We've just finished it. We've succeeded in melding Ear technology to a substrate of pseudoliving glass, and the result is unique. Take a look."

Brogg held out a fleshy palm. The technician dumped onto it a tiny metallic transponding plaque a few molecules in thickness, wholly invisible but snugly contained in a glossy little bead of some green plastic.

"What does it do?" Brogg asked.

"It functions normally as an Ear. But the spicule of the glass has a life-tropism of unusual character. Once the Ear is in place on the recipient's body, the glass goes into action and bores its way through the skin, generally looking for entry by way of the pores. It's a kind of artificial parasite, you see. It gets inside and stays there, where it can't possibly be removed by an itchy subject. And it broadcasts indefinitely. Surgical removal is necessary to shut off the information flow."

Brogg was impressed. There were plenty of models of Ear designed for internal use, of course, but they all had to be introduced through one of the bodily orifices of the victim, which presupposed certain difficulties for the agent. The usual method was to smuggle it into the victim's food. Since most people were reticent about eating in the presence of strangers, that required considerable planning. And in any event the Ear would be digested or excreted in short order. There were other bodily orifices, naturally, and Brogg had on occasion planted Ears in women who were off their guard in a throbbing moment of ecstatic passion, but the technique was a tricky one. This was infinitely better: to slap the Ear on externally, and let the device itself take care of the job of getting within the victim's body. Yes. Brogg liked the concept.

He spent an hour learning how to use the new model Ear. Then he went after Norm Pomrath.

The televector scanner located Pomrath quickly for him: at the Central Employment Register, doubtless punching the job machine in the customary prolet mood of total despair. Brogg changed into a shabby prolet tunic, suitable for Class Twelve slope vicinity, and headed for the domed building of the job machine.

He had no difficulty finding Pomrath In the crowd. Brogg knew approximately what the man was supposed to look like—stocky, dark, tense—and almost at once he found himself staring right at him. Brogg insinuated himself into the line not far from Pomrath and observed the CrimeSec's unhappy brother-in-law for a while. Pomrath spoke to no one. He peered at the red and green and blue banks of the job machine as though they were his personal enemies. His lips were tight with distress and his eyes were harshly shadowed. This man is in anguish, Brogg thought. No wonder he's planning to become a hopper. Well, we'll soon know a great deal about him, won't we?

Brogg sidled up behind Pomrath.

"Excuse me," he said, and stumbled. Pomrath reached out a hand to steady him. Brogg clasped his fingers around Pomrath's wrist and pressed the Ear firmly into the hairy skin just above the ulna. Straightening, he thanked Pomrath for his assistance, and all the while the pseudoliving glass in which the Ear was embedded was activating its tropism and drilling a path into Pomrath's living flesh.

By evening, the Ear would have migrated up Pomrath's arm to some nice warm fatty deposit where it could settle down and transmit its signals.

"Clumsy of me," Brogg muttered. He moved away. Pomrath did not show any sign of being aware that something had been affixed to him.

Returning to the office, Brogg examined the flow from the monitor device. Pomrath had left the job-machine building now, it appeared. The tracer line on the oscilloscope showed the minute neural explosions that told of footsteps. Pomrath walked for ten minutes. Then he halted. Complex muscular actions: he was entering a building with a manually operated door. Now came a voice pickup.

POMRATH: Here I am again, Jerry.

STRANGE VOICE: We got a couch all ready for you.

POMRATH: With a nice goddam hallucination, okay? Here I am fighting off the Crab People, you see, and there's this naked blonde panting to be rescued, while Kloofman is waiting to give me the Galactic Medal of Honor.

VOICE: I can't pick the effect for you, Norm. You know that. You pay your pieces and you get what comes. It's all what's stirring around inside your head that settles the picture for you.

POMRATH: There's plenty stirring around inside *my* head, pal. Where's the mask? I'm going to dream a beauty. Norm Pomrath, the destroyer of worlds. Disrupting time and space. The devourer of continua.

VOICE: You sure got a crazy imagination, Norm.

Brogg turned away. Pomrath was in a sniffer palace, evidently. Nothing meaningful was going to turn up on the monitor now—nothing but Pomrath asleep on the couch enjoying or perhaps not enjoying his hallucination.

In another room, Leeward was still interrogating the hapless prolet Brand. Brand looked disturbed. Brogg listened for a while, found little of significance going on, and checked out for the day. Quellen had already gone home, he observed. To Africa, maybe, for the evening.

Brogg reached his own apartment in a short while. As required, he had a roommate–a legal assistant in one of the judiciary divisions–but they had managed to work things out so that their paths rarely crossed. You had to make the best accommodation you could to the existing living conditions.

Tired, Brogg got quickly under the molecular bath and cleansed himself of the day's grime. He programmed dinner. Then he selected a book. He was pursuing a fascinating theme in his favorite subject, Roman history: Tiberius' handling of the rebellion of Sejanus. The interplay of character was irresistible: Sejanus, the sly favorite of the sinister old Caesar, overreaching himself at last and being cast down from the heights of power by Tiberius, the Capri-dwelling old goat.

Easily, Brogg drifted into contemplation of those distant and violent events.

If I had been Sejanus, he thought, how would I have handled the situation? More tactfully, no doubt. I would never have provoked the old boy that way. Brogg smiled. If he had been Sejanus, he knew, he would ultimately have come to hold the throne in his own name. On the other hand–

On the other hand, he was not Sejanus. He was Stanley Brogg of the Secretariat of Crime. More's the pity, Brogg thought. But we must make do with what we have.

10.

Night was closing in like a clamped fist. Quellen changed his clothes after a leisurely shower that used up nearly his entire week's quota of washing water. He dressed in clothes that were a bit on the gaudy side, in sullen rebellion against the sort of evening that Judith was going to inflict on him. The people who came to these communions of social regurgitation tended to be drab, consciously so. He despised their puritanical austerity. And so he donned a tunic shot through with iridescent threads, gleaming red and violet and azure as he shifted the angles of refraction.

He did not eat dinner. That would be an unpardonable faux pas, in view of this evening's planned ceremony. Still, he needed to keep his glucose level up after the tensions of the day. A few tablets took care of that. Refreshed, Quellen sealed his apartment and went out. He was meeting Judith at the communion. Afterward, perhaps, he might go home with her. She lived alone since she had joined him in Class Seven. It would be an act of good citizenship, Quellen knew, to marry her and combine their living quarters. Quellen was not prepared to be so patriotic just yet.

The cult session was being held, Judith had informed him, at the Class Four home of a certain Brose Cashdan, an administrator of the intercontinental stat nexus. It was interesting to Quellen that a transportation tycoon like Cashdan would get involved in such a cult. Of course, the cult of social regurgitation wasn't on the proscribed list. It might be esthetically distasteful, but it wasn't subversive like some of the others. Still, Quellen's experience with high administrators had taught him that they tended to be guardians of the status quo. Maybe Cashdan was different. In any case, Quellen was curious about the house. He had not seen many Class Four homes.

Brose Cashdan's villa lay just within the inner zone of the Appalachia stat radius. That meant that Quellen could not reach it by the instantaneous transmission of the stat, but had to take a quickboat. A pity, that; it was a waste of half an hour. He programmed his course northward. The screen within the quickboat gave him a simulated view of what was below; the Hudson River, silvery and serpentine in the moonlight, and then the furry hills of the Adirondack Forest Preserve, a thousand acres of unspoiled wilderness in the middle of the sprawl of the city, and finally the floodlit glitter of the landing ramp. Local transport took Quellen speedily to Cashdan's place. He was a little late, he knew, but it did not bother him.

It was quite a villa. Quellen was not prepared for such opulence. Of course, Cashdan was required to live in just one location, unlike the Class Two people who could have several homes in scattered parts of the world. Still, it was a magnificent establishment, constructed mainly of glass with axial poles of some spongy, tough-looking synthetic. There were at least six rooms, a small garden (!), and a rooftop landing stage. Even from the air the place had a warm, inviting glow. Quellen stepped into the vestibule, peering ahead in hopes of catching sight of Judith.

A portly, sixtyish man with a starched white tunic came out to greet him. Diagonally across the tunic was emblazoned the golden sash of power.

"I'm Brose Cashdan," the man said. His voice was deep, the voice of authority. Quellen could see this man making brisk decisions all day long and scarcely bothering to get a recommend from a High Government official.

"Joseph Quellen. I was invited by–"

"Judith da Silva. Of course. Judith's inside. Welcome, Mr. Quellen. We're honored that you've chosen to join us. Come in. Come in."

Cashdan managed to sound ingratiating and commanding at the same time. He propelled Quellen into an inner room twenty feet long and at least thirty feet in width, carpeted wall-to-wall with some gray foamy substance that possibly had a degree of pseudolife. There was certainly nothing austere or drab about this shining palatial residence.

Eight or nine people sat clustered on the floor in the very middle of the room. Judith was among them. To Quellen's surprise, Judith had not chosen to dress in the piously self-effacing manner that most communicants of this cult preferred. Obviously this upper-class gathering had different norms. She was wearing a highly immodest sprayon dress, blue with green undertones. A strip of fabric passed between her breasts, which otherwise were bare, and wound about her hips and loins. Her nakedness was covered, more or less, but since the covering was nothing but pigment she might just as well have come nude. Quellen understood that such extreme fashions were permissible only in sophisticated circles where the mode was Class Six or better. It was a trifle pushy, then, for Judith, a Class Seven to expose herself this way. Quellen sensed that he and Judith might well be the only Sevens in the room. He smiled at Judith. She had small breasts, the desirable kind to have these days, and she had called attention to them by pigmenting her nipples.

Beside her sat a thick-bodied, practically neckless man with a clipped blue-stained beard, moist lips, and a placid expression. He was flanked by another woman, somewhat older than Judith, who wore a sprayon rig not much more modest than hers. On Judith it looked good; but not on this other one, who had unfashionably bulging breasts and plump haunches. She simpered at Quellen, who rudely stared at her tastelessly exposed body.

The rest had a prosperous, earnestly intellectual look—mainly men, some of them a trifle on the epicene side, all of them well dressed and clearly high on the slope. Judith, rising to her feet, made the introductions. Quellen let most of the names glide past without sticking in his consciousness. The neckless man with the blue beard, he noted, was Dr. Richard Galuber, Judith's frood. The fleshy damsel was Mrs. Galuber. Interesting. Quellen hadn't known that the frood was married. He had long suspected that Judith was his mistress through some shameful reverse transference. Maybe so; but would Galuber bring his wife to meet his mistress at such a session? Quellen wasn't sure. Froods were often devious in their motivations, and for all Quellen knew Galuber was out to score some obscure therapeutic point on his wife by hauling her along.

Outside the group, Judith said, "I'm so glad you came, Joe. I was afraid you'd back out."

"I promised I'd come, didn't I?"

"Yes, I know. But you've got a tendency to withdraw from potentially hostile social experiences."

Quellen was annoyed. "There you go, frooding me again! Stop it, Judith. I came, didn't I?"

"Of course you did." Her smile was suddenly warm, authentically so. "I'm happy that you did. I didn't mean to impugn you. Come meet Dr. Galuber."

"Must I?"

She laughed. "As I said, you've got a tendency to withdraw from potentially—"

"All right. All right. Take me to Dr. Galuber."

They crossed the room. Quellen was unsettled by Judith's nakedness. A polymerized band of pigment wasn't clothing, really. He could make out the separate cheeks of her buttocks beneath the dark blue covering. It made her look more bare than actual nudity. The effect was provocative and disturbing. Her slender, angular body attracted him almost unbearably, especially in the social context of this urbane setting. On the other hand, Mrs. Galuber was just as exposed, practically, and Quellen's basic impulse was to throw a blanket over her shoulders to shield her shame.

The frood peered in a froodlike fashion at Quellen. "It's a delight to meet you, Mr. Quellen. I've heard a great deal about you."

"I'm sure you have," said Quellen nervously. He was disappointed that Galuber, despite his promisingly Teutonic name, did not fake the ritualistic Central European accent that most froods affected. "I didn't know that men in your profession belonged to cults like this."

"We accept spiritual experiences of all sorts," Galuber said. "Is there some reason why we should reject them?"

"Not really."

The frood nodded to his wife. "Jennifer and I have belonged to a social regurgitation group for more than a year, now. It's led us to some remarkable insights, hasn't it, beloved?"

Mrs. Galuber simpered again. She eyed Quellen in such a frankly sexual way that he rippled with shock. "It's been extremely enlightening," she agreed. Her voice was a warm, rich contralto. "Any kind of interpersonal communion is beneficial, don't you think? Which is to say, we achieve cathexis in the manner best suited to our needs." Jennifer Galuber's abundant flesh shook with genial laughter. Quellen found himself staring at the ugly upthrust mounds of her bare breasts, and he looked away, feeling guilty and sickened. The Galubers, he thought, must have a very odd marriage. But I will not let that fat witch sneak me off for a spot of instant interpersonal communion. Galuber may be bedding Judith, but it gains me nothing to bed his wife in turn, for the roles aren't equal.

Judith said, "I've been after Dr. Galuber to come to one of our communion group's meetings for months. But he's always resisted. He felt that until he and I had reached the right stage in my therapy, he couldn't let himself get involved on such an intimate level."

"There's more to it than that, of course," said the frood benevolently. "There always is. In this case, it was a matter of imposing my wife's handicap on the group, which would require special preparations. Jennifer's a galactose-deficient mutant, you see. She's got to stay on a galactose-free diet."

"I see," said Quellen blankly.

"It's a genetic fluke," Galuber went on. "She can't metabolize galactose at all, because of an enzyme deficit. Galactose precursors would pile up, and there'd be cell damage. So she's had to be on a galactose-free diet from birth, but that leads to other problems. Since there's the enzyme deficit, she can't synthesize galactose from endogenous carbohydrates, and if left uncompensated for that would lead to a partial replacement of galactolipids by glucolipids in the brain, a grossly defective blood group spectrum, poor immune reaction in organ transplants, abnormal brain development—oh, a great problem, in many ways."

"Can it be cured?" Quellen asked.

"Not in the sense of total remission of pathology. But it can be dealt with. Hereditary galactose metabolism defects can be controlled through enzyme synthesis. Nevertheless, she's got to remain on a special diet and avoid certain substances, among them the one that's the essence of tonight's ceremony. Which is why we had to substitute our own prepared material. An inconvenience to the host."

"Not at all, not at all," boomed Brose Cashdan unexpectedly. "A trivial matter! We're delighted that you could join with us, Mrs. Galuber!"

Quellen, bewildered by Galuber's stream of clinical verbiage, was relieved when Cashdan announced that the ceremony was about to begin. The frood had spouted all that stuff on purpose, Quellen thought resentfully, by way of establishing his intellectual supremacy. Instead of tossing forth the jargon on his own trade, which was easy enough to parry if you knew your way around cocktail-party froodianism, Galuber had chosen to engulf Quellen in a cascade of impenetrable technicalities of a medical sort. Quellen quietly cursed Jennifer Galuber's enzyme deficit, her wanton glances, her galactolipid accumulation, and her jiggling breasts. Slipping away from her, he followed Judith back across the room to the carpeted pit in the center where the ceremony was about to take place.

Judith said warningly, "Joe, please, don't back out the way you did the last time. You've got to learn to divorce yourself from tribal reactions. Look at things objectively. What's wrong with mixing a little saliva?"

"Nothing," he said. "I suppose."

"And digestive fluids—they can't harm you. It's all for

the sake of spiritual communion. You mustn't look at things in obsolete ways."

"Is that how you get up the nerve to come naked to a social gathering?" he asked. "By looking at things in a non-obsolete way?"

"I'm not naked," she said primly.

"No. You're wearing a coat of paint."

"It conceals what society requires us to conceal."

"It leaves your secondary sex characteristics exposed," Quellen pointed out. "That's pretty naked."

"But not the primary ones. See for yourself. I'm perfectly covered in that area, and so, I'm well within the norms. Why don't you look at me? You can be so absurd at times, Joe."

Since she insisted on it, he stared at her waist. His eyes traveled as far as her thighs. He had to admit it; she was decently enough clad there. She looked nude, but she wasn't. Cunning, he thought. Provocative. He wondered how she got the sprayon outfit off. Maybe she would show him that, too, before the night was out. Her lean body held a powerful attraction for him. Unlike Helaine, whose leanness was the result of erosion and general haggardness, Judith's body was perfect in its lithe, slim elegance. Quellen would gladly have walked out right now with her.

But there was the ceremony to endure.

The members of this communion group assembled themselves on the rim of the carpeted pit. Brose Cashdan, as the host, produced a shining metallic bowl in which reposed a doughy mass about the size of a man's head. This, Quellen knew, was the substance of the love feast; an indigestible algae product with emetic properties. Adapted, no doubt, to suit Mrs. Galuber's galactose deficit.

Cashdan said, "Dr. Galuber has kindly consented to be our first celebrant this evening."

The lights were dimmed. Galuber took the gleaming bowl from Cashdan and rested it on his knees. Then, solemnly, he broke loose a fistful of the dough and crammed it into his mouth. He began to chew.

There were many cults. Quellen was no joiner, but even he had now and then been drawn into their ceremonies, generally through the urging of Judith. She drifted everywhere in her search for spiritual fulfillment—from frood to frood, from cult to cult. Quellen suspected that she had frequented the proscribed cults, perhaps even the outlawed Flaming Bess religion. He could picture Judith dancing naked—no flimflam of sprayon to cover her shame—while a groveling pyrotic kindled an extrasensory blaze and raging voices called for the overthrow of the High Government. Pyrotics had actually assassinated several Class One leaders a generation ago. The cult still endured.

Mainly, though, the cults were more innocent things—revolting, perhaps, but not criminal. Such as this one, in which the chewing of the cud somehow led to a feeling of interpersonal harmony. Cashdan was intoning a digestive litany of some sort. Galuber was still stuffing resilient dough into his mouth. How much could that capacious belly hold? Jennifer Galuber was watching her husband with pride. The frood continued to devour. His face was transfigured, the eyes virtually sightless. Jennifer glowered. Her bare body seemed even more huge as she took vicarious pleasure from her husband's importance.

They were all chanting, now. Even Judith. Low, serious sounds of spirituality came from them.

She nudged him. "You too," she whispered.

"I don't know the words."

"Just drone along, then."

He shrugged. Galuber had ingested nearly every scrap of dough in the bowl. Surely his stomach was painfully distended, now. That stuff was like rubber. The emetic it contained worked on a critical-mass basis; once you had enough of the stuff in your gut, the peristalsis reflex was triggered and the sacred regurgitation began.

Judith, beside Quellen, was begging to be admitted into the realms of Oneness. Nirvana through up-chucking, Quellen thought coldly. How could it be? What am I doing here? The chant rebounded from the glass walls and deafened him. In a subtle antiphony currents of sound were sweeping round and round the room. He could not avoid swaying in rhythm. His lips moved. He would have joined in, if only he knew the words. He found himself humming tunelessly. Cashdan, still leading the ceremony, stepped up his volume. His voice was a fine, thick, black basso, with plenty of intensity to it.

Galuber sat motionless in the center of the pit. His eyes were closed. His hands were clasped on his abdomen. His face was flushed. He alone was in stasis in the midst of this swaying, chanting congregation. Quellen forced himself to stay aloof, observing. He watched the rhythmic side-to-side motions of Jennifer Galuber's offensively large breasts. He watched Judith's fine-boned face turn radiant with some inner ecstasy. A sexless young man with slicked-down maroon hair was jerking as though he had hold of a high-voltage wire. Around the room, the mysterious passion of social regurgitation was taking hold.

Dr. Galuber began to vomit, now.

The frood regurgitated with quiet dignity. His thick lips parted, and lumps of dough burst forth into the bowl. Sweat beaded his flushed face; there was effort in any kind of reverse peristalsis, even when the medulla was lulled, as it was by the drug within the dough. Yet he performed his function in the rite nobly. The bowl was filled.

It was passed around.

Hands clutched at moist dough. Take and eat, take and eat; here is the body, the authentic substance of the group. Join in the Oneness. Brose Cashdan was eating. Jennifer Galuber ate. Judith tranquilly accepted her portion. Quellen found a wet doughy mass in his hand.

Take. Eat.

Be objective. This is Oneness. His hand rose trembling toward his lips. He felt Judith's thigh warm against his own, beside him. Take and eat. Take and eat. Galuber lay prostrate in the pit, transfixed with ecstasy.

Quellen ate.

He chewed lustily, not allowing himself to hesitate. The particular property of the indigestible substance was that it could be digested upon contact with saliva *following* immersion in the alimentary tract. One swallowing wasn't enough; Galuber had merely prepared it for their intake. Quellen swallowed. Oddly, he felt no queasiness. He had eaten ants, raw whelks, sea urchins, other exotic delicacies, and had not even been granted a chance of a spiritual experience in the bargain. Why hesitate at this?

The other communicants were weeping in joy. Tears glistened on Judith's sprayon garment. Quellen still felt deplorably objective about the universe. He had not joined the mystic communion after all, dutifully though he had observed the rite. He waited patiently for the ecstasy to pass from the others.

Judith whispered to him, "Will you celebrate the next round?"

"Absolutely not."

"Joe–"

"Please. I came, didn't I? I'm participating. Don't ask me to be the star."

"It's customary for strangers to the group to–"

"I know. Not me. Someone else can have the honor."

She looked reproachfully at him. Quellen realized that he had failed her. Tonight had been some sort of a test, and he had nearly passed. Nearly.

Brose Cashdan had produced a second mass of ritual dough. Without a word, Jennifer Galuber accepted the bowl and began to stuff herself. The frood, exhausted by his efforts, sat slumped wearily beside her, hardly watching. The rite proceeded as had the first. Quellen took part as before, without ever becoming involved in the action.

Afterward, Brose Cashdan approached Quellen and said softly, "Would you care to lead us in our next communion?"

"I'm sorry," said Quellen. "I really can't. I've got to leave soon."

"I regret that. We had hoped you'd participate to the fullest." Cashdan smiled dreamily and handed the bowl to someone else.

Quellen tugged at Judith's wrist and drew her to one side. "Come home with me," he whispered urgently.

"How can you think of sex *here?*"

"You aren't dressed chastely, you know. You've had two communions. Will you leave with me?"

"No," she said firmly.

"If I wait until the next communion is over?"

"No. Not then. You'll have to take communion yourself, as a celebrant, and *mean* it. Otherwise I'd feel no kinship to you later. Honestly, Joe, how can I give myself to a man I don't relate to? It would be so utterly mechanical—it would harm us both."

Her nakedness that was not nakedness stabbed at him. He could not bear to look down at the alluring slenderness of her body. With pain he said, "Don't do this to me, Judith. Play fair. Let's leave now."

For answer, she turned away and rejoined her companions in the ritual pit. The third communion was about to begin. Cashdan looked invitingly at Quellen, who shook his head and quickly left the room. Outside, he glanced back through the transparent wall and saw Judith with her head thrown back and her lips parted in rapture. The Galubers likewise looked ecstatic. The image of Jennifer Galuber's obese body burned its way indelibly into Quellen's brain. He fled.

He was home not long after midnight, but his apartment gave him no comfort. He had to escape. Recklessly, he stepped into the stat field and let himself be hurled to Africa.

Morning had come, there. A light mistlike rain was falling, but the golden gleam of the sun cut through the gray haze. The crocodiles were in their usual places. A bird screeched. The leafy boughs, heavy with rain, trailed toward the rich wet black earth. Quellen tried to let the peace of the place enfold him. Kicking off his shoes, he walked down to the edge of the stream. The muck oozed voluptuously between his toes. Some small insect nipped at his calf. A frog leaped into the stream, making a pool of widening concentric circles in the dark surface of the water. One crocodile lazily opened a glistening eye. The sweet, heavy air surged into Quellen's lungs.

He took no comfort in any of it.

This place was his, but he had not earned it. He had stolen it. He could have no real peace here. Behind him, in Appalachia, he likewise found no repose. The world was too much with him, and he was too little of the world. He thought of Judith, sensuous in sprayon, ecstatic as she chewed the cud. She hates me, Quellen thought, or perhaps she pities me, but the effect is the same. She'll never see me again.

He did not wish to remain in these pleasant surroundings while he was in such a mood.

Quellen returned to the stat. He stepped into the field, and was hurled back across the sea to his own apartment, leaving morning and entering the fist of night. He slept poorly.

11.

At the office the following morning, Quellen found his two UnderSecs waiting for him with a third man, a tall, awkward, shabbily dressed fellow with a broken nose that projected beak-like from his face. Brogg turned the oxy vent up to full, Quellen noticed.

"Who's this?" Quellen asked. "You've made an arrest?" Could it be, he wondered, that this was Lanoy? It didn't seem likely. How could this seedy prolet—too poor, apparently, to afford a plastic job on his nose—be the force behind the hoppers?

"Tell the CrimeSec who you are," Brogg said, nudging the prolet roughly with his elbow.

"Name is Brand," the prolet said in a thin, whiningly high voice. "Class Fifteen. I didn't mean no harm, it was just that he promised me a home all my own, and a job, and fresh air—"

Brogg cut him off. "We ran up against this man in a drinker. He had had one or two too many and was telling everyone that he'd have a job soon."

"That's what the fellow said," Brand mumbled. "Just had to give him two hundred credits and he'd send me somewhere where everyone had a job. And I'd be able to send money back to bring my family along."

"That can't be right," said Quellen. "Sending money back? Contact *up* the time-path?"

"That's what he said. It sounded so good, sir."

"A phony inducement," Brogg suggested. "If there's two-way contact, it upsets all our calculations. But there isn't any such thing."

Quellen said, "What was this fellow's name?"

"Lanoy, sir."

Lanoy! Lanoy everywhere, tentacles reaching in all directions at once!

Brand muttered. "Someone gave me this and told me to get in touch with him."

He held out a crumpled minislip. Quellen unfolded it and read it. It said:

OUT OF WORK?
SEE LANOY

"These things are everywhere," Quellen said. He reached into his own pocket and pulled out the slip he had been handed on the flyramp. Quellen had been carrying it around for several days like a talisman. He laid it beside the first. They were identical.

OUT OF WORK?
SEE LANOY

"Lanoy's sent a lot of my friends there," Brand said. "He told me they were all working and happy there, sir—"

"Where does he send them?" Quellen asked gently.

"I don't know, sir. Lanoy said he was going to tell me when I gave him the two hundred units. I drew out all my savings. I was on my way to him, and I just dropped in for a short one, when–when–"

"When we found him," Brogg finished. "Telling everyone in sight that he was heading to Lanoy to get a job."

"Mmm. Do you know what the hoppers are, Brand?"

"No, sir."

"Never mind, then. Suppose you take us to Lanoy."

"I can't do that. It wouldn't be fair. All my friends–"

"Suppose we *make* you take us to Lanoy," Quellen said.

"But he was going to give me a job! I can't do it. Please, sir."

Brogg looked sharply at Quellen. "Let me try," he said. "Lanoy was going to give you a job, you say? For two hundred units?"

"Yes, sir."

"What if we tell you that we'll give you a job for nothing? No charge at all, just lead us to Lanoy and we'll send you where he was going to send you, only free. And we'll send your family along, too."

Quellen smiled. When it came to handling the lower prolets, Brogg was a far better psychologist than he was. He was forced to admit that.

"Sounds fair," Brand said. "Only I feel bad about it. Lanoy was nice to me. But if you say you'll send me for nix–"

"Quite right, Brand."

"I'll do it, then. I guess."

Quellen turned down the oxy vent. Brogg gestured to Leeward, who led Brand out of the room. Quellen said, "Let's go before he changes his mind. He's obviously wavering."

"Are you coming with us, sir?" Brogg asked. There was just a hint of sarcasm behind Brogg's obsequious tones. "It'll probably be a pretty filthy part of town. Vermin all over the place. The criminal section—"

Quellen scowled. "You're right," he said. "No need for me to go. You two take him. I've got plenty to do here."

As soon as they were gone, Quellen rang Koll.

"We're hot on the trail," he said. "Brogg and Leeward have traced a lead to the man who's behind the hoppers. They've gone out to make the arrest."

"Fine work," Koll said coldly. "It should be an interesting investigation."

"I'll report back to you as soon as—"

"Let it go for a while. Spanner and I are discussing departmental status changes. We'd prefer not to be disturbed during the next hour." He hung up.

What did that mean, Quellen wondered? The coldness in Koll's voice—well, that was nothing unusual, but it was significant. Koll had been harrying him all week for progress on the hopper business. Now that some progress had finally been made—now that a man was in custody who could lead them to the elusive Lanoy—Koll had been brusque, almost totally uninterested. Koll's hiding something, Quellen thought.

His conscience pricked him. The instant suspicion returned: Koll knows about Africa. That trip I made last night was monitored, and it was the last chunk of evidence in the case against me. Now they're getting the indictment ready.

No doubt Brogg had been offered a bigger price to talk than Quellen had been giving him to be silent, and he had sold out to the highest bidder. Koll knew everything, now. Demotion would be the least of Quellen's punishments.

Quellen's offense was a unique one. No one else, to his knowledge, had been shrewd enough to find that particular way out of heavily overpopulated Appalachia, the octopus of a city that spread all over the eastern half of North America. Of all the hundreds of millions of inhabitants of Appalachia, only Joseph Quellen, CrimeSec, had had the cleverness to find a bit of unknown and unregistered land in the heart of Africa and build himself a second home there. That was something for pride. He had the standard Class Seven cubicle of a room in Appalachia, plus a Class Two villa beyond the dreams of most mortals, beside a murky stream in the Congo. It was nice, very nice, for a man whose soul rebelled at the hellish conditions of Appalachian life.

But it took money to keep people bribed. Quellen had silenced everyone concerned who might know that he was living luxuriously in Africa instead of dwelling in a ten-by-ten cubicle in Northwest Appalachia, like a good Seven. Someone–Brogg, he was sure–had sold him out to Koll. And now Quellen was on very thin ice indeed.

A demotion would rob him even of the privilege of maintaining a private cubicle, and he would go back to sharing his home, as he had with the unlamented roommate Bruce Marok. It hadn't been so bad when Quellen had been below Class Twelve and had lived, first in the public bachelor dorms, then in gradually more private accommodations. He hadn't minded the presence of other people so much when he was younger. But when he had reached Class Eight and was put into a room with just one other person, that had been the most painful time of all, souring Quellen permanently.

In his own way, Marok was undoubtedly a genuinely fine fellow, Quellen reflected. But he had jarred on Quellen's nerves, crucifying him with his sloppiness and his unending visiphone calls and his constant presence. Quellen had longed for the day when he would reach Seven and could live alone, no longer with a roommate as a constant check.

Then he would be free—free to hide from the inpressing crowd.

Did Koll know the truth? Quellen soon would find that out.

Restlessly he walked down the echoing corridor to the monitoring wing. Might as well find out what they've learned about Norm, he thought. The brown metal gate slithered into its slot as Quellen palmed the door identification plaque. He went in. Instruments hummed all over the place. Technicians salaamed to him. The smell of some antiseptic chemical was in the air, as though this were a hospital.

"The Pomrath monitor bank," Quellen said.

"This way, CrimeSec."

"Who's watching it?"

"It's been on automatic, sir. Here we are." The man pulled out a pneumochair. Quellen planted himself before the turning spools of a tape pickup. The technician said, "Would you like to plug in on realtime first, or go over what we've taped since last night?"

"I'll do a little of both," Quellen said.

"This is the realtime jack, and this—"

"I know. I've used the equipment before."

The technician colored and went scuttering away. Quellen jacked himself into the realtime circuit, and abruptly jacked himself out again. His brother-in-law was performing natural bodily functions. Quellen bit his lip. With quick, edgy manipulation he activated the reserve spools and tuned in on what Norm Pomrath had been up to since Brogg had planted the Ear on him.

Quellen could not allow himself a one-to-one realtime correlation, of course, with Pomrath's activities. He had to be selective. Skimming along the tape, he found remarkably little conversation recorded. Pomrath had been to a sniffer palace last night. Then he had gone home. He had quarrelled with Helaine. Quellen listened.

POMRATH: I don't give a damn. I need my relaxation.

HELAINE: But we've waited dinner for you. And here you are all full of drugs. You don't even have an appetite!

POMRATH: What of it? I'm here. Put out the dinner. You program, I'll eat!

There was more of it, all relentlessly domestic and dreadfully dull. Quellen skipped ahead fifteen minutes and found the quarrel still going on, punctuated now by the snuffing sound of his nephew's tears and the annoyed comments of little Marina. It pained Quellen that the family disputes of the Pomraths should be so commonplace. He moved the tape on a short distance. The Ear had picked up different sounds. Harsh breathing sounds.

HELAINE: put your hand there again.

POMRATH: Oh, honey, you know I will.

HELAINE: Right there. Oh! Oh, Norm!

POMRATH: Are you ready yet?

HELAINE: A little while. Give me time. This is so nice, Norm.

Quellen stared shamefully at the floor. A faintly incestuous pleasure went through him as he eavesdropped on the lovemaking of the Pomraths. He reached for the dial, hesitated, listened to sudden pangs of ecstasy, clenched his jaws together as the words on the tape became more intimate and then dissolved into a rush of gasping sighs.

I ought to erase this section, Quellen thought. I ought at least not to listen to it myself. How disgustingly curious we can get sometimes!

With a quick jerky motion he sped the dial ahead. Nothing but sleep-sounds now. Then morning-sounds. Children pattering around. Pomrath under the molecular bath. Helaine yawning, asking about the breakfast menu.

POMRATH: I'm going out early today.

HELAINE: You think you have a line on that job opportunity?

POMRATH: What job opportunity?

HELAINE: You know, the minislip you were carrying. About the man to see if you're out of work.

POMRATH: Oh. Him.

Quellen waited for more. The telemetry showed unusual excitement in Pomrath, a surge of pulse intensity, a rise in skin temperature. Nevertheless, the conversation was truncated without any word about Lanoy. Quellen skimmed again. The timer told him that he was approaching realtime levels now. Quellen jacked in once more.

POMRATH: You can take me to Lanoy, can't you?

The monitor was programmed to trip an alarm when the name "Lanoy" was mentioned. There was an imperceptible lag while the computer analyzed the wave forms of Pomrath's speech, and then the alarm went off. A red light began to glow on the control panel of the monitor system. Signals blared around the room. A warning bell sounded. *Pong. Pong.*

Three technicians came running toward the instrument.

Pong.

Quellen said, "It's all right. I'll monitor it. Just shut off these damned alarms."

Pong. Pong.

Quellen leaned forward, and sweat poured down the palms of his hands as he listened to his brother-in-law commit the ultimate betrayal of his family.

Pomrath had traveled a considerable distance that

morning, unaware, of course, that his motions were being transmitted to the headquarters of the Secretariat of Crime and that his words and even his heartbeats were being recorded.

In the past several days he had asked many questions, mostly prior to the mounting of the Ear in his flesh. The minislips advertising Lanoy's services were widely distributed. Information about the actual whereabouts of Lanoy was not so easily had. But Pomrath had persistence.

He was determined to leave, now.

He had had all he could take. It was too bad about Helaine, of course, and the kids. He'd miss them. Yet he was fed up, and he sensed that he was on the edge of psychotic collapse. Words were losing their meaning for him. He'd stare up at a faxtape for half an hour, trying to puzzle out the significance of the rows of symbols on the yellow sheet. They had become squirming microbes to him. KLOOFMAN. UNEMPLOYMENT. TAX RATE. DANTON. MANKLOOF. LOYPMEMUNTNE. TONDAN. XAT RAET. KL. OOF. PLOYM. AX R. Dancing animalcules. EMPL. FMAN. Time to get away, ANTO. UNEM, THEM. FLOOK. FLOOK! FLOOK! FLOOK!

KLOOF!

A simpler world, that's what he needed. To hop to a place not yet this fouled with humanity—yes. Yes. Lanoy was the answer. Pomrath's head throbbed. It seemed to him that his frontal lobes were swelling, pushing against his forehead dangerously forward. "Can you direct me to Lanoy?" His head might burst, spewing brains all over the street. "I'm out of work. I want to see Lanoy." FLOOK! XAT RAET! "Lanoy?"

A squat, flabby-faced man with a row of natural teeth on top and a single seamless chopper below said, "I'll get you to Lanoy. Four pieces, huh?"

Pomrath paid him. "Where do I go? What do I do?"

"Quickboat. Number Sixteen Line."

"Where do I get off?"

"Just get on, that's all."

EMPL! FMAN! Pomrath headed for the quickboat ramp. He filed obediently aboard. It seemed a pleasant coincidence that someone would have been so conveniently available to tell him how to reach the elusive Lanoy, Norm thought. But a moment's reflection led him to think it was no coincidence at all. The flabby-faced man had probably been an agent of Lanoy, haunting him, ready to guide him in the right direction when the critical moment approached. Of course. His eyes were aching. Something coarse and gritty was in the air, a special eyeball-abrasive gas, perhaps, released by order of the High Government to bring about universal polishing of proletarian corneas. MANK! NOTD! Pomrath huddled in a corner of the quickboat. A cowled figure came up to him, a girl with shaven scalp, jutting cheekbones, no lips at all. "For Lanoy?" she asked.

"Why not?"

"Transfer to the Northpass Line."

"If you say so."

"It's the only way." She smiled at him. Her skin seemed to change color, cycling attractively through the spectrum from infragreen to ultralemon. PLOYM! XAT! Pomrath trembled. He wondered what Helaine would say when she knew. Would she weep? How soon would she remarry? Would his children bear his name? The line of Pomraths extinct? Yes. Yes. For he would have to bear some other name back there. FMANK! What if he called himself Kloofman? Sublime irony: my great-grandchild a member of the High Government. Some chance.

Pomrath got off the quickboat. The cowled girl remained aboard. How did they know who he was and where he was bound? He felt frightened. The world was full of specters. Pray for the repose of my soul, he thought. I'm so tired. OOF! TON!

He waited at the ramp. Around him the spires of ugly buildings of the previous century stabbed holes in the sky. He was out of the central slum-clearance zone now. Who knew what stinking warren he was heading toward? A new quickboat arrived. Pomrath boarded it unquestioningly. I am in your hands, he thought. LANOY! YONAL! Anyone. Anyone. Just get me out of here.

Out!

He journeyed northward. Was this still Appalachia? The sky was dark here. Programmed for rain, perhaps. A clean flush to purify the streets. What if Danton recommended a rain of sulfuric acid? The pavement hissing and smoking, citizens running to and fro as their flesh dissolved. The ultimate population control. Death from the skies. Serve you right for going outdoors. The quickboat halted. Pomrath got out and waited on the ramp. Rain was falling here, pocking against the sidewalk.

"I'm Pomrath," he said to a kindly old lady.

"Lanoy's waiting. Come on."

He found himself in rural surroundings ten minutes later. There was a shack by the edge of a lake. Figures moved mysteriously in and out. Pomrath was thrust forward. A purring voice said, "Lanoy's waiting for you out back."

He was a small man with a big nose. He wore clothing that seemed to be two hundred years old.

"Pomrath?"

"I think so."

"What are you, Class Twelve?"

"Fourteen," Pomrath confessed. "Get me out of here, will you please?"

"My pleasure," said Lanoy.

Pomrath looked at the lake. It was a hideous sight, crawling with pollution. Great greasy swatches of coarse algae roiled in the oily water.

Lanoy said, "Isn't it lovely? Six centuries of nonstop pollution interspersed with high-sounding official speeches. The renewal zone is still twenty years away by public count. Would you like to take a swim? We don't practice baptism here, but we can arrange a ceremony to fit anybody's religious preferences."

Pomrath shuddered. "I can't swim. Just get me out of here."

"The alga is *cladaphora.* Biologists sometimes come up here to admire it. It reaches lengths of ninety feet. We've also got anaerobic sludgeworms here, and fingernail clams. Quite primeval. I don't know how they survive. You'd be shocked if you knew the oxygen content of that water."

"Nothing shocks me," said Pomrath. "Please. Please."

"It's full of coliform intestinal bacteria also," Lanoy remarked. "I believe the current count is 10,000,000 per 100 milliliters. That's about 10,000 times the safe level for human contact. Lovely? Come inside, Pomrath. You know it's not easy, being a hopper."

"It's not easy being anything, these days."

"Consider the challenges, though." Lanoy led him within the shack. Pomrath was startled to see that the interior was out of keeping with the weatherbeaten exterior. Inside, everything was neat, spanking clean. A partition divided the building into two huge compartments. Lanoy dropped into a web and lay there, jiggling, like a spider. Pomrath remained standing. Lanoy said, "I can take you and dump you into the year 1990, if you'd like, or 2076, or most any other year. Don't be fooled by what you read in the fax-tapes. We're actually more versatile than the public knows. We're improving the process constantly."

"Send me anywhere," said Pomrath.

"The correct term is *anywhen.* But look here: I send you to 1990. Can you face it? You won't even be able to speak the language properly. You'll speak a weird jargon that they won't understand, all your grammar blurred. Do you know the distinction between 'who' and 'whom'? Between 'shall' and 'will'? Can you handle tenses?"

Pomrath could feel the blood surging in his arteries. He did not understand why Lanoy was weaving this cocoon of words about him. He had had enough words.

Lanoy laughed. "Don't let me frighten you. You don't need to know those things. They were forgotten, even then. People were sloppy in their speech. Not as sloppy as we are today, because we've had another few hundred years to erode the language. But they had blotted out all the conjugations and declensions already. Still, it'll take you a couple of weeks to learn how to communicate. You can get into a lot of trouble in a couple of weeks. Are you prepared to be sent to a lunatic asylum? Shock treatments, straight-jacket, all the barbarities of our ancestors?"

"Just get me out of here."

"The police will interrogate you. Don't give them your right name, Pomrath. You aren't listed in the hopper records, which means you never gave them your right name, and don't you dare try to do it. Make up a name. You can admit to being a hopper if you land in 1979 or later. If you go back earlier, you're entirely on your own. Frankly, I wouldn't try it. I don't think you've got the caliber for a free-lance trip like that. You're an intelligent man, Pomrath, but you're worn thin by care. Don't take risks. Go as an orthodox hopper and throw yourself on the mercies of the past. You'll make out."

"What does it cost?"

"Two hundred units. A token fee, really. Barely covers the energy costs."

"Is it safe?"

"As safe as taking a quickboat ride." Lanoy grinned. "It's disconcerting. No High Government to watch over you. Dozens of independent national states. Local rivalries. Conflicting taxing bodies. You'll have to cope, but that's all right. I think you'll manage."

"It can't be worse than what's here."

"Are you married, Pomrath?"

"Yes. Two children. I love them deeply."

"Want to take the whole family along?"

"Can it be done?"

"With uncertainties. We've got to send you separately: mass limits. You could get scattered over a range of as much as a dozen years. Your kids arriving first, then you and your wife a few years later, maybe."

Pomrath trembled. "Suppose I go first. Will you keep a record of where I'm sent—*when* I'm sent—so that my family can come after me if that's what my wife wants to do?"

"Of course. We look out for your welfare. I'll get in touch with Mrs. Pomrath. She'll have the option of following you. Not many wives do it, of course, but she'll have the option. Well, Pomrath? Still with us?"

"You know I am," Pomrath said.

Quellen, monitoring the conversation, sat trance-like and chilled. He could not see Lanoy, he had no real idea where the conversation was taking place, but yet he realized that his brother-in-law was about to enroll in the legion of hoppers, and there was nothing that could be done about it. Unless Brogg and Leeward reached Lanoy's headquarters in the nick of time, and came bursting in to make the arrest—

A voice said, "Sir, UnderSec Brogg is calling."

Quellen pulled himself away from the monitor. A visionless phone was rolled up. Quellen put it to his ear.

"Where are you?" he demanded. "Have you traced Lanoy yet?"

"We're working on it," Brogg said. "It turned out Brand didn't know the exact location. He just knew somebody who could take him to somebody who could bring him to Lanoy."

"I see."

"But we've got a geographical area pegged. We're cordoning it and closing in by televector. It's only a matter of time now before we put the intercept on Lanoy in person."

"How much time?" asked Quellen icily.

"I'd say six hours," Brogg replied. "Plus or minus ninety minutes. We're certain to nail him today."

Six hours, Quellen thought. Plus or minus. And then Lanoy would be in custody.

But Norm Pomrath would be a hopper by then.

12.

Brogg said in a relaxed tone, "I have to arrest you, of course. You understand that. It's regulations."

"Of course," Lanoy said. "It goes almost without saying. I wondered what took you people so long to get to me."

"Uncertainty in high places. There was a lot of dithering." Brogg smiled at the little man. "I don't mind telling you, you have the High Government quite upset. They're sweating to arrest you, but at the same time they're afraid of wrecking their position of power through some sort of rearrangement of past events. So they've been stalemated. It's the classic conflict situation: they must stop you, and they don't dare it."

"I appreciate their troubles," said Lanoy. "It's a terribly complicated life even for Them, isn't it? Well, you're here, now. Come outside. Let's watch the sunset, shall we?"

Brogg followed Lanoy from the shack. It was late, now, well into his overtime phase, but Brogg did not object. All day long he and Leeward had zeroed in on Lanoy, juggling televector constants until they had located him within a narrowing radius. As Brogg had told Quellen earlier in the day, it was only a matter of hours. In fact, it had taken four hours and some minutes from the time of Brogg's call. Deftly, Brogg had sent Leeward off on a wild goose chase an hour ago. Now Brogg and Lanoy were alone at this remote shack. Brogg had much to say to the hopper man.

A swollen golden sun hung suspended in the darkening sky. The track of illumination cast a purplish glow over the polluted lake. It took on an eerie glitter, and the slime-creatures that writhed on its surface seemed ennobled by the aura of the dying day. Lanoy stared raptly into the west.

"It is beautiful," he said finally. "I could never leave this era, UnderSec Brogg. I see the beauty within the ugliness. Regard that lake. Was there ever anything like it? I stand here at sunset each night in awe."

"Remarkable."

"Very. There's poetry in that ooze. The oxygen's just about gone, you see. There's been a devolution of organic life there, so that we've got only anaerobic forms. I like to think that the sludgeworms dance down there at sunset. About, about, in reel and rout. Look at the play of colors on that big swatch of algae. It grows as long as seaweed here. Do you care for poetry much, Brogg?"

"My passion's for history."

"What period?"

"Roman. The early Empire. Tiberius through Trajan, approximately. Trajan's time: a true golden age."

"The Republic doesn't interest you?" asked Lanoy. "The brave puritans? Cato? Lucius Junius Brutus? The Gracchi?"

Brogg was astounded. "You know such things?"

"I cast a wide net," said Lanoy. "You realize that I deal with the past on a daily basis. I've acquired a certain familiarity with history myself. Trajan, eh? You'd like to visit Rome of Trajan's era, would you?"

"Of course," Brogg said huskily.

"What about Hadrian? Still a golden age there. If you couldn't have Trajan, would you settle for Hadrian? Let us say, a margin of error covering a generation—we might miss Trajan, but in that case we'd land somewhere in Hadrian. We'd do better to aim for the forward end of Trajan's rule. Otherwise the error might take us the other way, and you wouldn't like that, eh? You'd come out in Titus, Domitian, one of that nasty bunch. Not at all to your liking."

Brogg could manage only a hoarse, croaking voice. "What are you talking about?"

"You know quite well." The sun had set. The magic glow ebbed from the ruined lake. "Shall we go in?" Lanoy asked. "I'll show you some of the equipment."

Brogg allowed himself to be led back inside. He towered over the little man; Lanoy was no bigger than Koll, and had something of Koll's nervous inner energy. Yet Koll brimmed with hatred and pustulence; Lanoy seemed utterly confident, with a core of tranquility within his active dynamism.

Lanoy opened a door in the partition that divided the building. Brogg peered in. He saw vertical bars of some gleaming material, an openwork cage, dials, switches, an array of rheostats. Rows of color-coded panels on the machinery radiated bright glows of data. It all seemed to be put together with an eye toward deliberate confusion.

"This is the time-travel machine?" Brogg asked.

"Part of it. There are extensions both in time and space. I won't plague you with the details. The principle is simple, anyway. A sudden strain on the fabric of the continuum; we thrust present-day material in, scoop out an equal bucketload of mass from the past. Conservation of matter, you understand. When our calculations are off by a few grams, it causes disturbances, implosions, meteorological effects. We try not to miss, but we sometimes do. There's a fusion plasma at the heart of it all. No better way to rip open the continuum; we use our own little sun to do it. We tap off the theta force, you see. Every time someone uses a stat, it builds up temporal potential that we grab and utilize. Even so, it's an expensive process."

"What do you charge for a trip?"

"Two hundred units, generally. That is, if we're willing to take money at all."

"You send some people free?" Brogg asked.

"Not exactly. We won't accept the money of certain individuals, I mean. We insist on payment of a different kind—services, information, that sort of thing. If they're not willing to render what we need, we don't transport them. For those people, no amount of money could hire us."

"I don't altogether follow."

"You will," Lanoy said. He closed the partition and returned to the office part of the shack. Sprawling out comfortably in his web, he asked Brogg, "What arrest procedure are you going to follow in my case?"

"You'll have to come down to the office to talk to CrimeSec Quellen. He'll have disposition of the case. Meanwhile we'll have to cordon this place off with a wide-band radion, and it'll remain sealed pending appeal. Any habeas corpus will go automatically to the High Government. Of course, if you can handle Quellen, the picture will change completely."

"But I must go to the office?"

"Yes."

"What sort of man is this Quellen. Malleable?"

"I think so. Especially if you use the right hammer on him," Brogg said.

"Does the hammer have a high rental cost?"

"Not very high." Brogg leaned forward. "Is your machine really limited to a reach of only five centuries?"

"Not at all. We keep improving. We've had a controlled reach of five centuries for quite some time, but an uncontrolled reach that's much greater."

"Yes," said Brogg. "The pigs and dogs thrown back to the twelfth century, and such."

"You know about those?"

"I've been very thorough. What's your controlled reach now?"

Lanoy shrugged. "It's variable. We can hit almost anywhere in two thousand years, but the built-in error gets wider the further the throw. We've got it down to plus or minus thirty years now, but that's quite a range. At the furthest, that is. We could hit 1492 or 1776 smack on the nose, I firmly believe." He smiled. "What's the hammer for pounding Quellen?"

"It'll cost you," said Brogg. "What's the cost of a ticket to Hadrian?"

"The hammer for Quellen."

"You won't take cash?"

"Not from you."

Brogg nodded. "Let's negotiate," he said. "I think we can strike a deal."

By sunset, Helaine Pomrath was convinced that her husband had become a hopper.

It was almost a telepathic thing. He had not come home for dinner, but he had been late for dinner quite frequently the last few weeks. Yet this was different. Helaine felt a strange sense of his absence. She had shared her life with him for so long that she had grown accustomed to his presence, even when he was not with her physically. Now she felt herself in the company of the presence of his absence.

The room seemed smaller, darker. The children's eyes were wide. Helaine said reassuring things to them. She tried not to think of Beth Wisnack and her grim prophecy that Norm was soon to become a hopper. Helaine asked the time, and the earwatch told her that it was half past eighteen. She gave the children their dinner, but did not eat herself.

At quarter after nineteen, she phoned her brother at his apartment.

"I hate to disturb you, Joe, but it's about Norm. He isn't home for dinner, and I'm worried."

There was a long silence at the other end. Helaine watched Quellen's face, but the expression on it baffled her. His lips were tightly compressed.

"Joe? Why aren't you answering me? Listen, I know I'm just a foolish woman who's worrying about nothing at all, but I can't help it. I've got this definite feeling that something terrible has happened."

"I'm sorry, Helaine. I did what I could."

"What are you talking about?"

"There's been an arrest. We've pulled in the slyster who ran the hopper outfit. But there just wasn't time to get Norm. He slipped right through."

She felt the chill sweeping up from her legs and invading her internal organs, turning them one by one to lumps of resonating ice. "Joe, I don't understand you. Do you know something about Norm?"

"We were monitoring him. Brogg put an Ear on him last night at my instruction. He went out to look for Lanoy this morning. The slyster."

"The one you arrested?"

"Yes. Lanoy's running the hopper game. *Was* running. He's in custody. I'll be interrogating him in the morning. Norm went to him. It was far out—the trip took him all morning. We were vectoring in on Lanoy, you understand, but there was absolutely no way to get to Norm in time. I've got a tape of the whole thing as it came out of the Ear."

"He's—gone?"

"Gone," Quellen said. "His destination was 2050. Lanoy wasn't sure that they could hit the year exactly, but he said the odds were in favor. I want you to know, Helaine, that Norm was thinking of you right up until he left. You can listen to the tapes yourself. He said he loved you and the children. He was trying to arrange things so you and the children could follow him to 2050. Lanoy agreed to do it. It's all on record."

"Gone. He just hopped like that."

"He was in bad shape, Helaine. The things he was saying this morning—he was practically insane."

"I know it. He's been like that for days. I tried to get him to go to a frood, but—"

"Is there anything I can do, Helaine? Do you want me to come over and stay with you?"

"No."

"I can have a registered consolation service come around."

"Don't bother."

"Helaine, you've got to believe me, I did everything that was in my power to prevent this from happening. And if you choose to follow him the hopper way, I'll see to it that you get the opportunity. That is, if the High Government permits further hopper operations, now that we've taken Lanoy into custody."

"I'll think about it," said Helaine quietly. "I don't know what I'll do. Just let me alone now. Thanks for everything, anyway, Joe."

She opaqued the screen and broke the contact. Now that the worst had happened, Helaine felt oddly calm. Glacially calm. She would not go into the past hunting for her husband. She was the widow Pomrath, betrayed, abandoned.

Joseph said, "Mommy, where's Daddy?"

"He's gone away, son."

"Will he be coming back soon?"

"I don't think so," Helaine said.

Marina looked up. "Does that mean that Daddy's dead?"

"Not quite," Helaine told her. "It's too complicated. I'll explain it some other time. Plug yourselves in and do your homework, children. It's almost bedtime."

She went to the drawer where they kept the alcohol tubes. Withdrawing one quickly, she pressed the snout against her skin and took a quick, subcutaneous jolt. It left her feeling neither more animated nor more depressed. She was frozen, at an emotional constant of zero.

The widow Pomrath. Beth Wisnack will be pleased to hear it. She can't bear the thought that any other woman might still have a husband.

Closing her eyes, she pictured Norm landing in 2050, a stranger and alone. He would make out, she knew. He had his medical skills. Dropped into the primitive past like that, he'd set up in business as a doctor, perhaps even concealing his hopper status–otherwise he'd have been on the roster of registered hoppers, wouldn't he? He'd be rich and successful. Patients would flock to him, especially women patients. He would lose his look of bleak defeat, and take on the glow of prosperity. He'd stand taller, and smile more often. Helaine wondered what sort of woman he would marry. *Had* married. It was all done. That was the weird part of it. Norm had already lived and died, perishing about the year 2100, and his body had turned to dust centuries ago, along with the bodies of his other wife and his other children. Perhaps his descendants in today's world were a numerous tribe. Perhaps I'm one of them myself, Helaine thought. And the book was sealed; his destiny had been written hundreds of years before their wedding day. Even then, it was fated that he would leave her and circle back into the past to die hundreds of years before he was born.

Helaine's mind reeled. She took a second alcohol tube, and it helped her, but not much. The children sat with their backs to her, plugged into their homework machine, assiduously pretending to study.

I am lost, she thought.

I am nothing.

I am the widow Pomrath.

On the third tube, a new thought occurred to her. I am fairly young. Given a few months to relax, I could even be attractive again. Joe can arrange it; there must be a special government pension for the deserted wives of hoppers. I'll go away, fill out, put some meat on my bones. Then I'll marry again. Of course, I'll have used up my reproductive quota, but that won't matter. I can find a man who's willing to forego fatherhood. He'll adopt Joseph and Marina. Someone tall and handsome, and high in slope. Can I catch a Class Six? A widower, maybe even a man whose wife turned hopper, if there are any.

I'll show Norm. I'll catch myself a real prize.

Already, she could feel her body blossoming, filling out, the sap rising in it. For months, years even, she had lived in a barren winter of terror, clinging to her husband and nurturing him through his mood of empty despair in the hope that she could prevent him from abandoning her. Now that he was gone, she no longer needed to fear that he would go. She was returning to life. She felt younger.

I'll fix Norm Pomrath, Helaine thought. I'll make him sorry he ever went away!

13.

It was morning. Quellen had deliberately allowed the captured slyster Lanoy to languish overnight in the custody tank, so that he could reflect on his crimes. Lanoy was in total sensory deprivation, floating in a warm bath of nutrients with all inputs plugged off, so that nothing would register on his mind but his own predicament. Such treatment often had a marked softening effect on the hardest of cases. And from what Brogg had said, Lanoy was the hardest case in a long while.

Quellen had received the news at home, late in the evening, not long before Helaine's call. He had given instructions for Lanoy's treatment, but he had not actually gone down to headquarters to view the slyster. Leeward had brought him in, Brogg remaining behind at the hopper place itself.

It had been a somber night for Quellen. He knew, of course, that Norm Pomrath had gone to the past. He had been listening helplessly, jacked into the realtime circuit, while Pomrath and Lanoy discussed the project and came to an agreement. Then and there, Pomrath had paid over his money—virtually wiping out the family savings—and had stepped up on the platform to be thrust into the year 2050. Ear transmissions had ceased at that point. The Ear was a sensitive device, but it had no way of broadcasting across a temporal gap.

Helaine's stony face had been unpleasant to behold. She blamed him for what had happened, Quellen knew, and she never would really forgive him. So his sister, his only relative, was lost to him. And Judith, too, was lost. Since the fiasco at the social regurgitation communion, she had refused to take any calls from him. He knew that he would never see her again. The slender bare form in the sprayon costume postured wantonly in Quellen's dreams, waking him often.

The only comfort in a generally bleak situation was the fact that Lanoy had been found and arrested. That meant the heat would be off the department soon. With the hopper ring smashed, life could revert to routine, and Quellen would be free to spend most of his time in Africa, once again. Unless, of course, Brogg had really betrayed him. Quellen had forgotten about that. Koll's unfriendly tone of yesterday—did it mean that his own arrest was in the offing, as soon as the Lanoy affair was wrapped up?

Quellen got his answer to that shortly before midnight, when Koll called. For Koll, office hours extended throughout the night and the day.

"I've just checked with the office," Koll said. "They tell me you've got the slyster."

"Yes. He was brought in around eighteen, nineteen this evening. Brogg and Leeward traced him. They've put him in the custody tank. I'll interrogate him in the morning."

"Good job," Koll said, and Quellen noticed the trace of an honest smile flickering on the small man's lips. "This keys nicely into the status meeting Spanner and I had this afternoon. I've just put through a promotion form for you. It seems unfair to let the CrimeSec live in a Class Seven unit when he rates at least a Six, don't you think? You'll be joining Spanner and me in your higher grade quite soon. Of course, that won't affect your slope in the office hierarchy, but I thought you'd be pleased."

Quellen was pleased. And relieved. So he doesn't know about Africa after all. It was just my guilty conscience stirring up fears. Then a new worry came: how could he move the illegal stat to new quarters without being detected? It had been hard enough to get it installed here. Perhaps Koll was only leading him deeper into a trap. Quellen pressed his palms against his temples and shivered, waiting for morning—and Lanoy.

"You admit you've been sending people into the past?" Quellen demanded.

"Sure," said the little man flippantly. Quellen stared at him, feeling an irrational pulse of anger throbbing in his skull. How could the slyster be so calm? "Sure," Lanoy said. "I'll send you back for two hundred units."

Leeward stood massively behind the little man, and Quellen faced him over the interrogation table. Brogg had not appeared at the office this morning. Koll and Spanner were listening from their own office next door. The slyster looked waxen-faced and limp from his night in the custody tank, and yet he held himself with dignity.

"You're Lanoy?" Quellen jabbed.

"That's my name." He was a small, dark, intense, rabbity sort of man, with thin lips constantly moving. "Sure, I'm Lanoy." The little slyster radiated a confident warmth. He was gaining strength from moment to moment. Now he sat with his legs crossed and his head thrown back.

"It was pretty nasty the way your boys tracked me down," Lanoy said. "It was bad enough that you fooled that poor dumb prolet into leading you to me, but you didn't have to dump me in the tank like that. I spent a lousy night. I'm not doing anything illegal, you know. I ought to sue."

"Nothing illegal? You're disturbing the past five hundred years!"

"I am not," Lanoy said calmly. "Nothing of the sort. They've already been disturbed. It's a matter of record, you know. I'm just seeing to it that past history gets to take place the way it took place, if you follow what I'm saying. I'm a public benefactor. What if I weren't fulfilling the records?"

Quellen glowered at the arrogant slyster. He turned to pace, found that he had no room to move in the tiny office, and sat down ineffectually at his desk. He felt strangely weak in the presence of the slyster. The man had power. Quellen said, "You admit that you're sending prolets back as hoppers. Why?"

Lanoy smiled. "To earn a living. Surely you understand that. I'm in possession of a very valuable process, and I want to make sure I get all I can out of it."

"Are you the inventor of the time-travel process?"

"I don't claim to be. But it doesn't matter," said Lanoy. "I control it."

"If you want to exploit your machine for money, why don't you simply go back in time and steal, or place bets on the arthropods, to make a living? Grab a quick killing on the outcome of a race that's in the records, then come back here."

"I could do that," Lanoy admitted. "But the process is irreversible, and there's no way of getting back to the present again with my winnings. Or my stealings. And I like it here, thank you."

Quellen scratched his head. He *liked* it here? It seemed

incredible that anyone would, but apparently Lanoy meant just what he said. One of those perverse estheticians, undoubtedly, who could find beauty in a dunghill.

He said, "Look, Lanoy, I'll be extremely frank with you: you're subject to penalties for operating this enterprise without the consent of the High Government. Kloofman has ordered your arrest. I'm not prepared to say what sort of a sentence you'll get, but it could be anything up to complete personality erasure, depending on your attitude. However, there's one option for you. The High Government wants control of your time-travel gimmick. Turn it over to my men—not just the device, you understand, but the method. Your cooperation will win you a remission of your sentence to some degree."

"Sorry," said Lanoy. "The machine's private property. You haven't got any right to it."

"The courts—"

"I'm not doing anything illegal, and so I don't need to worry about what kind of sentence I'll get. And I refuse to yield to your jurisdiction. The answer's no."

Quellen thought of the pressures that were on him from Koll and Spanner and even Kloofman to solve this case, and he got angry and frightened at the same time. He blurted, "When I get through with you, Lanoy, you'll wish you'd used your own machine and gone back a million years. We can induce cooperation. We can reduce you to jelly."

Lanoy's cool smile did not waver. His voice was measured as he said, "Come now, CrimeSec. You're starting to lose your temper, and that's always illogical. Not to add dangerous."

Quellen sensed the truth of Lanoy's warning. He struggled to calm himself, and lost the struggle. The muscles of his throat seemed to be writhing in knots. "I'll keep you in the tank until you rot," he snapped.

"Now where will that get you? I'll be so much moldy flesh, and you still won't be able to deliver the time process to the High Government." The slyster shrugged. "Would you mind giving me a little more oxy in here, please, by the way? I happen to be suffocating."

In his astonishment at the bold request, Quellen opened the vent wide. Leeward registered surprise at Lanoy's breach of taste. No doubt the watchers in the next room were startled at Quellen's abrupt capitulation, too.

Lanoy said, "If you arrest me, I'll break you, Quellen. I tell you there's nothing illegal in what I'm doing. Look here—I'm a registered slyster." Lanoy produced a card, properly stamped.

Quellen was stymied. Lanoy definitely had him off balance. Ordinarily, he was better equipped to deal with criminals, but the events of the last few trying days had weakened his fibers. Quellen chewed his lip, watched the little man closely, and fervently wished that he were back beside his Congo stream throwing rocks at the crocodiles.

"I'm going to put a stop to your time-travel business, anyway," Quellen finally said.

Lanoy chuckled. "I wouldn't advise trying it, Quellen."

"CrimeSec to you."

"I wouldn't advise making trouble for me, *Quellen*," Lanoy repeated. "If you cut off the flow of the hoppers now, you'll turn the past topsy-turvy. Those people went back. It's recorded in history. Some of them married and had children, and the descendants of those children are alive today."

"I know all that. We've discussed the theory in great detail."

"For all you know, Quellen, you may be the descendant of a hopper I'm scheduled to be sending back next week—and if that hopper never gets back, Quellen, you'll pop out of existence like a snuffed candle. I guess it's a pleasant way to die. But do you want to die?"

Quellen stared glumly. Lanoy's words chased round and round in his aching skull. It became apparent to him now that it was a plot to drive him insane. Marok, Koll, Spanner, Brogg, Judith, Helaine, and now Lanoy—they were all determined to see Quellen enmeshed. It was an unvoiced conspiracy. Silently he cursed the hundreds of millions of jostling inhabitants of Appalachia, and wondered if he would ever know a moment's solitude again.

He took a deep breath. "The past won't be changed, Lanoy. We'll lock you up, all right, and take away your machine, but we'll see to it ourselves that the hoppers go back. We're not fools, Lanoy. We'll see to it that everything goes as it's supposed to go."

Lanoy watched him almost with pity for a moment, as one might observe a particularly rare butterfly impaled on a mounting board.

"Is that your game, CrimeSec? Do you really think you'll learn to operate the machine?"

"I'm sure of it."

"In that case, I'll have to take steps to protect myself,"

Quellen felt like hiding. "What could you possibly do?"

"You'll see. Suppose you put me back in the custody tank for the time being, while you figure out your own set of options. Then come and get me and talk to me again. Privately. I've got some interesting things to tell you. You won't want anyone else to hear them, though."

An aperture yawned in the sky, as though a quick hand had unzipped it. Norm Pomrath dropped through. His stomach protested as he made a rapid descent, falling eight or nine feet without warning. Lanoy might have told me, he thought, that I'd come out in the middle of the air. At the last moment he twisted and landed on his hip and his left leg. His kneecap tapped the pavement. Pomrath gasped and lay in a huddled heap for a moment, throbbing where he had bruised himself.

It wouldn't do to lie here long, he knew. He pulled himself together and got unsteadily to his feet, brushing himself off. The street was remarkably filthy. Pomrath's entire left side ached. He hobbled up against the wall of a building, clinging to it for a moment, and, clenching his teeth, performed one of the suggested neural exercises for enhancing the flow of blood. The pain began to ebb from him as the capillaries he had crushed emptied out.

There. That was better. He'd ache for a few hours, but it wasn't serious.

Now he had his first chance to look about him at the world of A.D. 2050.

He wasn't impressed. The city looked cluttered, as it would look four and a half centuries hence, but the clutter was a random, asymmetrical thing. Spiky buildings in an archaic style stuck up everywhere. There were no quickboat ramps and no bridges above the street levels. The pavement was cracked. The streets were crowded with pedestrians, not noticeably fewer than he was accustomed to seeing on the streets, although he knew that world population was only a third of what it would be in his rightful era. The styles of clothing interested him. Although it was springtime and the air was warm, everyone was dressed for maximum concealment, the women bundled up from ankles to chin, the men affecting loose capes that blurred the outlines of their body. So Pomrath knew that Lanoy had sent him approximately to the right time.

Pomrath had done some homework. He knew that the middle of the twenty-first century had been a time of neo-puritan reaction against the fleshly excesses of the immediate past. He liked that. Nothing bored him more than an epoch of brazenly bare-breasted women and men in codpieces. True sensuality, he knew, thrived only in an era of erotic repression. Sensuality was one of the things he was looking for. After a decade as devoted father and faithful husband, Pomrath anticipated a fling.

He also knew that the neopuritan phase was soon to be struck down by another swing of the pendulum. So he would have the best of both cultures: first the covert pleasures of the inner revolt against the public morality, and then, in his declining days, the joys of witnessing the total breakdown of that morality. He had picked a good time. No wars to speak of, no particular crises. A man could enjoy himself here. Especially if he had useful skills, and a medical technician like Pomrath would thrive in this time of primitive medicine.

No one had seen him appear. At least, any witnesses to his materialization had quickly scurried on about their businesses, without meddling. Good.

He had to get his bearings, now.

He was in a city, presumably New York. Shops and offices all around. Pomrath drifted with the pedestrian tide. A kiosk at the corner was peddling what seemed to be the this-time equivalent of a faxtape. Pomrath stared. There was a date: May 6, 2051. Good old Lanoy. Within a year of the requested time. The yellow tape chuttered out of the slot in the machine. Pomrath had difficulty reading the ancient sans-serif type face. He hadn't realized how the shapes of the letters had changed. A moment though, and he had the hang of it.

Fine. Now all he needed was some money, an identity, a place to live. Within a week, he felt, he would be fully established in the matrix of this era.

He filled his lungs with air. He felt confident, bouncy,

buoyant. There was no job machine here. He could live by his own wits, doing solitary battle with the inexorable forces of the universe and actually getting the universe to yield a little. In his own time, he was just a number on a punched card, a patch of ions on a coded tape. Here he was free to select his own role and capitalize on it.

Pomrath stepped into a shop at random. They were selling books in there. Not spools; *books*. He looked at them in wonder. Cheap, sleazy paper; blurry ink; flimsy bindings. He picked up a novel, flipped its pages, put it down. He found what seemed to be a popular medical guide. It would be useful; Pomrath wondered how he could gain possession of it without money. He didn't want to admit to anyone that he was a hopper. He wanted to make the grade by his own devices.

A man whom he assumed was the proprietor came up to him—plump, grimy-faced, with watery blue eyes. Pomrath smiled. He knew that his clothing marked him as a stranger, but he hoped it didn't stamp him too clearly as a stranger out of time.

The man said in a soft, feathery voice, "There's better downstairs. Want to catch some haunch?"

Pomrath's smile grew broader. "Sorry, I be not easy speaking. My English very hard."

"Haunch, I said. *Haunch*. Downstairs. You from out of town?"

"Visitor from Slavic country. Incomplete grasp your language," Pomrath said, laying on what he hoped sounded like a thick Czech accent. "Maybe you help? Am feeling unsettled here."

"That's what I thought. A lonely foreigner. Well, go downstairs. The girls'll cheer you up. Twenty dollars. You got dollars?"

Pomrath began to see what was going on in the basement of the bookshop. He nodded vociferously and headed toward the rear of the store, still clutching his medical guide. The proprietor didn't appear to notice that he had taken the book.

Stairs led below. Stairs! Pomrath hardly knew what they were. He gripped the railing tightly, unsure of his footing as he descended. At the bottom, some sort of scanner beamed him and he heard a blipping sound that probably indicated he was carrying no weapons. A fleshy woman in bulky robes came swishing out to inspect him.

In his own time there were public sex cubicles available to all, without concealment. It figured that in this neopuritan era there would be girlie cribs hidden in the lower levels of musty old buildings. Vice, Pomrath thought, was probably more common here per capita than up yonder.

The woman said, "You're the foreigner Al said was coming down, huh? You sure look foreign to me. Where you from, France?"

"Slavic district. Praha."

"Where's that?"

Pomrath looked uncertain. "Europe. To the east."

The woman shrugged and led him with. Pomrath found himself in a small, low-ceilinged room which contained a bed, a washstand, and a pasty-faced blonde girl. The girl slipped off her robe. Her body was soft and slightly flabby, but the basic material was pretty good. She looked young and more intelligent than her job called on her to be.

"It's twenty dollars," she said patiently.

Pomrath knew that the moment of truth had arrived. He flicked a wary glance around the little room and saw no sign of any scanning devices. He couldn't be sure, naturally. Even way back here, they had been pretty sophisticated about espionage, and he didn't doubt that they pulled the same dirty tricks that were common in his own time. But he had to take the risk. Sooner or later, he had to find himself an ally in this other time, and now was a reasonable time to begin.

"I don't have any money," said Pomrath, dropping the phony accent.

"Then get the hell out of here."

"Shh. Not so fast. I've got some ideas. Sit down. Relax. How would you like to be rich?"

"Are you a cop?"

"I'm just a stranger in town, and I need a friend. I've got plans. Cooperate with me and you'll be out of the bed-girl business in a hurry. What's your name?"

"Lisa. You talk funny. What are you, a hopper or something?"

"Is it that obvious?"

"Just a guess." The girl's eyes were very blue, very wide. She picked up her robe and put it on again, as though she did not think it proper to hold a business conference in the nude. She kept her voice low as she said, "You just get here?"

"Yes. I'm a doctor. I can make us fabulously rich. With what I know—"

"We'll turn all the turbines, child!" she said. "You and me. What's your label?"

"Keystone," Pomrath said at random. "Mort Keystone."

"We're going to twist orbits, Mort."

"I know we are. How soon can you get out of this place?"

"Two more hours."

"Where should I meet you?"

"There's a park two blocks from here. You can sit there and wait and I'll come along."

"A what?"

"A park. You know, grass, benches, some trees. What's the matter, Mort?"

Pomrath was struck by the alienness of having trees and grass in the middle of a city. He managed a smile. "Nothing's the matter. I'll wait for you in the park." Then he handed her the book. "Here. Buy this for me when you leave the shop. I don't want to have to steal it."

She nodded. Then she said, "You sure you don't want anything else while you're down here?"

"There's time for that later," said Pomrath. "I'll be waiting in the park."

He went out. The bookstore proprietor waved cheerily to him. Pomrath replied in a string of improvised guttural sounds and stepped into the street. It was difficult for him to believe that he had been on the verge of psychotic collapse only a few hours ago and four hundred forty-nine years from now. He was utterly calm. This world held challenges for him, and he knew he could meet those challenges.

Poor Helaine, he thought. I wonder how she took the news.

He walked briskly down the street, only momentarily bothered by the lack of resilience in the pavement. I am Mort Keystone, he told himself. Mort Keystone. Mort Keystone. And Lisa will help me get together some money to start a medical practice. I'll be a rich man. I'll live like a Class Two. There's no High Government to slap me down.

I'll have power and status among these primitives, he told himself pleasantly. And after I'm established, I'll track down a few people from my own time, just so I don't feel too isolated from it. We'll reminisce, he thought.

We'll reminisce about the future.

14.

Quellen waited three hours, until Koll and Spanner both were tied up on other government business. Then he went down the hall to the custody tank. He opened the scanner slot and peered in. Lanoy floated peacefully on the dark green fluid, utterly relaxed, evidently enjoying himself. On the stippled metal wall of the tank the indicators announced the slyster's status. EEG and EKG bands wavered and criss-crossed. Heartbeat, respiration, everything was monitored.

Summoning a technician, Quellen said, "Get him out of there."

"Sir, we just put him back in a few hours ago."

"I want to interrogate him. Get him out!"

The technician obeyed. Lanoy was unplugged, filtered, and returned to consciousness. Attendant-robots wheeled him back to Quellen's office. In a short while his reflexes were working again and he could move under his own power.

Quellen shut down all recording devices in the office.

He had a strong hunch that he wanted this conversation to be strictly off the record. Since there were only the two of them in the room, he also moved to cut down the oxy vent.

"Leave it up, Quellen," Lanoy said. "I like to breathe well. It's at government expense."

"Let's finish our talk, then. What's your game?" Quellen was angry. Lanoy was a completely amoral creature, not even vicious in his criminality, who offended Quellen's pride and sense of personal dignity.

"I'll be blunt with you, CrimeSec," the slyster said. "I want my freedom, and I want to continue in business. I like it that way. That's what I want. You want to arrest me and let the government or perhaps the High Government take over my business. That's what *you* want. Right?"

"Right."

"Now, in a situation like that we have an interplay of mutually exclusive desires. So the stronger of the two forces wins—all the time. I'm stronger, and so you'll have to let me go and suppress all the findings of your investigation."

"Who says you're stronger, Lanoy?"

"I know I am. I'm strong and you're weak. I know a lot of things about you, Quellen. I know how you hate crowds and like fresh air and open spaces. These are pretty awkward idiosyncrasies to live with in a world like ours, aren't they?"

"Go on," said Quellen. He cursed Brogg silently. No one else could have revealed his secret to Lanoy. And obviously Lanoy knew too much about him.

"So you're going to let me walk out of here a free man," Lanoy continued, "or else you'll find yourself back in a Class Nine or maybe Eleven unit. You won't like it much there, CrimeSec. You'll have to share a room, and you may not like your roommate, but there'll be nothing you can do. And when you have a roommate, you won't be free to run away. He'll report you."

"What do you mean, run away?" Quellen's voice was little more than a husky whisper.

"I mean run away to Africa, Quellen."

That's it, then, Quellen thought. Now it's over; Brogg's sold me completely down the river. He knew that with Lanoy in possession of the secret, he was totally in the little slyster's power. He stood motionless before Lanoy, seething with the temptation to grab up a televector cable and knot it fatally around Lanoy's neck.

Lanoy said, "I hate to do this to you, Quellen. Actually. There's no personal animus in it at all. You're a pretty good sort, caught in a world you didn't make and don't especially like. But I can't help myself. It's either you or me, and you know who's got to win in a deal like that."

"How did you find out?"

"Brogg told me."

"Why would he do a thing like that? He was getting a good price from me."

"I gave him a better one," said Lanoy. "I sent him back to Hadrian's time. Possibly Trajan. He's gone back 2400 years, at any rate."

Quellen felt the floor turn to sticky rubber beneath his feet, writhing and squirming and pulsing with heat. He clung to his desk so he would not slide through into oblivion. Brogg a hopper! Brogg gone? Brogg a traitor?

"When did this happen?" Quellen asked.

"Yesterday evening, about sunset. Brogg and I discussed the problem of how I was going to avoid being put out of business. He suggested that you had a point of vulnerability. I got it from him in return for the one thing he really wanted. He's gone back to see Rome with his own eyes."

"That's impossible," Quellen insisted. "There are records on the known hoppers, and Brogg wasn't on the list."

Even as he spoke, he knew how foolish the words were.

The records went back only to A.D. 1979. Brogg—unless Lanoy were bluffing—was almost nineteen centuries further back. There'd be no record.

Quellen felt sick. He knew that Brogg had planted autonomic telltales all over Appalachia, with taped accounts of Quellen's crime in them. The telltales were programmed to march down to headquarters in the event of Brogg's death or disappearance. The little springy legs must have been in motion since last night. I'm finished, Quellen thought. Unless Brogg had the good grace to deactivate the telltales before he hopped. He could have done it with no great trouble. The boxes responded to telephoned instruction. One call would have shut them down. But had he? Otherwise, the High Government was even now in possession of the truth about Joseph Quellen.

Quellen had talked to Koll only this morning, though, and Koll had congratulated him on his promotion. Koll was guileful, but not to that degree. He would surely have been the recipient of one of Brogg's little telltales, and he wouldn't have been able to conceal his fury and envy at the discovery that Quellen had been living in Class Two luxury all this time.

So possibly Brogg had turned the telltales off. Or possibly he had never gone hopper at all.

Scowling, Quellen slammed on his communicator and said, "Get me Brogg."

"I'm sorry, UnderSec Brogg hasn't been in contact today."

"Not even to give a locus notice?"

"We haven't heard from him, sir."

"Ring his apartment. Check the district headquarters. If there's no word from him within the next fifteen minutes, initiate a televector search. I want to know where he is!"

Lanoy was beaming. "You're not going to find him,

Quellen. Believe me, he's in Rome. I set up the displacement myself–temporal and geographical. If everything worked out, he landed just south of the city, somewhere along the Via Appia."

Quellen's lips twitched. He was gripping the desk very, very tightly, now, so that his fingertips were beginning to make indentations in the top, which was thermal-sensitive and not designed to be handled that way. He said, "If you can send somebody back that far in time, how is it that 1979 has been the terminal date for the hopper phenomenon?"

"Lots of reasons."

"Such as?"

"For one, the process wasn't reliable beyond about five hundred years until recently. We've improved the process. New research. Now we can confidently shoot people back a couple of thousand years and know they'll get there."

"The pigs in the twelfth century?"

"Yes," Lanoy said. "Those were our experimental shots. Now, then: it also happens that such a concentration of hoppers got sent back to the 1979 nexus that the phenomenon came to the attention of authorities. Any hopper landing in a previous *elsewhere* would generally end up detained for insanity, or arrested for witchcraft, or something. So we tried to limit our hoppers to the 1979 to 2106 period because any hopper landing there would be recognized for what he was, and he'd have minimal troubles. We only exceeded that range upon special request, or sometimes by unintentional overshoot. You follow?"

"Yes," said Quellen glumly. "And Brogg went back to Rome?"

"He really did. For a price. And now you'd better let me go, promising to keep the results of your investigation from getting any higher, or I'll expose your little game. I'll let it be known that you've got a hideaway in Africa."

Quellen said coolly, "I could put a beam through your head right now and claim that you assaulted me."

"No good, Quellen. For one thing, the High Government wants the time-transport process. Kill me and you lose the process."

"We could dredge it out of your brain on a neural replay dead or alive."

"Not if you lase me through the head," Lanoy pointed out. "Anyway, the neural replay would also dredge up the Africa bit, wouldn't it? Besides that, you'd suffer if I died. Didn't you know that Brogg fed your story into a bunch of autonomic telltales programmed to walk into government headquarters if anything happened to him?"

"Yes, but–"

"He keyed them all over to me just before he hopped. Your fate is tied to mine, Quellen. You don't want to harm me. You want to let me go."

Quellen could feel the muscles of his face sag as the nastiness of his position came home. If he did not present Lanoy for prosecution, he ran the risk of demotion. If he turned Lanoy in, Lanoy would expose him. Nor could he simply let Lanoy walk out the way the slyster wished. It was already a matter of record that Lanoy was involved in the hopper affair. Koll knew. Spanner knew. Quellen could not easily expunge the knowledge from the records. If he tried to cover up for Lanoy, he would mire himself in lie upon lie. He was living one fraud as it was; he could not bear the strain of assuming another.

"Do I get what I want?" Lanoy asked.

A powerful surge of adrenalin rocked through Quellen. He was a man in a trap, and a trapped man fights fiercely. He found unexpected reserves of strength.

There was one thing he could try, a monumentally audacious thing, something so vastly bold that it seemed almost sensible in its way. Perhaps it would fail; probably it would fail. But it was better than making deals with Lanoy and slipping deeper into a morass of bribery and compromise.

"No," he said. "You don't get what you want. I'm not releasing you, Lanoy. I'm going to remand you for indictment."

"Are you crazy?"

"I don't think so." Quellen rang for attendants. "Put this man back in the custody tank," he said crisply. "Leave him there until further notice."

Lanoy was carried away, sputtering and protesting.

Now to secure the bait for the leviathan he hoped to snare.

Quellen jabbed communicator buttons. "Get me the Donald Mortensen file," he commanded.

The spool was brought to him. He threaded it through the projector and looked over Brogg's investigation. The face of Mortensen gleamed out at him, youthful, pink. He looked like some kind of albino, Quellen thought, with that white hair and eyebrows. But albinos have pink eyes, don't they? Mortensen's were blue. Pure Nordic. How had he preserved his bloodline so well, Quellen wondered? He examined Mortensen's dossier.

Quellen pored over the recorded texts of Brogg's pickups. Mortensen had quarreled with his wife; he had negotiated for a hopper trip several weeks hence; he had put money down, and was busily raising the rest of Lanoy's fee. Then the data ended with Brogg's notation: INVESTIGATION CONCLUDED BY OFFICIAL ORDER.

Quellen rang the listening room. He gave the number of the Ear that had been pressed into Mortensen's palm and asked if it was still functioning.

"The Ear's been deactivated, CrimeSec," he was told.

"Yes, I know. But can it be turned on again?"

They checked. A few minutes later they gave him the bad news; the Ear had dissolved a day or two ago, as it was designed to do. There were no further transmissions from Mortensen. Quellen was disappointed, but the setback was not critical. He ordered a televector check on Mortensen's whereabouts, hoping fiercely that he had not gone out of Appalachia.

He hadn't. The televector tracer reported that Mortensen was in a sniffer palace less than ten miles from Quellen's office. Excellent, Quellen thought. He would make the arrest himself. This was something far too delicate to leave it to a subordinate.

Catching a quickboat, Quellen crossed the city and stationed himself outside the sniffer palace, waiting on street level for Mortensen to come up from the depths. Seamy, shifty-eyed individuals kept shuttling past him. Quellen masked his discomfort and scanned everyone who emerged.

There was Mortensen now.

It was a long time since Quellen had made an arrest in person. He was a desk man, who left such contacts to underlings. Nevertheless he felt calm. He was well armed; taped to the palm of his hand was an anesthetic prong that would flip out at a command of his muscles, and beneath his armpit was a neural spray in case something went awry with the prong. He carried a laser pistol too, but the last thing he intended was to use it on Mortensen.

Moving in behind the man as he strode away from the sniffer palace, Quellen tapped him on the shoulder and said, "Just keep walking calmly, Mortensen. You're under arrest."

"What the hell–?"

"I'm from the Secretariat of Crime. I've got orders to bring you in. There's a prong in my palm and I'll slap it into you in a hurry if you attempt to resist. Walk quietly ahead of me until we get to that quickboat ramp. You do as I say and you won't get into trouble."

"I haven't done anything wrong. I want to know the charge."

"Later," said Quellen. "Keep walking."

"I have legal rights. A lawyer–"

"Later. Walk."

They ascended the flyramp. Mortensen continued to grumble, but he made no show of resistance. He was a tall man, taller than Quellen. He did not look particularly powerful, though. Quellen kept his prong-laden palm ready. His entire future depended on the successful completion of this maneuver.

The quickboat took them to Quellen's apartment building.

Mortensen looked puzzled. As they stepped out on the ramp, he grunted sullenly, "This doesn't look like a crime office to me."

"Down the ramp, please," Quellen said.

"What is this, a kidnapping?"

"I'll show you my credentials if you're worried. I'm an authentic peace officer. As a matter of fact, I hold the rank of CrimeSec. Step in here."

They entered Quellen's apartment. Mortensen, facing Quellen, stared at him incredulously.

"This is a private residence," he said.

"True. Mine."

"Somebody's clearly given you the wrong tip on my sexual orientation, friend. I'm not–"

"Neither am I," said Quellen sharply. "Mortensen, are you planning to go hopper the first week in May?"

Glaring, Mortensen said, "What's that to you?"

"A good deal. Is it true?"

"Maybe. I'm not saying."

Quellen sighed. "You're on the list of hoppers who went back, do you know that? A fully documented list giving your name, your date of birth, the day you arrived in the past, the day you left here. The list says you went back on May 4 of this year. Now do you want to deny that you're planning to hop?"

"I'm not saying anything. Get me a lawyer. Damn you, I didn't threaten you in any way! Why did you have to muck around with my life?"

"I can't explain that now," said Quellen. "It happens that you're the unfortunate victim of a situation that's getting out of hand. Mortensen, I'm going to send you on a journey. You're going to have a vacation. I can't say how long you'll be away, but at least you'll be comfortable there. You'll find a full food program; help yourself. And rest assured that I'll be looking out for your welfare. I'm on your side, actually. Deeply sympathetic to your position. But I've got to look out for myself, first."

The troubled Mortensen lifted a hand as though to lash out at Quellen. Smoothly, Quellen moved forward and activated the anesthetic prong on his hand. It bit into Mortensen's skin. The instantaneous anesthetic went to work, and Mortensen folded up into unconsciousness. He would be out for about an hour, which was more than enough time.

Quellen turned on the stat field and shoved Mortensen through. The blond man vanished. He would wake up in the CrimeSec's African cottage. No doubt that would add to his general bafflement, but Quellen had not been able to offer explanations.

A moment later the stat was turned off at Quellen's end. That would keep Mortensen from getting back until Quellen was ready to bring him back.

Waves of vertigo swept through him.

He had the bait. Now he had to play his fish. It seemed incredible that he would succeed, but he had gone too far to permit himself to turn back. And, if he failed, he was beginning to see, there was an alternative way out, less honorable but possibly more rational a solution than what he had in mind.

Can I get away with this, he wondered? Can I actually try to blackmail the High Government and make it stick? Or am I simply out of my mind altogether?

He would find that out soon enough. Meanwhile, he had a hostage—Mortensen. A hostage against the wrath of the High Government.

Now, just one small thing remained: to get an interview with Peter Kloofman. Himself. In person. Could it be arranged? It was a staggering dream. How could a Class Seven bureaucrat gain admission to the presence of Kloofman?

He'll see me, Quellen thought. When he learns that I've kidnapped Donald Mortensen.

15.

David Giacomin, who had been carrying out some quiet monitoring of the Mortensen situation himself, was the first to discover that there was trouble. A flashing red light informed him that Mortensen had vanished from the reach of the Appalachia televector field.

Giacomin experienced a sensation of disorientation. The critical day for Mortensen was May 4; and May 4 was still several weeks off. It wasn't possible for him to have gone hopper so soon, was it?

Yes, it *was* possible, Giacomin reflected. But if he had, why hadn't the fabric of space and time tottered? The past had been altered—or else the records had been in error in the first place. Giacomin ordered a full investigation into the Mortensen disappearance to be carried out, mobilizing every resource of the High Government. Kloofman had personally instructed Giacomin to see that nothing happened to Mortensen; and now it appeared as though something had indeed happened. The perspiring Giacomin reflected that he better damned well get Mortensen back before Kloofman found out he was missing.

Then, almost simultaneously, Giacomin learned that he was going to have to break the news to Kloofman after all.

A call came through from Koll in the Secretariat of Crime, the ratty-faced little Class Six through whom Giacomin supervised that wing of governmental activities. Koll looked upset, even dazed. His face was flushed and his eyes were fixed and glossy.

"I've got someone here who wants an interview with Kloofman," Koll said. "A Class Seven—no, he'll soon be Six—in my department."

"He's insane. Kloofman wouldn't see him, and you know it, so why are you bothering me with this?"

"He says he's kidnapped Mortensen, and he wants to discuss the situation with somebody in Class One."

Giacomin stiffened. His hands began to move in spasmodic jerks, and he fought to get them under control. "Who is this maniac?"

"Quellen. He's the CrimeSec here. He—"

"Yes, I know him. When did he make this request?"

"Ten minutes ago. First he tried to call Kloofman direct, but that didn't work. So now he's going through channels. He asked me and I'm asking you. What else can I do?"

"Nothing else, I suppose," said Giacomin hollowly. His quick mind sifted the possible things that could be done to the troublesome Quellen, beginning with slow disembowelment and proceeding from there. But Quellen had Mortensen, or said he did. And Kloofman was practically psychotic on the subject of Mortensen. He talked of little else.

There went Giacomin's carefully crafted plan to keep the news about Mortensen's disappearance from getting to the top man. He saw no way of avoiding that now. He could stall for time, but in the end Quellen would have his way.

"Well?" Koll said. The tip of his nose quivered. "Can I remand his request officially to your level?"

"Yes," Giacomin said. "I'll take it off your hands. Let me talk to Quellen."

A moment passed. Quellen appeared on the screen. He *looked* sane, Giacomin thought. A little frightened at his own audacity, no doubt, but generally rational. At least as rational as Koll, for that matter.

But determined. He wanted to see Kloofman. Yes, he had kidnapped Mortensen. No, he would not divulge the whereabouts of the kidnapped man. Moreover, any attempt to interfere with his freedom of action would result in the immediate death of Mortensen.

Was it a bluff? Giacomin didn't dare take the chance. He looked at Quellen in quiet wonder and said, "All right. You win, you madman. I'll pass your request for an audience along to Kloofman and we'll see what he says."

It was such a long time since Kloofman had consented to speak face to face with a member of the lower orders that he had nearly forgotten what the experience was like. He had some Class Threes and Fours and even Fives in attendance on him, of course, but they didn't converse with him. They could just as well have been robots. Kloofman tolerated no chitchat from such people. High on the lonely eminence of Class One, the world leader had cut himself off from contact with the masses.

He awaited the arrival of this person Quellen, then, with some curiosity. Resentment, of course; he was not accustomed to coercion. Anger. Irritation. Yet Kloofman was amused, as well. The pleasure of vulnerability had been denied him for many years. He could take a light approach to this unexpected crisis.

He was also frightened. So far as the televector men could tell, Quellen actually *did* have possession of Mortensen. That was distressing. It was a direct threat to Kloofman's power. He could not laugh at such a situation.

The subcranial probe murmured to Kloofman, "Quellen is here."

"Let him in."

The chamber wall rolled back. A lean, haggard-looking man walked awkwardly in and stood flatfooted before the huge pneumatic web in which Kloofman reposed. Between Kloofman and Quellen there rose a fine, almost imperceptible mist, an assassination screen extending from floor to ceiling. Any particle of solid matter attempting to cross that screen would be instantly volatilized, no matter what its mass or velocity. Robot wardens flanked Kloofman as an additional precaution. Kloofman waited patiently. The artificial systems within his reconstituted body purred smoothly, pumping blood through the vessels, bathing the inner meat with lymph. He saw that Quellen was uncomfortable in his presence. It scarcely surprised him.

At length Kloofman said, "You've had your wish. Here I am. What do you want?"

Quellen moved his lips, but there was a lag of several seconds before he produced words. "Do you know what I'm thinking?" he blurted finally. "I'm glad you exist. That's what I'm thinking. It's relieving to know that you're real."

Kloofman managed to smile. "How do you *know* I'm real?"

"Because—" Quellen stopped. "All right. I retract that. I hope you're real." His hands were quivering at his sides. Kloofman observed the man make a visible effort to pull himself together—an effort that seemed to be at least outwardly successful.

"Are you the man who kidnapped Mortensen?"

"Yes."

"Where is he?"

"I can't reveal that, sir. Not yet. I've got to propose a deal with you first."

"A deal with *me*?" Kloofman delivered himself of a rumbling chuckle. "You're incredible in your brazenness," he said mildly. "Don't you realize what I can do to you?"

"Yes."

"And yet you come here to bargain with me?"

"I have Mortensen," Quellen reminded him. "Unless I release him, he won't be free to hop on May 4. And that means—"

"Yes," said Kloofman sharply. He felt tension levels climbing within his body. This man had found his zone of vulnerability, all right. It was preposterous that he should be held at bay by a prolet, but that was the situation. Kloofman could take no chances with a man who threatened to change the past. No computer simulation could possibly calculate the effects of subtracting the hopper Donald Mortensen from his proper time destination. The world leader was helpless. Kloofman said, "You're playing a dangerous game, Quellen. State your business. Then you'll be removed and the location of Mortensen will be dredged from your mind."

"Mortensen is programmed to destruct in the event of any tampering with my brain," said Quellen.

Could that be true, Kloofman wondered? Or was this all some gigantic bluff?

"Your business."

Quellen nodded. He seemed to be gaining poise and strength, as though he had discovered that Kloofman was no superbeing, but merely a very old man with great power. Quellen said, "I was assigned to the investigation into the time-travel operation. I've succeeded in finding the man who controls it. He's under arrest now. Unfortunately, he's in possession of information that incriminates me in an illegal act."

"Are you a criminal, Quellen?"

"I've done something illegal. It could bring me demotion and worse. If I turn the slyster over to your people, he'll expose me. So I want immunity. That's the deal. I'll give you your man, and he'll blab about my crime, but you'll confirm me in my position and see to it that I'm not prosecuted or demoted."

"What's your crime, Quellen?"

"I maintain a Class Two villa in Africa."

Kloofman smiled. "You *are* a scoundrel, aren't you?" he said without rancor. "You connive out of your class, you blackmail the High Government—"

"Actually I regard myself as fairly honest, sir."

"I suppose you do. But you're a scoundrel all the same. Do you know what I'd do with a dangerous man like you, if I had my options? I'd put you in the time machine and hurl you far into the past. That's the safest way to deal with agitators. That's how we'll cope, once we—" Kloofman fell silent. After a moment he said, "Your boldness stupefies me. What if I lie to you? I grant you your immunity, you turn Mortensen over to me and surrender the time-travel slyster, and then I seize you and arrest you all the same."

"I have two other documented hoppers hidden away," said Quellen blandly. "One is due to depart later this year and the other one early next year. They're further insurance that you won't harm me after I've given you Mortensen."

"You're bluffing, Quellen. You've invented those other two hoppers on the spot. I'll put you under a neural probe and check on it."

"The moment the probe touches my brain," said Quellen, "Mortensen will die."

Kloofman felt unaccustomed anguish. He was certain that this infuriating prolet was piling bluff upon bluff—but there was no way of proving that without peering into his brain, and bluff number one made it too risky for Kloofman to try that. It might just not be a bluff.

He said, "What do you really want, Quellen?"

"I've told you. A pledge of immunity, before witnesses. I want you to guarantee that I won't be punished for maintaining my place in Africa, and that I'll come to no harm for having bearded you like this. Then I'll give you the slyster and Mortensen."

"And the other two hoppers."

"Those also. After I've become assured of your good faith."

"You're incredible, Quellen. But you seem to hold a strong position. I can't let you keep Mortensen. And I want that time machine. It's got many uses. Too dangerous to let it stay in private hands. All right. All right. You'll have your pledge. I'll give you more than that, Quellen."

"More, sir?"

"Your villa's Class Two, you say? I assume you want to go on living in it. We'll have to make you Class Two then, won't we?"

"Take me into the High Government, sir?"

"Of course," said Kloofman warmly. "Consider: how can I send you back to lower levels, after you've triumphed over me like this? You've won status. I'll put you up here. Giacomin will find room for you. A man who's done what you've done can't possibly remain in a low bureaucratic post, Quellen. So we'll arrange something. You've won more than you came looking for." Kloofman smiled. "I congratulate you, Quellen."

Quellen erupted into the upper air, after having risen level upon level upon level from that mythical catacomb that was the lair of Peter Kloofman. He staggered out into the street and planted himself solidly, feet on the pavement, head upturned to the towers far above. He saw the lacy connecting bridges, the gleaming cones atop the buildings, the faint patch of blue light beyond the summits.

I don't have much time, Quellen thought.

He was numb with shock after his interview with Kloofman. In retrospect he had no idea how he had carried off such an enterprise. To muscle his way into the lair of a Class One administrator, to stand there bluntly making demands and having Kloofman accede to them, to pile fraud upon fraud and carry his bluffs home—it was not real. It couldn't be. It had to be some sniffer palace fantasy, some dream of power that would fade with the ebbing of the drug from his brain.

Yet the buildings were real. The sky was real. The pavements were real. And the interview with Kloofman had been real, too. He had won. He had been invited to accept Class Two status. He had compelled Kloofman to retreat.

Quellen knew that he had not won a thing.

He had done his audacious maneuver with reasonable aplomb, but it had been a fool's maneuver, and he saw that more clearly now than he had an hour before. Any man could be proud of having had the nerve to confront Kloofman like that, but, having done it, Quellen knew that he had gained no real safety, only the temporary illusion of triumph. It would be necessary to activate the alternate plan that he had been nurturing for some hours. His mind had prepared itself for this eventuality, and he knew what he had to do, though he was not at all sure that he would have time to do it.

He was in mortal danger. He had to act fast.

Kloofman had not fooled him with his smiles, his words of praise, his promise of an uptwitch to High Government status, his apparent delight in Quellen's audacity. Kloofman was frightened that something might happen to Mortensen that could topple his own power, yes, but Kloofman could not be pushed around as easily as it seemed.

He'll get Lanoy and Mortensen from me, Quellen knew, and then he'll destroy me. I should have realized that from the start. How could I hope to outsmart Kloofman?

But he did not regret having made the attempt. A man is not a worm; he can stand up on his legs, he can fight for his position. He can try. Quellen had tried. He had done something foolhardy to the point of absurdity, and he had carried it off with honor, even if his success was probably unreal.

Now, though, he had to hasten to protect himself against Kloofman's wrath. He had at least a little time in which to operate. The euphoria of his meeting with Kloofman had worn off, and he was thinking clearly and rationally.

He reached the headquarters of the Secretariat of Crime and immediately gave orders for Lanoy to be taken from the custody tank once again. The slyster was brought to Quellen's office. He looked moody and downcast.

"You're going to be sorry for this, Quellen," Lanoy said bitterly. "I wasn't joking when I said Brogg had keyed all his telltales over to me. I can have the news of your African place in the hands of the High Government in—"

"You don't need to inform on me," said Quellen. "I'm letting you go."

Lanoy was startled. "But you said—"

"That was earlier. I'm releasing you and wiping out as much as I can of the records involving you."

"So you gave in after all, Quellen? You knew you couldn't take the risk that I'd expose you?"

"On the contrary. I haven't given in. I told the High Government about my African place myself. I let Kloofman himself know, in person. No sense wasting time talking to underlings. So your telltales won't be telling anything that isn't already known."

"You can't ask me to believe that, Quellen!"

"It's the truth, though. And therefore the price for my letting you go has changed. It isn't your silence any more. It's your services."

Lanoy's eyes widened. "What have you been up to?"

"Plenty. But there's no time for me to explain it now. I'll get you safely out of this building. You've got to get back to your lab on your own power. I'll join you there in about an hour." Quellen shook his head. "Not that I think you'll stay free for very long, Lanoy. Kloofman's hungry for your machine. He wants to use it to send political prisoners back. And to raise public revenues. He'll solve his unemployment problem by shooting the prolets back to 500,000 B.C. and letting them get eaten by tigers. You'll be picked up again, I'm sure of it. But at least it won't be my doing."

He escorted Lanoy from the building. The little slyster gave Quellen a baffled look as he scuttled away toward the quickboat ramp.

"I'll be seeing you in a little while," Quellen said.

He boarded a quickboat himself, a local, and headed for his apartment to perform one last chore. Had Kloofman taken steps against him yet? Doubtless They were having frantic conferences in the chambers of the High Government. It wouldn't be long now, though, and Quellen would be safe.

He had come to understand a great many things. Why Kloofman wanted the machine so badly, for one thing: as a tool to extend his own power over the world. Unscrupulous, it was. And I nearly helped him get it.

Then, too, Quellen saw why the recorded hoppers had all come from 2486–91. It didn't mean that the backward flow had been cut off next year, as he had assumed. It simply meant that control of the machine had passed then from Lanoy to Kloofman, and that all hoppers sent back after 2491 were hurled by the new process, which had a greater range, thrown back so far that they could be no possible threat to Kloofman's regime. And would not, of course, show up in any historical records. Quellen shuddered. He wanted no part of a world in which the government held such powers.

He entered his apartment and activated the stat. The glow of theta force enveloped him. Quellen stepped through, and emerged in his African cottage.

"Mortensen?" he shouted. "Where are you?"

"Down here!"

Quellen peered over the edge of the porch. Mortensen was fishing. Stripped to the waist, his pale skin partly red and partly tan, he waved to Quellen affably.

"Come on," Quellen said. "You're going home!"

"I'd rather stay, thank you. I like it here."

"Nonsense. You've got a date to hop."

"Why hop if I can hang out here?" Mortensen asked reasonably. "I don't understand why you brought me here, but I don't feel like leaving now."

Quellen had no time to argue. It did not fit into his plan to keep Mortensen from making his May 4 hop. Quellen had no vested interest in disturbing the recorded past, and Mortensen's value as a hostage would shortly be zero. It was conceivable that Mortensen's failure to hop on schedule would jeopardize Quellen's own continued existence, if he happened to be a descendant of the hopped Mortensen. Why take the risk? Mortensen would have to hop.

"Come," Quellen said.

"No."

Sighing, Quellen moved in and once again anesthetized

the man. He hauled the limp Mortensen into the cottage and thrust him through the stat, following a moment later himself. Mortensen lay sprawled out on the floor of Quellen's apartment. In a short while, he'd awaken and try to comprehend all that had been happening to him, and perhaps he'd attempt to get back to Africa. But by then he would have registered on the Appalachia televector field, and Kloofman's men would be on their way to pick him up. Kloofman would make sure that Mortensen hopped on schedule.

Quellen left the apartment for the last time. He ascended the flyramp and waited for the quickboat. He knew the route to Lanoy's place, thanks to Brogg.

He would rather have triumphed over Kloofman than have taken this route. But he had been in a trap, and a man in a trap must seek the sane path to freedom, not the most glamorous one. There was irony in the decision, of course: the man assigned to police the hopper problem becoming a hopper himself. Yet there was a kind of inevitability, Quellen saw, right from the start, that made him one with Norm Pomrath and Brogg and the others. He had begun to make his hop the day he secured the African retreat for himself. Now he was merely completing the logical course of action.

It was late afternoon by the time Quellen arrived. The sun was dipping to the horizon, and colors danced on the polluted lake. Lanoy was waiting for him.

"Everything's ready, Quellen," he said.

"Good. Can I rely on you to be honest!"

"You let me go, didn't you? There's honor even among slysters," said Lanoy. "You're sure you want to do this?"

"Positive. I can't stay here. I'm anathema to Kloofman now. I gave him an uncomfortable ten minutes, and he'll make me pay for it if he ever catches me. But he won't catch me. Thanks to you."

"Come inside," Lanoy said. "Damn you, I never thought I'd be helping you this way."

"If you're smart," said Quellen, "you'll go the same way. Kloofman's bound to catch you sooner or later. It can't be avoided."

"I'll take my chances, Quellen." Lanoy smiled. "When the time comes, I'll look Kloofman in the eye and see if I can't strike a deal with him. Come along. The machine's waiting."

16.

It was done.

There was a swirling and a twisting, and Quellen felt as if he had been turned inside out. He was floating on a purple cloud high above some indistinct terrain, and he was falling.

He dropped, heels over head, and landed in a scrambled heap on a long green carpet. He lay there for a moment or two, breathless, clutching at the carpet for stability in an uncertain world.

A handful of the carpet tore off in his hands. Quellen looked at it in puzzlement.

Grass.

Living grass. Strands of it in his clenched fingers.

The clean smell of the air hit him next, almost as a physical shock. It was painful to pull air like that down into his lungs. It was like inhaling in a room with full oxy turned on. But this was outdoors. The air in Africa was not like that, because it held an overstratum of residues from the more densely populated regions of the world.

Quellen gathered himself together and stood up. The grassy carpet extended in all directions, and in front of him there was a great thicket of trees. Quellen looked. A small gray bird came out on the overhanging branch of the nearest tree and began to chirp, unafraid, at Quellen.

He wondered how long Kloofman's minions would search for him before they concluded that he had hopped. Koll would be apoplectic. And would Kloofman cope with Lanoy? He hoped not; Kloofman was a sinister unreal monster, and Lanoy, despite his slyster habits, had a sense of honor.

Quellen began to move toward the forest. He would have to locate a likely stream and build some sort of house next to it, he decided. Improvised architecture—he'd make out, though his first attempts might not be very impressive. It would be *his* house, at any rate.

He felt no guilt at having taken this route. He had been a misfit, thrown into a world he could only hate and which could only ensnarl him. Norm Pomrath had taken this route. Brogg had. Now it was Quellen's turn. At least, before he had left, he had made a valiant try to defend himself against that world. It had been madness to think that he could match guile with the High Government. But he had shaken Kloofman, at least for a few minutes, and that was a worthy accomplishment. He had shown he was a man. Now valor's part dictated a quick exit, before Kloofman's superior might crushed him.

Two deer came bounding out of the forest. Quellen stood aghast. He had never seen land animals of that size, not even in Africa. The African mammals had long since been penned in preserves. Were these creatures dangerous? They looked gentle. They skipped off across the plain.

Quellen's heart began to throb as he filled his lungs with the sweet air. Marok, Koll, Spanner, Brogg. Kloofman.

Helaine. Judith. They began to fade and blur. Social regurgitation. Quickboats. Good old Lanoy, he thought. He'd kept his word after all. Back to an unspoiled continent.

The world is mine, Quellen thought.

A tall redskinned man emerged from the forest and leaned against a tree, regarding Quellen gravely. He was dressed in a leather belt, a pair of sandals, and nothing else. The redskinned man studied Quellen for a moment and then raised his arm in a gesture Quellen could not fail to interpret. A warm feeling of comradeship glowed in Quellen. This man welcomed him. This man did not fear him.

Palm upraised, smiling at last, Quellen went forward to meet him.